# STORM WARNING

**ALSO BY JAMES BYRNE**

*Chain Reaction*

*Deadlock*

*The Gatekeeper*

# STORM WARNING

*A Dez Limerick Thriller*

JAMES BYRNE

MINOTAUR
BOOKS
NEW YORK

This is a work of fiction. All of the names, characters, organizations, places, and events portrayed in this work are either products of the author's imagination or used fictitiously.

First published in the United States by Minotaur Books, an imprint of St. Martin's Publishing Group

*EU Representative:* Macmillan Publishers Ireland Ltd, 1st Floor, The Liffey Trust Centre, 117–126 Sheriff Street Upper, Dublin 1, D01 YC43


Printed in the United States of America. For information, address St. Martin's Publishing Group, 120 Broadway, New York, NY 10271.

www.minotaurbooks.com

Designed by Omar Chapa

The Library of Congress Cataloging-in-Publication Data is available upon request.

ISBN 978-1-250-31981-4 (hardcover)
ISBN 978-1-250-31982-1 (ebook)



First Edition: 2026

10 9 8 7 6 5 4 3 2

The people at Minotaur are amazing to work with and so appreciated. Big thanks to Keith Kahla, Grace Gay, Kelley Ragland, Hector DeJean, Stephen Erickson, Ryan Jenkins, David Rotstein, Omar Chapa, Ervin Serrano, Alisa Trager, Ginny Perrin, Diane Dilluvio, and Paul Hochman.

To the late Janet Reid, who saw my early potential and hung in there.

And, of course, to Katy King.

*The best thing to hold onto in life is each other.*

—AUDREY HEPBURN

# STORM WARNING

# PROLOGUE

## TEN MONTHS AGO, BUDAPEST

Ash is twenty-three. She stands five-foot-two, rail thin, with genetic roots in Europe, in the Middle East, in Asia. She studied dance and gymnastics, even competed in the latter, successfully. Her hair is dyed a pale blue. She doesn't speak often, but when she does, she is soft-spoken.

She has been taking assignments as a proofreader and copyeditor for technical treatises. She's also a hire-car driver. She gets a lot of foreign tourists, especially now, with Christmas approaching. Driving means she's learned a lot about this city she now calls home. She's picked up odd little hobbies, such as buying men's pocket watches at flea markets, plus a small packet of tools and a loupe, which she then uses to attempt to repair them. She hasn't actually repaired any yet. She also took a class on bookbinding and volunteers at a church's library, repairing old tomes. Like "fixing" men's watches, the end results don't matter to her, but the work appeals to her introverted nature and her need for quiet.

She waits in her tiny apartment near the Kiscelli Museum for the call.

The voice is always the same. Breathy, soft, slow speaking. Male. He always speaks in English, which is not Ash's first language.

"Hullo, Ash."

She squeezes her eyes shut. She says, "Day code: Edelweiss."

"You're to back up our Paris asset. Head there now."

This is a surprise; one assassin doesn't often meet another. "Target?"

"He will explain."

The Paris asset is a thin, wiry man. He introduces himself as Georges and she as Ash. Neither asks if these are real names or not. Georges has very curly hair, steely gray, and he's maybe in his fifties. At five-six, he is only four inches taller than Ash. He chain-smokes hand-rolled cigarettes and explains that the target will be an Egyptian in Paris to discuss medical shipments to Syria. He has photos of a tall man with a fierce beard and bushy eyebrows, wearing a long white thobe and gold wire-rimmed glasses.

"He'll have two bodyguards. We don't know much about them, other than that they are soldiers and appear competent. You'll run surveillance on those two men first. The target arrives in three days."

"Why is he a target?" Ash nudges the photo with her fingertip.

Georges rolls a cigarette and huffs a laugh. "Funny."

She's quite sure he never asked.

Ash follows the soldiers around Paris for two days. It's clear that they have arrived before the target and are using the time to take in the city's wonders. They walk most places and take the Métro to some. They visit the Musée d'Orsay and the Petit Palais. They drink a great deal of good coffee. They talk incessantly, nonstop, laughing, clearly friends. Ash so rarely carries on conversations with anyone, it seems quite alien to her.

The big man is called Dez. He isn't tall, five-eight, but powerfully built, with a thick neck and chest and biceps. He's bow-legged and walks with a sailor's rolling gait. He has sandy hair and blue eyes and smiles constantly. He sounds British (or Scots or Irish, possibly) and working-class.

His mate is as thin as a pipe cleaner. He's Saudi and named Rafik.

Ash is well trained in running surveillance, but twice she thinks the Brit catches her out. People often look right past Ash because she's young and, with her dyed hair and the right clothes, can look younger. She's also petite. Being young and small, people overlook her. But this man seems to have a keen eye for threat assessments.

Two days later, Georges tells her that he's established the kill box. The target and his two guardians will be meeting someone in a particular building in Paris's Third Arrondissement. The obvious foot route to the meeting place passes a bougainvillea-covered courtyard that has been under repair. Workers won't be there on a Sunday. Scaffolding covers two of three walls in the open-air courtyard. Plenty of painting supplies, including tarps, have been left on the scene. The two of them will climb up into the scaffolding, twenty feet off the ground, and will have the target and his bodyguards in a cross fire. A perfect, elevated enfilade. A logical position.

Ash has no interest in killing the two bodyguards, who've been nothing but polite to the French people they've met throughout their visit. But of course she and the Paris asset can't let them survive.

Georges and Ash arrive wearing painters' white overalls, cheap white sneakers, and white baseball-style caps. Also, KF94 masks, as one might if one is spray-painting. They both carry long duffels that could contain long-handled paint rollers, or could contain rifles and scopes, but when one hears hooves, one thinks horses, not zebras. Nobody on the street gives them a second glance.

It has begun to rain, but just a sprinkle.

They pass the big man, the one called Dez, who appears to be doing a reconnoiter prior to meeting the target. He hardly glances their way. They wear their masks, caps pulled low.

Before they climb up into the scaffolding, Ash turns to Georges. "Plant a microphone there, in the subpassage." Her thinking being: These two men never stop talking. She and Georges will hear them long before they're in sight.

The older assassin looks annoyed but, after a beat, does as she suggests.

They climb. Their scaffolding is rented and a little rusty, but it will hold the two of them. Ash's scaffolding is canted fifteen degrees differently than his. Her scaffolding hides a mural that she thinks might date back to the Napoleonic era. It is faded and chipped but quite beautiful, a horse on a grassy rise, his rider beside him, one hand on the reins, the other on his sheathed sword.

They both lie on their bellies under paint-spackled tarps. Both remove their rifles and attach their scopes. Their rifles are loaded. Ash will be firing down from ten o'clock; Georges will be firing down from twelve o'clock. If it takes them more than three shots each, they are losing their game.

Both wear earpieces. They hear the footsteps of the three men as they hit the subpassage, well before they enter the kill box.

A second before she expects them to emerge, they hear the Brit, Dez, say, "Hang on."

Their footsteps stop.

The thin one, Rafik, says, "Trouble, *chef*?"

She's heard him call Dez that several times.

"Painting gear, in the square."

"Yeah?"

"Passed two painters whilst I was on recce. Both had clean shoes."

Rafik says, "Unusual for painters."

The third man speaks in English but with a Cairene accent, his voice deep and nicotine-roughened. "This plan, my visit. It is not without opposition."

Dez says, "Hang on a wee sec."

He enters the courtyard first, moving fast, and immediately dives behind a small cement mixer that the real workers had left.

Georges fires at him. Foolishly. Even before the actual target has emerged. Georges's bullet pangs off the rough iron of the cement mixer.

They hear receding footfalls. Rafik and the target, sprinting away.

"Fuck!" Georges hisses.

They both calculate what will happen next. This man Dez will attempt to sprint back the way he came, through the exit. No other option is logical: armed opposition ahead of him, his friend behind. Of course he'll retreat. Ash and Georges will be able to cut him down before he takes three steps.

Dez is up and running. Georges fires off another shot that ricochets off cobblestone; firing where he expects Dez to be.

Not where he is.

Dez is sprinting toward the scaffolding. Toward the assassins.

Ash has not yet fired a shot. Killing the bodyguard is a secondary goal.

Dez runs as fast as he can and slams his shoulder into Georges's scaffolding.

The metal reverberates like a tuning fork. Two empty buckets fall and a tarp drifts away.

Ash watches in shock as the scaffolding begins to collapse. The Englishman hits the structure hard enough to break it. Or at least to jar loose a few rusty bolted connections. If you weaken a narrow vertical latticework at the base, you threaten the entire structure's integrity.

Georges's scaffolding begins disintegrating, long bits of aluminum shaking themselves free from their geometric grid pattern.

On the ground Dez dodges falling debris.

Ash is on her knees, throwing off her tarpaulin, when Georges's scaffolding begins leaning hazardously into her own.

She drops her rifle and grabs both handrails.

She sees, from the corner of her eye, Georges moving toward her, shouting, "Ash!" Then he tumbles, cartwheeling, from twenty feet up.

Ash's wood-and-metal support sways like a ship caught in a storm at sea, the platform undulating under her shoes.

She runs for the far, western end of her plank, hanging on for dear life, as Georges's scaffolding takes out the eastern support braces of her own scaffolding.

There's a chance she can ride it down and tumble free. She's athletic, a former gymnast who competed for her native country in the Olympics. She watches her rifle tumble away. She grabs both handrails and, as the boards under her feet begin buckling, she stays aloft. Like a surfboarder.

She hits the ground and rolls like the gymnast she once was. Relishing that she still has the skills.

She keeps rolling, and something—perhaps a piece of brick, which the painters used to hold down their tarps—cracks off the back of her skull.

She collapses, half-awake, her head in searing pain.

Through a swirling fog of brick dust, she catches a glimpse of Georges, who landed in such a way as to snap his spine. He is upside down, head and shoulders and arms on the ground, his leg and torso caught in a giant's game of long aluminum pickup sticks. His eyes are open and glazed.

As her vision warbled, she spots the man called Dez. Standing, staring down at her.

"Your mate called you Ash, yeah? Hallo, Ash."

He picks up her rifle.

Ash always knew this is how her life was going to end. She didn't know when, but the how was as inevitable as the rain. She would fail a mission, and a target would kill her.

She waits for it.

Dez holds the gun like a cricket bat, swinging hard for the cement mixer. The rifle cracks in two, a bit of the butt spinning away.

He tosses the ruined weapon aside and turns and leaves.

Miraculously, Ash has kept her earpiece. She begins trying to rise. Dizziness engulfs her, her ball cap askew, her hair matted in blood.

She makes it to her feet and hears voices through the mic they'd left hidden in the subpassage.

"We go around," Dez says. "Two snipers. One's dead. Other's injured and unarmed."

The Arab speaks. "We should kill the second one. Quickly."

"We'll not be killing her, mate. She's no threat t'you. Not no more. More's the point, she's no threat to me. Come along now. Spritely, if you will."

Ash finds a water hose the workers had coiled up. She washes blood and dust off her head and neck, doffs the blood-soaked overalls. She painfully jams the ball cap over her head wound, hoping it will stanch the bleeding. She stumbles to the nearest Métro station. She takes the very first train that pulls in. She spots a pass sticking out of another woman's change purse and swaps her own with that one, then takes a lateral train, then another and another. She rides with no destination for two hours.

She gets to the safe house at dusk and finds the burner phone that Georges had hidden behind the refrigerator. She calls the emergency line.

She explains that she is injured, Georges is dead, the target has escaped.

The line disconnects.

The people to whom she is indentured now will come to her aid. Or will come to kill her. She has no idea which, and no option but to wait.

The big man. The one called Dez. He had the means, the motive, and the opportunity to kill the woman who'd attempted to kill him, and his friend, and the target.

And he hadn't.

*She's no threat t'you. Not no more. More's the point, she's no threat to me.*

The man could kill. Had killed Georges.

But he also could make the other call.

Ash sits and thinks about that.

Someone shows up and lets himself into the flat. A man in a suit. Ash doesn't recognize him. She is seated cross-legged on Georges's couch, holding a cold, wet kitchen towel to the jagged cut to the back of her skull.

The man stares down at her. "Well, this is a bloody mess. The target is untouched and we are out a skilled operative." He sounds British.

Ash nods. She speaks barely above a whisper. "Did you come to help take care of my injury?"

He peers down his nose at her. "That's why you think I'm here? For your needs?"

Ash says, "Did you come to kill me?"

The man says, "Young lady, I am not at all sure you have grasped the gravity of this situation. This mess—"

Ash sighs. Uncrosses her legs and stands. The man is still lecturing her as she drives the sole of her sneaker into the inside of his knee. His eyes bulge as his leg gives out.

As he falls, Ash takes a knee. She grabs a fistful of his hair, twists, and slams his throat onto her upturned knee.

The force and angle of the fall snap his neck. He's dead before his body falls fully to the old carpet.

Ash rinses the kitchen towel in Georges's sink, gets it cold again, and sits with it against her aching skull. She reaches for the burner phone.

Whoever picks up doesn't speak.

"Please send someone to tend to my head injury. Or to kill me. Please do not send another man to lecture me."

She hangs up.

Thirty minutes later, a messenger leaves a grocery bag on the stoop. Ash finds painkillers and wrapped sandwiches and crisps and bottled water.

Ash eats and scans newspaper websites. There is no mention of a dead man at a Paris construction site. It's as if Georges never existed.

Someone else walks in. This time a middle-aged woman. She stares at the dead man on the oval carpet, his eyes fixed on the ceiling and a look of surprise on his face.

"He always was one to harp. Apologies." This one also sounds British.

"Congratulations," she says, turning to Ash. "You've just inherited your next post. We will have your things shipped here immediately. You'll find this posting more to your liking, I daresay."

Ash holds the compress against her skull. "I don't want this post. I didn't want the last one."

"Your debt is not yet paid off."

"Will it ever be?"

The woman smiles blandly. "There are assets and targets, my dear Ash. Most people do not get to choose which they are. You do. Which shall it be?"

She waits patiently. Ash mulls over the events of this week. And the way Georges's body disappeared so completely.

She whispers, "Asset."

"Ever so glad," the woman says, and turns to leave. She gestures to the corpse. "Oh, and we'll have that cleaned up in a jiff, my dear."

# CHAPTER 1

## TODAY

Desmond Aloysius Limerick ties a red apron around his white tunic and stares at the hemp bag on the butcher-block table. "What's all this, then?"

Sly Colehouse is tying her very long dreads into a single rope that hangs down to the small of her back. Some of the dreads are dyed red and blue. She's just returned from the Monday farmers market in Queens. She says, "Leeks."

"How many d'you need?"

She says, "All of them."

Desmond—Dez to his friends—laughs. "Jay-sus, girl! How many did ye buy?"

She smiles. "All of them."

She laughs at the face he makes. She reaches over and touches his biceps through his white, button-down cook's tunic. "Ahhh. Are the nasty old leeks too much for your big muscly arms?"

"Y'know, there's a reason I retired young," he grumbles, reaching for his paring knife, "so nobody can order me around."

Three weeks ago, Dez was enjoying the New York art scene, picking up some gigs as a bass player and pianist, when one of his bandmates told him about the Cheshire Cat. The owners were running into some trouble with a protection racket, and would Dez be willing to help? Dez has no love for bullies. He met the owners, plus the up-and-coming chef, Sly, and quickly agreed to help.

His second day there, the dudes running protection showed up. Dez chatted them up in the alley in the back, explaining that the owners wished no further visits from the gentlemen. They talked a bit. Dez returned to the kitchen and called an ambulance for them. And that was all of that. They never returned.

That was two weeks ago. Dez has been hanging around just to be on the safe side, and because he surprised himself by falling in love with the rhythm of being a cook in a high-end restaurant. He's learning things every day. Plus, he has nowhere else to be. Why not be here?

Also, as luck would have it, Sly Colehouse has taken to the notion of sleeping with him. No strings, ships passing in the night, as it were. She's quite a lovely bird, and she makes him laugh. This arrangement is working out quite splendidly.

He's renting a tiny room, really, no more than a bedsitter, from a plump and pleasant Englishwoman, a Mrs. Welliver, not four blocks from the restaurant. She favors paint-speckled overalls and Crocs, and she smiles incessantly, apple-cheeked. She ribs Dez about his "lady friend" staying over. Dez thinks she's a hoot.

One day he finds her struggling with the door to the apartment building's cellar. She rattles the handle, yanking on the door.

"Morning, Mrs. Welliver. Need a hand?"

She says, "Are you any good with doors, Desmond?"

Dez laughs. "A bit."

It's late morning, and the kitchen of the Cheshire Cat has obtained the proper level of insanity. It's hot and humid. Sly Colehouse barks orders, and her four cooks hop to. Sly is the chef de cuisine. She calls the shots, and everyone does as told.

Dez stands out among the five people working the kitchen. First, he has the least experience and the least talent, having only worked as a short-order cook a few times in his life, among many other jobs. Second, he's from the UK, and the others are all from somewhere along the Eastern Seaboard. Third, he's put together like a bulldozer. It took Sly ages to find a chef's tunic big enough for his neck, chest, and biceps.

"Gonna get rich!" Sly sings out from where she's deveining shrimp.

The four cooks shout, "*Oui, chef!*"

"Gonna get me that Michelin star!"

"*Oui, chef!*"

"Gonna beat Bobby Fucking Flay!"

"*Oui, chef!*"

The call-and-response is something Sly Colehouse gets going most days, within an hour of the hostess opening the front of the shop. Her team cracks up, going along with it. There are only thirty tables at the Cheshire Cat. Thirty of the thirty will fill for lunch. And for dinner; the tables will turn over thrice. And so on and so on. It opened five months ago and the place is all the rage in this part of New York City.

The lunch rush goes by in a sweaty blur. The place shuts down from two to four to restock and to prepare for whatever entrées Sly has conjured up for that day; they differ often. Dez gulps water, joshes with the others.

Natasha, a honey blonde who serves as the hostess, steps into the kitchen. "Dez? There's a guy in a suit here to see you."

Sly doesn't look up from dicing shallots at her station. "If it's a cop, pretend you don't speak English. I've heard you talk; it's mostly true."

Dez washes his hands and hangs a towel over his shoulder and steps out into the front of the house.

A guy is waiting for him. Dez's eyes pop wide. "Special Agent! Now there's a nice surprise!"

Tom Fairweather is a team leader of the FBI's elite Hostage Rescue Team. He and Dez had met earlier in the year.

The man is a bit of a legend. He's only in his late forties but with prematurely gray hair. He's not that tall, not that strongly built. He has largish ears and downturned eyes. No one alive has ever heard him shout or swear or express anger or anxiousness. He leads the Federal Bureau of Investigation's number one counterterrorism force but to look at him, you'd assume he was an accountant.

He offers his hand. "Mr. Limerick. How are you?"

They shake. "Nary a complaint. Surprised to see yez."

Fairweather nods. "We have a door we can't open. I could use a gatekeeper."

Dez says, "How long's it likely t'take? The dinner rush starts soon."

Tom Fairweather says, "It's in a remote part of Canada. It's in the path of a series of very nasty North Atlantic storms. And we suspect we'll meet violence."

Dez says, "Best get my coat."

Dez returns to the kitchen and tells Sly Colehouse. She leads him out to the little corridor for some privacy, doffing her apron. She hugs him. "Is this goodbye?"

He hugs her back. "Likely. An' the restaurant's safe now."

She arranges her dreads over one shoulder. "Dez. Look. Ah, this isn't easy to say. This thing between us? It's—"

Dez smiles. "Run its course?"

Her shoulders drop in relief. "Yeah. Probably. I think. You okay?"

He hugs her again. "Am. You're amazing, but aye. I'm fine."

She buries her head in his chest. "Thank you so much. For everything. Now get out of my kitchen and make room for a real cook."

"You know I saved your restaurant from the ravages of evil men."

She pecks him on the cheek, palms on his chest. "Yeah, but I tasted your béchamel, too. It evens out."

Dez laughs and heads to the front of the house. "Ta, love. Be well."

# CHAPTER 2

Special Agent Tom Fairweather could have sent any junior FBI officer to collect Dez, but he came himself. That alone tells Dez something. Fairweather has a driver; he and Dez sit in back as they head to the FBI New York field office.

"Would you mind if I brief you there? I have to brief State, as well. I'd prefer to do it once."

Dez nods.

Fairweather dons reading glasses and draws his mobile and checks incoming messages, responding to a few.

They ride in silence.

The Hostage Rescue Team has taken over a briefing space within the FBI field office. Fairweather is consulting his own people. Dez spots a couple who don't appear to be FBI, so he approaches them first.

"How d'you do. Dez Limerick. Know what this is all about yet?"

It's a woman and a man. She's stout, in her late fifties, with blond hair going to gray, cut haphazardly, and in a shapeless suit. She wears a lanyard with the logo of the U.S. Department of State. "Hi. Trisha Jean Jackson, deputy assistant secretary, State."

The man is in his mid-thirties maybe, with a boyish face. Small-boned, his hair thinning. He's wearing a forgettable suit with running shoes designed to look like dress shoes. "Rusty Townsend, Secret Service. I'm Secretary Jackson's security."

The slightish fellow doesn't appear likely to be anyone's security, but Dez lets it go without a word. "I'm a consultant, I suppose."

Trisha Jean has a strong Southern accent. She says, "Your area of expertise?"

"Of late? Dicing leeks."

None of them had spotted Special Agent Fairchild approach. "But before that, Mr. Limerick was what is known in military circles as a gatekeeper. He's good with locked doors."

Dez racks up his sleeve and shows them the tattoo of a two-faced Roman god on his forearm. "Janus. Roman god o' beginnings an' gates, dimensions an' doors, transitions an' times, passages an' endings. Sigil of the trainin' I received. Can open any door. Keep it open for as long as them what's in charge deem necessary, and control who does, and who does not, pass through."

Rusty Townsend says, "For real?"

"Guess we'll find out, yeah?"

Fairweather doesn't raise his voice but says, simply, "Folks?" And about thirty people in the room take seats or turn in his direction. He applies his reading glasses and reaches for a remote control. Behind his neatly trimmed gray hair, a flat-screen monitor blinks to life.

The people in the briefing room see an image of a cluster of metal buildings amid a vast pile of snow. "Does anyone here know what the Fuchs Underground Neutrino Collector is?"

Rusty Townsend says, "Oh, sure. Their gift shop is legendary."

Dez thinks he's going to like the Secret Service lad.

Fairweather might be amused or annoyed; his voice and face don't change. "Fuchs is a scientific research facility in Eastern Canada. It's underneath a mining site on the coast of Newfoundland and Labrador. The project head is Dr. William Sato, who won the Nobel Prize for . . ." He checks a spiral-topped notepad. "Oscillation variants in antineutrinos. And no, I do not have any idea what that means."

A slide of Dr. Sato appears. He's Asian, mid- to late fifties, Dez guesses.

"Approximately twenty hours ago, we received word that the facility went into lockdown. Canadian authorities have tried getting through to the town that sits atop the facility, but it's in total communications blackout. For reasons that are too technical for me to understand, when a neutrino facility goes into lockdown, it's virtually impossible to get it unlocked from the outside."

"Too technical for *me* to understand," Trisha Jean murmurs to Dez and Rusty. "And I've got a civil engineering degree from Georgia Tech."

Townsend continues. "The Fuchs facility is an international operation, which is why State will be giving the FBI its marching orders on this thing. The land itself is Canadian and the Canadians have green-lit HRT taking point up there. The mining operation is, ostensibly, run by the Canadian government. And the neutrino research site is run by the Americans and Swiss but received some big grants from our government and the private sector to set it up."

Dez nudges Trisha Jean Jackson. "Care to wager that 'ostensibly' ends up being the operative word therein?"

Fairweather says, "The mining operation is searching for a mineral called cerite. From cerite, they're extracting cerium, which is used in—"

Dez says, "Monitors. TVs, computers, smartphones, an' the like."

"Very good, Mr. Limerick. And here's the wrinkle. The company handling the extraction of cerium is Syever Mineralnaya."

Trisha Jean groans. "And relations with the Russians are so good right now."

"Yes, ma'am. Which explains why State will be telling the FBI what we can, and cannot, do in this matter. Like it or not, you're now my boss."

Rusty Townsend raises his hand. "So, what? We've got a full-blown deputy assistant secretary of state to run downfield interference with the Canadians and the Russians. We've got Mr. Limerick here to open some sort of door. And we've got the Hostage Rescue Team to . . . rescue hostages?"

Dez says, "Dez to me mates."

Tom Fairweather removes his glasses. "Mr. Limerick, we do think we might need your expertise getting into the underground facility. Until we get there, we just won't know for sure. But . . . I also didn't tell you everything. One of the private donors to the scientific expedition is Petra Alexandris."

Dez says, "CEO, Triton Expediters. The bank for much of the world's military an' government infrastructure. Petra an' me were . . . close, for a minute."

"I'm aware of that, sir. And it's one of the reasons I reached out to you. Ms. Alexandris apparently was greatly concerned about her investment at the neutrino facility. Concerned enough to, well, conduct an inspection."

Dez stiffens. "Wait."

"I'm afraid so, Mr. Limerick. Ms. Alexandris is at the site right now. And she's behind the door we need you to open."

# CHAPTER 3

Special Agent Tom Fairweather says, "First thing in the morning, we'll have a C-130 ready at Newark Liberty. Madam Secretary, I've had an office here made ready for you. Or you can work out of Washington. Whatever you think is best."

Trisha Jean says, "Whatever I think's best?"

"Yes, ma'am."

"Then I'm gonna be on that C-130. Right beside y'all."

Rusty Townsend, her bodyguard, groans. "Are you kidding me? Anyone here catch the weather report? There's a hell of a storm blanketing Eastern Canada."

Fairweather uses the remote, and a satellite image of the Atlantic Ocean pops up. "Agent Townsend is correct. Right now, one storm is pummeling the area. But there's a much bigger storm waiting over the Atlantic and heading toward Canada. So we have a needle to thread between the storm fronts. Ms. Jackson: Are you sure you want to head up there with us?"

"You do your best business on main street, Special Agent. If I'm there, I'll know more, and quicker. Simple as that."

She turns to Rusty. "Sorry. I don't suppose Nova Scotia was on your plans for the week."

Rusty sighs. "I gotta ask the boss."

"Justice? One phone call from me, and we're wheels up."

"I meant Lauren."

Trisha Jean grins. "Well, your wife does outrank me. Go."

Rusty steps away, drawing his cell phone.

Trisha Jean says, "You're in, Mr. Limerick?"

"Dez to me mates. We'll be needing cold-weather gear."

Tom Fairweather says, "That's being taken care of. We are wheels up at oh eight hundred tomorrow. Madam Secretary, I need you to make sure the Canadians are okay with all this."

Trisha Jean gives him the thumbs-up.

An FBI agent drives Dez to the apartment run by Mrs. Welliver. He calls Sly and lets her know he's heading out of town to help a mate. "Next time you're in New York, come look me up?" she asks.

"Ye know I will."

"Dez. Thank you. For everything."

Dez dines at a shawarma place around the corner, chatting up the owners in Arabic.

It's going on 10 P.M. when he hears a knock on the door of his fifth-floor room. FBI, he wonders? Maybe moving up the timeline because of the storms heading toward Canada?

Three men, strangers, stand outside his room. All three look beefy and capable. The guy in the lead wears sunglasses and has a wooden toothpick between his teeth. Beneath his winter jacket, he wears a sweatshirt with the logo for something called Skyhook Technologies.

"Desmond Limerick?"

Dez says, "Am, aye. Help ye?"

"Can we come in?"

"But of course!"

It isn't a big room, and it's smaller now with these three guys, all of whom are taller than Dez, if not as buff. Everyone remains standing. There wouldn't be room for a fifth man in this space.

"How can I be of assistance, gents?"

The guy with the sunglasses is the clear leader. The other two stand behind him, flanking him. "It's come to our attention that you're climbing on an aircraft tomorrow and flying to a mining facility in Newfoundland. We very, very much want to catch a lift with you."

And how the hell could these gentlemen know that? Dez smiles and doesn't bother denying anything. "Not my plane. Not my ride t'give."

"Yes, but you're going as a civilian contractor, to help with the situation at the Fuchs facility. You could say we're associates of yours, and you'll require our assistance. That would get us there."

They're remarkably knowledgeable.

"I could say that, aye, but it'd be a lie. Don't know you lot from Adam's off ox."

The guy with the Skyhook Technologies sweatshirt reaches into the chest pocket of his coat. In these tight confines, it would be interesting to see if he's going for a gun, Dez thinks. Instead, he produces a stack of one-hundred-dollar bills with a blue latex ribbon around it, widthwise. The stack is quite thick.

Skyhook tosses it onto Dez's bed. "Please?"

"I've no wish to get crosswise with the U.S. government, my lad. I'm a guest in this fair country."

Skyhook produces a second bundle of the same dimensions and tosses it onto the bed. "Pretty please?"

Dez whistles, high-low, and scratches his head. "Dunno . . ."

A third packet of hundreds lands on the bed. "Pretty please with a cherry on top?"

Dez gestures to the three packets of money. "May I?"

"Sure."

Dez picks them up and thumbs through them. He's not sure how much is here, but it's got to be at or near fifty thousand dollars. He crosses the room, his back to them, thumbing through each. When he's near the window, he says, "Honestly? I've never held this much cash in me life."

"That'd be the down payment. That gets us on the plane to Newfoundland. The same amount when we get back."

"This much again?" Dez marvels.

Skyhook smiles around the toothpick. "Absolutely."

Dez opens the window and tosses the money out onto the sidewalk from five floors up. "Nah."

The guys are startled. Even from five stories up, they can hear cars honking and loud voices coming from the street.

Skyhook is in total shock. "The fuck did you just do?"

Dez has crossed back to them now. "Turned down your kind offer, gents. A question: Do thugs in the States always work in groups of three? Is it a union thing?"

The two pit bulls behind Skyhook look ready to fight. Skyhook raises a hand, stops them.

"That was really stupid."

"Ye'd not be the first to call me stupid. Nor the hundredth."

"You know the cliché: There's an easy way and the hard way," the leader says. "The money was the easy way. We—"

Dez throws a very fast punch into the man's nose. Cartilage crackles.

The blow rocks the man back into his mates. Blood flows onto his lips and chin, staining his nice coat and the sweatshirt.

"Thought that might speed up the speechifying."

"Fug you!"

This is where the tightness of the bedsitter plays to Dez's advantage. Unless the gorillas plan to step back away from him, draw guns and shoot him, he's in the catbird seat. Without climbing onto the bed, they can't easily get around their boss with his broken nose.

Dez raises both hands and shoves the leader in the chest. The guy slams into his mates again.

Dez wades into their space. The guy on his right has drawn a combat knife from a coat pocket. He's a lefty. Dez grabs the man's left wrist to immobilize his arm, makes a blade of his hands by curling his fingers in, and jams his big, calloused knuckles into the hollow of the man's left shoulder. The blow doesn't dislocate his shoulder but the nerve cluster sends shock waves through his body. The knife drops to the floor.

Using Skyhook as leverage, Dez raises his boot and brings it down on the right knee of the third man. The leg gives out from under him, and all three men crumble to the tight confines between the bed and the short hall to the bathroom, closet, and the door to the fifth-floor corridor.

Dez scoops up the fallen knife and crouches, setting the blade against the underside of Skyhook's chin. "Get your lads out of me room, please. An' if ye bleed on the carpet an' the landlady keeps me security deposit, there'll be the devil t'pay."

Shocked at how the whole thing went—and how quickly—the men rise and back out of the room. One man's arm hangs limply at his side, his other hand supporting his shoulder. One man limps on knee tendons that are stretched, maybe even torn.

"This was a fugging mishtake." Skyhook holds his busted nose in both palms. "A big fugging mishtake."

"Was," Dez concurs. "But it could be a teachable moment, as well. Think on your errors, me darlings. And have a lovely evening."

Dez closes the door on their surprised mugs.

He can still hear a commotion from the street, from where something like fifty thousand dollars rained down like manna from the heavens. He calls Rusty Townsend—the Secret Service man had given him his card—and tells him what happened.

"You're kidding! So my first questions are: Who the hell are these guys? And how'd they know we're flying to Newfoundland tomorrow?"

"Same questions I had."

"Okay, I'll have a car at your apartment in ten minutes. You're not safe there."

"Nah. Safe as houses. They'll not bother me again. See ye in the morning, as planned."

Dez hangs up, washes up, strips to his boxers, climbs onto the bed, and falls asleep in seconds.

# CHAPTER 4

At six thirty A.M. sharp, an FBI driver picks up Dez, his U.S. military surplus duffel, and his guitar case.

They stop by a row of apartments in Brooklyn and a pretty redhead gives Rusty Townsend of the Secret Service a rolling suitcase and a kiss.

Back in the sedan, Dez says, "Far be it for me to mention it, lad, but you married well outside your league."

The FBI driver laughs. Rusty does, too. "You don't know the half of it, man."

They move through traffic, heading for New Jersey. Rusty says, "So tell me about this Petra Alexandris."

"Her company, Triton Expediters, serves as the bank for much of the world's military. Her old man, ah, retired recently. Petra went from lead legal counsel to CEO."

"And you two were, um . . ."

Dez says, simply, "Aye."

Once they're into the Holland Tunnel, the driver uses his siren and the red-and-blue lights hidden behind the grille, and they race out of the city.

Not one, but two C-130 Hercules cargo planes await them at Newark Liberty, and an Air Force Humvee escorts the FBI vehicle to it. Several military types are standing around, and a Cadillac Escalade, black, is parked under one of the gargantuan wings. Dez spots Trisha Jean Jackson, in back, on her phone.

An Air Force officer whistles high-low when he spots Dez. "I don't know if we've got a parka and gloves that'll fit you, sir, but we'll do our best."

Rusty glances at Dez. "What are you grinning about?"

Dez gestures to the hulking cargo planes. They're standing under one of them. "Herky Bird. I've lived in smaller villages. As ungainly as fuck, and them big Allison engines'll vibrate your fillings loose. But damned if I don't love these planes."

Rusty looks a little awestruck, staring up at the behemoth. "My first time in one."

Dez pats him on the shoulder. "A Hercules is too damn dumb to fall out of the sky, my son. We was in more danger in the Holland Tunnel."

Quartermaster comes up with parkas and hats and gloves and thermal underwear for Trisha Jean and Rusty and, miraculously, for Dez, who sports a fifty-inch chest.

Special Agent Tom Fairweather explains that a twenty-member unit of the FBI's Hostage Rescue Team will fly in one of the massive cargo airplanes. Trisha Jean, Rusty, and Dez will be in the other. "FBI regulation about having people other than the HRT on a flight en route to a mission. Sorry. I don't make up the rules. Is everyone ready?"

Everyone is.

* * *

Fairchild invites the non-FBI members of the expedition onto the first plane, so they can listen in on his briefing of the Hostage Rescue Team. He does so in his usual laconic style.

"This thing is a layer cake. There's a small town on top. A mining operation under that. And the neutrino research facility under that," he explains to his twenty people and the State team.

"We have lost communications with the town, the mine, and the research facility. The miners went on strike last week, so they're accounted for and elsewhere. That leaves the townies and the scientists. The reason HRT is being sent in is the communications for the town have nothing to do with the communications within the underground facility. For both sets to be offline, we have to assume hostile intent. Our goal number one is to secure the town and to look for hostages, civilians, survivors, or corpses. Our goal number two is to get inside the mine. The gentleman behind me is a civilian. Desmond Limerick. He's very good getting locked doors unlocked, so that'll be his job. Once the doors are open, Mr. Limerick will fall back with the State Department folks, and we will take point. Questions."

Someone says, "No threats? No demands?"

"No communications whatsoever. From anyone."

Another hand goes up. "I'm monitoring the weather, sir. This is gonna be a tight, tight fit. Right between two Atlantic doozies. I'm not sanguine that the Hercules will get us there in time. The math doesn't look good."

"Understood, and thank you. If we have to land elsewhere and wait, then we do. That's not ideal. Anything else?"

Another hand. An FBI guy looks glum, crossing his arms over his chest. He says, simply, "Russians."

"Yes, there are Russian interests in the mine. But we do not make assumptions. We get to the site and we see what's what. Questions?"

There are no more.

Dez, Trisha Jean, and Rusty head over to the second C-130 Hercules.

Airborne. Dez had warned them that the Allison engines are so loud they shake your bones, and he wasn't exaggerating. He, Trisha Jean, and Rusty don thick, foam-padded headsets and go to channel three.

Dez asks, "Why are there no miners in this mine?"

Trisha Jean tells them. "It looks like the mining operation itself shut down seventy-two hours before everyone lost communications. Apparently, a number of serious accidents occurred within the past week. Enough that the unions pulled all their workers out in protest. Shortly after that, someone in the neutrino detection unit shut down all access to the entire underground facility: the science part and the mining part."

"I've a little experience with the Hostage Rescue Team," Dez says. His own voice echoes mechanically through the headset but he's used to that. In his life, he's flown in far more military aircraft than civilian aircraft. "They're bloody good. Best I've ever seen." He turns to Trisha Jean. "D'you have a schematic of the place?"

Trisha Jean is wearing cheap half-glasses on their beaded lanyard. She opens her laptop. "This is Fuchstown. A couple dozen homes, a store, a bar. It's an actual, incorporated municipality, with a mayor and everything. Population about twenty-five or so, I'm told, and none of the miners actually live in the town. They're flown in for shifts. Six days on, four days off. No police force in the town, but the region is served by the Royal Canadian Mounted Police."

She switches the image to a schematic, showing a sideways depiction of an underground facility.

"This mine is important. There's a worldwide shortage of cerium. The U.S., Western allies, the Russians, the Chinese; everyone wants this mine back open."

Rusty turns to Dez. "I looked into that company you asked about. Skyhook Technologies? The guys who visited you. They make mining equipment. One of the largest companies of its type in the world. They've got facilities on five continents."

"And those men wanted to bribe you to get a lift in this plane?" Trisha Jean asks. Rusty briefed her earlier on what happened in Manhattan.

Dez gestures to the laptop. "Tell us about the underground levels."

Trisha Jean brings up a new image. She uses the nether end of a ballpoint pen, pointing at the first, highest underground level; the first of five levels in the drawing. Like a barbell, the first and fifth levels are the largest.

"Admin, storage, a gym, a cafeteria, et cetera, all surrounded by a ring of small apartments."

Her pen hovers over the next three levels. "Here's the actual mining operation. Now, this is just the layout of the main silo. The mining operations aren't shown here, but they extend laterally, and in almost every direction. At any given time, about eighty men were working down there before they pulled out. Bunked there, too. People in the town could go days without ever seeing a miner. This was designed to be a low-impact mining operation. As green as you can get within the extraction industry."

Her pen drops down to the fifth of five levels: by far the largest, round and shaped like a massive lozenge.

"The Fuchs Underground Neutrino Collector. Cofinanced by private enterprise, MIT, and CERN, with major grants from the U.S. Fermilab. Los Alamos National Lab threw money in, too. And, of course, Triton Expediters."

Rusty says, "CERN?"

Dez says, "Organisation européenne pour la recherche nucléaire. A whacking-great underground facility in Switzerland. Studying subatomic particles, thanks to a supercollider."

The other two glance at each other, surprised by his knowledge and his fluent French.

Trisha Jean says, "Anyway, this research facility initially was excavated for the mining, but they discovered that the cerite seams don't go that deep. MIT and CERN reached out to Canada and asked to lease the space. That was, ah, like five years ago, if I remember."

Rusty says, "If I'm reading this right, that fifth level is huge. You could play baseball down there."

"Only in scuba gear," Dez says. "My guess is most of it's flooded."

Trisha Jean leans back, appraising him. "How did you know?"

"Neutrinos are nearly massless subatomic particles, yeah? Passin' harmlessly through you, me, the Hercules, the planet Earth, right now. Can't detect 'em. To do that, you need a vast body of something liquid. If a neutrino runs smack into an atom of the liquid, it should strip off a couple of the atom's subatomic particles, aye? An' create a brief, dim trail. That's how ye know them little buggers is about."

Trisha Jean looks to Rusty, who says, "How the hell do you know stuff like that?"

"Bein' in the military is five percent action and adrenaline, and ninety-five percent sitting on your arse, awaitin' orders. Ye either learn to read or go mad."

# CHAPTER 5

Stormy conditions make for a bumpy ride and the C-130's T56 turboprops hammer the civilians with both vibrations and a dull roar, made only marginally better with the thick, padded ear protectors Dez's old unit used to call Mickey Mouse earphones.

Which is why Trisha Jean and Rusty are surprised when Dez lies on his back on a canvas rack, folds his arms over his chest, and quickly drifts to sleep.

An airman shakes Dez's shoulder to wake him up. He checks his beloved and well-beat-up Ancre 15 Rubis wristwatch. He's been out nearly an hour.

"Call, sir. We're routing it back. Go to two."

Dez sits up and rubs his eyes. He'd been sleeping in his Mickey Mouse ears, but not attuned to any frequency, just using them for their noise-canceling quality. The State Department official and her Secret Service bodyguard are both engrossed in their respective laptops. The airman brings Dez a lidded cup of coffee. "Here you go, sir."

"Ta." Dez switches to two.

*"Dez? It's Alonzo Diaz."*

He rubs his eyes. "Hallo, mate."

*"Oh Jesus Christ Jesus Christ Jesus Christ . . ."*

Alonzo serves as cook, house staff, majordomo, and consigliere for Petra Alexandris. In the vast, multibillion-dollar organization that she runs, Triton Expediters, Alonzo is probably the only man she trusts.

"Alonzo. I'm on me way to get her. Okay?"

*"You are?"*

"Aye. Airborne now, mate."

He can hear Alonzo holding back tears. He says, *"Fuck. Of course you are. That's so fucking on brand for you. Thank you."*

Dez laughs. "Don't talk daft, lad! Would Petra come, were it me in the barney? 'Course she would."

*"She really does love you. Dez. So do I. Thank you."*

"We're not there yet, mate, and the flyboys tell me we're threadin' a needle twixt blizzards. Dunno if we'll get to this Fuchs Underground Neutrino Collector. Which, now as I think on it, has the acronym FUNC. Didn't think that through, the boffins, did they?"

*"I can't believe she . . . herself. Stupid!"* Alonzo's signal is breaking up a bit.

"Mind me asking: What's she looking for there at the aft end of the buttocks of the world?"

His friend's voice sounds tinny and distant, and it fades in and out. Sunspot activity, Dez assumes.

*". . . scientists running the . . . unpredictable and stubborn. They've been ignoring communication protocols. They . . . outside access to their data. Both CERN and MIT are locked out of their computers. Petra wanted to figure out why. She reads—"*

Dez finishes the sentence. "—reads people better'n anyone else either of us has met. She had to go herself. Smart."

*"Stupid. Now she's trapped there. She should've sent me!"*

"Meaning no offense, but you graduated Juilliard with degrees in acting and dance."

*"Yeah. Meaning . . . ?"*

"Not a bloody thing, lad. You'd've been my first choice to go. But Petra's Petra, yeah. Trying to get her to *not* do something's . . ."

Alonzo sighs. *"I know."* The transmission fades in and out. *"I'm sorry if . . . trouble. No idea . . . could be nothing."*

"Well, no need to worry until we know the score up there. I'll get back t'you as soon as I can."

He listens to the hiss and snap of electromagnetic interference. Then hears Alonzo's voice.

*"—nk you. God, thank you."*

"Was gettin' bored with New York," Dez says. "This is better."

# CHAPTER 6

As it turns out, getting to Fuchstown that day ends up being hopelessly optimistic.

An airman asks the passengers to go to channel three and informs them of the situation. *"The storm seems to have stalled over the coast. Looks like we'll be turning around."*

Dez asks, "Can we get to St. John's?"

*"We can . . . I think. Not the other Hercules. She's a lot heavier than we are and well behind us. But I'm not sure I want to try."*

Trisha Jean says, "We think some civilians and some scientists could be in trouble up there. The nearer we are, the better. If you think you can land in St. John's, that would be my vote."

Dez says, "An' mine. Although hers is the only one that matters."

The pilot says, *"Lemme check with the FBI."*

Ten minutes later, and all three civilians hear a crackle, then the voice of Special Agent Tom Fairweather from the other plane. *"Ms.*

*Jackson, our plane will not make it to St. John's. We've fallen a good twenty minutes behind your plane. Are you sure you want to risk landing there?"*

Trisha Jean tells him what she'd told the pilot.

"All right. You guys try. We're rerouting to Quebec City and we'll rejoin you as soon as possible. Good luck."

The copilot, who looks to be no older than twenty-four, steps out of the flight deck and gives Trisha Jean the thumbs-up to indicate he was listening in.

"The second storm," she says. "The one still over the Atlantic? Did it stall, too?"

The kid shakes his head. "No, ma'am. That one's barreling ashore. We're being told they're mostly just one big superstorm, or they will be soon. When that happens, we'll be stuck in St. John's for days. At a minimum."

Dez feels the massive, four-engine plane begin to change directions.

He catches Trisha Jean's attention. "Is there another way t'get to Fuchstown? A land route?"

"From the briefing I got: no. I mean, in good enough weather, yes. Which this ain't."

"So they've no comms, and we're sitting on our arses, fat, dumb, and happy."

Rusty Townsend says, "Think positive. They might get the radios working again before we get there."

Trisha Jean shakes her head. "Communications with the town may be offline, but the radios underground *are* working, Rusty. So's the computer uplink. They've been turned off at the source. Level five. The neutrino facility."

# CHAPTER 7

Dez feels the thud as the landing gear is deployed.

From a port-side window, peering out, he can't even see the city of St. John's, or the airport tower or the runway. It's a white-out.

Trisha Jean and Rusty are staring out the starboard windows. They look to Dez, fear in their eyes, as another gust shakes the plane like a baby's rattle.

Dez winks at them. "It's a Hercules!" he bellows over the racket. "Ye can't hurt this beast! I love 'em!"

Wind shear drops the bird about twenty feet straight down. Dez's stomach is in his throat. But this isn't his first airborne rodeo.

He still can't see the ground. And he doesn't until a second before the wheels touch down.

The C-130 makes a rocking, hard-buffeted landing. Bouncing once, then two more times. The wind shear is brutal, the plane gliding sideways between the first touchdown of the wheels and the next. She skews laterally but rights herself, right wing dipping dangerously close to the tarmac. The fuselage shakes like a martini mixer.

Trisha Jean Jackson and Rusty Townsend look petrified, knuckles white, eyes wide.

The plane hugs the runway and begins to slow down.

"There!" Dez shouts. "Wasn't so bad!"

The other two stare at him with wide eyes.

Theirs is a nonscheduled, noncommercial flight, so air traffic control routes them around the terminal and into a ginormous Quonset hut, well away from the airliners. The copilot emerges from the flight deck as the C-130 rolls into its curved metal cocoon. "We just heard: We're the last bird landing. St. John's airspace is closed for business."

Dez says, "Any idea how long we'll be here?"

"No, sir. But they're putting us up at the airport hotel, so the upside is: There'll be booze."

"I appreciate an optimistic man, mate."

A pair of burly Land Rovers arrive in the Quonset hut, and the crew and passengers are encouraged to bring all of their gear. The wind punches the sturdy, heavy vehicles the moment they're clear of the hut. Snow whirls around them, making the terminal building all but invisible from where they are.

The hotel is barely a quarter mile away, and the storm punishes the tough SUVs the whole way.

The U.S. Air Force crew, Trisha Jean Jackson, Rusty Townsend, and Dez are the only guests in the spacious lobby, and Dez hadn't spotted a lot of cars in the parking lot. St. John's probably is a rollicking tourist attraction, when it's not getting its bell rung by back-to-back-to-back storms.

They get checked in and are given rooms. A man in a blue suit and hotel pin on his lapel points out where the restaurant and bar are located, just to their left. "We have a pool on B1, and a rather well-appointed gym," he says. "I believe the others may already be in the bar."

Rusty says, "Others?" The bodyguard is suddenly on alert.

"The other party heading up north."

After that flight, Dez's body is longing for a good, solid workout. But he's as curious as the Secret Service man. "Any one you walk away from's a good landing, but I wouldn't say no to a drink."

Trisha Jean shakes her head. "I need a shower. Followed by a nap and a shower. And maybe a nap. I'm too old for this shit."

"You?" Dez laughs. "You handled that landing like a pro, love."

She barks her very unladylike laugh.

"Rusty?"

"A shower, some aspirin, and a couple of Hail Marys for taking the Lord's name in vain during the landing."

The others head for the elevators, Dez shoulders his secondhand, Vietnam-era U.S. Army surplus duffel and his guitar case, and heads to the bar.

Outside, the wind buffets the hotel hard enough to make the lobby chandeliers jingle.

The restaurant is to his left and mostly empty. The drinking establishment is to his right and he spots a cluster of three people standing around the small, black, acrylic bar. A bartender is pouring mixed drinks. Dez rolls in their direction.

"You lot heading to Fuchstown?"

They turn.

It's two men and a woman.

The woman spots Dez and sets her drink down on the bar. She was about to take her first sip. The drink splashes a little. She sets her feet shoulder-width apart, one slightly ahead of the other, hands free.

She is maybe five-two, with hair cut short and dyed white-blond. Mid-twenties, Dez thinks, and Eurasian, or possibly Middle Eastern. And right now, she looks ready to land the first blow in a fight.

Dez has seen it before. Many, many times. A fight-or-flight reflex.

The other two are men: one white, one Black. The Black guy has an easy, laid-back, off-kilter smile. "Yeah. You?"

Dez offers his massive hand. The Black guy shakes first, then the white guy.

The woman glances at a knife the bartender used to cut a trim of orange peel for a drink.

"Dyson Patterson," the Black guy says. "Royal Canadian Air Force. I'm a doc. They're sending me to see if there's a medical mission. And because someone somewhere hates my ass."

He says it with a smile.

The white guy says, "Frank Watts, RCMP."

"I know naught of the Royal Canadian Mounted Police. Are ye a military operation? Paramilitary?"

"Para," Watts says. "I'm a homicide inspector. I'm supposed to ascertain what the hell's going on up there. Which I'm going to do by having several drinks over the next few days and catching an Oilers game on that big screen tonight." He gestures to the bar's television.

"Dez Limerick. I'm representin' one of the investors. Triton Expediters." That's sort of the truth. He doesn't want to represent himself as an FBI asset.

Dr. Patterson turns to the bartender. "Triton. He's buying the first round."

Dez laughs and makes eye contact with the bartender. "Whiskey sour, squire. Well whiskey'll do. And yeah, this round's on me."

The bartender nods.

Dez turns to the woman. Her suit and riding boots look inexpensive but fit her well. She's petite but somehow he gets the sense she's well put together: strong shoulders, strong legs. It's in her stance. She's athletic and works out. And, Dez knows, she can fight. It's in her body language.

She's also lovely.

The two men turn to her. Both seem surprised she hasn't introduced herself.

She studies Dez. Who smiles and waits.

"My apologies," she says, and offers her hand. "We have not met?"

"Haven't."

"Elisabet LeCroix. I am representing the Conseil National de Recherches Canada."

Dez nods. "National Research Council. Makes sense. Your lot oversees the neutrino facility, yeah?"

"Only in an advisory capacity, with CERN and MIT."

And as Dez studies her dark eyes, he, too, thinks they might have met before. But he's fairly certain he'd have remembered such a beauty.

Ash is shocked. She damn near grabbed the knife to defend herself.

It's the big man who bested her and the Paris asset known as Georges, when they'd been assigned to kill an Egyptian delegate. By bulling his way into a scaffolding so hard he knocked the thing down, killing her cohort and paving the way for her to inherit the Paris branch. Whether she wanted to or not.

At first, she's absolutely certain he will recognize her. But her mind flashes back to the hit: She'd been wearing a baseball cap and a painter's mask, her exposed face covered in chalky white dust from the masonry, blood leaking down her left ear and the left side of her neck. And she'd dyed her hair blue that year, not its current chalk-white.

Of course he hadn't recognized her.

Meaning there was no reason to kill this man.

Yet.

# CHAPTER 8

Dez accepts his drink and slides a five into the bartender's tip glass and flashes his room key to put the drinks on the bill. "D'you take U.S. currency?"

The bartender says, "Sure do. Thanks."

Dez turns to the other travelers. "What, collectively, do we know about this fecking lunacy?"

The RCMP cop, Frank Watts, answers the way cops usually do. "What do you know?"

"Way too little to be of any bloody value. Mate of mine working for Triton is caught up there. Alls I care about is getting her home safe."

The doctor, Dyson Patterson, reaches for a small bowl of mixed nuts on the bar. "The town itself is just a bunch of metal buildings. Most of the mining and research personnel live on the first of five levels belowground. Or they did, before the miners pulled out last week."

"Something to do with unexplained injuries in the mine?" Watts says it like it's a question, but Dez is sure the cop is just sizing up how much everyone else knows.

"Seen a schematic," Dez says, keeping an eye on the quiet French-Canadian woman. "One floor of residence, three of mining, and the neutrino facility, yeah?"

Elisabet LeCroix has said nothing. She holds her drink, eyes down.

Frank Watts gulps his drink. "You represent the money, right? You're not here 'cause of one person."

"Am," Dez says, smiling.

The cop shakes his head. "Look, even if we can get up there, I'm told we might not be able to get inside the facility. If it's in lockdown, we're going to have to reestablish communications from topside. Get them to open the damn doors."

"Might be other options." Dez shrugs. "None of which matter a bit if we're stuck here in St. John's."

"I'm in no rush to get up there," Dr. Patterson says. "I'm a city guy, and this drink's pretty good."

"An' you, ma'am?" Dez asks Ms. LeCroix.

She hesitates, eyes taking in the anonymous, unremarkable hotel bar, designed to look exactly like ten thousand other hotel bars. "I am here in an advisory capacity only," she repeats.

She remains on high alert, her body fairly vibrating. Dez has seen this before: Some women, and some men, are simply uncomfortable in his presence. It's his bulk. It's often women who have been victims of sexual assault. Dez's mass sends danger signals to their brains. He finds a stool and sits; a less intimidating position.

"What will your role be up there, Madame LeCroix?" he asks in French.

She hesitates. "We shall see."

She downs her drink, sets the glass on the bar, glances at the others. *"Merci. Bonne nuit."*

And leaves.

Patterson and Watts keep their eyes on her as she leaves. Her shoulders are up, her legs stiff-kneed as she all but sprints for the door.

Patterson sips his drink. "Was it something we said?"

# CHAPTER 9

The winter storm rages outside the hotel.

Dez discovers that the health center in the basement rents togs, and by chance has some that will fit his physique. He heads to his room, drops off his bag and guitar, then works out with free weights and a Nautilus device for an hour.

He showers and changes into what he normally wears: a black T-shirt, black denim jeans, and lace-up boots. He's added a black jacket.

Down on the lobby level, he finds that most of the two groups heading to Fuchstown have joined up for dinner: Trisha Jean Jackson and Rusty Townsend are seated at a large round table with Inspector Frank Watts of the RCMP and Dr. Dyson Patterson, the Canadian Air Force physician. Trisha Jean is telling some sort of story and the others are laughing along. She's one of those persons who talks with her hands, gesturing evocatively, adding to the punch lines.

Dez joins them. He suspects the food will be bland and forgettable, but he orders a burger and a salad and a beer. The others had just ordered so, when the food comes, it comes more or less together.

Dez eats like a man who's just worked out for an hour. He wolfs it down.

Frank Watts listens more than he talks. And when he does talk, it's to ask questions. If he has a family or a favorite hobby or a dog, none of them discover any of that during the meal.

Dyson Patterson is very chill. Dez discovers he's another guitar player, an amateur, and they compare great guitarists over the past few decades, finding they've many of the same favorites, but some surprises each.

Patterson says, "I think Prince was overrated."

Dez says, "I think you're mad as a hatter!"

Rusty turns to his protectee. "Tell them about the Saudi general. *That* guy was mad as a hatter."

Trisha Jean grins and looks like a little kid getting away with something. "I was supposed to be negotiating with this general, who also was a cousin of a crown prince, right? Only this guy had never negotiated with 'girls' before." She makes air quotes around "girls." "I challenged him to a round of poker. He wins, I head back to the States, and they send a man in my stead. I win, and we do the sit-down."

Rusty grins. "And she beat three nines with triple jacks. I thought I was honestly going to have to draw my gun, that dude was so angry. Around State, they still call the secretary Trip Jacks."

Everyone laughs.

Dez pauses, listening to the piped-in music that, until that moment, he'd ignored. He smiles. "Listen."

It's a pop song. A female vocalist, really belting it out. Dez's smile widens.

“She’s good,” Trisha Jean says. “She’s got some range.”

“I know who that is. Her name’s Raziah Swann,” Dr. Patterson drawls. “This season’s earworm. This is, like, her breakout hit. She came out of nowhere.”

Dez’s smile is contagious, and Rusty feels his own growing. “What’re you grinning at?”

“’ang on. Wait a bit . . . there.”

They hear a bass guitar kick in, supplementing and complementing Raziah Swann’s vocals. Dez says, “That’s me. We recorded it in LA last spring. Raz was so stone broke, I had to offer to fix a leaky roof in the studio in return for a mixer and thirty minutes of their time.”

The song ends. Dez shakes his head and rises. “Funny oul’ world, innit? Be right back.”

Dez excuses himself to use the men’s room. He washes up.

In the hotel lobby, he comes face-to-face with a strikingly beautiful woman. His very first take on her is: She’s rich. There’s something in the clothing and hairstyle and stance of rich people that are just different from the non-rich. She’s tall, perhaps a few years his senior, with cascading auburn hair. She’s wearing a cashmere sweater and fitted jeans and boots with blocky, two-inch heels. Hers is a body that was dealt a good hand by genetics to begin with, and which she’s cared for since.

“You’re Desmond Limerick.”

He smiles. “Ma’am.”

The woman sounds British and posh. “Hullo. My name is Valerie Cray. My husband and I own Skyhook Technologies.”

“Ah. I met some of your lads in New York.”

Valerie Cray smiles innocently. “Really? Small world. Can we talk?”

“’Course.”

She leads the way into the bar, well away from Dez’s friends in the restaurant. He gets the sense that she's comfortable leading and others following. It also would be sexist and wrong to point out how much he enjoys watching her walk ahead of him, so he keeps that to himself.

The same barman is there. Valerie Cray says, "Gin martini. Bombay Dry. One olive. Mr. Limerick?"

"Harp." The barman cracks open a bottle for Dez, who eschews a glass. "Ta, mate."

The guy starts mixing the martini.

"Do you know much about Skyhook Technologies?" Valerie asks. Her voice is lower than he might have expected. Her voice sounds the way good cognac tastes.

"You're a big to-do in the mining industry."

She smiles. "We have a strong interest in what's going on at the Fuchs facility. Some of our people and equipment are there already. We need to make sure they're safe."

"Did your people get out when the miners walked? Last week?"

"We . . . don't know for sure. Not everyone is accounted for."

"If an' when me and mine get to Fuchstown, I'll see if we can report back to you on our progress. That'd be up to the FBI an' the U.S. State Department, mind ye. I'm not callin' the shots in this thing."

Her drink arrives. She makes no acknowledgment to the bartender. "We were hoping that your C-130 can get us to the site once this storm abates a bit. If any aircraft can make it first to Fuchstown, it would be your Hercules."

"Ye'll have to speak to the lady in charge." Dez sips from his bottle.

"I'm not sure that State will want us up there. I'm hoping you can speak on our behalf."

"Won't," he says, smiling softly.

Valerie Cray is just about to sip her drink but pauses, eyes on Dez. If he were to guess, this woman can count on one hand the number of men who've said "no" to one of her requests. She radiates power as well as a far-from-subtle sexuality.

"May I ask why?"

"Because of that bloody great idiot ye sent to me hotel room and his two Dobermans, ma'am. Their goal was to bribe me or intimidate me. Makes for a bad first impression of your company." He sips beer. "And its leadership."

Meaning Valerie Cray.

She sips her drink. Love it, hate it, Dez can't tell by her facial expression. Is she angry? Is she anxious? She gives away nothing except a sort of smoldering . . . presence. He can't think of another way to describe her.

"We didn't send anyone to your hotel room. If someone claims we did, well, they're lying."

"Lead hooligan? He wore a Skyhook Technologies sweatshirt. Which, not for naught, but he'll want to expense that. Got a bit of blood on it after I broke his beak."

Dez smiles broadly, waiting.

Valerie Cray covers well. "Again, I have no idea who that could have been. However, I'm traveling with my own security. If you like, I could have someone watch your hotel room. Just to play it safe."

Dez's smile broadens.

She says, "What?"

"Ms. Cray, ma'am. Do I give ye the impression of a man who plays it safe?"

"That's the very reason we're talking. We've tried to look into your background. Prior to this year, you're a cipher."

"There's a fine line 'twixt cipher and just plain boring."

"You're not boring. What we have found, regarding your activities on the East and West Coasts, is that you can hold your own. There's no denying that you're a fast thinker and capable. I'm inviting you to come on board as our chief adviser for this Fuchstown operation. You'd answer directly to my husband, Vincent, and myself. My security detail would answer to you. You could tell them what to do or even send them back to our corporate office in New York, if you'd prefer. Vincent and I would agree to follow your lead in this matter. And in return, you could be looking at a contract worth one million dollars, American. Plus, an office at our headquarters. Which is about a quarter mile that direction."

She points east.

"Your headquarters is in the Atlantic?"

"It's in the bay. It floats. You'd have an office, and staff, and insurance, and a retirement plan, and company cars, and access to the corporate jets. And"—she sips her drink, eyes gliding sideways—"fringe benefits."

She smiles softly as she says this. The innuendo isn't lost on Dez.

Dez finishes his beer. He draws his room key and hands it to the bartender.

Valerie says, "The beer is on me."

"The beer is not. Was a pleasure meeting you, ma'am. You have a lovely rest of your evening."

Dez signs the bill and adds a hefty tip.

Valerie Cray's voice takes on a colder tone. "I might not have been clear. My company *needs* to get there first. It's imperative. And it would be wise of you to find a way to make that happen."

"Ye know that circus act, wherein they fire a clown out of a cannon? Never seen it tried in real life. We could try finding a big enough cannon. Fire you up there. Parabolic arc. Do the math right. Could work."

A ripple of something—"anger" is too anemic a word for it—skitters under the taut skin of her face.

Dez smiles blandly and waits.

She drains her drink. Her knuckles are white.

"We will get there first," she says.

"Nice meeting ye, ma'am."

Dez ambles out of the bar.

There's a better than even chance that Skyhook Technologies bulldogs will be coming for him. Sooner rather than later.

But at least he's getting a sense for who the players are in this pantomime.

After dinner, Dez heads up to his room.

In this modern age, many doors feature electronic security. So Dez's gatekeeper training includes a bit of computer hacking. He gets into the hotel's computer inside of about eight minutes, then finds out that the room opposite his is unoccupied and not reserved.

Next, he pulls a small packet of tools out of his messenger bag and disassembles the security system on his own door. He studies it; knows it to be a fairly standard system that he's seen before. Easy enough to bollux, if you've the training. He reassembles the system.

It's going on eleven at night in St. John's, and the storm outside rattles the double-pane windows of his seventh-floor room. Dez opens his door and checks the corridor. He spots no one. He uses his picks to open the door opposite—Room 715, opposite his Room 716—steps in, removes the cover of the security system, and bypasses it quickly.

Then closes the door and sits on the floor, right inside the door, knees drawn up, forearms on his knees. He's brought his phone, keeps the screen light low, and begins checking football scores from the Premier League.

# CHAPTER 10

Vincent and Valerie Cray didn't want to stay in a hotel while stuck in St. John's, Newfoundland and Labrador. Normally, they would have stayed in their private office, which isn't that far away, but with the weather such as it is, that seemed impractical. So they had someone in the real estate arm of the company purchase a house in town. The owners weren't selling, so Skyhook offered five times the price of the last house to sell on that block.

The Skyhook board of directors won't grumble. Much. The board gives Vincent and Valerie plenty of room to play, so long as they stay out of the media and out of criminal courts.

It's a massive, rambling Victorian with a view of the Atlantic and the Cape Spear Lighthouse. The Crays and their immediate staff are only going to be here until the situation at the Fuchstown mine is settled. Which, once the weather cooperates, shouldn't take long.

It took four Range Rovers to get the Crays and their staff and security detail to the house. Both Vincent and Valerie have their own executive assistants. They've brought tech people, who will be sitting bored until they can get up to the Fuchs facility. And they brought a portion of their highly paid mercenary corps.

Valerie's driver gets her from the airport hotel to the Victorian house, the wind buffeting the big, four-wheel-drive the entire way. If she's frightened, inside her fur coat and tall fur hat, she doesn't show it.

She's just royally pissed off.

At the house, Vincent greets her right inside the door, with a tight embrace and a sustained kiss. He can feel the tension in her back and in her lips. He's a tall man, early fifties, handsome, with graying hair clipped short and a strong jaw. He works out every day.

Valerie doesn't respond romantically to the kiss but he sustains it anyway. Their daily battle for dominance in their relationship is part of what's kept them madly in love, twenty years in.

She finally pulls back, eyes glistening with righteous anger.

"What?" he asks, smiling. She's English, he's American.

"Limerick turned me down. Flat."

"Then he's gay. Maybe I should take a run at him. Nobody's ever turned us *both* down."

"I think we're going to want to take a simpler approach. Are Loesser and his men here?"

"Downstairs."

The security personnel have turned the Victorian's basement into a bivouac. Valerie doffs her fur and her gloves, and they take the stairs down.

Craig Loesser, head of security, greets them. He has tape across his nose, and both eyes are blackened. He stands at parade rest, gun and shoulder holster strapped to his chest.

Valerie spots a tall, red-haired man with diamond studs in his earlobes. He's easily six-four. She glides to a halt, eyes sparkling. "We've met."

The tall man also stands at parade rest. "I was part of your security detail in Sebastopol, ma'am. Last June."

"When that bomb went off," she says. "You reacted quickly. Impressive."

Craig Loesser puffs up his chest. "I selected Finn myself, ma'am. The best guy I got."

The tall man smiles. "Aiyden Finn, ma'am. Good to see you again."

Valerie says, "Aiyden. I like it. May I see your gun, please?"

Finn's eyes flicker to those of Craig Loesser, then he unsnaps his shoulder holster, draws his SIG Sauer, hands it to her butt-first.

Valerie dogs the slide, just an inch, to confirm he has a bullet in the pipe. "Very good," she says. "It's smart to be prepared."

Then she turns to her right and shoots Craig Loesser in the chest.

The man flies back, arms flailing, a perfect arc of blood following him.

The sound of the shot is deafening. Every soldier in the basement flinches.

Valerie turns to Vincent, who's lighting a cigarette with an old-school wooden match. A soft smile plays on his lips.

She says, "When Loesser confronted Limerick, he wore . . . wait for it. Waiiiit . . . a Skyhook sweatshirt."

A beat, then Vincent blows out his wooden match and smiles. "You are fucking kidding me."

Valerie reverses the SIG and holds it out to Aiyden Finn. He pauses, then takes it back.

"Please dispose of the rubbish on the floor. You've just been promoted, Aiyden. I'm sure you won't disappoint us."

He says, "Ah . . . yes, ma'am."

"Desmond Limerick is supposedly a trained soldier. Have you studied his dossier?"

"Yes, ma'am."

"You know where he's staying. Take as many men as you think you'll require."

Finn says, "Dead or incapacitated?"

"I couldn't care less. Whatever's expedient." She turns to her husband. "I don't know why the FBI brought him along, but he's an X factor. We need to get there first. If the State Department plane won't take us, we need to delay them while we figure out another way. Eliminate him, and we slow down the FBI."

Vincent shrugs, smoke swirling around his startlingly gray eyes.

Aiyden Finn throws off the shock he's feeling. He picks four guys by nodding to them. "Saddle up."

The Crays head for the stairs. Vincent's eyes often squeeze shut when he smiles. "Oh. Finn?" he says over his shoulder. "If you could avoid wearing any of the company merch, that'd be good."

# CHAPTER 11

Dez sits in the near dark, reading up on the recent acquisition of a young Namibian striker for Arsenal. If the lad's half of what the pundits say, he'll add depth to an already deep squad.

Dez stands up every twenty minutes or so, flexes his knees and his back and his neck, then sits again, knees up. He goes to the Council on Foreign Relations site and reads the daily circulars. Dez has friends working in many of the world's war zones. Also, enemies.

He checks his emails. Nothing of importance.

Dez hears a shuffle outside the door, against which his shoulder rests. It sounds like the soft shush of canvas trousers rubbing together.

Dez kneels, his face to the floor as if he were observing the Maghrib prayer. He can see a bit of light coming from the seventh-floor hotel corridor.

Boots pass by, making the light blink as if tapping out Morse code.

Men in the corridor. More than one. He can't be sure, but he thinks there are five of them.

He hears no other sounds. No boot tread, no idle chatter. Good unit discipline. He wonders if the dunderheaded lad with the broken nose is leading the pack again. He hopes so. There's no character trait he enjoys more in a villain than incompetence.

He hears a sound he recognizes. Someone is running a bypass on the electronic lock on Dez's door. So: not total amateurs.

Dez rises.

He could wade out there and confront these lads, but he's unarmed and outnumbered. Not that it wouldn't be a chance for some good crack, but it also might be more than he can handle.

Better he should wait.

Dez had borrowed a very old trick from about a hundred movies: He'd left pillows bunched up under the heavy, winter-weight blanket on his bed, to simulate a sleeping form.

He hears the very, very familiar *whut whut whut* of silenced gunfire. Someone just committed premeditated, first-degree pillowcide.

So. Not here to offer him more money. Or to chat.

That alone tells Dez something.

He hears whispering. Soft, but somehow also angry. He guesses the men just realized he's made monkeys of them.

He presses his ear against the wooden door of Room 715.

He can hear an American voice in the corridor. Whispering, but with steely authority. "This guy's a baller."

Someone else whispers, "Fucker saw us coming."

The first voice says, "Simms, Jennings: Take the rear parking lot. Gordo, you and me out front. Moncton . . ."

Dez tenses as the doorknob near his hip jiggles softly.

"I'll have one of the geeks reserve this room. Wait for him in there."

The doorknob rattles again. Someone begins running a bypass on the room in which Dez is hiding.

In the military, Dez's best friend was a jovial soldier named Rafik, who used to say, *"It's good to be good, chef, but it's better to be lucky."*

Dez says a soft prayer to his old friend and steps away from the hotel room door, fading into the dark.

# CHAPTER 12

The mercenary called Moncton gets the door to Room 715 open and slips in, as the other four head quietly for the exit. Two will run surveillance on the front of the hotel, and two in back.

Dez knows that surveillance in a bitterly cold night is a slice of hell. He has no idea how long these lads will hold out before calling it a night.

This man Moncton quietly shuts the door. He wears a winter-weight coat and canvas trousers and lace-up boots, very similar to Dez's boots. He stands close to the door, ear to the wood.

Dez steps up behind him and kicks the man in the middle of his back.

Moncton's face smashes into the door. Dez grabs the man by the scruff of his neck and realizes he is wearing a ballistic vest under his winter coat.

He drags the man back into the room, which is the mirror opposite of his own; bed on his right, TV on his left, one window that looks out to the rear of the hotel, not the front. Surveillance will be setting up out there, so Dez keeps the lights low, turning on only two small, shallow, blue lights over the bed. It's enough for him to see but the light won't travel far.

The mercenary called Moncton is dazed, barely conscious. Dez rids him of his shoulder-holstered SIG, pats him down, comes away with a metal-cored, folding battle truncheon. As fine a non-trenchant hand-to-hand combat weapon as they make, Dez thinks.

The man wears an earpiece, Bluetoothed to a radio pack on his belt. He removes both, screws the receiver into his own ear. He hears naught.

It's then that he spots the man's brass knuckles, gracing his right hand.

Moncton lies on his back, arms akimbo, moaning. Blood trickles from his split right cheek and his right eyebrow.

Dez stands over him. And waits.

"Wha . . ."

Dez smiles in the semidark. "Hallo, Moncton, my lad. How's with you?"

"Who . . . ?"

"I've some questions for ye. Keep your voice low, kindly, an' answer with honesty and gusto, if ye could."

Moncton is coming around, realizing his situation. His left hand checks his left ear: no comms.

"What's the goal here? What does Skyhook want from us?"

"Go . . . fuck your . . . self."

"The theory behind brass knuckles is simple, me oul' darling. Hit a man in the face with your knuckle, with bone an' flesh an' tendons, and you're as likely to hurt your hand as you will your opponent. But when bone meets metal, well, metal wins. Every time."

Dez raises his boot and stomps on the man's right hand.

The brass knuckles hold their shape. Moncton's finger bones do not.

The man groans, his face going death-white.

"What's the goal here? What does Skyhook want from us?"

"Fu . . . fuck . . ."

"Yes. Fuck, my son. Of course. But first: What's the goal here? What does Skyhook want from us?"

Moncton moans.

Dez raises his boot over the man's ruined right hand.

"Stop it stop it stop it," he wheezes out, screwing his eyes shut. "Keep you . . . outta Fuchs."

"How come?"

"They don't tell us . . . jack, man. Just . . . needed to . . . slow you down." Sweat and blood slick Moncton's face. His unruined left hand drifts toward the small, tubular holster on his belt, which formerly held his truncheon. Dez waits until the man realizes it's missing.

"What's the end play?"

"You . . . broke my fucking hand, man."

"Yes. Yes, I did. You're a shooter? Ye won't be shooting with your right, mate. Not no more. Sorry. What's the end play?"

Moncton shakes his head, blood now coating half of his face. "Need-to-know only and . . . we . . . we don't need to know."

"Solid logic, that. Nothing but respect. Mr. Moncton, sir?"

The guy looks up.

Dez stomps on his head.

# CHAPTER 13

Dez goes back to his room, keeps the lights off, and changes into his winter coat and watch cap and gloves. He calls Rusty Townsend of the Secret Service and tells him to stay with Trisha Jean and to keep her safe. A threat against a single member of their party might be a one-off, but who knows?

Next, he asks the front desk to call Inspector Frank Watts of the RCMP, who agrees to meet him in the lobby. There, Dez outlines what just happened, and what he knows.

Watts studies him with unbridled doubt. "You're something more than an adviser for the Yanks."

"Am, aye." Dez waits.

"What do you want to do?"

Dez outlines a plan.

A longish pause, then Watts mutters, "Well, Jesus." He reaches for his cell phone.

* * *

Dez goes through the hotel restaurant's darkened kitchen and borrows a meat cleaver that looks like something out of *Dungeons & Dragons*. It's a fearsome bit of iron, the metal blade and wooden handle stained from the countless carcasses it's hacked apart.

He sneaks out by way of a kitchen door that leads to a dumpster.

Military types are very consistent when it comes to moving surveillance. No weak-engined cars. No subcompacts. They want heft, in case they need to ram someone, and speed, if it's a chase. They won't pick some color in the jewel spectrum. No reds, purples, what have you.

Dez has heard not a single peep from the radio he confiscated. Whoever's running this show runs it with admirable discipline.

The snow is blowing horizontally. Dez is a strong man, built low to the ground, but the storm damn near blows him on his ass before he's a dozen paces. He's wrapped a dark scarf over his mouth and nose, and quickly feels his exhalations turn to ice in the folds of the scarf.

He spots a black or dark gray SUV that's backed into a spot with a straight-on view of the window of Room 716. Dez's room.

No sign of exhaust. No dome lights. These lads must be freezing but they maintain protocols.

The windows are shaded but he knows there'll be two men in this vehicle. One is the ramrod of this outfit.

He trudges slowly and as silently as possible through snowdrifts, circling the SUV. He keeps low, the blizzard punishing him.

He's keeping his gloved, left hand in his coat pocket, so when his mobile vibrates, he feels it. He pauses, his back to the SUV, draws the phone, and peers at the message from Inspector Frank Watts.

st johns police here

Dez tucks the phone away and turns back, advancing on the darkened vehicle.

When he's close enough, he rears back and slams the meat cleaver into the left rear tire. He slides it all the way through, Dez's arm jolted by the feel of the iron cleaver hitting metal. The air in the tire is warmer than outside, and it sends up a plume of steam.

He yanks the cleaver free.

"Freeze!"

The voice has come through the whirling wind from behind Dez. From his blind spot.

He hears the *chick-chack* of a SIG slide being thrown.

The voice had come from his left rear. But the sound of the gun came from his right rear.

The car before him is empty. These lads either had seen him coming or had anticipated he would.

The voice he hears is that of the leader, the one who'd whispered orders to the others in the seventh-floor corridor. Now the man says, "Target is out front."

He's speaking to the guys parked in the rear of the hotel parking lot. Meaning the men had realized their guy upstairs is incapacitated. Likely he missed a check-in. And the other four had switched frequencies.

Pros, these.

The leader says, "Hands."

Dez lifts his, drops the cleaver.

At the north end of the parking lot, and at the south end, police cars pop on their revolving bubblegum lights. Dez and these two lads can't see the prowl cars, just their lights.

From in front of the SUV, Inspector Frank Watts shouts over the blistering wind, "RCMP! Freeze!"

The leader doesn't hesitate. Dez winces as he hears a *crack!* But he feels no impact.

Barely visible, fifteen feet away, Frank Watts grunts and falls straight back into the snow.

*"Go go go!"*

Dez turns but the two men are racing away into the night. The one he thinks might be the leader is very tall with red hair. And fast as hell. He's in Dez's vision one second, then gobbled up by the swirling snow the next.

The other man runs the opposite direction.

Dez picks up the cleaver from a snowbank and begins racing after the leader.

The local city cops won't leave their vehicle until Frank Watts tells them the score. Their job was to hit their lights and let the attackers know they're outnumbered.

So Dez is racing into the dark and the cold with no serious backup.

He can't see the leader but he can see the man's fast-fading boot prints. The lad had to be a good hundred and ninety centimeters tall; six-four or thereabouts. The man's legs are a far sight longer than Dez's, and all things being equal, there's no doubt who would win in a footrace.

But all things aren't equal. In the summer months, the leader would blow Dez out of the water. But in deep snow, it's a question of who's got the stronger legs, not just the longer legs.

Based on the boot prints, Dez thinks he's gaining on the fellow.

His breath is raggedly, the wind and the cold taking their toll. He's fighting the fallen snow, yes, but he also has to judge where the cement parking chocks are. They're painted yellow, but most of them are buried, and if he trips on one, he'll go face-first, splat, into the asphalt. That'd slow him down.

The chase winds between parked cars, but not many of them. The hotel isn't doing gangbuster business in this blizzard.

They're circling the big hotel.

If Watts is alive and calling for him on his phone, Dez is none the wiser; the phone's in his left-side coat pocket, and he's pumping his arms, trying to catch up to the tall lad.

They're running clockwise. And Dez knows, the leader is heading toward the two men parked in back.

He races on, heart trip-hammering in his chest. Most of Dez's military work has been in deserts and Mediterranean climes. Snow is not his friend.

He doesn't hear the bullet that whizzes past his sturdy back but he sees it shatter the windshield of a pickup truck four meters ahead of him.

Dez shifts in mid-stride and dives to the left. Putting the pickup between him and this new shooter.

Two more bullets ping off the bonnet and side panel.

Dez does a barrel roll and ends up on his boots, crouched behind the pickup. He has a tall man with a gun ahead of him, and an unseen man with a gun behind him, and they've both switched frequencies on their comms, meaning they can speak to each other, but Dez will hear naught. This is a bad combination. Dez snatches the useless earbud away and tosses it to the snow.

Dez belly flops and crawls under the pickup, using his right arm and right leg to brush snow out of his way. He's freezing, his teeth chattering.

Dez took out the man named Moncton in the hotel room but didn't bring Moncton's gun. That's because the last thing Dez wants is a running firefight amid civilians. So it's the cleaver or nothing.

Well, and Moncton's collapsible truncheon.

The shadow of a man emerges from the maelstrom. Just a dark blob at first, then a coat, and trousers, and a gun. Dez can barely make him out, peering up from under the pickup. This is one of the two men who was parked in back. The one who just fired at him.

He saw Dez dive to the left of the pickup. His gun is raised, left hand supporting his right, shoulder hunched up.

Dez lies in the snow, under the pickup. The man doesn't spot him.

The guy slow-walks behind the pickup.

Dez crawls out and rises in the guy's blind spot, drawing the truncheon.

He circles behind the lad. He snaps his wrist to extend the nightstick to its fullest length.

Someone else, a third man, fires a gun from behind him. Dez never feels the impact, doesn't see any impact, hears nothing. This third shooter missed by a mile.

But the man before him heard it, too, and spins around.

Dez whips the baton downward, taking out the shooter's left forearm. The gun hits the snow at his feet. Dez tosses the nightstick in midair and grabs it with his other hand, then drives the nightstick in a powerful uppercut, straight into the man's balls.

The man's torso arches upward and forward, shoulders snapping toward Dez. Like a jazz dance move from the fifties. His eyes go wide, his mouth an oval. The blow likely sent reverberations through his stomach, his duodenum, as far north as his lungs.

There's a chance it's a killing blow. Dez doesn't know for sure and also doesn't care.

He grabs the man by the back of his ballistic vest and spins him around, so the man and his vest are between Dez and the third bad guy, the unseen man who just fired from the darkness a second ago.

The man he's just injured is dead weight. Dez lets the man drop to his knees and he does so, too. The man is held aloft only by the strength of Dez's arm.

Dez waits behind his human shield. Wondering what will happen next.

He hears an engine rev. He turns and barely spots an SUV through the whirling gloom. It screeches to a halt, twenty meters behind him. The dome light pops on and the tall, red-haired man he'd spotted—the leader—climbs in on the passenger side. The door's not even closed yet as the SUV screeches off into the night.

Five men came for him. One, he defeated in a hotel room. One, he's holding up, hoping to make the man's vest work in his favor. Two just departed, fast as they could.

And no. 5 is somewhere in the dark. Ahead of him, maybe. The man who fired moments ago.

Dez waits.

Red and blue revolving lights begin to reflect off the falling snow. Cops. He sees multiple people moving his way, backlit by the car lights.

"Right here!" Dez shouts. He releases the man in front of him, who collapses straight forward, his face and torso taking the impact. Dez refolds the truncheon, sets it by his knee, drops the cleaver. He raises his hands over his head. "I'm here!"

Inspector Frank Watts spots him first. Two men in navy blue winter coats trail behind him. Local police.

Watts, gun drawn, limps to him. He's wearing a Kevlar vest. When the leader shot him, it must have hurt like hell, but he's alive.

"Limerick!"

Dez rises, still showing them his palms.

He points. "Two got away in an SUV! Thataways. One more in the parking lot. Fired at me from over there!"

The national cop and the local ones call it in.

More prowl cars appear. More dome racks, spitting lava red and glacier blue.

More cops on foot.

Inspector Watts leads Dez back inside the hotel. Dez can barely feel his hands in his gloves, but he brings the cleaver and truncheon along.

"You okay?" the cop asks.

"Am I okay? I'm not the one took a slug to the chest, mate."

Watts rubs his chest and winces. "They warn you those damn things hurt, despite the vest. That was my first one."

"Aye."

"Give me a count."

Dez doffs his gloves and blows on his ice-white hands. "Five. One's upstairs in the room opposite mine. Room seven fifteen. One you saw me with. I might've done some damage to that lad's internal organs. He should see a doc, right quick."

"That's the St. John's PD's call."

"Right. So five in total. Two fled by vehicle. One more fired at me from somewheres in the dark."

The glass doors slide open, swirls of snow blowing in, plus two townie cops. One of them makes a chin-jutting gesture to Watts, who says, "Excuse me a second." He points to a coffee station near the reservation desk. "Get yourself some."

Dez doesn't hesitate. He doesn't drink the coffee, just holds the hot cup in both palms.

After a bit of discussion, Watts heads back to him. "The fifth guy. The guy who fired at you. You confronted him?"

"Never saw him through the snow, mate. Only confronted the one upstairs, plus the one by the pickup."

"Well, SJPD's rushing both those guys to a hospital. You did a number on them."

Dez smiles. "Came at me with guns. They called the tune. Don't get to complain if they don't like the dance."

Watts studies him, steely-eyed, unsmiling. "Sure you didn't see the one who fired last?"

"Am."

"He's dead."

"How?"

"His throat was slit."

"Wasn't me, mate. Pro move. Especially in the dark, in the snow, against a man with a gun."

Watts says, "Yeah." And doesn't bother hiding his suspicion.

Dez cups the coffee in both palms, feeling his fingers tingle. "You get the sense we've yet another player in this game?"

"Could be."

Dez shakes his head. "Jay-sus, but I need a scorecard to keep 'em straight."

Ash returns unseen to her hotel room. She slips in, doffs her coat and stocking hat and gloves. She goes to the bathroom and begins cleaning blood off her butterfly knife.

It could be she was deeply stupid, saving the life of this man.

But there's still a chance this party can get to the Fuchstown facility. And if they do, she'll be in need of a way in.

And the others claimed that this man Limerick is her way in.

# CHAPTER 14

Most of the Fuchstown party—Trisha Jean Jackson and Rusty Townsend, plus Inspector Frank Watts and Dr. Dyson Patterson—join Dez in the now-closed restaurant. Dez has changed to warm, dry clothes, and Dr. Patterson has brought him a brandy from the bar. Dez doesn't know if there's any medicinal benefit from brandy after being so cold, but he doesn't argue.

Patterson smiles at him wryly. "I took a look at the guy up in the hotel room," he says. "You went through him like a tornado looking for a trailer park. And the guy outside you hit in the nutmegs isn't going to die on us, but he won't be auditioning for any tenor roles for a while."

"They had guns and came for me. Didn't feel the need to abide by the Marquess of Queensberry."

Frank Watts also has changed to dry clothing. His fingers rub at the bruise just above his sternum. "Mr. Limerick, you're my lead suspect in the death of one of these men, so the whole trip to Fuchstown just became pretty damned academic."

Dez smiles at him. "Look at me. Do I look like a fella what needs a knife t'kill a man?"

Rusty Townsend turns to the RCMP inspector. "C'mon. Limerick called you in before he confronted those guys. Gave you time to call the local cops. He didn't go looking for trouble. Maybe we shouldn't be busting his ass about his surviving out there."

Watts is a study in irony. "The advice of the U.S. Secret Service is greatly appreciated, thank you, Agent Townsend."

"Inspector," Trisha Jean cuts in, smiling. She's old enough to be his mother, and the use of the title is intentional. "Fuchstown, and the Fuchs Underground Neutrino Collector, both fall within the charge of the RCMP. True?"

Watts nods.

"This woman from Skyhook bribed Dez, saying her party *had* to get their first. She also told Dez that if her party couldn't be first, she didn't want another party to stake that claim."

"That's what Mr. Limerick says their private conversation was about, yes." Watts, not conceding an inch.

"First, they bribe and threaten Dez while he's in New York, regarding getting to the facility up north. Here, they sent five armed men to stop him. Someone has a considerable amount of ill intent, and they seem focused on keeping us from getting those people out of the Fuchstown facility. And by *us*, I mean you, too."

Watts sighs. "Yes, ma'am. All that's true. Still—"

She keeps her tone soft as she rides over him. "The people with the guns don't want us to get up there. Limerick's our ticket for getting those people out of the facility, and until he does, we're really not going to know what the hell's going on here. Dez is my ticket to getting my job done right. And I think he's yours, too."

Watts rubs his eyes with the pads of his thumb and forefinger. Her diplomatic logic is breaking through his cop's instincts.

Dez sips his brandy. "Has anyone seen Elisabet LeCroix, then?"

Trisha Jean turns to him. "Who?"

"National Research Council," Dr. Patterson says. "She arrived in the same plane as Frank and me. Dez met her when we had drinks. She didn't come down for dinner."

"An' ye've not seen her since?"

Watts lets loose a mirthless laugh. "Any normal person, in this hotel, in this blizzard, with no way to get out, would be in their pajamas, in bed, watching HBO. It's a measure of how screwed up this whole thing is that we think the one person probably doing just that suddenly seems suspicious."

"Might not be a bad idea to check on her, all the same," Dez says. "Make sure she's all right. I'll do it."

Watts holds up a palm. "No, you gave her the heebie-jeebies when she met you. I'll do it. You get some rest. This isn't over."

The cop turns to Trisha Jean. "What you said makes sense. My mission is to get up there and see what's ailing that town. And to get those people out of that damn bunker. You say Limerick's our best chance of making that happen, so, for now, we'll play it your way, ma'am. But please understand: This is police business now. And at the end of the day, we will play it my way."

He walks out of the darkened restaurant.

When Wednesday morning arrives, Trisha Jean meets with Dez and Rusty in the otherwise empty restaurant, and Dez uses his tech to place a video conference call to FBI Special Agent Tom Fairweather in Quebec City.

In lean, emotionless sentences, Trisha Jean explains to the FBI leader about last night's violence.

"And you're okay, Mr. Limerick?"

"Fit as a fiddle."

"You think it's Skyhook. And Valerie Cray."

"Well, she and some of her people are here in St. John's. Not a lot of players in our cast of characters can say that, aye? She said Skyhook needs t'be first on scene at Fuchstown. And she indicated she don't much care about what steps she'd need t'take to make that happen."

Fairweather ponders that.

"Well, I might be able to add a little good news," he says. "There's still no communications with Fuchstown or with the mine and neutrino research facility. But the Canadians have loaned us a team of meteorologists who think the storm might—*might*—be letting up a bit."

Trisha Jean says, "Slim good news is better than none."

"There is a window in the meteorologists' forecast, which says our plane might be able to make it from Quebec City to Fuchstown. But maybe not your plane. The weather between you and Fuchstown is different than the path we could take. You're on an island, obviously. Closer to the Atlantic."

Dez snaps his fingers. "Atlantic."

Rusty sips coffee. "I literally saw the light bulb go on over your head."

"Thomas, my lad. Can ye contact Canadian Coast Guard? Ask 'em if they can whistle up an H225."

Trisha Jean and Rusty look at him.

"Airbus helicopter. Big, ungainly beast, but the only helo I've ever ridden in that's got full deicing tech."

Special Agent Fairweather says, "You know a lot about military aircraft."

Dez smiles. "Also, twenty-first-century Eurovision contestants. Go ahead: Ask me anything."

Fairweather doesn't smile, exactly. This man would be hell to play poker against. "We'll call the Canadian Coast Guard. Not bad, Mr. Limerick. They just might have one of your birds."

And in fact, the Canadian Coast Guard does have an H225 stationed near St. John's. They've got a pair of them. They're the ideal aircraft for ocean rescues in rough seas.

It takes a combination of the FBI's cajoling, the U.S. State Department's pleading, and Frank Watts's RCMP connections, but the Coast Guard agrees to consider the entreaty.

The traveling party wastes another full day in St. John's, waiting to hear.

But at least no thugs try to kill Dez, and the hotel restaurant offers bangers and mash, one of his favorites. All in all, he's not complaining. Dez has had worse days.

The next morning, Thursday, they get the call from the Canadian Coast Guard.

The storm has died down a little, as the Quebec City meteorologists have predicted. But it's a temporary reprieve. The next front is moving in fast off the Atlantic. But yes, if the party is prepared to leave immediately, the Coast Guard thinks there's a likelihood it can get them to Fuchstown.

Frank Watts goes up to the room of the Canadian National Research Council official, Elisabet LeCroix, to tell her. The others haven't seen her since their first night in St. John's.

Trisha Jean contacts the FBI and is told their Hercules is airborne and threading a needle between storms, bound for Fuchstown.

With that, the big Land Rovers with their fat snow tires return to the hotel to pick up the northbound party. Trisha Jean and Dez say goodbye to the Hercules pilots and thank them for their service.

The storm doesn't seem noticeably better as they head back to the airport.

Riding in the first car are Dez, Trisha Jean, and Rusty Townsend. Riding in the second car are Inspector Watts, Dr. Patterson, and Ash, whom they know as Elisabet LeCroix.

Crews have already moved the teams' cold-weather gear from their fixed-wing planes to the bulky, orange Coast Guard helicopter. Dez grins when he spots it, climbing out into the bitter wind. He grabs his bulging backpack and the beloved guitar case, a shoulder for each.

Inspector Watts sees his smile. "Is this the bird you wanted?" he shouts over the wind.

"This? Much better than what I suggested! I thought of an H225. This here's an H225M. The military version of the Super Puma. Designed for combat-zone search and rescue. This thing's a feckin' beast, this!"

Rusty Townsend grouses, "There's a fine line between liking aircraft and a fetish."

Inside the big, orange-and-white rescue copter, they're greeted by the lead pilot. She waits until the whole party has climbed up into the fuselage.

"Captain Cora Charbonneau," she says. She appears to be Indigenous. The rotors have begun spooling up, and she shouts over the din. "A quick Bible lesson: God gave man dominion over all the world, but he gave dominion onboard aircraft to pilots. It's me, then it's God. That's your org chart. No one argues. No one pitches a fit at my decisions. At the end of the day, my number one goal is to get my copilot home. He's got kids and a labradoodle. And I care about him a whole hell of a lot more than I care about you. My number two goal is to get you people to Fuchstown. I will accomplish goal number two, so long as it does not interfere with goal number one. Am I clear?"

Trisha Jean lets loose with a hoot of a laugh. "Now, that's how you chair a meeting. All in favor: Aye?"

Everyone nods their consent.

"Captain?" the diplomat says. "We're in your hands."

# CHAPTER 15

For the next several hours, the Super Puma takes an ever-loving beating. Captain Charbonneau hugs the coastline. It takes them the better part of three hours to get to Indian Harbour and Lake Melville. Rusty Townsend loses his breakfast in a barf bag. Twice. Dr. Patterson looks like he's a second away from doing the same.

Dez points out the giant lake out the port side. They're all on frequency one. "Lake Melville!" he shouts to Trisha Jean. "Ye have to love the Canadians! They named a lake after a fella, his most famous novel is about men lost an' dying at sea!"

Dez hears an odd noise through his headset and turns to see Ash, whom he knows as Elisabet, stifling a laugh.

It's the first non-threatened reaction he's gotten out of her.

The burly, brightly painted helicopter powers on, heading north and west along the coast. Cora Charbonneau's copilot comes back at one point, standing with his boots well spread, holding on to an overhead bracket. They hear his voice through their headsets.

"Skipper says the storm's picking up! We're maybe twenty minutes out! But it's gonna be the wind at the site that tells us if we can land! Plus, we're running low on fuel! Skipper will make the go/no-go call when we get there! Are we clear?"

Everyone is.

"Also, get this: The Coast Guard has two Super Pumas assigned to the Rock. This one and her sister. You're not gonna believe it, but someone just stole her sister!"

Dez toggles his voice wand. "Was anyone injured?"

The copilot looks grim. "Two men dead. We just got the word over the radio. Goddamnedest thing I ever heard of. Who'd want to steal an SAR bird?"

Dez turns to the others. "So now it's a fecking race."

About twenty minutes later, they spot Fuchstown. They've seen photos before; they know it to be a cluster of about two dozen metal prefabricated buildings, more like cargo containers than domiciles. They're laid out with an east–west main drag and two north–south side streets. Nearby, they spot the long runway that serves the mining and research facility.

They see the world's largest igloo: A forty-feet-tall, half-globe-shaped structure that stands taller than everything else in Fuchstown. It has sliding, garage-style doors, and it's surrounded by large industrial vehicles, all painted vivid yellow, including some with tank treads instead of tires.

Their helicopter is being buffeted like crazy. Everyone holds on to the iron handles that dot the interior of the fuselage. Ash stands and crosses to starboard to get a better look at the village. Dez can't help but notice she's lithe and well-balanced, handling the strain of the storm's punishment like a lifelong sailor on the high seas.

She glances his way, her vision darting to the starboard window again.

Inspector Watts points out the window. "Look. That one, there." He gestures toward one of the buildings on the main drag. "Soot marks. And windows are broken," he says. "Fire."

From the flight deck, Captain Charbonneau switches to their frequency. *"My gut tells me to turn tail and run. But there are people trapped up here. For that reason only, I'm setting her down. Everyone strap in. This will not be fun."*

Rusty leans in toward Trisha Jean. "Remind me when we get back home: I'm gonna ask for a raise!"

She shouts, "Me, too!"

The captain makes the decision to land the helicopter on the town's runway. It's flat, obviously, and away from habitation. The only nearby building looks like a small, metal terminal building, rudimentary and ugly.

Over their earphones, they hear the captain's strained voice. *"Everybody hang on! We got nasty crosswinds, plus the runway looks iced over! That's a bad combination!"*

They're five meters off the ground and being shaken like a martini.

Four meters.

Two.

As the wheels touch the icy runway, a gust of wind grabs the Super Puma and shoves it laterally.

They touch down but slide sideways. They hit something under a pile of snow and one of the landing skids buckles.

The great helicopter leans over onto its side and, with a roar, they hear the big, overhead rotors touch snowdrifts, and then ice. And then tarmac.

One propellor arm shears off and goes flying into the blizzard.

The helo skids, shuddering. Everything inside is strapped down professionally by Coast Guard crew who know their business.

Everything but the passengers. People go flying. Dez grabs a handhold with his left fist and reaches out to snatch Rusty Townsend as the man almost flies past him. He gathers Rusty into a one-armed bear hug and holds him tight.

The aft end of the bird dips and the stabilizing rotor in back screams, coming into contact with ice and asphalt.

Still the big thing glides across the ice, spinning clockwise as it does.

The Puma slams to a stop against a one-story metal building.

The entire helo is canted to the aft and port.

Sparks fly overhead. Something shorts out.

Dez releases Rusty Townsend and stands, reaching for a fire extinguisher.

Ash gets there first, standing assuredly on the madly slanted deck. She hits the shorted circuits with one quick, deft burst of fire retardant.

Dez nods to her, standing. *"Il est bien fait. Merci."*

She nods, sets the red canister down. *"De rien."*

He realizes he saw her lips move but can't hear her. He doffs his headset, the radio circuits dead. He reaches out and taps people on their shoulders. They begin removing their Mickey Mouse ears, too.

"Frank: Get everyone inside the metal building, if ye will. I want well away from this helo, lest anything else catches fire. I'll get the flight crew."

The cop is holding his left arm against his side, his face a rictus of sweat and pain. He nods.

Dez fights against gravity and climbs the canted floor up to the flight deck. The nose of the helo faces upward about fifteen degrees.

Captain Charbonneau is jerking on the buckle of her safety harness, trying to get it free. She's taken a deep cut over her right brow, her right eye pasted shut with blood.

Her copilot is unconscious.

"I got him, Cap. Can't believe you got us down in one piece."

As she coaxes her buckle undone, she looks up sharply to see if he's being sarcastic. He's not.

Dez gets the four-point harness off the copilot and hefts him easily over his shoulder, a fireman's carry. He begins edging back out of the tight space, his boots slipping on the off-kilter deck.

Everyone else is off the helicopter and the sliding side door has been shoved one-quarter open. It jammed there.

Copilot over one shoulder, Dez grabs his U.S. Air Force backpack, leaving behind his guitar case. Sensing Captain Charbonneau on his six, he edges himself out and jumps down into a now well-trampled snow mound. The copilot moans. Footprints lead from there to the building their bird settled against.

The inside of the place is a miniaturized version of a terminal building. Two mismatched couches, several plastic chairs, a station for making coffee and tea, a unisex bathroom, a small desk with an ancient PC and an enormous old printer. The calendar on the wall advertises car parts and is seven months out of date. The space is maybe thirty paces long and fifteen paces wide. It's cold inside; warmer than outside, but not by much.

There is no power; the only light coming through windows.

The prefab building must have been solidly mounted on its deck, because it didn't budge under the impact of the sliding Super Puma.

Dez gets the copilot lying on his back on one of the couches. The man's breathing. "Doc?" he says.

Dyson Patterson looks up from where he's helping Frank Watts. "Right there."

Watts's left arm is broken below the elbow. He's sweat-sheened and pale, but he's standing upright while the doctor takes a look at it. One tough cop, Dez thinks.

"Trip Jacks?"

She smiles a little at the nickname, her breathing shallow and quick. "I'm okay. Rusty?"

Rusty Townsend sits by her side, also gasping. "My mom wanted me to be a lawyer. It's looking better and better."

Dez grins. He looks toward the woman from the National Research Council.

Ash has her eyes on him. She nods back.

Dyson Patterson rises, reaching for his backpack of medical supplies. Dez says, "Copilot's out but his irises look good, mate. Just wacked his melon, I think. Check the captain, please."

Dyson gets her seated and begins cleaning the wound over her right eyebrow. The wound isn't as deep as Dez initially thought, but given where it is, it's bleeding like mad.

Dez has the layout of Fuchstown in his head. He peers out a window, into the whirling, drifting snow. "We're in the easternmost building in town. I don't see anyone comin' a-running to rescue us, which bodes poorly, I think. On t'other hand, the Puma hasn't exploded."

"It won't," Captain Charbonneau says. "Also, we have battery-powered space heaters on board. We can get this place warmed up."

"Ta. We're here until the FBI arrives, looks like."

The captain nods. "I think they . . . were more than an hour out," she says, wincing.

"Ye've weapons on board?"

She shakes her head as Dyson puts a pressure bandage on her forehead and wraps her skull in gauze. It's clear that the blow rang her chimes, and she grips the arm of her chair as waves of dizziness pass through her.

"Expected as much. Doc, you stay here and tend to the wounded, please. Trip Jacks, you as well, kindly. Me, Rusty, and Ms. LeCroix will head into the town, reconnoiter a bit, see what's what."

Frank Watts says, "I'm coming with you."

Dyson, kneeling by the captain, says, "No, you're going into shock. In about ninety seconds. Sit your ass down, Frank. Please."

Watts hesitates, then almost collapses onto one of the chairs.

Trisha Jean Jackson says, "I'm old and fat and out of shape, but I grew up on a farm. I can handle a little goddamn snow, England."

Rusty touches her arm. "I'm sure you could. But we can do it faster alone. Ma'am."

She glowers at her bodyguard, then blanches and nods. "I can get the space heaters out of the plane, at the very least."

"'Sides," Dez says, "the FBI'll be here soon an' Frank's got a gun."

The cop, pale and sweaty, gives them a thumbs-up.

"Frank, my lad, remember: Someone stole the other Puma. She's headin' this way, an' that's a certainty."

Captain Charbonneau shoots him a look. "Wait. What?"

"Aye. I was both bribed and threatened into not coming here, Captain. That shooting at the hotel in St. John's? That was the oppo. They couldn't stop us whilst we was down there. Their only hope is doing so here."

"Why?"

"Haven't the foggiest."

The aviator looks grim. She lifts the bottom of her leather bomber with its fleece lining and shows them a Colt 1911 in a belt holster. "Make that two guns."

Rusty raises his hand. "Three."

"We've that, then. Better yet, we've a feckin' great pilot who got us down in one piece. The villains may have a pilot, ma'am, but they sure as fuck don't have you."

Cora Charbonneau gives him a hint of a smile and a nod. "They do not."

Dyson stuffs a roll of stretch tape into his backpack. "You got a gun, Dez?"

Dez shows them the retracting truncheon he stole from one of the mercenaries in St. John's. "I'm all set."

He peers out windows on all four sides. The wind is howling and, even if the stolen second helicopter is overhead, he doubts he could hear it. He stands in the middle of the room.

"Right, then. Special Agent Fairweather should be calling in soon. And when he can't reach us, he'll know we're in it, but good. We'll look for our own sat phone when we get into town. Ms. LeCroix? I'm Dez to me mates. Can I call you Elisabet?"

Ash nods, silent.

"We're not being paid by the hour, mates. Let's look lively."

As she packs her things, Ash doesn't reveal to the others that she, too, has a handgun. And a silencer.

# CHAPTER 16

In their parkas, watch caps, scarves, gloves, snow pants, and boots, Dez, Rusty Townsend, and Ash look like cosplay versions of the Michelin Man. Ash, at five-two, looks particularly spherical in her puffy outfit.

Rusty has stuffed his service auto into the outer pocket of his parka. Dez leads the way as they begin climbing through snowdrifts, westward, into the tiny, quiet village of Fuchstown.

In summer, it might look like any small town anywhere. Two dozen single-story, metal-sided buildings laid out on a partial tic-tac-toe grid of one main street, which they're on, and two streets heading north and south. All of the buildings appear prefabricated and identical, more like U-Stor-It bins than homes. Metal is the only material they spot. They see no cars, but they notice a parking lot of Caterpillars and construction vehicles, closer to the big domed entrance to what Dez assumes is the Fuchs Underground Neutrino Collector and the three-story mining facility.

The dome itself looms over the town, although a good one hundred yards away. They're too far away to tell what it's made of. It dominates the landscape, oddly alien in the otherwise sterile little metal village.

The wind whips through Fuchstown. No lights show in any windows. They spot no boot prints in the drifting snow. There's no second helicopter in the sky; so that's something.

Rusty shouts over the wind. "Last weekend, Lauren and I took in an off-off-Broadway show! It was nice! Nicer than, you know, this!"

Dez shouts, too. "Last weekend, I learned how to make a roux!"

"A what?"

"Roux!"

Rusty blinks at him. "Like a sauce?"

"The basis for a lot of sauces, yeah. Isn't that a thing?"

Rusty laughs. "We get outta this: Show me!"

"Deal!" He turns the other way. "D'you cook, Elisabet?"

Ash trudges through shin-high snow. *"Non."*

The first small building they come to might be a home. It's got lace curtains in the windows. Dez veers off the street, into the deeper snow in front of the place. He adjusts the straps of his backpack, cups his gloved hands against the windowpane, and peers in between them.

The place is deserted but doesn't appear to be damaged. He turns to the others and shakes his head.

They keep treading westward.

The next building has a carved wooden sign over the door that reads HANK'S PROVISIONS. It's larger than the house they passed but not by much. Ash and Dez both peer through windows.

Ash tries the front door. It's unlocked. She has to kick snow away to open it.

Inside, the place is dark. Dez, right behind her, tries the light switch. Nothing.

Here, it's called "provisions." In most American towns, it'd be called a 7-Eleven. A few rows of processed foods. One half row of household goods, including light bulbs and plungers and toilet paper and rolls of aluminum foil and plastic wrap. One row of candy and salty snacks and microwave popcorn. A whole lot of cheap liquor behind the cashier's stand. One of frozen entrees against an exterior wall; the freezer isn't working, but it's cold enough in the room not to make a difference.

Dez circles the stand and crouches, looking for a weapon. Some store clerks keep them; anything from a shotgun to a baseball bat. He spots a pair of brackets where a long gun or a bat might've been stored. They're empty now.

"Not where ye come for the meat and veg, yeah?" Dez checks the office, which is tiny and cluttered. And empty.

Ash tries the single restroom and a janitor's closet. In the main room, they shake their heads to each other.

"No bodies," she says.

"But you was expecting bodies. Me, too."

Rusty stands just inside the doorway. "You guys see this?"

He's peering down. Dez and Ash head his way. A beat, then they both crouch.

A brownish stain marks the lower corner of an end rack filled with bags of jerky.

"Blood," Dez says. "Dried."

Ash nods.

They stand.

Together, the three of them head back out and toward the center of town.

"This is foolish," Ash says.

"How so?"

"There is no power out here. Everyone's underground. We should head there."

Rusty says, "You're probably right, but I want to check out the building that looked like it'd been on fire."

They trudge on.

The next building appears to be another house. Dez approaches the front-facing window and realizes the glass has been shattered. He sweeps the snow with his boot, sees no shards of glass. He steps closer.

The window shattered inward. A small living room features glass on a cheap area rug, plus piles of snow. There's a small dining room table with room for two chairs. The table has been smashed, two legs broken, salt and pepper shakers lying on the floor, on their side.

More blood. A lot more of it.

No body. But Dez can see from the blood tracks where someone has dragged a body away.

He turns to the others. "Someone died in there. The body's been moved. C'mon."

Rusty grips his gun in his pocket a little tighter.

They get to the building with the soot marks. It's pretty much the largest of the single-story metal buildings in town. A sign out front reads FUCHSTOWN—DEALOUS FUCHS FOUNDER—2017.

"Must've been founded after they discovered cerite deposits," Dez says.

Rusty sighs. "You can't fight city hall. Unless city hall is a single-wide trailer."

One of the windows on the front-facing side is shattered. They see soot traces along the metal surface and they smell smoke, although whatever burned was doused some time ago, likely by the storm.

Dez doffs his left glove and grips the truncheon in his pocket. He leads the way into city hall.

It's what one would expect: A chest-high counter with a service bell and laminated cards explaining how one can pay city taxes online, and how to file a complaint. Framed photos on the walls of three white men who look self-important. A Canadian flag in a stand, and a second flag Dez assumes is that of Newfoundland and Labrador. It features mostly white, with a few filled-in blue triangles, not-filled-in red triangles, and a horizontal gold arrow.

Rusty points to it. "The white symbolizes snow. The blue, the sea. The red is for human effort and the gold's for confidence in the future."

Dez and Ash blink at him.

He rolls his eyes. "I like to do research on the places my protectee travels to. It makes the trips more interesting."

Dez says, "Quick: official bird of Newfoundland."

"Atlantic puffin."

"Seek help."

They keep looking around. One door is marked MAYOR. It's vacant, the furniture IKEA bland, a steelhead trout mounted on one wall.

The next door is marked CLERK. Pretty much the same as the other. Dez notes that the mayor's office and the clerk's office are the same size. For some reason, he likes that.

There's a small and windowless meeting room; no more than eight chairs. A cheap wooden gavel rests on the center of the table.

The room at the end of the hall is where the fire was. There, they find the skeletal remains of technical equipment, which likely included telephone equipment and routers. They also find the skeletal remains of, well, a skeleton.

Dez says, "And the gold's for confidence in the future."

Rusty keeps a little cross on a chain around his neck. He reaches up and rubs its outline through his sweater.

Ash does not react to the sight, or the smell, of the badly burned body.

Snow has drifted into this room. That's what put out the fire, they assume.

Rusty says, "Do you smell wine?"

Dez says, "They used ethyl alcohol as the accelerant, them. Smells like wine."

Rusty looks his way. "They?"

"Whoever firebombed this place an' killed this gent. And left blood in that house back there, and the general store."

Dez crouches. If the man had identification, it's gone now. Whoever used accelerant to spread the fire also doused him, head to foot. No clothes remain.

Dez is assuming it's a man. Could be a woman.

He rises. "If we was going to find a sat phone, this is where it'd be."

"Or at the facility entrance," Ash says. "Can we go there now?"

"No. We head back an' tell the others. No need to go to the dome until the FBI gets here."

Dez slips his glove back on, and the trio leave city hall.

They trudge past the little convenience store again. With their hoods up, none of them note the glint of light on the lenses of the binoculars following their path.

# CHAPTER 17

The trio returns to the terminal building by the runway to warm up a little, and to report that they found no satellite phone, no living residents, blood in two buildings, one arson-caused fire, and an incinerated skeleton.

"In case we had any lingering doubts about this being a freak accident," Trisha Jean says. She and the others have retrieved two battery-powered space heaters from the helicopter, and the terminal building is becoming warmer by the moment.

"I thought some twenty-five people live here," Rusty says, blowing into his cupped hands to warm them. "We're short about twenty-four so far."

"We didn't search every building. There's gotta be a dozen more," Dez reminds him. "Time enough for that later. We'll—"

Trisha Jean's cell phone blinks to life with an incoming call. She says, "The literal and metaphorical cavalry," and connects. "Special Agent Fairchild?"

The voice on the other end is tinny with static. "This is FBI Special Agent Neal Conway! Get me Deputy Assistant Secretary Jackson!"

He sounds as if he's shouting over the storm.

"This is she. Where are you guys?"

"We're grounded, ma'am!"

Trisha Jean and Dez glance at each other. Dez moves closer to her.

"It's this storm! We lost an engine. Somewhere over rural Quebec!"

Dez speaks loud. "Did ye turn back? Or find a runway long enough for a Hercules?"

"We landed on a damn rural road! The pilot thinks we might've damaged the port landing gear!"

Trisha Jean says, "Tom Fairweather?"

"Unconscious, ma'am! It was a rough landing! He took a fire extinguisher off his skull. I think he's concussed!"

His voice fades out in a blizzard of static. All around Dez and Trisha Jean, the others are quiet, unmoving. There's no need to explain to any of them why this is exceedingly bad news.

Neal Conway's voice comes back. "—can't get this engine running, or if we did fracture the landing gear, then this bird isn't going anywhere, ma'am! We'll hunker down and wait for the Canadian military to send trucks to get us. No idea how long that'll take! What's the status of your plane?"

Dez says, "Left it in St. John's. We came in a Super Puma helo. Military-grade. An' it's as damaged as your bird."

Special Agent Conway says, "Well, Jesus."

"Aptly summed up, aye."

They listen to the hiss of static and the storm. The FBI man says, "Look, the closest HRT unit is in Kansas City! They've got a hostage crisis and should be wrapped up in a day!"

Behind him, Dez hears Dr. Patterson mutter, "HRT?" and Rusty replies, "FBI. Hostage Rescue Team."

Over the sat phone, Conway shouts, "That team will be rerouted to New York. Another Hercules is waiting for them! Their priority is to get you out! If we catch a break with these storms, it shouldn't be more than a few days!"

Trisha Jean says, "That's swell and peachy, but we're pretty sure whoever's behind this is coming for us. And they'll be here in fewer than a few days."

They wait.

Conway says, "Ah . . . Do you . . . Can you hide? Is there a safe place to hide out?"

Rusty sighs and speaks directly to Dez. "Not aboveground, there isn't."

# CHAPTER 18

Trisha Jean disconnects and the survivors of the Super Puma crash study one another in the warmed-up terminal building.

Dez says, "We make for the dome, I reckon."

Frank Watts, holding his broken arm by his side, grunts a ruthless laugh. "Without the FBI and their fancy-dan armament and weapons? This is likely a hostage crisis, remember? You want to put us in front of that?"

Trisha Jean says, "Our best guess is that the Skyhook people who attacked Dez in St. John's stole the other helicopter and are on their way here. Now, this storm's been hell on aircraft, fixed wing or not, but I don't want to have to take my chances against those guys with your three guns and my good looks."

Everyone's quiet.

Rusty raises his hand. "We *think* there's a hostage situation underground, but we don't know that. We're pretty sure the Skyhook people are on our trail." He glances around, makes an all-encompassing gesture to the metal terminal building. "This look like the Alamo to you, Frank?"

"Academic," Dez adds. "Dunno if I can get the door to the mine open. Don't see as how we have much choice, yeah?"

A beat, and Frank Watts nods. Dr. Patterson does, too.

"Okay. Rusty, Elisabet, and me, we go see if it's even possible. You lot hear the other helicopter, you come runnin' fast, aye?"

More nods.

"Shall we?"

The three explorers bundle up again, gather their backpacks, and trudge back out into the storm.

The entrance to the mine and the Fuchs Underground Neutrino Collector site is in the dome, forty feet high, that looks to be made of blocks of ice, à la an igloo. But only from a distance. Closer, they realize the blocks are made of a lightweight, pale blue material that, to the touch, could be ceramic. "Solid, light, easy to stack." Dez smacks the surface with the palm of a gloved hand. "Sturdy, too. Not bad. Learned a trick or two from Brunelleschi, yeah?"

Rusty raises his brows in question.

Ash says, simply, "Florence. The Duomo."

Dez beams at her. "That's right. Filippo Brunelleschi. Designed the domed Cathedral of Santa Maria del Fiore, early fourteen hundreds or thereabouts. His duomo is still the largest masonry vault ever conceived."

Ash says, "And the most beautiful."

The laconic one's getting chatty, Dez marvels.

The half dome contains large, garage-sized double doors big enough for the nearby construction equipment to enter. Plus, a human-sized door. Dez tries that first. It's locked. It has a ten-key security pad to the left of the knob. Dez opens his parka and pulls out some of his lockpicking equipment, including a short screwdriver. "Let's get this off, shall we?"

He removes the cover of the ten-key pad. He peers into it. He deftly picks two wires, cuts them with plastic snips from his pack, then adds tiny, red alligator clips, and reattaches them both.

The door clacks open.

Rusty Townsend says, "Gatekeeper?"

Ash looks up, not getting the reference.

Dez leads them inside. "I'm not half bad with doors an' such," Dez tells her. "Explains why I'm not in Queens dicing up a mirepoix right this moment."

She says, "That's why they brought you. To open doors."

"Aye." He pauses. "Why do I keep havin' the feeling as if we've met somewhere?"

"We have not," she lies.

There are no windows on the dome, and they didn't realize until he breached the door that the interior is lit up. It's the first hint of electricity they've seen since they crash-landed. The interior is cold, but not the bone-cracking cold of outside. Dez doffs his fur-lined hood and watch cap.

The inside of the dome is all one room. They spot a parked Jeep with massive, fat snow tires. Some technical equipment, stacked on metal shelves. There's a forklift with the stylized logo of Skyhook Technologies.

He sees dumpsters in various colors, for paper, metal, and plastic recycling. Handy, this far north. Dez suspects there's another out back for food waste, which would stink up this igloo pretty badly, if left inside. He glances through the bins and spots several empty paint cans.

A small quadrant is blocked off with run-of-the-mill cyclone fencing, the type found in many a backyard. Within the enclosure is a wide array of tools, ranging from hammers and screwdrivers to a gas-powered snowblower and loops of hoses. All neatly stowed.

If the exterior is a dome, the interior isn't exactly. Three-fourths of the wall is concave, shaped like the outside, but the far wall is flat. In the center of that is a very large set of elevator doors; much wider than most commercial elevators. More like the type one might see at a construction site. Dez doesn't know how deep the elevator car is, but the door is wide enough that ten people could stand shoulder to shoulder and enter the car together.

Facing the big door, a dozen feet away from it, is a standing control panel. Dez grins. "Know what this reminds me of? The transporter room in every *Star Trek* series, ever. Stand here, control the elevator."

Rusty says, "But Atlantic puffin, and I'm the nerd."

The trio step up to the elevator controls.

If there is light and heat in the dome, there's none flowing to this control panel. Dez touches several buttons. Nothing.

He takes one knee and begins unscrewing a square, steel access panel below the controls. The screws are in place but not tightened.

"In me past, I visited mining operations a time or two. Found two kinds: pigsties, and them what's as neat and tidy as an operating room. This is the latter."

Which is why these loosened screws are sending warning signals to his brain. Two screws done, he gets the others off in no time. Inside, he finds wires ripped out and circuit boards that have taken direct hits from some sort of solid object, like a hammer. He shows the damage to the others.

"The elevator'll have interior controls an' exterior controls. Smash this one, topside, and ye can still control the lot of it from below."

Rusty says, "I guess you do know something about doors."

Ash takes one knee, too. "Is this fixable?"

"Likely, but not quickly. Might have to cobble together an alternative."

She looks at him. Their shoulders touch. "You could do that?"

"Hate to overpromise, but it's not undoable. My guess is, that's why the electronics at city hall were destroyed. So no one could fix this."

He rises. "Rusty. Go get the others, will ye? We'll relocate 'em here. I'll walk back t' the general store and get some bottled waters and prepared foods. Should hold us whilst I cobble another elevator control panel."

"Sure." Rusty gathers his stocking cap and gloves and moves to the human-sized door to the outside.

The second the door is open, they hear it.

The whoop of an airborne helicopter.

Dez says, "Both of yez. Go, an' right quick. Help get the injured back here."

"Maybe it's safer to stay in the terminal building?" Rusty asks.

"The villains of the piece? They didn't steal an H225 helo. They stole an H225M. The military variant of the Super Puma. Did ye notice on our bus? It had a sideboard pintle. Designed to hold a fifty-caliber machine gun. That, or even a twenty-millimeter cannon."

Rusty says, "Holy Mary."

"Them lads I tangled with in St. John's? Had all the moves and tech of mercenaries. Maybe they don't have access to military weapons. Maybe they do. I'd prefer not to gamble, either way."

# CHAPTER 19

Dez steps out into the storm and peers up into the sky. The cloud roof is very, very low; lower now than it was when they'd arrived. He can't see the helo, but he can still hear it, and he gets the sense it's not directly overhead.

"That cloud covering is a blessing!" he shouts over the wind, then leans in toward Rusty and Ash. "You two, scoot. Get the others back here, double-quick. I'll see to fixing the elevator controls."

Ash looks up and nods. She's dragged her scarf over her nose and mouth, and she's pulled her navy blue, woolen watch cap so low it nearly touches her eyebrows. All he can see of her is her hazel eyes.

And again, Dez is awash in a feeling that they've met before. A few images pop into his head but evaporate before he can snare them.

Don't push it, he tells himself. You'll remember when you remember.

"Elisabet? Ask the captain if she can disconnect the helo radio and bring it along, will ye?"

Ash nods.

Back inside the dome, Dez sits cross-legged in front of the elevator controls and begins pulling some of the damaged parts out and away from the rest. He's brought along his bespoke tablet computer, which, like his mobile, is a bit thicker than commercial brands. Both contain apps that he needed when he was deployed as a gatekeeper. He's retired these days but has kept the tricks of the trade in case they might come in handy.

He connects his tablet to the elevator console and begins running a diagnostic on the circuits. He can't make the system work until he knows what's broken and what isn't.

What are the chances that the mob chasing them stole the other Super Puma from the Canadian Coast Guard? Dez puts it at 100 percent. What are the chances that they've got access to either a mounted machine gun or a cannon? Unknown. But not zero.

Dez's diagnostic program is running, so he stands and crosses to the fenced-off portion of the dome that contains tools and equipment. He picks the lock, steps inside. It's an array of the things you'd pretty much expect. The tools necessary to keep an isolated town running. A lot of this stuff you'd find in any decently outfitted garage in the States. Some of it is very specific for a snowy, isolated place like Fuchstown, including the snowblower, road flares, and five barrels of deicer. The small forklift he noticed earlier is painted in the universal workplace-danger colors: striped yellow and black.

There's a box of air-activated hand warmers. Dez grabs a fistful of those and stuffs them in one of the voluminous pockets of his parka.

He spots coils of wire; metal piping; drawers full of nuts, bolts, screws, and nails; and all the tools one could hope for, all neatly tucked into their appropriate spaces. Someone took good care of this equipment.

He finds three small but well-maintained portable generators. Also, an array of space heaters. He spots plenty of barrels with plenty of petrol, which makes sense in a place like this.

He thinks he hears the helicopter again but it's hard to tell, being inside the dome.

A thought hits him.

He drags out one of the generators. Also, some of the precut piping and several flares.

# CHAPTER 20

Rusty Townsend and Ash return to the terminal building by the runway and the ruined helicopter. Trisha Jean Jackson sees them from a window and waves.

They get inside. It's warmed up considerably.

Dr. Patterson says, "We heard a helicopter."

Rusty says, "We did, too. Captain?"

Cora Charbonneau looks up.

"Dez thinks there's a possibility your helicopters could be turned into gunships."

"I guess," she says. "If they stole the other Super Puma to chase you people, they might have armed her."

"Okay. We're inside the dome that leads to the mining and research site. Dez thinks it'd be better to move everyone there. I mean, if the helicopter's armed, this place isn't going to be much of a shield. Also, Captain? He wants to see if you can disconnect your radio and bring it with us."

She rises, fighting off her vertigo.

The cop, Frank Watts, looks a little better now that the pain meds have kicked in. Dyson Patterson has fixed a sling for the inspector's broken arm. "Even if they haven't armed the chopper, they could land," Frank says. "I'm pretty sure they brought weapons, after what we saw at the hotel in St. John's."

Trisha Jean asks, "Can you walk?"

"Yes."

She turns to the pilot. "Captain?"

"I cleaned my clock pretty good, and Tulsa hasn't woken up yet." She nods toward the unconscious copilot.

Trisha Jean says, "If we take apart some of the seats on the chopper, I bet we could use the frame and the cloth to create a travois. We can drag your copilot with us."

Captain Charbonneau says, "Not necessary. We have an actual, handheld gurney on board. It's got a backboard and head restraints. That should do."

She and Dr. Patterson head for the helicopter.

Twenty minutes later, the party is moving. The petite Ash supports the cop, which looks a little silly, since he's so much larger than she is. She's stronger than her ballet dancer's frame suggests.

Before they get moving, Dr. Patterson takes her aside. "Elisabet? Frank's got a compound fracture in his arm. I doped him up, best I could, but he's in a lot of pain. Go gentle with him."

Ash nods.

Rusty and the doctor work together to drag the unconscious copilot strapped to the search-and-rescue helicopter's back brace turned travois.

Trisha Jean escorts Captain Charbonneau, her skull wrapped in gauze. The pilot is still feeling spells of dizziness and nausea from her head injury. Those two lead the way. The travois crew comes next. Ash and the cop third.

Which is why nobody notices when Ash lifts Frank Watts's service weapon and stores it in her parka, next to her own gun. The groggy Watts is entirely unawares.

They hear the helicopter more clearly now. It's up there, fighting the same savage winds that they'd faced. The cloud ceiling is low and thick, the winds this close to the Atlantic unpredictable and capricious.

They're about two-thirds of the way to the geodesic dome when the winds die a bit. Rusty says, "Uh-oh."

The stolen Super Puma breaks free from the clouds. It's hovering over the town itself, to the north and west of them.

"Gun!" It's Trisha Jean who spots the fifty-caliber machine gun on a turret, mounted on the side of the helo.

Someone in a parka and goggles is manning the big gun. He fires, strafing the town and the walkway ahead of them.

Trisha Jean looks around, trying to calculate how far they are from the dome. The answer is: too goddamn far.

She spots Dez. He's stepped out of the dome and he has something with him. A portable generator? And, maybe a pipe, six feet long or so? Together, they look like a weird and bulky upright vacuum cleaner. She wonders what the hell he's playing at, when Dez aims his pipe assembly thing at the Super Puma in the sky.

The tall redhead, Aiyden Finn, stands behind his gunner. Both wear goggles, the side door of the gunship open to deploy the fifty-cal.

He looks back inside. He's got a total of twelve men, himself included. All armed like they're about to occupy some banana republic in Southeast Asia.

He speaks into the voice wand of his headset. "Collins! Hold this fucking bird steady!"

He hears the pilot over the comms. *"In this weather? No can do!"*

"Fire again," he tells his gunner.

The big helo reverberates as the wind punishes them. His man fires but, as unstable as their platform is, he hits shit.

That's okay. They've got lots of bullets.

"Hit 'em again. We got—"

*"Incoming!"* the pilot screams.

A red streamer is heading their way. It was fired from the dome.

Finn grabs his gunner by his jacket and yanks him back inside the bird. He slams shut the side sliding door.

"They got a fucking antiaircraft mortar!" he screams into his comms. "Climb! Climb!"

But the pilot is already pushing the Super Puma back up into the cloud roof. Well away from the arcing, red-glowing ordnance aimed at them.

The party double-times it toward the dome. Dez waves them forward.

The red mortar he fired at the gunship arcs gently downward, landing somewhere in the streets of Fuchstown.

Nothing blows up.

The travois party gets inside first, followed by Trisha Jean and the pilot, then Ash and the cop.

Dez drags in his portable generator, then slams the door shut.

Everyone's gasping. Most of them plop down on the tiled floor, heaving, whisking off goggles and wool caps and mittens.

Trisha Jean Jackson says, "Holy . . . Someone just fired a goddamn Gatling gun at us!"

"Fifty-cal," Dez says. "Vicious weapon, that. Them fuckers."

Rusty is gasping. "What . . . What'd you . . . fire at them?"

Dez says, "Used the genny to create an air pump. Fired a lit flare at 'em."

The assassin from Paris spins on him, her mouth open. *Such a gambit!* Ash marvels. *Like running into our fire that day, eighteen months ago, in Paris. Not away from our fire, as any sane man would do. The kind of chess move that nobody could have predicted!*

Trisha Jean says, "Could you have downed that helo with a flare?"

Dez laughs. "Not even hypothetically! Had I hit it—and in this wind, are ye daft? I had no chance whatsoever. But if I had, it would've bounced harmlessly off the fuselage, yeah?"

Rusty shakes his head. "Then why?"

But it's the wolfish laugh of Captain Cora Charbonneau that catches everyone's attention. "Because those assholes didn't know it was a flare. Dez chased them out of our airspace with a bluff." She grins up at Dez. "You have any Comanche genes in you?"

He laughs. "'Fraid not."

She nods respectfully. "Nice move. That's what my people call 'counting coup.'"

# CHAPTER 21

They hear a ping. Dez crouches in front of the standing controls for the freight elevator. His tablet computer has finished running a diagnosis.

"Someone bolluxed this, then took the time to close the access hatch and return all four screws."

Rusty is standing by the elevator doors, peering at the flat metal wall. "I'm not seeing any other controls over here. Thought there might be a mechanical bypass."

"Had the same thought," Dez says, scanning the readout with the tablet in the crook of his arm. He sits cross-legged, studying. "Captain?"

The helo pilot also sits on the floor, her back to the concave wall of the dome. "Yes?"

"You brought your ship's radio. If I give you a power source, can you tap into the comms of that other bird?"

"Can I . . . ?" She sits bolt upright. "Yes! I mean, I think so. Yeah."

Ash takes the radio from her and crosses to Dez. She hands it to him. He begins rigging it to the power flowing through the elevator controls.

"This is clever," she says in English, softly and for his ears only.

"Ta. Where are you from, ye mind me askin'?"

A beat, and she says, "Montreal."

Dez smiles at her.

Dez spent the greater part of his adult life speaking French amid a wide array of people who were not native French speakers. And he has a good ear for dialect. He's absolutely sure that the woman claiming to be from the Conseil National de Recherches Canada just lied to him. She's most definitely not from Quebec, nor any other part of Canada. If he were to guess, he'd say she's from the Middle East, or was, a long time ago.

He says, "Captain? Got this thing hooked up."

Trisha Jean helps the pilot to rise.

Cora Charbonneau leans on the elevator controls, waiting for another surge of dizziness to pass, then begins modulating the frequency of the radio. They hear a great deal of static. Then:

*". . . fuel reserves! We got, maybe, thirty minutes!"*

Some of the people in the dome cheer. Dez begins snipping wires inside the elevator controls and using his alligator clips to realign them.

He knows that helo has to leave or land, and the decision time is fast approaching. Given all they've done so far, he assumes they'll land.

And they'll be armed to the teeth.

But at least Dez and his traveling companions will know when they're coming.

★ ★ ★

In the Super Puma, Aiyden Finn sees the red light on his sat phone blink three times. He doffs his helicopter headset and connects. "Bukowski? Status!"

Finn has a man hiding in Fuchstown; the same man who destroyed the town's telephone system and killed some of the townies.

*"They're all in the dome,"* his man says. *"I got the binoculars on 'em. They ain't coming out."*

"Understood. Keep watching."

*"Boss? That wasn't no mortar they fired at you. It was a fucking road flare."*

Finn pauses. He squints his eyes shut tight. "Are you fucking . . . They chased me out of the goddamn sky with a *flare*?"

*"That's affirmative, boss. It was that big moose of a guy. The one built like Popeye."*

Limerick.

"Understood. Keep watch."

Finn disconnects. His grimace shifts into a grim smile and a shake of his head.

*All right, Mr. Limerick,* he thinks. *Not too shabby. Not too fucking shabby at all.*

He looks around the interior of his gunship. Dez Limerick crafted an air cannon and a road flare to scare them, and it worked.

But Aiyden Finn has twelve men, counting himself, and they're armed with Heckler & Koch MG4 light machine guns and SIG Sauer sidearms.

*Let's see some more of your fancy tricks now, you son of a bitch.*

# CHAPTER 22

Dez has taken out a couple of yards of wiring from the sabotaged elevator controls and has reconnected much of it into a new pattern of spaghetti logic. He sits on the floor, cross-legged, smiling a bit because he enjoys puzzling out engineering problems. It's cold enough in the high-tech igloo that everyone's still wearing their coats, and everyone's breath mists.

The radio retrieved from their downed helicopter sits on the belt-high cabinet that houses the elevator controls. It chirps, and they hear a voice they've heard before.

*"Collins, get below the fucking ceiling and hold her steady."*

Collins, Dez realizes, is the pilot of the stolen gunship.

*"Jesus, Finn! This storm's kicking my ass!"*

Which makes Finn the tall, redheaded fella with whom Dez tangoed outside the hotel in St. John's? Seems likely.

*"Just do it!"*

Dez speaks up. "Ah. That could be a cue, friends."

The others look his direction.

"See the nice, thick, iron forklift in the cage, there? What say everyone gathers around it, please."

The sardonic Dr. Patterson goes to his haunches and gives Dez that slow, stoner smile of his. "These guys can't see in here. My guess: They'll land and walk in."

Dez, still seated and fiddling with the innards of the control panel, nods toward the human-sized door they used to get in here. "Them fuckwits can't know how many weapons we have. Unless they brought flash-bangs, gettin' through that door could be a challenge. And they'll be out in the storm with no cover. The more I cogitate on it, the more I think they'll try'n soften us up whilst airborne."

Patterson says, "They have a fifty-cal, dude. You don't think they brought flash-bangs? And what if—"

A string of fifty-caliber bullets rips through the ceramic bricks that make up the curved walls. The shots come in high, starting thirty feet off the floor inside this forty-foot-tall half globe. The line of bullets runs left to right, dropping to maybe twenty feet off the floor.

Some bullets ping around inside the dome, ricocheting. Some gouge into the cement floor.

Dr. Patterson was on his haunches but, in shock, he falls on this ass. *"Jesus Christ!"*

Half of their party already is inside the fenced-off tool area. The wounded get assistance. Everyone tries to huddle behind the small forklift.

Dez is aware that helicopters move, of course. There's no guarantee that the next salvo will come from the same angle.

Trisha Jean shouts at him, "Limerick! Get your ass in here!"

He winks at her. "We're safer underground than we are up here, love. And—"

More heavy bullets rip through the wall. Lower this time and farther to Dez's right. Bits of white ceramic fly free and bounce off the floor like a broken string of pearls. Bullets gouge into the far, curved walls, and ping off the floor. Two hit the elevator doors.

Dr. Patterson, who'd been the most shocked by the aerial assault, was the last guy behind the forklift. "Dez! Let's go!"

Above Dez's head, the elevator controls blink to life.

"Ah!" He grins. "Better."

He stands, studies the controls. Snowflakes are beginning to drift lazily into the dome via bullet holes.

He hears the telltale sounds of another volley, but the dome holds this time. The voice of the assault leader, Finn, erupts from the radio. *"Goddamn it! Where'd you learn to fly?"*

The pilot: *"Fuck you! Losing control of the tail rudder! The fucking storm! Probably froze up the hydraulic cable!"*

A third voice: *"Get back to civilization, boss?"*

The pilot: *"With a balky rudder? We're dropping, people! That's a given. Just gotta goose this piece of shit and hope for the best!"*

Cora Charbonneau, sitting on the floor and with her copilot's unconscious form before her, his head on her lap, glowers. "Amateurs."

Dez says, "I'll say it again: Damn glad we had you at the stick, Captain."

They hear a ping. A recessed light over the massive elevator doors lights up.

It shows a glowing up arrow.

Dez types quickly on his tablet computer. "Our ride's here. Best case scenario, them twats die in a ball of flame and the rest of this mission's a holiday, yeah? Worst case: They survive and come gunnin' for us. So next stop: the mine."

Rusty Townsend rises from behind the forklift, helping to get the RCMP inspector, Frank Watts, to his feet. Rusty says, "What's to stop them from following us?"

Dez waggles his tablet in the air. "I can whistle up the elevator car with this. But the control panel is still busted. Whoever's down below can control the elevator, too."

Ash, the quiet woman, nods her approval.

They hear a *thunk*. The elevator car—wide enough for ten people to line up—has arrived.

The twin elevator doors begin sliding open.

"Ladies and gents?"

Dez steps toward the elevator.

That's when he notices a rope, strung from one door to the other. And as the doors separate, the rope stretches taut.

The door to Dez's left glides open, and he spots a cylinder of propane. Standing upright in the car. The rope is attached to it.

*"Bomb! Down down down!"*

Dez is airborne, diving over the top of the elevator controls, hoping to hide behind the central leg of the thing.

The others react quickly for the most part; Ash and Trisha Jean and Dr. Patterson drag the others back behind the forklift.

The twin elevator doors fully open. The rope yanks on a mechanism atop the propane tank.

And a fireball erupts from the car.

# CHAPTER 23

The gout of flame roars past the single leg of the elevator controls, to Dez's left and to his right. The good news: There's no carpeting in the igloo, and the concrete floor isn't flammable. Dez's U.S. Air Force snow pants are another matter, but he quickly beats out the part that catches fire.

He's holding his breath. But the flash of flame is brief and there's not too much smoke.

He stands.

The elevator car—fifteen feet wide, ten feet deep and tall—is blackened inside by the incendiary device. Soot has charred the flat wall around the doors, too, and also in an oval pattern on the floor outside the car. Smoke roiled out of the blast but the igloo is forty feet high at the center, and the hot smoke quickly floats aloft.

A couple of people are coughing as they rise, but nobody looks reinjured. Except the Canadian cop, Frank Watts, who is holding his busted arm against his side, eyes squeezed shut, teeth clenched.

Tentatively, Dez circles the elevator controls and approaches the toppled propane canister. Fire devoured the rope that triggered the explosion.

Ash softly approaches from his left, as does Rusty Townsend.

Dez studies the makeshift incendiary, turns to them, his blue eyes wide. "Did ye see that? That was . . . that was fecking rude! I mean it! It was inhospitable, it was dangerous, an' if I'm being honest, I'm not feeling very welcomed!"

Rusty bends over, hands on his knees, and expels a long-held breath.

Trisha Jean says, "You okay there?"

He looks her in the eye. "There's no place like home, there's no place like home, there's no place like home. . . ."

She hugs him. "Lemme know if that works."

Dez looks around for Ash but she's picked the helicopter radio up off the concrete floor. She makes eye contact, shakes her head, and drops it again.

No more eavesdropping on the mercenaries from Skyhook Technologies.

"We have to assume they landed safe-like and are on their way here," Dez says.

Dr. Patterson is seeing to Frank Watts's broken arm.

Rusty says, "We got guys behind us trying to kill us, and people below us trying to kill us. I say we leave the igloo, head for city hall, and hope our opponents behind and below annihilate each other."

Ash ponders it a moment, turns to Dez. "It is an option. It's not ideal but . . . ?" She shrugs.

The more he hears her, the more Dez is sure she's neither French nor Canadienne.

"Nah," he says, kicking at the overturned metal container. "Didn't try t'kill us, tried to scare us. An incendiary? In a vast hall like this? Very little chance it was a killin' weapon. Now, a fragmentation device would've been a different kettle of nettles, as Sister Agnes used to say."

Ash nods. "A fragmenting explosive would have hurled bits of metal through the air at the speed of sound, *oui*. All this was—was . . . pyrotechnics."

Dez smiles at her. "Bureaucrat with the National Research Council, are we?"

She looks him dead in the eye. "The council does research on many topics."

He laughs. "Fair play t'you. Captain Charbonneau?"

The helo pilot turns to him.

"D'you and your mate carry walkie-talkies?"

Cora Charbonneau unzips her parka and shows him the walkie-talkie clipped to her belt. "I brought both of them."

"Excellent. Mind if I put one of 'em in the elevator and send it back down to whomsoever sent us the souvenir?"

Trisha Jean Jackson says, "The elevator's still working?"

"Industrial-grade machine, this is. For use on mining sites. Tougher than your average bit of technology. It's charred a bit, but it'll run, I wager."

"And you want to talk to whoever's down there?"

"No, you're the professional diplomat. I want you t'talk to whoever's down there."

Trisha Jean nods.

Rusty says, "And the guys from the helicopter?"

Dez scratches his head. "Why come up with an original idea when our downstairs neighbors gave us such a good one?"

"Limerick." It's the wounded cop, being tended to by the physician. Frank Watts, seated on the floor and leaning against the forklift, juts his chin in Dez's direction.

Dez walks over and goes down on his haunches before the man.

"I was pretty dizzy on the walk over here. Plus, the pain meds. Plus, running when we saw the gunship."

"Aye?"

Watts looks as much embarrassed as he does in pain and nauseous. "I . . . dropped my service piece. It's not here."

So they have two guns, not three. As far as Dez knows. "No worries, mate. Expect the unexpected, that's my motto."

"I'm . . . I'm better than this, goddamn it. I'm not some rank amateur."

Dez grips him on his good shoulder. "I've the serenity to accept the things I cannot change, mate. The courage to change the things I can, an' wisdom to know the difference."

Dr. Patterson gives him that loopy smile and a nod. Grateful, perhaps, that Dez didn't make his patient feel more guilty than he already does.

Dez rises and moves to the wall of tools inside the fenced-off portion of the igloo. Time to get busy.

# CHAPTER 24

Fifteen minutes later, Dez sets one of the Canadian Coast Guard walkie-talkies in the massive elevator. He's found a legal pad and felt markers amid the tools. He sets the radio on a note that reads WE'RE THE RESCUE TEAM.

Rusty Townsend smiles at that. "Quick question: Who rescues us?"

"Maybe we rescue each other." Dez glances over his shoulder at the human-sized door, through which they all entered. Ash drove the forklift out of the caged area and parked it laterally against the door. As she did that, Dez disabled the motor of the vehicle-sized door.

Now Dez taps his tablet computer. The soot-stained elevator doors hiss closed. They hear the motor engage, and a lighted down arrow appears over the doors.

Rusty says, "Hang on. You're meeting your friend. Petra . . . Alexander? Alexandris? Why not have her vouch for you?"

Trisha Jean answers. "This is a really, really small town, even by rural Georgia standards. She's a fabulously rich lady from California. I don't know how much stock the townies will be giving her."

Dez nods. "My thoughts as well. Rusty? Captain? If the elevator comes back up, you've got our only two guns."

Cora Charbonneau nods. She and the Secret Service agent placed themselves to the left and right of the big doors.

Everyone can hear the elevator motor stop.

The down arrow disappears.

They wait, one of two walkie-talkies in the hands of Trisha Jean Jackson, their diplomat. The other down in the mine.

Aiyden Finn leads the crew of mercenaries as they approach the forty-foot-tall igloo on foot. Everyone wears winter camo gear over ballistic vests, and everyone carries their Heckler & Koch MG4 light machine guns. The crew is Finn plus eight men, now. Three of his guys died when their stolen helo crashed. The rest are okay but a little banged up. Nothing they can't handle.

*Nine is enough*, Finn thinks. Nine battle-hardened guys from the U.S. and from Western Europe. He knows these guys; trusts them.

Their tenth man waits outside the igloo. Bukowski. One of two guys hired by Skyhook Technologies to create havoc in the village, and to kill or drive away as many of the residents as they could.

Bukowski's winter gear doesn't match theirs; his is designed to look civilian; theirs is covered in white, off-white, and gray blotches; snow camo.

"They're in there!" Bukowski shouts over the wind and snow. "Take a look at the surprise they left us with!"

Aiyden Finn does, then steps ten paces away from the human door to study the igloo. "Can we get the big door open?"

"It's got a motor but it looks like power's been cut off to the controls on this side."

Finn steps closer to the obstacle in front of the human door. It's a barrel, three feet high. It's plastic. On the outside, he sees the logo of a popular brand of deicer. It would make sense, a place this far north would stock this.

But someone has written on the barrel with a paint brush.

WE HAVE A FRAGMENTATION BOMB. TAMPER WITH IT AT YOUR OWN PERIL.

The barrel is wrapped in several yards of chain.

Finn peers over the top of the barrel. Someone drilled two holes in the bottom of the door, and the chains extend through there to the inside of the igloo. He sees no immediate way of moving the barrel away from the door.

"Sanchez!" Finn yells over the storm, waving one of his guys forward.

The guy trudges forward. He peers at the note, then up at his very tall boss.

"You're our explosives expert. Defuse it."

Sanchez is a Spaniard and has worked with the mercenary crew for six years. Everyone respects his expertise on things that go boom. He says, "This is that guy, that Limerick. He's got military experience. He's more dangerous than we figured."

"Yeah, but can you do it?"

Sanchez shrugs. "Let me look at it. Back everyone else up."

"Shit!" Finn growls. It's too cold to stand around in this vengeful wind; a factor that the English asshole, Limerick, was counting on. If it takes Sanchez long enough, Finn's guys will be fighting off frostbite as well as the U.S. State Department party inside.

He turns to Bukowski. "Get everyone inside the nearest home. I'll stay and cover Sanchez. Go."

Eight of the ten men stomp through shin-high snow toward the ghost town.

Sanchez goes to one knee and doffs his swollen backpack. He

unzips and pulls out a stethoscope and other tools of the bomb squads' trade.

Inside the igloo, everyone waits. Dez and most of the people keep their eyes on the elevator. Rusty Townsend and Captain Charbonneau, handguns at the ready, also keep their eyes on the door barricaded by the forklift.

But even those two turn when the walkie-talkie in Trisha Jean Jackson's hand chirps.

*"Who is this? Over?"*

Dez whispers, "Press here to send. Say 'over' when you're done."

She whispers back, "You mean like they do in every damn army movie ever made?"

Dez blushes. "Sorry. Shouldn't've assumed."

She depresses the key. "This is Trisha Jean Jackson. I'm from the U.S. State Department. I have a party with me and we are armed. No one was hurt by your firebomb, by the way. Over."

They wait.

Click. *"How do we know you're who you say you are? Over."*

"Well, who were you expecting? I'm from the State Department. We've got a representative of Triton Expediters, the Canadian National Research Council, an RCMP cop, plus people from the Canadian Air Force and Coast Guard. Over."

It's an impressive-sounding list. Most of the people she just mentioned are injured or unarmed. Still, Dez remembers the story of Trip Jacks beating a Saudi general at poker. She makes their party sound like the Royal Regiment of Scotland.

The wait this time is even longer. Every time Dez moves, the left leg of his polyester snow pants crackles from where the firebomb half melted the material.

Rusty and the helicopter captain keep their guns trained on the exterior door.

Click. *"You're not with the Russians? Over."*

Trisha Jean says, "I'm from Georgia. And not *that* Georgia. The one with peanuts, the Braves, and Scarlett O'Hara. Over."

Click. *"We're sending the car up to you. Be careful. There are Russians in Fuchstown. They already killed some of our friends. Over."*

# CHAPTER 25

Sanchez, the Skyhook explosives expert, has to stop and reach into his parka every twenty seconds. He's got air-activated hand warmers in each. With work this tricky, he can't do it wearing mittens.

Aiyden Finn is standing guard, and he's as bitterly cold as Sanchez.

Sanchez has confirmed that there is no counterweight holding on to the chains from behind the door. If there had been, then severing the chains could have triggered the fragmentation device from inside. He's used a small, palm-sized torch to melt through one of the two chains, and has unwrapped it, freeing the lower half of the barrel. He's listened via the stethoscope but can detect no sounds from within the barrel. Although that means nothing. You can listen to a hand grenade for a week and not hear anything; doesn't mean it won't explode.

It takes Sanchez fifteen minutes to get the second chain off the barrel.

He loops the chain around the freestanding barrel, near the bottom. He hands one end of the twenty-foot-long chain to Finn. "We're going to pull the barrel, slowly, away from the door. There are no connecting wires, I've checked. There could be a plummet trigger inside, or a spirit-level trigger, so we're doing this nice and slow, boss."

Finn nods. He shoulders his H&K. Sanchez does the same, putting his mittens back on. The men take one end of the chain each. Both go down on one knee.

"Slowly. Now."

Finn nods and they both pull.

The barrel slides on snow away from the door. It does not topple or wobble.

They get it two feet from the door. Then four feet. Then ten.

Both stand. Finn claps the Spaniard on the shoulder. "They don't know we're through their guard. Let's get to the house and warm up before we breach the door."

"Roger that."

They see lights in the nearest single-wide trailer. Bukowski and the others have set up a bivouac there, and they've got a gas-powered space heater that belonged to the resident. The place is up to about fifty degrees.

Finn and Sanchez warm their hands and get a little food and water in themselves. They explain the situation at the igloo.

"Was it really a frag bomb?" one of the guys asks.

The Spaniard shrugs. "Who knows? Easier to just move it out of the way. We can try to detonate it later, when we're done and our ride is on the way to get us out of here."

Finn's feeling better already. He flexes his hands, making fists, over and over, restoring circulation. "Bukowski, you and Collins lead the assault. Get the door open, toss in the flash-bangs. Then back out, left and right. We give it a count of five. Then I lead the assault. This is a spray and pray. No one and nothing that moves in there is our concern."

The guys look at one another. Someone says, "Boss? We got people on the inside."

"We're soldiers. We get paid to take risks," Aiyden Finn says, getting back into his parka and stocking cap. "Everyone knows the score. Let's go."

Frank Watts says, "I don't know we can trust whoever's on the other side of the radio, ma'am. They did greet us with a goddamn firebomb."

Trisha Jean ponders that, tapping the stubby antenna of the walkie-talkie against her lower lip. "My gut says we trust 'em."

Her Secret Service bodyguard speaks from farther away, still guarding the door to the outside. "And my gut tells me the dudes coming from that helicopter definitely want to kill us. The devil you know versus the devil you don't, Inspector."

Dez nods. "I agree."

The elevator arrives. The double doors hiss open.

Nothing goes boom this time.

Dez says, "Right, people. In we go. Let's—"

Captain Cora Charbonneau says, "Shh. Outside. I heard something."

Dez says, "Go. Into the elevator. Captain, Rusty? You, too. We—"

The outside door bursts open.

Exactly ten inches. Then slams into the parked forklift.

Out in the blizzard, Bukowski and Collins, their helo pilot, shove their shoulders into the door, as hard as they can. It opens, but just ten inches.

Bukowski literally ricochets off the door, arms flailing. His boots slip on the ice and snow, and he lands on his ass.

Collins stumbles back but stands his ground.

He can see light from inside the door. He sees the flank of a forklift blocking their way. Also, several stacked paint cans just to the right of the door. And a broom, standing straight up.

The broom handle was leaning against the door. With the door open, it begins leaning out toward them. Like the arm of a metronome. The bristled part of the broom is near the floor, surrounded by the paint cans.

A sheet of legal paper flutters from the broom handle like a flag.

Collins peers at it. "It says . . . 'Told you.'"

Aiyden Finn shouts, "Back! Get b—"

Dez has rigged the paint cans to be fragment explosives; not the barrel. He created a simple toggle trigger activated by the tipping of the broom. The purpose of the chained barrel was to slow the mercenaries down, and to make sure they were nice and cold. The misdirection of warning them about a bomb—by making them think it was in the barrel outside, not the paint cans within the igloo—was to play fair. Dez has no intention of accidentally blowing up a townie who survived in hiding and came to the igloo seeking shelter.

The concussive force of an explosion normally travels in three dimensions equally. But the paint cans are stacked against the forklift, so the high-pressure wave exits through the ten-inch gap in the door, or straight up toward the curved ceiling.

The pilot, Collins, is blown in half. His hips and legs fall to the left; his chest, arms, and head to the right.

Stumbling as he did saves Bukowski's life. Most of the nails, screws, and bolts Dez packed into the paint cans sail over his head. But he's on his back, soles of his boots on the ground, his knees up. He takes several blows to his calves. He screams in agony. But he'll live.

A big, gangly soldier from Florida, whom Aiyden Finn has

known for a decade, was right behind Collins. Bolts, nuts, and nails sail through the remains of Collins and hit the Floridian straight on. The puffiness of his snow suit and his Kevlar vest stop most of the impact to his torso, but nothing stops three bits of fast-moving iron from penetrating his face and ricocheting around inside his skull. He's dead long before his body hits the ground.

Everyone else is far enough away to survive. Several took hits, but not life-threatening ones.

Inside the igloo, and inside the massive elevator, the State Department team see swirls of snow enter the igloo, then hear the explosion Dez has rigged.

As the elevator doors hiss closed, they hear a man scream.

# CHAPTER 26

The big elevator begins rumbling downward. Trisha Jean Jackson says, “Jesus.”

Rusty Townsend rubs the little gold cross hanging inside his sweater.

Dez side-eyes the allegedly French-Canadian woman; she appears unshaken by the scream they heard.

Trisha Jean says, “Dez . . . The forklift could have blocked the door. Did we need to . . . ?”

He replies softly. “They have a fifty-caliber gun that can shoot through our walls. Stopping them from entering was never the same as stopping them.”

“Okay. I know. But . . .”

“A leader of the FBI’s Hostage Rescue Team said he needed me because I’m good with doors, ma’am. He told ye I’d had military trainin’. Ye had to know that meant I’m more than good at opening doors. I’m good at defendin’ ’em. Aye?”

"No, you're right," Trisha Jean says quietly, facing the big door, and not Dez. "I knew. I knew what you'd be capable of. I just chose not to dwell on it at the time."

The solid, metal elevator shudders as it descends.

Dez has drawn the retractable truncheon but holds it down by his side. "Turn around," he advises. "It's the door behind us that'll open below."

Everyone turns and spots an identical door on the wall opposite of where they entered. So they turn that way.

Rusty and Captain Charbonneau hold their guns.

The car comes to a rest. Everyone tenses up except Dez and Ash.

The aft doors open to the left and to the right, but on this level, outside of them, heavy metal grates retract like accordions, both upward and downward, as well.

They face several people in civilian garb. Men, mostly, and a couple of women. Dez spots three shotguns and a couple of rifles. One person's holding the leash of a gray-muzzled German shepherd.

The townies—he's assuming that's who they are—inhale deeply as the elevator dumps a load of fresh air into the large, musty room. The place is big enough to store two small forklifts and a hydraulic excavator bearing the Skyhook Technologies logo.

One woman steps forward and sighs.

Dez does, too, sliding the truncheon away. They step together and hug. The hug lingers.

Petra Alexandris holds him very tight. She says, simply, "Dez."

He says, simply, "'Course."

When they separate, Petra uses the pads of her thumbs to wipe tears from her cheeks. She says, "Desmond Aloysius Limerick, this is Burt Brandywine. He's the mayor of Fuchstown. Mr. Mayor, Dez is probably the only man on this continent who could get the elevator working again."

The mayor steps forward and offers his hand. He and Dez shake.

The guy is in his fifties, tall and pudgy, with a poorly considered comb-over. He's wearing what most everyone down here is wearing: snow pants and a plaid woolen shirt with a thick undershirt. It's in the mid-sixties down here.

"Mr. . . . Limerick, was it? We're sure glad to see some friendly faces."

Someone coughs. A few people look red in the face. Dez counts ten townies in all.

He turns to his party. "Trisha Jean Jackson, leader of our expedition. She's U.S. State Department. We've got some wounded. D'you have an infirmary?"

Burt Brandywine nods. "We do. I don't know how well stocked the medical supplies are."

Dyson Patterson, who's steadying Inspector Watts, says, "I'm a doctor. I've got some supplies."

"That's dang good news," the mayor says.

Silent, Ash has been studying Petra Alexandris. She is not what she expected as far as the all-powerful CEO of Triton Expediters. She's tall, athletically built, mid-thirties, with long, black hair. She wears a flannel shirt and jeans and thick-soled Timberlands. If she's worth billions, it's not obvious right now.

A big, rangy guy with a full beard and a Montreal Canadiens cap speaks up behind the mayor. He's one of the ones holding a shotgun. "We thought we felt something rumble? On the surface?"

"We was attacked," Dez says. "Used an explosive to delay 'em. Same as you."

One of the townies mutters, "Goddamn Russians."

Dez and Rusty Townsend exchange looks.

Dr. Patterson clears his throat. "Can we . . . ?"

Trisha Jean takes over. "Yes. Let's get everyone who needs to be to the infirmary. Then, Mr. Mayor, maybe we can brief each other? Get a sense of what's what and who's who here?"

# CHAPTER 27

The infirmary is on the first level of the mine and the Fuchs Underground Neutrino Collector site. This level has a doughnut of living quarters surrounding common areas such as a dining room, an exercise room, little offices, and storage. The actual mining happens on levels two, three, and four. And below all that is the neutrino facility.

The infirmary is unimpressive; two camp cots and a few standing cabinets of medical supplies. Dyson Patterson stays there with Frank Watts, Captain Charbonneau, and her still-unconscious copilot.

Mayor Brandywine asks some of his constituents to haul in some more beds.

The mayor leads the others to a break room that includes a dozen round tables, plastic chairs, a microwave station, a large fridge, and coin-operated vending machines filled with chips and candy in one; soda, bottled water, and energy drinks in another; packaged sandwiches and cups of soup and ramen in the third.

Someone pushes two tables together and they gather enough seating for Mayor Burt Brandywine along with Dez, Petra Alexandris, Trisha Jean, Rusty, and Ash. Trisha Jean makes the introductions, identifying Ash as Elisabet LeCroix of the Conseil National de Recherches Canada.

For Trisha Jean, this is as much a fact-finding mission as it is a rescue mission. "Tell us what happened. Please."

The mayor walks to one of the vending machines and gets a Sprite. The dispensary machines have been opened, so coins aren't necessary. Rusty Townsend gets a bottled water for his protectee.

Dez and Petra sit together and Petra rests her hand on Dez's thigh.

"Let me start at the top," the mayor says. "We've been having some big, big problems here in the mine for more than two weeks. Three miners died in accidents. Two more inhaled lead fumes and had to be airlifted out. Another got compound fractures to both legs when one of the hydraulic front loaders overturned. Pretty soon, the union shop steward called a temporary work stoppage. There was a whole lot of arguing, and accusations going to and fro. The negotiators from Syever Mineralnaya really got into it with the union chief, accusing the workers of negligence and of working drunk or stoned. That's when the miners voted for a full work stoppage and hitched a ride on the next cargo plane heading south."

Trisha Jean sips her water. "That's about the last that we heard. After that, you went radio-dark."

Burt Brandywine shakes his head. He's red in the face and seems to have a little trouble breathing. "Not us. It was the eggheads down in the Swimming Pool. They stopped sending whatever gobbledygook they normally sent to the universities and whatever. Then they established whatcha call 'lockdown protocols.'"

He makes quote marks with his fingers.

"All that stuff's so much Greek to me, but whatever. Anyway, shortly after that, things went to heck in a handbasket, topside. Someone destroyed our radio and the telephone system in city hall. There went our internet. We had a couple of satellite radios but they went missing. Poof."

He makes a hand gesture like a stage magician.

Dez says, "We saw blood."

Burt Brandywine frowns, lengthening his jowly face. "Big Charlie Wentworth was the first to go. Found him dead in his home, in his bedroom. He'd been gutted with a knife. Hank Whitebird, he ran the convenience store. He got hit in the head. Cracked his skull open. Then Sarah Anne Bricknell. She was the city clerk and my good right hand. Sarah Anne died in a fire at city hall. That's when we realized these dang Russians weren't just here to handle the cerite from the mine. They was killing us off, one by one. The rest of us hightailed it down here. Only, not fast enough."

He's starting to tear up. Trisha Jean makes a gesture to the others: *Give him a minute.*

Ash speaks softly, and mostly for Dez's ears. "Carbon dioxide."

"Aye. Noticed it, too."

There is a buildup of dioxide down here, and it's affecting everyone's breathing.

Petra Alexandris overhears this. "The engineers in this group tell me the scrubbers aren't working. Like, when we lost the elevator, we lost some of the venting."

"Lost?" Dez says. "Wasn't it you who sabotaged the elevator?"

Petra shakes her head. "We think the Russians did it."

"Then . . . they're down here, too?"

"I'm afraid so. The Fuchstown residents have levels one and two. This level and the first of the mining levels. The Russians are holding levels three and four. And they have guns."

Ash addresses Petra for the first time. "Are you in contact with the scientists on level five?"

"No. We've been down here since Sunday. Oh my God. I . . . What's today?"

Dez says, "Thursday."

Petra shakes her head. "Good lord. I'd lost track. But no, we haven't heard from the scientists, and the Russians have barricaded their level. They fired at us when we tried to get through, so we know they're armed. And they know a couple of the townies are armed. It's been a standoff."

"Except you've got the food and drink, thanks to the vending machines," Rusty points out.

"Oh, and a lot more food and potable water in the storage areas," the mayor says. "This place was designed for upwards of eighty miners."

"And they lived down here? Not in Fuchstown?" Trisha Jean asks.

Brandywine nods. "For the most part, yeah. It's a pilot project. Only five or so miners topside at any given moment, to get some sunshine and air, and to raid Hank's little store. But very little impact on the town as a whole. You noticed there were no mounds of rock everywhere, like at a lot of mines? That's because they dug good, useful tunnels, and tunnels where there ain't no cerite. Then they transfer the tailings from the good tunnels into the others. The landscape's more or less pristine."

"I'd read about that on my way up here," Trisha Jean says. "But to see it in reality? Impressive."

The mayor says, "We're good to go, as far as provisions and water. We're hoping to starve out those Russians."

Dez shrugs. "If they planned for a siege, who knows what provisions they brung, yeah? Could be well stocked, them."

Trisha Jean catches the mayor's attention. "Sir? Do you know anything about an outfit called Skyhook Technologies?"

Brandywine frowns. "Sort of. They provide a lot of the mining equipment. We don't interact with them much in town, but we see their logos everywhere. They had some folks here to inspect the site from time to time."

She chooses her words carefully. "Someone in New York tried to bribe and threaten Dez from coming here. Someone tried to kill him in a hotel in St. John's. Then they stole a Coast Guard helicopter and chased us up here."

He shakes his head. "Those Russkies. What the heck do they want?"

"That's just it. These weren't Russians, Mr. Mayor. They were mercenaries. Mostly . . . American, Dez? Is that right?"

"Aye."

She resumes the story. "They were mercenaries, mostly American. And we think they're on the payroll of Skyhook Technologies."

Burt Brandywine frowns. "What for?"

Trisha Jean gives him an elaborate shrug. "We were hoping you could tell us."

"The guys up top? They're not Russians?"

"No, sir."

"Then . . . Well, forgive me for saying this, ma'am. But your so-called rescue mission just brought more bad guys to our doorstep."

She laughs without mirth. "They were coming anyway, Mr. Mayor. Our presence slowed them down. Or more accurately, Dez slowed them down. If they'd have gotten the elevator working, rather than us, you'd really be in the thick of it."

# CHAPTER 28

This level of the mine is equipped with a public-address system in some rooms. They call Dr. Patterson in the infirmary to check on his patients, who are doing all right. So far.

Then the mayor and the State Department team start strategizing.

"I've got to speak to the Russians," Trisha Jean says. "I'm a trained negotiator and a diplomat. This is my specialty."

Her Secret Service bodyguard rolls his eyes. "Oh, joy."

Dez says, "May I suggest ye add Petra to your team? She's the former chief legal counsel for Triton. She's not a half-bad negotiator herself."

Petra says, "If I'm not in the way."

Trisha Jean laughs. "Ma'am, you've negotiated billion-dollar deals with the likes of Putin and Xi. So, yeah, pull up a chair, we'll deal you in. Whites are a buck, blues are five, and reds are ten."

"Good. And it's Petra, please."

Dez says, "I'd say the carbon dioxide scrubbers should be my priority."

The mayor says, "We have an engineer who's been trying to do just that. I'll connect you two."

"Ta, mate. How many people d'you have down here?"

"Nineteen."

"An' no idea how many the Russians have?"

Petra says, "Unknown for sure. Fewer than ten is a best guess."

He turns to Ash. "And the neutrino team?"

Ash shrugs. "I do not know."

And yet a representative of the National Research Council would know that, he thinks.

Trisha Jean says, "The briefing I got said the neutrino team has a total of ten personnel. Including the lead researchers, Professor William Sato of MIT and Dr. Sophia Araki of CERN. They've got living quarters on that level. They should have food and water, but again, with the air running out."

"Air's not runnin' out," Dez says. "The stuff we breathe out, the carbon dioxide, is buildin' up too fast. If we've got ten folks on the research level, nineteen here, and, say, ten maximum amongst the Russians, that's fewer'n forty. That gives me a baseline for how much $CO_2$ we need to pump out."

He turns again to Ash. "Where d'you best fit in, till we can get to your scientists?"

The assassin from Paris, who has two guns Dez doesn't know about, says, "I'll assist Madam Jackson, if that is all right?"

Trisha Jean smiles her way. "Glad to have you."

Everyone stands. Mayor Brandywine says, "I'll head to the infirmary, see what your doctor needs."

"Ta, sir."

When he's gone, Dez gestures to Petra and to Rusty Townsend. "Rusty: Captain Charbonneau has a revolver. I think you should ask her for it, yeah? Petra: Tell me if I've got this right. People starting dyin' topside. The Russians sneak into the mine first. That's why they've got the lower levels. Then the townies get down here next. Then the elevator gets bolluxed."

She simply nods.

"Then that means the Russians didn't feck with the elevator controls on this level, excuse me language. Someone amongst the townies did."

Rusty groans. "We've got either a Russian covert agent, or a Skyhook ringer, hiding down here among the civilians. Swell. I'll get the pilot's gun."

"Good. You lot keep your eyes peeled. We don't know all the dangers down here, an' that's for certain."

Rusty runs to the infirmary and returns with the Colt 1911 that Captain Charbonneau lent him. He holds it by the barrel and offers it to Petra. She waves it off. "I go to a firing range twice a month, because some of Triton's customers operate out of developing nations. But I'm not comfortable being armed in a civilian population."

Ash shakes her head and lies. "The same as well for me."

"Gimme that," Trisha Jean says. "I'm from Georgia. My mama had a mobile of these dangling over my crib."

Rusty hands it over. "Our chief negotiator is Calamity Jane. I don't see how that could end badly."

"I'll worry about the $CO_2$, but first I'll go with you lot," Dez says. "I need t'get a sense of the layout of this place. *And* a sense of the Russians. I do that, then I'll get to work on the air scrubbers."

Petra leads him, along with Trisha Jean, Rusty, and Ash, to a set of iron stairs that run about twenty feet down to the next level. A pair of iron doors stand open at the top of the stairs. "In the event of a fire, each level can be sealed off," Petra explains.

Level two, like level one, shows no exposed dirt or rocks. It looks like the man-made tunnel system it is, not like a mine. The walls, floors, and low ceilings are all concrete. From the briefing they received earlier, Trisha Jean and Rusty know that the mines extend laterally, and in almost every direction, from the prefabricated silo they're in now.

They pass another townie with another rifle, who's on guard. He glowers at Petra en passant. When they're out of earshot, she whispers to the others, "The townsfolk aren't wildly excited about outsiders."

Dez's head is on a swivel, taking in every detail of the place. Yes, he's seen the schematics. The map is not the territory.

At the next level, Petra puts a finger to her lips. They walk a bit slower. The double fire doors atop the next set of stairs are half-closed and iron debris has been stacked up in the two-foot gap between them. They spot overturned wheelbarrows and pickaxes and massive chunks of stone, wedged into the entrance. The pile stands four feet high.

Petra gestures and they all stand well to the left of the double doors. "Hello?" she calls out.

A guttural voice from level three responds. "What do you want?"

It's a man, and he sounds Slavic.

"We have a delegation from outside," she calls out. "They're from the U.S. State Department. They're here to negotiate."

A bullet pings through the space between the doors and embeds itself in a far wall.

Trisha Jean surprises the others with a smile and a rueful shake of her head. "It's good to not underestimate the animosity of the opposition."

Stepping a few inches closer to the pile of rubble, she raises her voice. "My name is Trisha Jean Jackson and I'm from the U.S. State Department. Now you know, and I know, that this stalemate can't last forever. For the simple reason that the air's getting foul down here. So, at some point, you guys need to tell me what it is you want. Once we know that, we can see about finding some compromise. Okay?"

Another bullet whizzes through the opening.

"And if that was supposed to intimidate me, I should tell you I've had diplomatic postings in Kosovo, Yemen, and Afghanistan. And growing up, my daddy was the Democratic Committee chairman in Glascock County, Georgia, which won't mean diddly to you, but believe me: If you think you're the first dude to fire a bullet over my head, let me set that record straight."

She waits quietly. Behind her, Dez and the others do the same.

The wait lasts nearly a minute.

The guttural voice says, "When, in Kosovo?"

Trisha Jean lets out a silent sigh. "Two thousand and five to twenty-ten."

"I was there in twenty-twelve," the voice says. "Was not good."

"That's an understatement."

The voice says, "Stay on your side. Do not attempt to come down here. If we wish to talk, we will."

"That works for me," she shouts. "But the air ain't getting any fresher."

She makes a head gesture, and the party moves back the way they came.

When they get to the shotgun guy on guard duty, Trisha Jean says, "What's your name?"

The guy says, "Corey." And stands, shotgun at his side.

"Corey, they're gonna try to reach out to me. Maybe soon, maybe not. Get closer and keep your ears open."

The townie says, "Why the hell would I take orders from a tourist?"

Dez is about to intervene but Trisha Jean steps inside Corey's personal space, shotgun be damned. She narrows her eyes and drops her voice. "Because I'm the mean-ass mother who's gonna get your pencil neck out of this jam, Sonny Jim. And when I do, that means I'll be getting out every resident of Fuchstown. Every last one of you. Now, if your goal is to spend your remaining years here, be my guest. If you want a peaceful way to the surface again, you're gonna salute smartly. You're gonna follow my orders. And you're gonna keep a civil tongue in your head. Do I make myself clear?"

Corey gulps. "Yes."

"I'm sorry?"

"Yes, ma'am."

She smiles and steps back. "Outstanding. Thank you for your assistance."

# CHAPTER 29

Back on level one, Dez is introduced to an engineer who has been trying to solve the problem of the carbon dioxide buildup in the facility. He'd seen the man when the team first arrived; a tall, rangy fellow with a full beard and a Montreal Canadiens cap. They shake hands. "Joel de Brienne. Are you an engineer, too?"

Now, this fella sounds French-Canadian, Dez thinks. "Aye. If an extra set of eyes an' hands can help . . . ?"

De Brienne says, "I'll show you. Come."

There's a workroom on level two with a belt-high table surrounded by metal stools. Dez has doffed his puffy winter clothes—including his singed snow pants—and is, again, in his unform of a black jacket and T-shirt, black jeans, black boots. He's glad he brought the change of clothes in his borrowed backpack.

De Brienne unrolls a five-by-five-foot schematic drawing of the industrial-sized elevator and the air-ducting system. He leans over the table. He's a big fellow, six-one and muscled, a guy who's made a living working outdoors. "All this was built at the same time. Assembled together, too. When the Russians sabotaged the elevator, the $CO_2$ scrubbers were affected, *hein*? Don't know how."

Dez leans over on his elbows and studies the fine-detail drawing. He uses one stubby finger, follows conduit paths.

He also doesn't tell the big man that he suspects it wasn't Russians who sabotaged the elevator. Because at this stage, outside of Petra Alexandris, he has no idea who he can trust.

"There's no obvious flaw to this design," he says, scratching his head. "If we figure out how the oppo bolluxed the controls, maybe we can get the scrubbers back up to maximum."

"Been trying," De Brienne says.

"I know. No offense intended." He studies the drawings more. He usually carries a small notepad and pen in his messenger bag—which he brought along in his backpack, along with his tablet computer. He draws them out and makes notes to himself.

"Ye've tried to reestablish comms with the scientists on five?"

The man snorts. "The Swimming Pool. Yes. There's nothing wrong on our end. The scientists just turned theirs off, is what I think. Never had much use for theorists."

Dez grins over at him. "Best part of engineering is the chance to get your hands greasy, yeah?"

"My father and my brothers taught me to strip a hemi before I could read."

"Lovely." Liking the man. "This access shaft, here. We could get in there, get a visual."

De Brienne laughs. "Okay, that was the one design flaw. That shaft is far too small for me, *hein*? Believe me, I've tried. I'm taller than you, but you're wider in the shoulders and chest."

"Well, I'm travelin' with someone what stands just about five-foot-two and looks t'be a size two. We might get our visual after all."

The problem being: Dez doesn't know who amongst the townies he can trust. And he can say the same for the woman he knows as Elisabet LeCroix.

# CHAPTER 30

## ST. JOHN'S

Vincent and Valerie Cray lie in bed in the sprawling Victorian, both sweat-sheened, both breathing shallow. They were fucking for close to forty minutes and have kicked almost all of the sheets and all four pillows to the floor. Vincent has a magnum of champagne on the side table; they've been drinking from the bottle, not bothering with glasses.

Vincent rubs his palm over his face, blinking sweat out of his eyes. "Holy hell, woman."

Valerie laughs. She's all but purring, well satisfied. Vincent hands her the bottle and she takes a long pull.

"The board of directors called," Vincent says. "Okay, their sniveling lapdog, Wendell, called. Something about a girl who was badly beaten? In Berlin? And about German law enforcement demanding some answers."

Valerie shrugs. "It was a whore. She was injured. It's Berlin. It happens."

He smiles. "That's more or less what I told Wendell. His people will pay off . . . I don't know. Whoever they need to pay off. Without the board of directors having a conniption fit."

Valerie's cell phone, which they knocked to the floor, lights up. She peers down at it. It's an alert. Their satellite phone just received an incoming call.

"It's Finn," she says.

Vincent stands. Naked, he pads out to the room that they designated as their temporary office upon arriving in St. John's. Outside, the storm rages. He returns with the encrypted sat phone. "Finn's pretty fucking hot. I'd screw him."

His wife laughs. "Stand in line, baby."

Vincent calls their lead mercenary back, puts it on speaker mode, and drops the phone on the sweat-soaked cover sheet. Naked, Valerie sits up into the lotus position and hands him the magnum.

"Mr. Cray? Ms. Cray?"

"We're both here, Aiyden," Valerie says, reaching for the tank top she doffed and using it to wipe sweat from her carved abs and between her breasts. "You're calling to report unparalleled success, naturally."

She's sure Finn remembers the fate of the previous mercenary team leader. So she's expecting crowing or groveling. Not anger.

"The situation here is *not* what we were told! They have a trained special forces soldier with them! That asshole Limerick! I don't know what you thought he was, but he's a fucking lot more!"

The Crays look at each other. Vincent raises his eyebrows and purses his lips. He hands his wife the champagne. He says, "Finn? You have . . . what? Twelve men?"

"Not any goddamn longer! I've got dead and injured because this bastard rigged a frag-bomb at the mine entrance!"

Valerie says, "Wow. Mr. Limerick is not unimpressive. Aiyden? Are you in the mine?"

"Negative, ma'am. The elevator has been screwed with."

Vincent wipes wine off his lips with the back of his hand. "Is the FBI team in the mine?"

"The State Department team, yeah. The FBI is in a second Hercules. They haven't made it yet. We don't know why."

Valerie reaches for the sat phone and mutes it. She looks up at her naked husband, standing at the edge of the bed.

"We had the mine elevator taken down until Finn's team could get up there," she says, speaking more or less to herself, to make sure she understands what's happening. "If the State Department team is in the mine, then someone got the elevator running again. Then screwed with it again once they were safe."

Vincent says, "Looks like."

"Limerick."

"Looks like." He smiles and shakes his head ruefully. "We didn't know why the FBI brought him along. I think maybe now we know."

They hear Finn's voice. "Hello? Are you still there?"

Valerie taps the phone. "Aiyden? Please hold." She returns it to mute mode.

Vincent says, "If Finn's crew can't get into the mine, we're screwed. They can't shoot their way in. They don't have the munitions to blow their way in. And our asset in the mine is competent enough, but if this Limerick guy is special forces . . ." He shrugs.

"We don't have unlimited time." Valerie sips from the bottle and hands it up to him.

"Could we drop a bunker-buster bomb on the site? Smash our way in?"

She laughs. "Oh, I like how you think. We could, in theory, get our hands on one, yes. It would kill Finn's crew, of course, unless they could evacuate to a safe distance."

"Which would take time."

"Which we don't have in unlimited quantities. And it might kill everyone inside the mine."

Vincent shrugs. "Maybe not the scientists on level five. But we don't care about them. The question is: Would a bomb big enough to get us in also destroy the find?"

"And even if it didn't, could we get away with blowing up a town in Newfoundland? And could we get what we want and get out of Canada in time?"

He says, "Well, that's what Wendell and the board of directors is for. To handle public relations. Right?"

They stare at each other. Vincent sips from the bottle. Valerie laughs. She reaches out and softly grips her husband's penis. It stirs. "Go big or go home?"

Vincent grins. "He who dares, wins."

He picks up the sat phone and unmutes it. "Finn? Hold position. Make sure they don't get out of the mine. We'll send . . . reinforcements."

"Reinforcements? What? The Seventh Cav? Just tell your asshole in the mine to get that elevator running! My team can handle Limerick and whatever surprises they have down there! But get us in that fucking mine!"

Vincent smiles as his wife caresses him. "Finn? Hold position. Await further orders. Out."

He says, "Go big or go home."

Valerie grins up at him. "Speaking of big . . ."

# CHAPTER 31

Dez meets in the level one break room with the French-Canadian engineer, Joel de Brienne. Also, Mayor Burt Brandywine, Trisha Jean Jackson, and her Secret Service bodyguard, plus Ash.

Petra is checking on the wounded in the infirmary.

"We made contact with the Russians," Trisha Jean tells the others, doctoring her coffee with sugar and powdered cream. "It's a start."

The mayor shakes his head. He has a jowly, basset-hound look. "They can't be trusted."

Trisha Jean gives him a smile and a shrug. "I'm a negotiator, Mr. Mayor. I don't actually trust anyone. When my mama told me my daddy was my daddy, I asked for a second source. But if we're getting out of here, I think it's gonna mean getting *everyone* out. Enemies or not."

She turns to Dez and the bearded engineer. "Any luck with the air? It's getting pretty stuffy down here."

Dez nods to Ash. "There's an access shaft, but neither Joel nor meself can fit in there. You might. If you could get in there and pipe video back to us, we'd have a better sense of what needs fixin'."

Ash doesn't do a very good job of hiding her disinclination. She's here with one mission only, and crawling through maintenance tunnels isn't it. But she's not sure how she can decline without raising suspicions.

She settles on, "I have . . . claustrophobia issues."

Trisha Jean lays a hand reassuringly on hers. Ash doesn't like being touched but she forces herself not to recoil.

"This isn't easy for anyone, Elisabet. But I need time to pour oil on troubled waters. If you can help Dez, it might buy me that time."

Seeing no way out, Ash nods.

Dez says, "Ta." He turns to the mayor. "I've an odd sort of question for ye, sir."

"Shoot."

"Did ye actually see the Russians killing your people topside?"

Brandywine gives him a deep scowl. "What do you mean?"

"Did ye see the killer? Or killers?"

"Well, no. But Jiminy Cricket! Who else could it have been? You think a bear killed our friends?"

It's Trisha Jean who responds. "We're just trying to get a better picture of exactly what happened. If I want to get a temporary ceasefire with the Russians, it's important I know as much as possible."

The mayor still looks disgruntled. "Well, I guess. But the Russkies can't get away with murder. They gotta pay for what they did to our friends."

"That's tomorrow's problem," she says. "Today's problem is getting your residents out of the mine. And the scientists on five, too. And I can't get them out without getting the Russians to stand down."

Brandywine studies the tabletop. "Well . . . I guess."

"Excellent. Can I ask your people to take shifts close enough to the Russians' barricade to hear if they reach out?"

"No more citizens of Fuchstown are gonna get shot, I can tell you that for darn sure!"

Rusty says, "They can stay well back from the barricade and tell us what they hear. And every time Secretary Jackson goes down, she's got me watching her back. I can watch your people, too."

Joel de Brienne smiles down at the much smaller Rusty Townsend. "You don't mind my asking, how did a guy built like you join the Secret Service security detail?"

Dez expects Rusty to take umbrage, but he just looks up at the Canadian and says, "High school aptitude test."

Trisha Jean turns to Ash. "Elisabet? You'll help Dez and, ah, Joel, was it?"

De Brienne nods.

Ash says, "Is there somewhere safe I can store my belongings?"

De Brienne stands. "*Oui*. I'll show you one of the miners' rooms. They lock."

Dez grins. "Let's to it, then."

The rangy engineer leads Ash around the doughnut-shaped residence wing of level one, which surrounds the commons areas. He finds an empty one-room apartment with a key in the door and hands it to her. "Freshen up and meet us at the elevator, *hein*?"

She nods.

As soon as he's gone, Ash locks the door. She hides her handgun, and its silencer, under the single bed's mattress. She reaches into her backpack and hides Inspector Frank Watts's gun, too.

# CHAPTER 32

Back in the break room, Petra Alexandris makes eye contact with Dez. "Can I have a second?"

They move to a table with some privacy.

"How are ye holdin' up, love?"

She places a hand on his chest. "Better now that you're here. First: thank you. I mean it."

He hugs her. "Any time."

"Okay, that's *how* I'm doing. Now, as to *what* I'm doing."

"You came because them scientists went radio-dark, yeah?"

"That's part of it. Even before I took over from my father, I insisted Triton invest in this facility. Then the scientists broke communication protocols, both with their host universities and with Triton. I wanted to see if I could talk to them, figure out what happened. But I also wanted to look into an outfit that's been pouring money into the mining operation."

Dez says, "Skyhook Technologies."

"Absolutely."

"Them's the fuckers been tryin' their best to bribe me, scare me, shoot me, or seduce me outta coming up here. We think they hired the soldiers up top who've trapped us in here. I've spotted the Skyhook logo on bits of tech, on the surface an' down here."

"That makes sense. I couldn't possibly care less about the mining of cerite. I do care about this pilot project for a more environmentally friendly type of mining."

"The miners living underground. Minimal impact on the town above. No tailings. Yeah, I thought it might be something like that. Never been near a mine had less impact on its surroundings than here."

"I'm willing to invest the company's money in that concept, yes. But mostly I'm backing the scientists. So when Skyhook Technologies started pouring money into the mining operation, I took notice."

Dez says, "Skyhook's reputation's not sterling, I assume."

"The company's run by a board of directors. Very respectable. Bankers, lawyers, international investors. All up-and-up. But I've been doing some digging and the board also spends a great deal of its time covering for the married couple, Vincent and Valerie Cray, who serve as copresidents. My investigators found a long, long line of DUIs, arrests, charges, brawling, whatever, connected to the Crays. The board probably spends as much time painting that lily as it does actually running a mining technologies company."

"I met the missus. Or a Canadian snow lynx. Not sure which."

Petra laughs. "Oh, yes. That definitely is her reputation. His, too, actually. I'm told they're swingers." Petra holds out both palms. "I'm not kink-shaming. I'm the last person in the world to judge how consenting adults get off."

"Same."

"But I do care that the company's main business is providing heavy equipment for mining operations, shipping operations all over the world."

Dez sees where this is going. "They've a side hustle, Skyhook?"

"I think so, yes. Rumor has it they provide the same heavy equipment for third-world warlords. They've provided the infrastructure for the overthrow of legally elected governments in Africa, in Southeast Asia, in South America. All of which is perfectly legal, by the way."

Dez says, "Triton's the bank for more'n half of the world's militaries."

"Trust me, I know. My father wrote the how-to manual for war profiteering. But even he drew the line at profiting from failed nations and drug lords who want to become dictators."

Dez sits back, fingers of both hands laced behind his head, elbows akimbo. "Well, that brings us to the tricky bit, don't it? Skyhook's a billion-dollar operation, working on five continents. What could possibly be down in this mine that's worth slaughtering the residents of Fuchstown and sending mercenaries after us?"

"Honestly, I was hoping you could tell me."

"It's not cerite," Dez says, his eyes raking the popcorn ceiling as if looking for answers up there. "That's a silicate mineral, an' it's valuable enough, given all the high tech it's used in. But it's not *that* valuable. Not on the scale that the Crays operate."

"I don't think it's the neutrino search team, either," she whispers. "Knowing the fundamental building blocks of the cosmos is fascinating. But I don't see where the profit is for people like the Crays."

"Nor I. Which leads us to door number three."

Petra nods. "The miners might have found something else down here. Gold, or silver, or, I don't know, *something*. Something that would make even billionaires sit up and take notice."

"Was thinkin' the same. Absolutely no idea what that might be. But it's gotta be dearer than eyesight, space, an' liberty."

Petra smiles. *"King Lear."*

Dez rises. "We should join the others. One last thought: After the killing's started in Fuchstown, the Russians got here first. Which is why they hold levels three an' four. Which means—"

"It wasn't them who sabotaged the elevator," Petra cuts in, rising, too. "Skyhook has a spy among the civilians here. I don't think the mayor has figured that out yet. He's focused on hating the Russians."

"Right. Gets a bit complicated, this."

Petra places a palm on his barrel chest. "I really am glad you're here. I cannot even—"

Dez laughs and draws her into a tight hug. They hold each other a moment, then Petra pulls back and kisses him, softly, on the lips.

"Of all the people I wanted to see walk through that door, Desmond Aloysius . . ."

"Happy t'serve."

Ash has just passed by the break-room door and spots the hug and the kiss, and the kindly way these two smile at each other. Clearly, they were lovers. But Ash remembers the warm relationship Dez shared with his friend, Rafik, in France. How the two of them talked and laughed nonstop.

Ash doesn't understand it. And, for a second, her heart cracks a little. She knows she will never have that kind of connection to any other human being.

# CHAPTER 33

Joel de Brienne joins Dez at the elevator again. Dez is down on one knee, unscrewing the cover of the access shaft, which is low to the floor. "She's on her way, the cute one."

Dez gets two screws undone. "Ask ye a question?"

"Sure."

"Elisabet sound Québécois t'you?"

The man shrugs. "We got a big immigrant community. Lot of people in Quebec don't sound Québécois."

"Fair, that."

Dez removes the metal mesh cover and stands. Both men turn as Ash approaches.

She's changed into a two-piece exercise outfit: a cropped, T-back, spandex tank and leggings. Also, trainers. She still looks petite but Dez now sees the tautly honed muscles of a ballerina or a gymnast. Muscles ripple across her back as she turns. She's beautiful.

"Have your phone?" he asks.

She hands it to him.

Dez calls his own larger phone. He establishes a video call.

He also took a photo of the elevator blueprints and now shows it to Ash on his tablet. "Ye see this junction? This is the airflow for all five levels. You're lookin' for a blockage here."

Ash peers at it for about twenty seconds, then nods.

"We appreciate this, love."

She moves to the access panel and crouches, weight on the balls of her feet. She possesses a dancer's strong core strength, Dez can see. And likely she practices yoga. She contorts herself to get one arm and shoulder into the square opening, then her head, then her other arm, then her torso, narrow hips, and toned legs.

When she's out of sight, De Brienne whispers, "Is it wrong I enjoyed watching that?"

Dez also whispers. "Our lass is put together."

He holds his phone so both of them can see the screen. What they see is a blend of black nothingness and blurred flashes of gunmetal gray. Ash is pulling herself upward inside the aluminum vent, her phone in her hand.

De Brienne rubs his forehead with the pad of this thumb.

"Headache?"

The big man nods.

"Me, too."

Headaches being one of the first symptoms of carbon dioxide poisoning.

Ash contorts herself in the maintenance shaft. It's a tight fit and she's caked in dust and particulate. She's hoping it isn't asbestos.

She is blessed with a keen sense of direction and spatial geometry. She memorized the blueprint segment Dez showed her. She gets to the place where she can see laterally—both to her left and to her right—and brings her camera up to begin showing the video.

★ ★ ★

Dr. Dyson Patterson strolls up to Dez and De Brienne, hands in his pockets, loose-limbed and chill. "Yo."

Dez says, "Elisabet's inside the elevator controls. Tryin' to find out why we're not pumping out more carbon dioxide."

"Yeah. About that. Everyone in the infirmary's got a headache now. Me, too."

De Brienne says, "Us, too."

"Couple of people reported feeling dizzy. I think sooner's better than later for fixing this."

Dez keeps his eyes on the video images being transmitted to his phone. "Aye. Joel, see that?"

They both peer at the image Ash is transmitting.

A largish more-or-less rectangular sheet of metal lies twenty feet from the laconic woman. It doesn't appear to belong where it is; like it fell off something above her.

"Elisabet? You hearin' me, love?"

"Yes."

"You see the obstruction?"

"Yes."

"Can you reach it, then?"

"Hold on."

The image goes black. Her phone is still sending video, but she's set her phone down.

The doctor says, "Joel? I'm Dyson."

They shake.

"You got any idea where the miners stored their backup medical supplies?"

"Sure. I can show you. Dez?"

"Scoot. I'll keep an eye on our girl."

De Brienne gives him a wink and a sly shake of his head. "I bet you will."

The physician and the engineer amble off.

Dez keeps watching the blackness being transmitted to his screen.

Petra Alexandris places a hand on the curved wall of the level one ring corridor and waits for a wave of dizziness to pass. Her head is throbbing. She takes a second, then continues on to the break room and finds Trisha Jean Jackson and her bodyguard, Rusty Townsend.

"The Russians want to talk to, and I quote, 'the woman.'"

Trisha Jean shakes her head and smiles. "I like to think of myself as da man, but okay." She begins to rise and falls back into her chair. Rusty is at her side, a hand on her shoulder, steadying her.

"Jeez, that was embarrassing."

Rusty spots the bottle of aspirin on the break-room table. He shakes out two and hands them to his protectee with a bottle of water.

"Were the headaches and dizziness this bad before we showed up?" Trisha Jean asks, capping the bottle and sliding it into the front pocket of her baggy snow pants.

Petra says, "It wasn't this bad. You brought eight more people with you, which added to the problem."

Trisha Jean rises again. "Well, let's go make with the diplomacy."

The three of them head toward the stairs that lead to level two. Rusty says, "So. You and Dez are close?"

Petra smiles at him. "We were for a time. When he lived in Los Angeles. This is the first I've seen him since."

Trisha Jean says, "He's a good man. I'm glad he's here."

Petra just smiles but also changes the subject. "Why does Dez call you Trip Jacks?"

Rusty grins. "Now, that's a good story."

On the second level, they find another townie standing guard duty with a shotgun. "You the U.S. State Department bigwig?"

"Medium-size wig; yes."

"One of the *assholes from Moss-cow* wants to talk to you." He shouts the middle part of that declaration.

"Thanks. I'm sure you made my job easier, there."

Rusty draws his Glock. He checks to make sure no one is visible in the barricade that's been erected, holding open the door to the third level. "This is close enough."

"Thank you, mother." Trisha Jean takes three steps closer. "Hello? It's Trisha Jean Jackson, U.S. State. You want to talk?"

A voice echoes from the gloom beyond the barricade. It's the same Slavic voice who spoke to her before.

"The air is bad."

"Yep. For us, too. We think that when the elevator to the surface was disabled, it affected the air filtration system. We have people working on it right now."

"Could be this is true. Could be you are hoarding all the good air, yes?"

She says, "Yeah, the good air wanted to flow through this gap in the door you've created, but I gave it a stern talking-to."

She waits.

The Russian guy chuckles. "Yes, is fair."

"Are you in contact with the scientists on level five? Do you know how their air is holding up?"

The Russian doesn't answer.

"Hello? Sir?"

"Elevator is working. You and your people got down here."

"Yes, it is working. But a crew of gunmen tried to kill us when we were up there, so we've disabled it again."

She waits. Petra and Rusty stand by.

"Who is this, who tries to kill you with guns?"

Trisha Jean says, "Well, they aren't Russians. We're pretty sure of that."

The man says, "Yes, I would have known if I tried to kill you with guns. I am not on surface. My men are not on surface. This is not something that I do not know that you are telling me."

"So you don't have any more men on the surface? That means there are now four sets of armed people here. You have guns. The citizens of Fuchstown have guns. The law enforcement and military guys I'm with have guns. The guys who tried to kill us have guns. That's pretty odd for Canada, don't you think?"

Another pause. "Newfoundland is not wild, wild west. As you say. How do I know any of this is real?"

She says, "Because what's it net me to lie about it?"

She waits.

"Is good point."

Trisha Jean is happy about this exchange. Because it's precisely that: an exchange. It's step one in any new diplomatic outreach. "We're without communications," she tells the stranger. "As I understand it, people on the mining levels could only communicate with the town. All of the communications gear in the town was destroyed by whoever that other group of gunmen is. Now, the scientists on five should be able to communicate with universities and research groups. But we think they turned their comms off, and we don't know why."

The Russian coughs. The air isn't getting any fresher down here.

"I got the mother of all headaches right now," Trisha Jean says honestly. "You, too?"

"Is dioxide, yes?"

"Yup."

The man says, "We want that you fix the air. Everything else is second problem. Only air is first problem. You understand this?"

"I do. The air is the first problem. But it'd help mightily if I knew the scientists in the neutrino research facility are okay. Can you speak to them? Can you confirm they're okay?"

They wait. The wait lasts nearly sixty seconds. She thinks she hears muttering in Russian, between at least two men.

The Russian says, "You fix air. Do that, then come talk. That is all."

Trisha Jean says, "You know what I'm gonna do? I'm gonna step up to the barricade here so you can see me."

Rusty hisses, sotto voce, "No no no no no . . ."

Trisha Jean waves him off.

"You will stay away from barricade," the Russian says.

But she steps gingerly over some of the debris on the ground.

Rusty reaches for her, and Petra holds him back. When Rusty's head snaps around, she whispers, "She's right. Let her play it out."

Trisha Jean winks at Petra. "I'm stepping up to the barricade now, mister. You're gonna see me in five seconds."

A shot rings out.

But a bullet does not fly into their side of the stairwell door. As if the Russian just fired into the air.

Her heart trip-hammering, her headache rising, Trisha Jean takes another step forward. "All righty, then. Here I go. Two seconds."

"Stay back," the man says, but with more confusion than malice in his voice.

Rusty braces his gun hand, left hand around his right wrist, also stepping forward in her wake.

Trisha Jean steps fully up to the chest-high barricade of debris.

Light from level three limns her face.

She smiles. She waves a little.

Two men stand on the far side, on an iron-grid platform at the top of the set of stairs. One of them is hulking. The other decidedly smaller and wiry. Both in their mid-forties, she guesses.

She says, "Howdy. I'm Trisha Jean. Okay. Heading back to check on the air. In the meantime: here."

And she chucks the bottle of aspirin through the stairwell door and into level three.

# CHAPTER 34

Over his phone, Dez hears Ash say, "I . . . I can't reach it." She sounds like she's straining.

"Hang on a bit. I've an idea. Right back."

His headache ramping up, Dez dashes to the break room. Several townies look up as he barges in, reaching for his little tool kit in his messenger bag, and unplugs the microwave oven.

Someone says, "What're you . . . Hey!"

Dez sets the microwave on one of the tables and begins unscrewing the back plate. "I need one of the magnets in here."

"What for?" Two guys approach him.

"To get the air scrubbers working again."

The guys look at each other. "How do you know there's a magnet in there?"

Dez glances their way. "It's a microwave oven."

"Yeah?"

"Well, it's a big, oul' cavity magnetron, innit? Uses oscillating currents to create microwave radio-frequency energy to . . . Ah!"

He removes both ring-shaped magnets. "Here we go, then. Ta, mates!"

He spots a dish towel near the communal sink. He grabs it en passant and dashes out again.

At the elevator doors, Dez again draws his phone. He goes down on one knee before the access hatch, whisking off his belt. "Elisabet? I'm tying a magnet to me belt. That bit of metal in there, could be it's magnetic, could be it's not. We'll try this an' see if it works."

From his perspective, two small hands emerge from the square hole in the floor. They are blackened by dust and soot. Dez gives her the magnet tied to his belt. "All's you gotta do is—"

"I know." Her voice sounds tinny and echoic coming from the maintenance shaft.

He hears her scrambling upward again.

He stares at the broadcast blackness on his phone. She still hasn't picked up her phone.

He waits.

He hears her sneeze.

"Sorry 'bout the dust, love."

She doesn't respond. He hears the clanging noise of metal on metal. Hears it again.

"Elisabet?"

The image on his phone shifts. Suddenly, her face comes into view. She says, "I have the thing. It looks like a metal panel that fell off something. As soon as I moved it, I felt the air in here change."

Dez laughs. Her hair is matted and black-gray. Her eyes shine brightly, surrounded by a grubby forehead and cheeks. "Ye look like a chimney sweep from *Mary Poppins*."

"I have not seen that. Not, I think, a compliment."

"Ye look fine, love. Hurry back down. Then we'll get you a

nice shower and a gold star for HVAC heroism above and beyond the call o' duty."

Pretty soon, her filthy hands emerge from the access panel, and Dez takes back the magnet and his belt. He wipes the latter clean, threads it through his belt loops. Yes: He can tell the air is better already. Or maybe that's just wishful thinking.

Her hands disappear again. Next comes Ash's now very dusty sneakers. Followed by her calves and thighs, then her upper body, her head and arms snaking out last.

She smiles shyly. "It's working."

Dez hands her the dish towel. "I think so, aye. You did splendid, love."

She bends at the waist and runs her hands briskly through her hair. Particulate and dust fall to the floor like dirty snow, her white-blond hair reemerging. She takes the towel and wipes the area around her eyes, first, then her cheeks, nose, and mouth.

She looks at Dez, holding the cloth up like a bandit's bandana.

Dez smiles down at her. It's an odd sort of smile.

Ash says, "What?"

"Ever been to Paris, love?"

The woman called Ash twirls and kicks him in the head.

# CHAPTER 35

The big, bearded engineer, Joel de Brienne, is in one of the level two storage areas with Dr. Dyson Patterson. The room is nearly filled with crates on pallets. Together, they've moved several large boxes out of the far, left-hand corner of the storage area. De Brienne turns to the next crate, upon which the word AIR COMPRESSORS has been stenciled.

"Here."

The lid of the crate has been opened already, so he simply lifts it off. He reaches in and retrieves a satellite radio, handing it to Dr. Patterson. He reaches in again and draws two fully loaded Sten guns.

Patterson adjusts the settings on the phone. A text message scrolls across the phone's face. He reads it, then places an outbound call.

In the ghost town above them, Aiyden Finn greets him with, "About fucking time."

Dr. Patterson says, "Status?"

"The status is, that fucker Limerick killed two of my men and injured nearly everybody. He's down there, we're up here. Get the elevator working. I'm going to kill him myself."

Patterson glances again at the text message that awaits him. "The Crays have ordered you to stand by, Finn. So stand by."

"Get! The goddamned elevator! *Working!*"

Patterson sighs. "Yeah, see, the problem is, I work for the Crays, not for you. They tell me to hold position, just like they told you. So what we're going to do is: hold position."

"De Brienne! You answer to me! If you have to kill that bastard in front of you, do it! Then get me down there!"

The big man ponders that a moment. Patterson waits. De Brienne is holding both machine guns.

Finn tries to sound calmer. "Look, there are too many armed people in the State Department party. You need backup. You know it."

Patterson chuckles. "Dude, I wasn't just a battlefield medic. I was Delta, okay? Outside of Limerick and the scrawny Secret Service dude, the biggest threats are the RCMP cop and the two helo pilots. I've been keeping all three of them too doped up to be any kinda threat. Hell, the cop even dropped his gun in the snow."

"That leaves two threats!"

"The Secret Service guy looks like a featherweight. I'm not worried about him. Which means it's me and De Brienne against one tough but unarmed guy. And, bruh, we got machine guns, yo."

Finn's faux calm evaporates. "De Brienne! You work for me! Get the doors open!"

The big, bearded man contemplates that. He still has both of the Sten guns.

He clears his throat. "Hey, Finn? Before you were in charge, it was Loesser. From what I'm told, he made one screwup and that psycho broad we work for shot him in the chest, *hein*? I think I'm gonna follow orders."

They wait.

Topside, Finn disconnects.

"I'm a mercenary," De Brienne says to Patterson. "I don't fight for glory. I fight for money. The money says hold, I hold."

Dyson Patterson gives him that languid, stoner smile of his. "Well, I got the search-and-rescue pilots and the inspector KO'd. Think you can handle Limerick?"

De Brienne holds his hand up more or less five feet, eight inches off the floor. "Guy this big? *Oui.* Him, I can handle."

Dez says, "Ow!"

The toe of Ash's shoe caught him in his left ear. He stumbles sideways, flinching.

Ash backs off, then stands her ground. She seems to be hopping a little bit, bouncing off the balls of her feet, legs spread shoulder-width apart, fists down by her side.

"That bloody well hurt!"

She bounces in place, light as a meringue.

Dez rubs his ear. "You're a pro? Assume so. Who's your target?"

Ash bobs in place.

"Well, you're not armed now." He gestures to the skintight spandex top and leggings. "We'll just park you in one of the storage rooms where ye can't get into mischief, shall we?"

He advances on her.

Dez weighs in at around 280 and a great deal of that is muscle. The woman before him might weigh a hundred pounds, but then again, might not quite hit that mark.

He reaches for her and she's not where she was. She sidesteps his reach, drops to the floor, and goes for the coffee grinder, sweeping his boots out from under him.

Dez lands on his ass.

Ash makes an X of her forearms and, up on one knee, drives the cross where her wrist bones meet into Dez's throat.

Dez has fast hands. He blocks the blow, but barely. He reaches for her and she does a back somersault out of his reach, landing on her feet. Again, bobbing in place.

Dust shakes loose from her whenever she moves.

Dez recognizes the blow he just blocked. The bones of her crossed wrists would have crushed his windpipe. She'd gone for the kill shot.

He rises to his feet. "Well, ye've training. That much is certain."

But so has Dez.

He moves deftly and quickly into her space but Ash is a will-o'-the-wisp. She's gone by the time his massive hand arrives.

She spins and drives a bent elbow into Dez's side.

She blinks, surprised by how little the blow hurt him. And how much it hurt her elbow. It's the first emotion she's shown since Dez identified her.

Dez reaches for her but it's a feint, going to his left now.

Ash recognizes the feint for what it is. She barrel-rolls low, just to the right of his leg. As he adjusts, turns her way, she braces both hands on the floor and kicks his knee with the heels of both shoes.

Dez's leg folds out from beneath him.

She's on her feet and drives her knee into the bridge of his nose. He dodges, and the blow misses its target.

Dez rises.

"I've seen fast before. I've naught seen the likes of you, love. I don't even know what martial arts style that is."

They spar for another sixty seconds. Dez has yet to lay a hand on her. She's tried counter-striking but seems to finally realize that it's like punching a rhinoceros. You might score points, but all you'll do is rile the rhino. Which nobody wants.

The next time he reaches for her, she pirouettes out of reach, a half-inch shy of his thick fingers. And as he's slightly off-balance, Ash turns and sprints out of the elevator room.

There one blink. Gone the next.

Dez stands his ground. He rubs his left ear; the one truly solid blow that hurt him.

He looks up at Petra jogging into the room, Trisha Jean and Rusty on her six.

"I can smell the air! It's already better!" Petra hugs him. "You're a genius."

"'Twasn't I. Our petite friend done it."

Trisha Jean glances around the empty room. "Elisabet? Where is she?"

"Funny story . . ."

# CHAPTER 36

The foursome race toward the ring of living quarters and run headlong into Joel de Brienne, who has an olive-colored duffel over one shoulder. The kind of bag used for carrying long tools.

Dez says, "Where'd ye park the wee Québécois, mate?"

The bearded man says, "I'll show you." He doesn't ask what's up.

They get to the one-room apartment he led Ash to earlier. The door is unlocked. Her backpack is there, along with the borrowed U.S. Air Force winter coat and snow pants, stocking hat and mittens.

Dez unzips and upends her backpack on the floor. It's filled with women's clothing and a toiletry kit and a paperback book in French.

Trisha Jean says, "She's an assassin? Are you serious?"

"Aye. Met her in Paris about eighteen months ago. Tried to kill someone me mate and me was protecting. Name's Ash."

He lifts the mattress of the single bed. He spots the indentation that could have come from two guns.

"Think she ran here, armed up. De Brienne? Are there security cameras this level?"

"No."

Petra is sorting through Ash's clothes, looking for a phone or any other electronics. "How did you recognize her?"

"In Paris, she was covered in dust an' wore a mask. Saw her just now more or less the same. Should've recognized her earlier, but I'm thick as paste, me."

The big engineer blinks. "Wait. I'm sorry." He holds his hand up, palm down, five feet off the floor. "*La petite femme* is an assassin?"

Rusty Townsend is in the hallway; the room's too small for all five of them. He peers both directions, his gun in hand. "Is she targeting Trip Jacks?"

Trisha Jean grins at him. "You just called me Trip Jacks."

Rusty blinks. "No, I didn't."

"Ye did, mate. An' no." Dez turns to Trisha Jean. "Killin' you'd have been a far sight easier in St. John's, yeah? She wanted t'get here. Her target's here."

Trisha Jean says, "How do you like them apples? I don't even rate an assassin."

Rusty says, "She didn't come to kill Mayor Brandywine. Or any of the townies, I guess. Then it's the neutrino team."

Dez stands, nods. "Process of elimination, aye."

Trisha Jean says, "And she can't get to them without going through the Russians. So the scientists are safe. For now."

"'Safe' being a relative term, love. Joel: She has the full access to levels one an' two, aye? Lots of places t'hide?"

"*Oui.* When fully operational, the mine ran eighty men per shift. You haven't even seen the mining operation itself yet. Just the residential quarters. She could hide out down here for months."

Everyone ponders a bit. Trisha Jean says, "The wounded?"

"Your doc sedated them," De Brienne says. "Says they'd produce less carbon dioxide that way."

"Smart, that." Dez rubs his ear. His knee, where she kicked him, feels like it might be swelling just a bit. "Trip: Any luck with the Russians?"

"Dialogue," she says. "Got them communicating. Got them thinking of me as a person, not the opposition. But you fixing the oxygen's going to go a long ways toward gaining their trust."

Rusty grumbles, "Why did you want them to see your face? That was a dumb risk."

Petra stands, leaving behind the pile of Ash's things. "I'm not a negotiator on Secretary Jackson's level, but I do put together a lot of deals for my company. Letting them see her face imbued her with . . . I don't know. Personhood, I suppose. Made her real to them. Now they won't be talking to 'the American woman.' They'll be talking to someone they've met."

Trisha Jean winks at Petra. "Bingo."

Dez says, "I don't think I want Ash runnin' around armed. De Brienne? Can we put together a plan to search this level in a systemic way? Make sure we don't miss her?"

The engineer shrugs.

"Ta. Trip, we need t'get the Russians on board before we try to take on them Skyhook lads up top. Did ye tell 'em about the oppo up there?"

"I did. Now that the air is flowing, I'll talk to them again. And you're right: We have a chance with the Russians helping us against the thugs up there. And I don't much like our chances without them."

"Same. I'd like t'come with you when you talk to the Russians. I need t'get a sense of who they are. Joel? Let's see some more schematics. Figure out a way t'flush Ash out in the open."

"Okay," the big man says, "but I gave my rifle to one of the townies. I wouldn't mind having a gun."

Trisha Jean has been holding Captain Charbonneau's Colt 1911. She draws it from her belt now, reverses it, and hands it to De Brienne. "Here ya go."

*"Merci."* De Brienne reaches for the gun, shifting the duffel on his back that carries two Sten guns.

The walls in the residential doughnut aren't very thick, the insulation not very good. There are eighty apartments down here and Ash could be in any of them. But, in fact, she sits in the very next room over, listening to them through the wall.

She'd raced back to her room, retrieved her guns and some clothes and other tech from her backpack, then moved next door, picking the lock, sneaking in. She took a very quick, ten-second shower to get all the dust and particulate off her skin and hair. She doesn't want to be tramping dust everywhere, and she doesn't want to spend her time sneezing. The shower seems like a good tactical move. She switched to another set of exercise togs, much the same as the last but these are matte black with bloodred piping down both legs. She cleaned her sneakers as best she could. She tucked her white hair up into a black baseball cap with no logo. She has short, wrist-length gloves that have been reinforced with thin metal bands sewn in along the backs of all four fingers. Not brass knuckles, but close enough.

She's sitting, ear to the wall, knees up. Four extra ten-round magazines for her G43X Glock lie by her hip. Also, her butterfly knife. She wears a combat holster strapped low on her thigh. She's breaking down the cop's stolen gun; too bulky for her to haul around. The reason she carries the G43X is that it's sized for a woman's hand, and her hands are smaller than most.

By listening through the wall, Ash knows that their diplomat is heading back down to talk to the Russians, and that Dez is organizing a search party. So once again, she knows more than they do.

She has no chance of reaching her target. Not yet. So the best thing she can do is hide and bide her time.

When the moment is right, she'll be ready.

## ST. JOHN'S

Vincent and Valerie Cray receive a satellite call routed through two continents and filtered to make it untraceable. The caller says, "I received your twenty-one million euros. You will have your bunker-buster bomb and your extraction team. They are airborne, coming your way from Central America even as we speak."

Valerie says, "Have them set down in Quebec. I'll join the extraction team there."

"It's your money." He hangs up.

Vincent smiles at his wife. "That takes care of us getting into the mine. Next question: Finn and his men? Do we tell them we plan to blow our way into the mine?"

She says, "I've thought about that. I don't think we should sacrifice them. I mean, if we need to, fine. Whatever. But I say we warn them before the bomb arrives and tell them to seek shelter here."

She spins her laptop to show Vincent the screen. "This was a NORAD watch site in the 1960s, when Canada was on the lookout for Russian bombers or missiles coming over Greenland. It's been long abandoned. It's two miles north of Fuchstown. Sturdy, concrete construction. This should be a safe distance from the bunker buster."

Her husband nods. "And do we tell Finn about the second wave of mercenaries?"

"Not . . . yet," she says. "Finn is expressing more self-determination than I prefer in my soldiers. We might yet need to replace his leadership."

Vincent smiles. "That we might."

# CHAPTER 37

Dez, Trisha Jean Jackson, and Rusty Townsend head back down to the barricade blocking open the fire doors between levels two and three. Trisha Jean says, "I knew the Russians wanted to talk. They were looking for an excuse. Why block the door open, if not?"

"So they can shoot through and pick off the townies," Rusty says.

"You're a glass-half-empty kinda guy, you know that?"

"I'm a 'glass half full of cyanide and wondering why I'm not thirsty anymore' kinda guy."

She laughs. "Come step up to the barricade with me. I want them to see you guys, too."

"Why?"

"What Ms. Alexandris said. Establishing us as people. If it's gonna be the Russians and us versus the Skyhook group up top, I need the Russians to think of us as real people."

Dez gets that, nodding.

They're closer now. Trisha Jean sings out, "It's us. Don't shoot. Our guys got the airflow fixed."

She steps up to the barricade, peering over it. She spots the same two men: the hulking, bearded guy and the smaller, wiry guy on the platform at the top of the stairs. "Hi, guys."

She gestures to Dez and Rusty to join her. They do. All the Russians can see are their faces, necks, and shoulders.

"This is Dez and this is Rusty. Dez is the guy who got the air flowing again."

Dez waves. "Mates."

The wiry guy says, "You fixed air? Is better. We can tell."

He tosses the bottle of aspirin back to Trisha Jean. They're separated by about fifteen feet. She catches it in both hands. "Softball in college. Starting shortstop."

The more they identify her as a normal human being, the more likely they are to talk.

"Is elevator working?" the wiry Russian asks.

Dez says, "Aye. But we figure them gunmen Trisha Jean told ye about are still up there. We go up there, it'll be the OK Corral."

The Russians glance at each other.

"It'll be a shoot-out," Trisha Jean translates. "Unless I can get the word out to the authorities. Have the Canadian military or RCMP intervene. And now I'm wondering: What are the chances you guys came here without an emergency communications plan?"

"We represent Syever Mineralnaya, yes? We ship cerite, extract cerium. We did not come here expecting this cowboy, pow-pow, American violence. We have no communications."

"Yeah, see, that's one possible answer. But I also think you guys look more like military than a mineralogical operation. You know?"

Wiry Guy glances at his companion, who must stand six-six and who's as muscled as Dez. He turns back to Trisha Jean. "My friend is farm boy. He is strong like ox, but he's no soldier. Same, too, is me. I am janitor."

"Sure. But the thing is, my daddy taught me a lot about guns, growing up. I mean, we're talking Georgia here. And you remember I served a diplomatic tour in Kosovo? Now, a lot of those guys carried a Russian-made sidearm called a Grach. Which looks a lot like the guns you got holstered there on your hips. And if I'm remembering my Kosovar briefings, that's the gun of choice for Russian special forces. So you see where a suspicious gal such as myself might think you guys are military. And if that were true, well, you might have a way of communicating with the outside."

Dez hasn't really gotten to see the diplomat in action. He's more than impressed.

Wiry Guy smiles. He points to his friend and then to himself. "Farm boy. Janitor."

"Right, right," Trisha Jean says. "I just plain forgot. So if you can't send out a mayday signal, and we can't send out a mayday signal, and those guys are still up there, armed for bear, then it looks like a stalemate. We can't move. You can't move. And at some point, the storm's going to end and the Canadian military will send everything they've got to figure out what's going on here. So you're right: If we're all just patient, this thing will sort itself out."

The Russians glance at each other.

Clearly, waiting for the Canadian military to intervene isn't in their best interests.

"Look, why don't you fellas think on it a bit. Who knows? Something might come to you. Okay?"

Wiry Guy nods. "We will think, yes."

"Okay. Again: Trisha Jean, Dez, and Rusty. What do I call you?"

He makes the same two-part gesture. "Farm boy. Janitor."

"Gotcha. Do you need anything? You got water? Food?"

"We need nothing."

"All right. I got someone standing by within earshot. You wanna talk, sing out."

Wiry Guy nods.

Trisha Jean steps over the rubble, Dez and Rusty follow.

They move well away, and Dez speaks softly. "Janitor and farm boy, me arse. Them's soldiers, plain and simple. The shorter fella outranks the bigger guy."

Trisha Jean says, "Agreed. I was trying to get their names. An essential trick in hostile negotiations."

Rusty says, "I'm going with: 'Look, darlink, is Moose and Squirrel.'"

Dez laughs and slaps him on the back. "Perfect! Moose and Squirrel, it is."

# CHAPTER 38

Dez splits with Trisha Jean and Rusty, who head for the break room and some food. He finds the big engineer, Joel de Brienne, talking to a cluster of the townies. "Mr. Mayor, you take your people and move through the residence hall, okay? Here." He hands him a passkey. "This will get you in every room."

Dez says, "Ash is armed, but she's also shown restraint. She's a pro. If she's not paid to kill you, you're safe. But don't get in a fight with her and make her make that choice, yeah?"

The mayor stands with three other townies. He does not look happy.

"The mines themselves are a little less stable," De Brienne says. "I'll take Limerick and we'll scout them. Well, level two, anyway."

Because that's the only part of the mine the townies currently control.

De Brienne has a walkie-talkie and so does Mayor Brandywine. Dez says, "Pipe up if ye catch sight of her. Don't provoke her."

One of the Fuchstown residents raises his hand. "Wouldn't it be easier just to leave her alone?"

"She's here t'kill someone. One of the scientists, I'm bettin'. I'd rather have her under wraps before Trip Jacks finds a way to get the Russians on our side, which would clear the path between Ash an' her target."

The townies don't look enthusiastic. De Brienne raises his hand. "Anyone here sleeping well, knowing we've got an armed killer on the loose? No? Then do as Limerick says, *hein*?"

With a little more grumbling, they part ways.

De Brienne stops at the infirmary to drop off whatever's in the long canvas bag hanging off one shoulder. He has tucked the helicopter pilot's gun in his belt. He says, "Everyone's tired and scared. At least you got the $CO_2$ scrubbers online. Everyone's headaches have gone away."

"Aye. And whilst I've only known Trip Jacks for a few days, I've the feeling that if anyone can get the Russians t'stand down, 'tis she. Meant what I said about corralling Ash before that happens."

The big man adjusts his Montreal Canadiens cap and leads the way. They stop in the break room to fill in Trisha Jean, as well as Rusty and Petra. Rusty says, "Want me to join you?"

De Brienne says, "Mayor Brandywine and some of his folks are searching the residences. They ain't too happy. Would appreciate having a professional join them."

"I got it. Ms. Alexandris? You'll stay with Trip Ja . . . with Secretary Jackson?"

Everyone laughs at the faux pas. "Of course. And it's Petra, please."

With that, Dez and De Brienne head down to two.

At the bottom of the stairs, the engineer turns left, not right, as Trisha Jean's party has done repeatedly. Dez sees signs that read HARD HAT ZONE—PPE REQUIRED. Also, one that reads DAYS WITHOUT

A WORKPLACE ACCIDENT, with chalkboard space before DAYS to write in a number. Right now, the number reads ZERO. Which is why the miners went on strike and are in St. John's now, safe as houses.

They reach an entryway with no doors, but with yellow and black stripes painted on both sides and over the top, the universal sign for danger. "How long've you been in Fuchstown?" Dez asks.

"Couple of years."

They head through the portal. On the other side, Dez expects to see the Hollywood version of a mine: dark, narrow, with a bunch of two-by-fours clapped together. This isn't that. The mine shaft is wide and well lit by a string of work lights inside metal cages that line the roof. Instead of wooden beams, the roof and walls are supported by latticelike metal pillars and plates bolted together. Right down the middle of the mine are narrow-gauge train tracks. Dez spots the little, electric-powered dump truck that runs on the rails. It's about thirty meters straight down the main tunnel.

"So, amongst the townies down here, who's the most recent addition?"

De Brienne says, "How come?"

"Just wondering who to trust."

De Brienne doesn't comment on that. "You know what a cerite seam looks like?"

"Don't."

De Brienne picks up a clawed hammer. The handle is a good fifteen inches long. "C'mon. I'll show you."

He starts walking down the main tunnel, following the tracks toward the electric car. They could walk side by side, but Dez trails behind him.

"I was a soldier of sorts, for a bit. Protected a few mines, but I never worked in one."

"This one's better than most. Cleaner."

"Can see that."

They get to the topless electric car. De Brienne passes by it. Then Dez.

Then the big man spins fast, swinging the clawed hammer in a horizontal arc.

Dez ducks, and it misses him. But by an inch at best.

The electric car is behind Dez, so there's no room to back up. Instead, he plows forward and throws a punch into the big man's abdomen.

De Brienne is no slouch. He spins a bit with the punch, absorbs some of its energy. He grabs Dez by the back of his collar, continues his spin, and throws him farther into the mine.

Dez lands on his side and rolls and comes up to his feet.

De Brienne swings the long hammer again.

Dez bops backward, hopping, watching the wicked weapon whiz past his gut.

De Brienne has longer arms, longer legs, and he's got the long-handled hammer. All advantages.

Dez keeps backing up, and the engineer keeps advancing.

"This what they call Canadian hospitality, then?"

The big man doesn't respond. He swings the hammer again. Misses again. Dez keeps backing up.

"Work for the Crays?"

Swing. Miss.

"Not the most jocular of villains, you. Less chatty than I'm used to."

Swing.

And this time Dez doesn't back up. He advances on the nether side of that swing. He grabs De Brienne's wrist and shoves the same way the big man swung. He also draws the collapsible truncheon he stole from another Cray mercenary in a hotel in St. John's. He doesn't fully deploy it but uses the base of it to whack De Brienne across the knuckles.

The hammer slams into the one of the latticelike metal braces holding the rocky walls up. Metal on metal; the reverberation runs through De Brienne's right arm. That and the blow from Dez's truncheon, and the big man drops the hammer.

He also headbutts Dez.

Dez staggers backward. Lands on his ass.

De Brienne shakes out his right arm, still aching from hitting the metal brace. He casually picks up the hammer with his left hand, straightens up.

Dez rises.

With a rock the size of a racquetball in his left fist.

He lets fly.

Years of cricket and darts have given Dez great eye-hand coordination, and years of boxing and martial arts have given him strong arms.

The rock hits De Brienne on his left cheek.

Bone cracks.

The man spins to his left, the impact to his face staggering him.

Dez is on him in a heartbeat, racing forward. He springs into the air and brings the heels of both boots down on De Brienne's right knee.

Dez lands 280 pounds of muscle on the engineer's knee, and the knee breaks. Ligaments shred. Leg bones above and below the knee crack like lobster claws. The man howls and falls, his leg cocked at a right angle, but not the right angle that a million years of evolution intended.

The knee is ruined.

Dez only now realizes that the rock he threw broke De Brienne's cheekbone. He's bleeding from his eye, too.

The big man lies on his back. His legs form the number 4. He keens in exquisite pain, then passes out.

Dez stows the retractable billy club in his back pocket. He takes a knee and retrieves the helo pilot's gun out of De Brienne's belt. Dez realizes the man didn't shoot him because he'd have had to explain the gunshot, which everyone would have heard. Even the Russians. His better plan was to beat Dez to death, dump his body farther down in the mine, then claim he had no idea what happened and to suggest that Ash killed him.

Dez pats down the man's pockets, hoping for some sort of communication device. He finds nothing.

He grunts and lifts the man up onto his shoulder in a fireman's carry. "Jay-sus but you're a big un!" he huffs.

And starts walking back toward the stairs to level one.

Ash steps gingerly out from a side tunnel, watching Dez's broad back retreat.

She observed the fight. She can now confirm that which she speculated upon in Paris: Dez is the most gifted and the smartest fighter she's ever faced.

# CHAPTER 39

Up on level one, Dez passes a townie and wheezes, "Oi. Get to the infirmary and get Doc Patterson, will ye? Ask him t'meet me in the break room."

The Fuchstown resident says, "Is that Joel?"

"It's a fecking manatee, if me back is to be believed. Scram, please."

He gets to the break room and dumps the unconscious man on his back across one of the tables. Several townsfolk are there and rise to their feet.

De Brienne's face is ruined.

"Someone want t'go to the habitat ring and get Mayor Brandywine, please." Dez looks around for the bottle of aspirin he'd seen in here earlier but can't spot it. That headbutt was a thing of beauty, he thinks, massaging his forehead.

"What happened to Joel?"

"Get the mayor, yeah?"

Dez has time now to search the man more thoroughly. He thumbs through his wallet and finds no ID, nor driver's license, nor credit cards or debit cards. Just a lot of cash.

His pockets are otherwise empty of anything important.

Burt Brandywine enters with three more townies.

Dr. Dyson Patterson arrives on their six and stops in his tracks. "Whoa."

"'allo, Doc. This man's got facial injuries and a badly busted knee. More'n you can do for him, I'd wager, but you're the best we got."

Patterson moves forward.

The mayor says, "What happened? Did that woman get him?"

"Hmm? No. Our Monsieur De Brienne here tried t'kill me with a clawed hammer. In the mines. He works for the same outfit as them up top."

Trisha Jean, Rusty, and Petra make the scene now. Dez repeats his story to them. More townsfolk pour into the room.

A townie says, "Joel tried to kill you? How do we know that's true?"

"Told me he'd lived in Fuchstown for, an' I quote, 'a couple of years.' This true?"

People glance at each other. Brandywine says, "Joel moved here maybe three weeks ago."

"There ye go. Was the advance man for the lot that killed your people up top."

"He works for the Russians?"

Trisha Jean cuts in. "I'm afraid not, Mr. Mayor. In St. John's, Dez was attacked by professional soldiers working for Skyhook Technologies."

"Skyhook?" someone bleats. "The mining construction folks?"

She says, "Yes," addressing everyone. "They sent more mercenaries after us when we got to Fuchstown. They're armed to the teeth.

The Russians, we suspect, are fully down here. On levels three and four. The threat on the surface are these mercenaries from Skyhook."

The mayor shakes his head, his jowls bouncing. "I don't know. That sounds like a lot of horse hockey pucks."

Someone points to Dez. "This guy brutalized Joel. That's for sure! How much of this story of theirs is bullshit?"

Burt Brandywine says, "Language."

Another townie grumbles, "Look, we know it's the goddamn Russians, okay? I don't know why we're even talking about this!"

Dyson Patterson looks up from his patient and eyes Dez. "You did a number on this guy. The damage to his cheekbone and his eye socket? That's not something I can fix. He needs a Level One trauma hospital. And I'm pretty sure he's going to lose this leg."

Trisha Jean says, "You're not really helping here, Doctor."

And he isn't. The townies are grumbling louder.

Dez holds up both palms, faces the residents. He notices that Petra moves to his side, facing them as well.

"Friends? I was mindin' me own business in New York when the State Department asked me to help, because I'm sort of good at opening doors. That's all. I'd not heard of your town, nor the mine, nor the Fuchs Underground Neutrino Collector, till a few days ago."

Trisha Jean says, "I can confirm that."

The mayor rubs the back of his neck. "It's just that there's a girl running around out there younger than my daughters, and you tell us she's an international assassin? I'd sure like to hear her side of that. And Joel's only lived here a few weeks, but he's an amiable sort. A good neighbor. You say he's some kind of mercenary soldier? It's all just a little far-fetched is all."

A voice rings out. "I bet that girl's dead! Bet he killed her and concocted that silly story about her being an assassin!"

People rumble their assent.

And some of them have shotguns and rifles. And at least one hunting dog.

Trisha Jean addresses the mayor directly. "Sir, emotions are running high here. Think we can lower the temperature a little? Just talk?"

Brandywine pulls on his lower lip as he ponders the situation. Then he turns to his town's residents. "Let's calm down, all right? I'm gonna talk to these folks and try to get to the bottom of this. Sound good?"

Reluctantly, the crowd bows to his leadership.

"I've set up one of the smaller offices, down this way."

"Thank you, sir," Trisha Jean says. "I'd like Dez to join us. He brings a unique perspective to everything."

With that, she, her bodyguard, the mayor, and Dez exit.

Dr. Patterson points to Petra. "You should go with them. Let's create some physical space between everyone."

Petra nods and joins the others.

As that group leaves, Dyson Patterson's mind reels.

His only ally down in this hellhole lies broken on a break-room table! Limerick stands just five-eight. And he looks like he works out plenty, but Patterson knows that De Brienne was a skilled and highly decorated special forces soldier. Patterson held no doubt that the big man could take out Limerick, thus eliminating their biggest threat.

So much for that theory.

Patterson himself was a well-trained and proficient killer when he was a Ranger. But the reason he became a battlefield medic is because he prefers to use his brain rather than his brawn.

As soon as the others are gone, he turns to the remainder of the Fuchstown residents. He shrugs. "I honestly don't know what to believe. I mean, I just met these people a couple of days ago in St. John's."

Someone says, "You don't trust them?"

"I don't *know* them. And that Limerick guy?" Patterson shakes his head. "Mrs. Jackson says she's from the U.S. State Department, and I don't know. I guess she could be. But that guy isn't. He isn't even an American."

Townies mumble and nod.

"Joel seemed nice enough to me. Was he some sort of, what? A secret agent or something?" Patterson scoffs.

Someone shouts, "Hell no!"

"And the blond girl? I'd believe it if you told me she was a grad student. Art history or some such liberal arts bullshit, am I right?"

People mutter, agreeing.

"She's what? The Black Widow. Please."

The crowd is definitely re-riled. They're where he wants them.

"Look, I trust Mayor Brandywine. He says chill, we should chill. Can I get a couple of you guys to help me carry Joel to the infirmary?"

Several guys volunteer.

But Dyson Patterson's pretty sure the fuse is lit. The townies are looking at this Limerick prick like he's the Creature escaped from Castle Frankenstein.

Only, these villagers aren't carrying pitchforks and torches. They've got rifles and shotguns.

And with a little bit of luck, they'll do Patterson's job for him.

# CHAPTER 40

Burt Brandywine sits behind a plain, unadorned desk in an office on the residence level, rubbing his face. He glances at his watch.

"The problem with being trapped underground is you've got no sense of time. Heck, it's three in the morning. It's . . . Wow. It's . . . Friday?"

"It is, sir," Dez says, taking Captain Charbonneau's Colt from his belt and setting it on the table. He slides it across the distance, closer to Brandywine. "This belongs to our helicopter pilot. Want to hold on to it till she's on her feet?"

Brandywine studies it, then studies Dez. "You don't want it?"

"I'm a former soldier, sir. Means I strongly believe in the concept of elected, civilian oversight for soldiers like me. Right now, enough folks seem scared of me. I'd like to take steps to address that."

Trisha Jean nods approvingly. It's the sort of de-escalation move she, herself, might have picked.

A few seconds pass, then Brandywine shoves the gun to the

middle of the table. "I'm a rock-ribbed conservative, Mr. Limerick. I'm a hunter, and I contribute to the National Rifle Association in the States. But honestly, I do not particularly like guns. They scare me. And I'll deny saying that to any registered voter in Fuchstown."

"Then you're a smart man," Trisha Jean says to him, leaning forward in her chair. She stopped briefly in the room where they'd stored their backpacks. Now she hands him her U.S. State Department credentials, which include her photo.

"I am who I say I am, sir, and the FBI invited Dez up here because they were told he could get us into the mine. They vetted him before inviting him. He's got fans in the U.S. Marshals Service, in the FBI, and in the halls of several municipal police departments. I've only known him since Monday, but I've put my life in his hands. Rusty's, too."

Rusty sits next to her. He says, "Well, technically, you put your life in *my* hands, and I put mine in Dez's, but—"

She smiles serenely at him. "Rusty?"

He says, "Yes, ma'am," and clams up.

Petra stands near the door, arms folded, her back to the wall. "I run a . . . pretty big company, Mr. Mayor. And I do it well. But not when I'm sleep deprived."

Brandywine chuckles. "My late wife used to say, 'Sleep on it, dummy, and talk to me in the morning.' I'll check in with my folks. Let's everyone get a little sleep. But, just let me say this."

He leans forward, eyes on Dez.

"Near as I could tell, you maimed Joel. If we got him to the best hospital in Ottawa, ten minutes from now, he'd be a one-eyed cripple for life. So despite *this* . . ."

He nudges the gun on the table with his fingertip. It spins clockwise a few degrees.

". . . despite this? I'm not feeling an overabundance of trust here."

He stands. "Mrs. Jackson. Let's get your people settled into some of the rooms. Everyone get some sleep. I'll talk to my folks. Then we'll figure things out tomorrow."

He glances again at his watch. "Or, later today, I mean. That work for you folks?"

Everyone stands. Trisha Jean offers her hand, and they shake.

"Thank you, Mr. Mayor."

Dez shakes the man's hand, too.

Knowing full well that, in defending himself against Joel de Brienne's attack, Dez actually made their situation more precarious.

Out in the hall, Petra touches Dez's shoulder. "Hey. I don't know if . . . I'm saying, I already have a room. If you'd like . . . ?"

Dez grins. "I would like. Didn't want to presume."

She links her arm with his. "I was kind of hoping you'd say yes."

**ST. JOHN'S**

Vincent Cray gets a text message on their encrypted sat phone.

> Your package has cleared U.S. airspace. It should be over Canada in less than 10 hours.

Valerie is en route by truck to Quebec, where she'll join the backup mercenaries. And oversee the delivery of the bunker-buster bomb.

# CHAPTER 41

Dez and Petra make love.

They haven't been together since much earlier in the year, when Dez was in LA and had helped her, and Triton Expediters, out of a jam. They fall back into their old grooves quickly. The sex is comfortable and slow, both of them needing the release equally.

They lie in bed together after. Petra says, "What I wouldn't give for a good bottle of Sancerre right now."

"Dunno if you ventured into Hank's Provisions in Fuchstown, but a box of blended reds may be the best we could hope for."

She laughs.

"Love? Your being here makes not one ounce of sense. You've, what? A dozen advisers who could've come check on this place? Five dozen?"

She's quiet for a time. They both lie on their backs, Petra's head on Dez's forearm.

She says, "I ran away from home to join the circus."

He laughs.

"I'm actually serious. I ran away from Triton. When you met me, I was chief legal counsel and my father was CEO. My job was to negotiate with the leadership of whole nations. With generals and admirals."

"I remember."

"I knew with granular detail the makes and models of the armaments or defense systems Triton money would go to purchasing. I could tell you the five primary differences between a French Mistral missile and a Russian Igla-S missile. I just never had to think about what they'd be used for. Or on whom they'd be used."

Dez is silent, letting her tell the tale in the way he senses she needs to.

"I'm good at running Triton. I've got us back on track after that trouble you got us out of. But now I have to think about where our money is spent. Who benefits. Who suffers. I hate it. I hate every minute of it."

"So ye financed both a beta test of a clean mining method and a neutrino research facility."

She turns to him. "That's right. That's the kind of things Triton should be financing. Not just paying for war."

"Defense systems sometimes keep the wars at bay, yeah?"

"*Si vis pacem, para bellum*. Believe me, I know. Still, it's . . . overwhelming. I had to get out of there. I had to think about something other than war."

"Well, here's as good a place as any," he says, leaning her way and kissing the top of her head. "If ye don't count the Russians, an' the mercenaries, and whatnot."

Petra laughs. "And the ultra-processed food. Don't forget the ultra-processed food."

And she snuggles closer to him.

★ ★ ★

They both log a solid eight hours of sleep. It's noon Friday when they stir.

Dez ponders his to-do list. Today's problems are pretty simple, really.

One: Get the Russians to give up levels three and four.

Two: Get to the neutrino hunters and find out what kicked off this whole mess. They went radio-dark first. That was before the killings up topside, and the destruction of Fuchstown's communications infrastructure. Dez has a strong belief in the concept of inciting incidents. Figure out what that was all about, and the rest of this might achieve some level of clarity.

Three: Figure out how to bollux the Skyhook thugs currently occupying the igloo and their only means of egress. (Dez is an optimistic man but he can't hope that his fragment bomb got all of them. No one's that lucky.)

Four: Try not to rile the locals any more than he already has.

Five: Get some breakfast.

Petra showers first. While she's drying her hair, Dez jumps in. He's sitting on the room's plain-as-dirt couch, tying his boot laces, when it comes to his attention that someone is standing outside his door. He spots the shadow play under the door. Whoever it is shifts his weight from time to time. One of the townies.

Here to ask him a question and too timid to knock? Or is Dez under house arrest? Given the relatively friendly conversation they had with the mayor at three this morning, the latter would be a significant downgrade in the situation.

"Love?"

He gestures. She spots it. He waits till she's finished dressing in a man's button-down shirt, her jeans and boots with Spanish heels.

He opts not to grab his jacket, so it's obvious he's not armed. He opens his room's door.

One of the Fuchstown residents stands outside. With his shotgun.

Dez beams at the man. "Morning! I slept like the dead. A new man, me. Breakfast?"

The guy takes a pugnacious step forward, blocking Dez's exit. "You're under house arrest, dude. Just get your ass back in your room. Someone will bring you something to eat."

Dez keeps smiling. "And coffee, kindly. Tout de suite. Cream, two sugars, for me. Ms. Alexandris prefers black tea. Also, two eggs, scrambled is fine. An Eccles cake is too much to hope for, I've no doubt, but I wouldn't turn down a crumpet. Barring that, sourdough toast would do. Jam, of course. Goes without saying, don't it? A fried tomato would be just the very thing. If there's a potato to be had, in any form known to man or god, I'd not turn it down."

He smiles back at Petra. "Forget anything?"

She is playing with her phone. "Avocado toast, please."

The guy looks more pissed off than ever. He grips the shotgun in both hands, his knuckles white. "You tried to kill Joel and you probably killed that girl. Now shut your fucking mouth, get back in your room, and we'll decide when . . . and if . . . to bring you a sandwich. You got me, fuck head?"

Dez is stronger than people think, and they think he looks plenty strong. But Dez also is faster than people think.

He whisks the gun from the man's hands.

It takes a moment for the guy to even realize it's happened. He actually looks down to confirm what his fingers are telling him; that his hands are empty. His eyes go from angry to scared in a snap. He stumbles, backing up.

Dez takes a step out of the room, shotgun in one hand. "And if by chance I forgot to mention bacon, well, that'd be an oversight on my part, now, wouldn't it?"

The man turns and sprints down the hall.

Dez ejects both shells. He sets the shotgun down in the hallway, butt down, barrel leaning against the wall. He sets the shells, standing, next to the butt. Then he returns to Petra's room, closes the door.

"I suggest we wait a wee bit."

He can tell that Petra is fuming. But she nods, agreeing.

Burt Brandywine listens as Bobby Schultz, one of his constituents, tells him that Dez snuck up on him, stole his shotgun, and threatened him.

Brandywine and Schultz head toward the oval of residential rooms that encircle the commons area. First, they both grab two more guns. They stop at Trisha Jean Jackson's room, and the mayor raps on the door with his knuckle.

When she pops open the door, he explains the situation and asks that she accompany him. She listens, says nothing, then steps out.

They make it a quarter of the way around the doughnut of residences to Petra's designated room, which she's occupied since arriving on Monday. They spot the shotgun leaning against the wall. And the shells.

Brandywine's headache is back; this one from lack of sleep, not an overabundance of carbon dioxide. He pinches the bridge of his nose. "Bobby," he says, "I've known you for going on ten years now, and you are a hotheaded sort of guy. You also drink more than I think you should, but I'm not your mom. If I were to guess, I'd say Mr. Limerick did not sneak up on you while you were standing outside his door, watching for him. He might have taken your weapon, but he did not threaten you with it. Maybe just the opposite."

The guy called Bobby is seething. Taking his weapon from him so casually was one insult. Leaving it outside in the corridor was another. "I'm gonna—"

Brandywine keeps his voice down. "What you're gonna do is go get yourself a cup of joe and count to ten. Go on, now."

Bobby doesn't budge.

"Bobby?"

The man turns and stalks down the hall on stiff legs.

"This seems like a good time to speak," Trisha Jean says, and she allows true anger to color her voice. Brandywine turns to her, blushing, embarrassed. "Why did you put Dez under house arrest, Mr. Mayor?"

There's steel in her voice. He hadn't heard it before.

"I'm sorry, ma'am. After you all went to bed, we had a brief town meeting. The upshot of which is: My people don't trust this Limerick character. We don't want him wandering the mine on his own."

Trisha glares at him. She has a ferocious glare.

He raises both palms, placatingly. "You're absolutely right, ma'am. I should have told you. I'm sorry."

"I understand fear, Mr. Mayor. And I understand your constituents are under a great deal of pressure. But oh yeah. You definitely should have spoken to me."

Dez and Petra are reading on their smartphones when someone knocks on their door. Even the knocking sounds contrite.

Petra pats Dez's thigh, then stands and answers the door.

It's Mayor Brandywine and Trisha Jean. She's picked up the shotgun Dez left by the door. They spot him behind Petra, reading.

Petra stares into the mayor's eyes with no emotion on his face.

Brandywine sighs. "I understand there was some sort of miscommunication this morning, ma'am. I want to—"

Petra shows him her phone. It's set on audio recording. She taps a button.

*"You tried to kill Joel and you probably killed that girl. Now shut your*

*fucking mouth, get back in your room, and we'll decide when . . . and if . . . to bring you a sandwich. You got me, fuck head?"*

She clicks it off.

She knows the mayor neither swears nor appreciates swearing in others. She played him the tape to make as strong a case as she can without speaking a word.

Brandywine turns about four shades of red. "Mrs. Alexandris, I just . . . I am truly sorry. I owe you both an apology. I shouldn't have posted a hotheaded guy who hasn't had a wink of sleep in three days."

Petra steps a bit into his space, and he steps back. "The woman to your left is *Madam Secretary.* I'm *Ms. Alexandris,* Mr. Mayor. And as of this second, I am in dire need of caffeine. Shall we?"

Burt Brandywine takes two meek steps back, head bowed.

Petra nods to Trisha Jean. Who manages not to pull a muscle hiding her big grin.

Dez steps out, too, and slaps the mayor on the shoulder.

"Dez to me mates, guv'nor!"

# CHAPTER 42

In the break room, plenty of townies glare at Dez and the other outsiders as they beeline for their caffeine of choice. As they do, Rusty Townsend hustles in.

"It's the Russians, ma'am. They want to talk to you."

Trisha Jean dips a tea bag in her cup of hot water. "I take that as a good sign. Mr. Mayor? Would you care to accompany us this time?"

They trudge down to level two, and to the stairwell door to three that's been jammed open. They pass the townie on watch, carrying a Winchester Model 70 hunting rifle, its strap over one shoulder. He juts his chin in Dez's direction and mutters to the mayor, "That asshole tried to kill Joel."

Brandywine gives the man one of his patented sighs.

They get closer to the doors, and Trisha Jean sings out before she shows her face. "I'm back. I brought the mayor of Fuchstown, in case you wanted to ask him some questions."

Dez hangs back with Petra and Rusty.

The guy they'd dubbed Squirrel stands, again, next to the towering Moose. "We want to leave of our own accord. We want you to make the elevator work. We want you to clear a path of your residents. We will exit. What you do after that is not our concern. Go. Stay. But we want to leave."

Meaning they've come to the conclusion that Trisha Jean led them to: that the Canadian military likely will be the next set of visitors to Fuchstown, and the Russians hope to be long gone by then.

The mayor frowns and gestures to Trisha Jean. She addresses the Russians. "Is it okay if the town's mayor speaks to you?"

The men exchange looks. Moose shrugs. The man's so big Trisha Jean imagines the floor shakes under her shoes when he does.

She gestures Burt Brandywine forward. He hesitates, then speaks from a foot or so to her left. Meaning the Russians cannot see him or (perhaps, more important, from his point of view) shoot at him.

"You people killed citizens in my town. Including the city hall clerk, who I've known for more years than I can count! Why should we let you leave?"

Squirrel says, "We killed no one in your village. We *know* no one in your village. Our only goals are here, in mine. You speak mistaken."

"The heck I do!"

Trisha Jean makes no effort to calm him down. His genuine show of moral outrage might give her a bargaining chip. "There wasn't anybody else here!"

Squirrel addresses Trisha Jean. "You tell me there is mercenary cadre on surface, yes? Mayor says different. Who am I to trust?"

"The mayor didn't see who killed his residents but he knows you're here. He put two and two together and came up with four. A logical deduction. We arrived later. After y'all were in here. So only we saw the mercenaries we've been chased by. So far, the mayor's had only our word that they're for real. Same as you have only our word."

"What does this cadre want?"

"Someone or something that's down here. Same as you. But I don't know their goals any more than I know yours. Honestly, if you told me what you're after, it might help clarify some things."

Dez leans in close and whispers to Petra, "She's good, that one."

"Beyond words. This is a master class."

Squirrel says, "Our goals are not your concern. Will you do as we ask?"

"Are you in contact with the scientists on level five?" she counters.

Squirrel studies her. "I ask that you let us pass."

"I ask for more information."

He says, "We have bigger guns. Also, more of them."

Trisha Jean says, "Positive about that, are you?"

It's a standoff. She doesn't flinch, she doesn't threaten, and she doesn't raise her voice. Dez is enjoying the show.

"What is it you want?" Squirrel finally asks.

"I want to come down there. Just me and one other person. I want to find out if the scientists are all right. We'll come unarmed."

Rusty whispers, "Great, good, I love this plan, this is awesome."

Dez grips his shoulder and gives it a reassuring squeeze.

Moose nudges his cohort. The men turn around and whisper.

Mayor Brandywine whispers, "They can't just leave!"

Trisha Jean nods his way; she heard him and understands his concerns. But she holds her ground.

The Russians talk for nearly a minute. Then turn back to her.

"You and one person."

"That's right."

"And no guns."

"No guns."

"Then you do as we say. You get elevator working, you clear path, we leave."

"Let's not get ahead of ourselves. I need to know the scientists are safe first."

She waits. She's a sphinx, showing no impatience, no anger, nothing.

Squirrel says, "Is all right. Barricade stays. Bring ladder, you climb over."

Trisha Jean barks a laugh. "Twenty years ago and fifty pounds ago, I bet I coulda done that. But today . . . ?"

Squirrel smiles and nods. "Okay, yes. We will set up platform on our end. You climb over barricade; we make it how you say 'easy-peasy' on our side. Yes?"

"Done."

# CHAPTER 43

The State Department team and Mayor Brandywine huddle about a dozen feet from the barricade. Rusty Townsend says, "This is a huge risk."

"This is what diplomacy is," Trisha Jean responds, gripping his upper arm and squeezing. "The impasse can't last forever. That's not good for the townies, the Russians, the scientists, or us. My taking a leap of faith seems like the best way to get a W up on the board."

Rusty groans, rolling his eyes. "Okay, okay. I hate it, but okay."

He draws his service weapon, reverses it, and holds it out toward Dez.

Trisha Jean says, "Oh dear."

When Dez makes no play to take the gun, the penny drops. Rusty's eyes go wide. He keeps his voice low. "No. No. You are my protectee. You are not going in there without me!"

"Goddamn, I like you," she says with a total lack of irony. "You are one hell of a good man, Russell William Townsend. They don't make 'em better. But Dez is going in with me."

"Dez is built like a tank. But did you get a look at Moose in there?" Rusty turns to Dez. "No offense."

"None taken, mate. An' she's not takin' me because I could win a fight. If she gets in there, and they take her hostage, we've already lost this round, and it'll only escalate from there."

Trisha Jean nods. "Right. I'm taking Dez because between me and those scientists will be a door. A door I need him to examine. I don't need a bodyguard on the other side of the barricade. I need a gatekeeper."

"'Tis why I was brung in the first place."

Rusty looks like he's about to burst an appendix. Petra speaks softly. "If it works well, the secretary will get what she needs, which will give her the leverage to give the Russians *some* of what they need. Then they give some more, and she gives some more, and that's the game."

Trisha Jean eyes her anew. "Come work for me."

"You're the federal government. You couldn't afford me."

Rusty says, "We could wait out the storm. Let the Canadian military handle the crazies topside."

Trisha Jean shakes her head. "Emotions among the townies are at a tipping point. Sorry, Mr. Mayor."

Brandywine nods his agreement.

"I'm shocked this whole thing hasn't gone tits up already," she says. "If and when the storms abate and the military can move in, either they'll be unprepared for the Skyhook mercenaries. Or they'll best them, then have no idea how to get down to us or to let us know the coast is clear. Dez rigged the elevator controls to his computer, remember?"

Dez says, "Our best play: The Russians know about the oppo on the surface. We let them outta here to run downfield interference for us, yeah? Let them an' the mercs soften each other up."

Rusty holsters his weapon again.

"I hate this."

Trisha Jean throws an arm over his shoulder. "Which is why you're the best there is at what you do."

# CHAPTER 44

Following the mayor's orders, two of the townies bring a sturdy metal A-frame ladder, and they set it up in front of the four-foot-high barricade. Dez has a folding knife in his pocket, plus the collapsible battle truncheon; he leaves both with Petra.

Who hugs him. She doesn't say *be careful.* She doesn't have to.

They hear the clatter of metal on metal from the other side. Squirrel's voice rings out. "Platform is ready. Only two of you. And no weapons."

Despite her sangfroid, Trisha Jean looks flushed, and her smile is a brittle cover for fear. "Well . . . wish us luck."

The others nod.

Dez mounts the ladder first. At the top, the Russians eye him. He shows them his open palms, then crawls on hands and knees over the debris that holds the doors open.

He glances at the two Russians, Moose and Squirrel. It takes every ounce of energy not to bark a laugh, seeing the two of them now.

They've set up a metal riser at the top of the stairs and appear to have spot-welded it in place. The stable platform is made of iron lattice. Once through, Dez plants one knee and one boot on the surface, then reaches back through for the diplomat.

Trisha Jean Jackson crawls through on her hands and knees. "I am too damn old and too damn fat for this shit," she mutters.

"Too damn brave and too damn logical to see any other path forward."

She gives him a flash grin and a wink.

He helps her through, helps her to stand on the iron platform. He hears her left knee pop, and she winces.

Dez makes eye contact with the Russians, holds his arms out, and does a slow spin. He doffed his jacket; with just a T-shirt, it's clear he's unarmed.

Squirrel nods. "Come down."

The platform includes a ladder. Dez hops down onto the landing at the top of the staircase, then helps Trisha Jean down.

As soon as they both get down to the floor, Trisha Jean turns to Squirrel and offers her hand. "Trisha Jean Jackson, U.S. State Department."

A beat, then he shakes her hand.

She has her diplomatic ID with her and hands it to him. "You read English?"

"I read English," he says. The man is maybe forty, Dez thinks, five-six or so, slight in build. But he also looks like his skin is made of deer jerky and his insides are sinew, gristle, and barbed wire. Give this man a knife or a length of chain, and Dez would put money on him to fight dirty and win against nearly any opponent.

Squirrel studies the ID, then hands it back.

"May I know who I have the honor of addressing, sir?" When she goes into full diplo-speak, Trisha Jean tends to sound like a character in an antebellum romance novel.

Squirrel says, "I am Bob."

"Uh-huh. And your compatriot."

"He is not Bob."

Dez says, "Desmond Aloysius Limerick. Civilian." He smiles up at Moose, who's easily six-six, all of it muscle. "They fed you good growing up."

The big man rumbles in a language Dez assumes is Russian. Dez is a polyglot, but that's not one of his tongues.

Trisha Jean says, "Can I see level five please?"

Squirrel still isn't sure about this. He studies her eyes. She waits.

"Tell your people, if anyone else comes through, they are to be shot on sight."

Trisha Jean inhales deeply. "Mr. Mayor! Rusty! You boys stay in the yard till supper time, you hear?"

They do.

"Is good. Please." Squirrel gestures for them to descend the stairs, and toward the darkened areas beyond, which no one on the Canadian side of the barricade can see.

Dez and Trisha Jean Jackson are in terra incognita.

"Now what?" Burt Brandywine asks in a whisper. His shirt is sweat stained. He is not happy being in conversation with the men he still believes killed his fellow citizens.

"The secretary has a way of getting people to see reason," Rusty says. "I've seen her do amazing things."

Petra says, "I believe it. She's . . ."

Her voice drains away. She's looking over their shoulders.

Rusty and the mayor turn.

Ash stands behind them. Holding her Glock in her right hand, left hand bracing her right wrist, her feet shoulder-width apart, her balance perfect.

"Draw your weapon left-handed," she tells Rusty. "Do anything foolish, and I shoot the mayor."

Smart, Petra thinks. The man's a bodyguard. Protecting a civilian is baked into his DNA.

Rusty draws the weapon awkwardly.

"Throw it, down that direction. Hard as you can."

He mutters, "Oh, man," then turns and overhands the gun into the dark tunnel. It disappears as soon as it's clear of the work lights that limn their side of the barricade.

She circles around them, pivoting her aim, the opening of the barrel unmoving. As she reaches the A-frame ladder, Petra speaks. "They promised to shoot anyone who goes through."

Ash does not reply. She climbs the ladder. She quickly falls to her hands and knees and crawls over the debris.

Once she's gone, Petra dashes forward and quietly mounts the ladder, peering through.

Nobody has fired any shots.

And Ash is nowhere to be seen.

Petra turns her eyes to the mayor. "You know all your residents who were ready to convict Dez of killing her? Guess what . . ."

The mayor averts his eyes. "We do owe him another apology."

# CHAPTER 45

To Dez's mind, level three of the Fuchstown mine looks exactly like level two, down to the metal bracings for the carved-out floor, walls, and ceilings of the mined area; the string of work lights up high; the narrow-gauge track; the electric car that rides the track and hauls rocks and precious finds away from the workers. It's no colder than the other levels, and again he's surprised by how clean everything is. This pilot project, for a new kind of mining, seems to be innovative and smart.

Squirrel leads the way, followed by Dez and Trisha Jean, then Moose.

Dez remembers from his briefing that the man-made parts of the underground facility are largest on levels one and five: the commons area and habitat ring on the highest level, and the neutrino site down below. On two, three, and four, the center parts are smaller and are mostly used to store mining equipment and rows of lockers for the workers. This level has a much smaller break room that they walk past; three tables, fifteen chairs total. The only vending machine here dispenses nothing but water, and it's free. Dez imagines that dehydration is a constant concern for those working underground.

They pass one more Russian. This one cradles a Heckler & Koch MP7, a stocky little submachine gun that has a maximum effective range of less than 200 meters; round it to 650 feet or so. Out in the open, in the snowbanks and widely separated prefab buildings of Fuchstown, the bullpup gun wouldn't be anyone's first choice. Down here in the tight confines of the mine, its thirty-three-millimeter rounds could turn the entire survival party on level one into confetti in two heartbeats.

Squirrel speaks to this guy in Russian, then the man walks back the way Dez and Trisha Jean just came. Likely to guard the entrance.

They are heading toward the stairs to level four. When they get there, Trisha Jean uses the handrail and eases herself down, her left knee stiff from crawling even a few short feet through the barricade.

"You all right, love?"

"I'm fine."

Squirrel turns briefly and glances at her. The man has an easy smile, although it's only a few degrees separated from a sneer. "My mother was diplomat."

"Was she good at it?"

"She was corrupt as hell."

Trisha Jean says, "Some parts of the world, that's the only way to stay in the game and make changes."

Squirrel stops walking, studies her. He purses his lips and shrugs. "Is true. But I did not know Americans knew this."

"Old dogs, new tricks."

Squirrel starts walking again. "Is good."

The manufactured portions of level four look like level three, which look like level two. Functional and bland. The same sand-colored paint on the walls, the same cement floors. Dez spots a fourth Russian, who also carries an H&K bullpup.

The favorite submachine gun of the Russian FSB, if he remembers correctly.

So much for being representatives of Syever Mineralnaya, the Russian contractor extracting cerium from the mined cerite.

When Dez was doing the math to calculate how much carbon dioxide would be too much, Petra told him as many as ten Russians were down here. He's starting to think it's nowhere near that many.

They come to the next set of stairs. Beyond this, they'll see something new. At least, if the schematics hold true.

They do.

These stairs are much longer than between the other levels. They lead down thirty feet to a well-lit, concrete room; concrete on the floors, three of the walls, the ceiling. The room is narrow, maybe forty feet wide but only about fifteen feet deep.

The one wall not made of concrete is made of steel. It's the wall they're facing. It reminds Dez of the elevator entrance inside the igloo up top: flat and unadorned metal, with a sliding door in the middle. This door, however, has a viewing pane to see through to the other side.

To the state-of-the-art neutrino detector facility.

Dez spots a control panel built into the wall, just to the left of the door. It's hinged at the bottom, designed to swivel outward, much like an old-fashioned mail slot, or the rubbish chute of an apartment building. It's deployed now, revealing a keyboard and other controls.

"You've spoken to them?" Trisha Jean asks.

Squirrel nods. "We have."

"Are you in regular contact with them?"

"No. We ask them to come out. They politely decline. We don't talk much since then."

Dez smiles at the wiry guy. "Politely decline?"

"These are scientists, yes? Advanced degrees. Physicists. They do not say, 'Nikolai, go fuck yourself.' But is more or less their message."

Dez laughs. So Squirrel's given name is Nikolai. He tucks that bit away.

Trisha Jean says, "Can you talk to them, Dez?"

"Can try."

He studies the panel. It seems simple enough. It includes controls for an audio system.

"All the money in the world, an' what do they install? A bloody doorbell."

He depresses a button. They hear a muted buzz from behind the sliding metal door.

They wait.

Dez smiles up at Moose. "Good fences make good neighbors, yeah?"

Moose glowers down at him.

They wait.

Dez presses the control again. They hear the buzz again. He presses it three times quickly. Three times slowly. Three times quickly.

Trisha Jean says, "SOS. Smart."

He waits and tries the combination again.

A shadow flits past a surface on the far side of the view port. Dez can tell by the degree of distortion at the edge of the glass that it is many inches thick. It might not even be glass; might be a much tougher form of Plexiglas.

Someone steps up to the window from the far side.

It's a woman. She's likely ten years younger than Trisha Jean and ten years older than Dez. She has gray hair, worn short and a bit tousled. She has glasses hanging from a lanyard around her neck. She appears to be Middle Eastern. Dez realizes he'd been expecting white lab coats, because he's seen way too many science fiction films, and those scientists all wear white lab coats. She's wearing a hoodie with the letters CERN stenciled across her chest.

Her eyes go wide at the sight of them.

Dez plays with the controls. "Trip Jacks: You're up."

Trisha Jean steps up to the window, smiling. She shows the woman her State Department ID. "Dr. Sophia Araki?"

Trisha Jean has memorized the files on the science staff.

They hear the woman's electronically distorted voice through a tiny speaker in the control panel. "You're American!"

"I am, ma'am. Deputy Assistant Secretary Trisha Jean Jackson, U.S. State Department. This man is Desmond Limerick, a civilian adviser."

"Ma'am," Dez says.

The woman's eyes dart from Trisha Jean to the smallish Russian standing behind her and to her right. She ignores Dez.

"Dr. Araki, the Russians are asking for us to clear the way for them to leave this facility. I told them I couldn't do that unless they let me talk to you, to find out if you and Professor Sato, and your staff, are all right."

"We're fine," the woman says. "We're not opening these doors until the Russians leave."

"Have they been inside the neutrino facility?"

The physicist shakes her head.

"Have they threatened you?"

Squirrel says, "I am civilized man. I threaten no one."

Trisha Jean smiles sweetly over her shoulder. "You fired two rounds in the general direction of my head the first time we spoke."

"Is not threatening. Is emphatic."

Dez laughs. "Hard t'argue with that."

Trisha Jean turns back to the viewing window. "Doctor, why did you shut down all communications with MIT and CERN?"

Dr. Araki's eyes dart. She does not reply.

"Are you being coerced, Doctor?"

"No."

"May I speak with Professor Sato?"

She says, simply, "No."

"Is he all right?"

She says, "We want the Russians to leave. If you can make that happen, I can open this door. But not before."

Trisha Jean glances in Dez's direction. He gives her the faintest of shrugs.

Can he open the door from out here? Maybe. But neither of them sees much to be had in explaining his gatekeeper training to the Russians, so they stay mum on that point.

Trisha Jean turns to Squirrel. "You told me you wish to leave the facility. You want us to unlock the elevator and clear a path for you."

"Yes."

"And this sudden change of heart . . . ?"

"Canadian military."

Which had been her assumption anyway. His apparently true answer is what she'd hoped to hear.

Trisha Jean angles herself so she can address Dr. Araki through the glass and Squirrel on this side. "Things are more complicated than y'all realize. On the surface, my party was attacked by a paramilitary organization. Mercenaries, we think. We fled into the mine and shut down the elevator behind us."

Araki shakes her head. "Wait. There's another hostile force?"

Squirrel says, "Implying we are hostile force. You are very judgmental woman, Doctor."

Trisha Jean says, "Be that as it may. Yes, Dr. Araki, there's a hostile force topside that has nothing to do with the Russians. There's also a blizzard, which is keeping our reinforcements at bay. For now.

I think our Russian friends may be correct in saying they should git while the gittin's good."

Dr. Araki and Squirrel say more or less together, "I don't know what that means."

"Sorry. Something my mama used to say. I think our Russian friends may be correct in saying they should get off Canadian soil before the Canadian military arrives. The Russians want to leave. Dr. Araki, you say you want them to leave. I'm State Department, not Defense Department, so my mission does not require me to make them stay or make them go. I'm agnostic on that issue."

She turns. "Dez?"

Dez says, "Nikolai. We've no idea how big the oppo is up there. We do know they're backed by very rich people. The Skyhook Technologies group. Ye've heard of 'em?"

Squirrel says something in Russian to Moose, who shrugs. Squirrel says, "We have not."

"They've got unlimited financing and excellent training. When they came at us, they brought a bloody gunship with a fifty-cal."

Squirrel's eyes go big.

"Aye," Dez says. "They're for real. T'get gone before the Canuck military gets here, ye'll have t'go through them fuckers first. Sorry, ladies."

Squirrel consults his hulking friend in Russian.

Squirrel turns to Trisha Jean. "Is possible I mislead when I say we are mineral consulting firm only. Admitting nothing, I do acknowledge that my colleagues and I have some small understanding of weapons and combat. We need to get out of Canada. We will take our chances with this Skyhook cadre."

"All right. I need to make sure the Fuchstown crowd is okay with this. They still believe you killed some of their residents topside."

"Why would we? How would this benefit us?"

"Okay. I'll talk to them." She turns to the view port. "Dr. Araki? I really would like to speak to Professor Sato, to confirm he's all right."

The physicist shakes her head. "No."

"Then you're withholding information from me, which complicates my ability to meet everyone's goals. Y'all understand that."

Araki says nothing.

"All right. I'm going to go talk to the town residents next. And their mayor. If they're all right with this plan, we'll begin helping the Russians to get out of the mine. Hopefully quickly. I'll report back to you when that's done."

"How could I believe you?" Araki asks. "How will I know you're not being forced to say whatever they want?"

"Because I'm a goddamned awful liar, ma'am. If I'm lying, everyone always knows it. I wouldn't know how to bluff you if I tried."

Dez bites his tongue.

A few beats, then Araki nods. "All right. Come back without them, tell me they're gone. And I'll open this door."

"Thank you, Doctor. My friend and I will return as quickly as we can."

Dr. Araki shuts off the comms from inside the chamber and disappears back into the dark.

Squirrel says, "Satisfied?"

"Well, I'd like to have seen the MIT professor. I asked twice."

"So she is not one hundred percent honest with you." He shrugs. "I have little use for scientists. Most can tell you speed of light but not to cross street without looking for traffic."

Trisha Jean laughs. "Honestly, that's how I feel about most of 'em, too. I have an engineering degree. At least engineering's practical."

Squirrel looks at her anew. "Structural?"

"Civil."

He smiles. "Mine is electrical engineering. Small world."

She says, "Yes, it is."

Squirrel makes an *after you* gesture, and they head for the stairs that lead up to level four.

# CHAPTER 46

Again, they pass one armed Russian on level four, and one guarding the egress to the upper levels. Dez thinks that may be the lot of them. Others could be hiding but why not make a show of strength?

They get to the stairs leading up to the platform welded to this side of the barricade. Trisha Jean says, “Well, so much for my knees.”

Squirrel says, “I will gather my men. You talk to the villagers, yes? Then we leave.”

“That is the plan. But it depends on the residents agreeing. I’ll get back to you as quickly as I can.”

They mount the stairs, then the lattice-iron scaffolding, and Dez lets Trisha Jean crawl through first. He calls out, and Rusty Townsend appears on the other side to help her through.

Dez turns back to look down on their hosts at the bottom of the stairs. “Would be a pleasant surprise if this thing ends peacefully.”

“We are soldiers, you and me,” Squirrel says. “We can make

sure everything underground is peaceful. But on surface. That will be firefight."

"It will."

"I would ask if you want to join. Another gun on our side, this would not be so bad a thing."

"I've a few cross words I'd love t'share with the Skyhook mob, but I'm here for Trisha Jean and me friend. Their needs come first."

Squirrel nods.

Dez kneels and crawls through.

Trisha Jean is on the ground talking quietly to Rusty, Petra, and the mayor. And rubbing her left knee. Dez joins them.

Petra says, "The assassin. Ash. She showed up, got past us, and went through. She's on that side. With a handgun."

Dez scratches the back of his head. "Confirmin' that her target's either the Russians, or the scientists. As we figured. If she was after any of us, she'd've made her move in St. John's."

Trisha Jean lays out the situation to the mayor. His scowl grows deeper; his theatrical sighs, as well.

"I say those men might've killed my townspeople."

"Or the Skyhook mercenaries might have. And from our perspective, that's the more likely scenario."

He ponders it a bit, deeply unhappy. "Let's take it upstairs. See what the residents think."

"Thank you, sir."

They head toward the stairs. They pass the townie guard they'd seen before, but now he's regaining consciousness and his rifle trigger has been bent out of shape. Ash's work. One fewer guns down here may not be a bad thing, Dez ponders.

The guy's coming to, sitting up, rubbing his skull. Dez pauses. "You all right?"

"Go fuck yourself."

"Splendid. Ta."

Mayor Brandywine says, "Sorry."

They get to the much larger level one and find most everyone in the break room, which has become something of a de facto city hall. Dr. Dyson Patterson is there as well. No one appears to be in a swell mood.

Brandywine lays out the scenario for everyone.

One of the townies stands with his arms crossed, a belligerent frown locked in place. "We been talking about it, Burt. These goddamn Russians are never gonna see the inside of a Canadian jail, and everyone here gets that. It rubs us wrong. But if getting them outta the mine gets them outta Fuchstown, we're okay with that."

The mayor says, "Thank you."

The guy points a pugnacious finger at Dez. "But he goes with them."

"Now, look—"

The guy holds up a palm. "I'm sorry, Burt, but you're outvoted on this one. You're mayor, not some lord of the manor. We don't trust him. If the Russians go, he goes with them."

Trisha Jean says, "There's an armed gang up there."

"So you say."

Petra cuts in. "Dez fixed your air filter. We'd all be suffocating if—"

"He says he fixed it. How do we know Joel didn't figure it out, before this guy damn near killed him?"

Trisha Jean turns to the physician. "Dyson?"

He shrugs. "Look, I'm just trying to keep my patients alive. I never met Limerick before we got to St. John's. I don't have a dog in this fight."

She studies the doctor a moment, calculating.

Dez says, "It's fine. The Russians'll be outmanned up there. I know a thing or two about firefights. I'll help."

Petra says, "Dez . . ."

"I'm with her." Rusty Townsend steps up next to Dez, facing the crowd.

Trisha Jean touches Dez's shoulder. "Look, there has to be—"

"If ye pull off this bit of diplomatic prestidigitation, love, ye'll not need me. You'll open sesame this thing all by your lonesome. Up top, I could be of some use. And I wouldn't mind boxing the ears of them Skyhook twats, if ye'll excuse me English."

The mayor glowers at his people, his jowls shaking. "I don't like this."

The leader of the mob says, "Yeah, well, we recommend you don't run for reelection, Burt. There's a lotta shit we don't like going on."

"It's settled," Dez says, as much for Petra, Trisha Jean, and the mayor as for the townsfolk. "Let's get the Russians outta here."

# CHAPTER 47

Dez returns to the barricade and asks to be let through. The platforms are still there on either end. This time he brings a lidless bin of thick, white, corrugated plastic with handles, the kind the U.S. Postal Service uses.

"Here's the plan. Ye'll put your weapons in this. I'll carry 'em. We get to the elevator, an' you lot get in. Huddle to the right. We'll put the box down on the left, close the doors, and send ye up. You'll be armed for the Skyhook arseholes but not in front of the townies."

Squirrel speaks to Moose in Russian, then to Dez. "Is acceptable."

"One more thing. I'm takin' ye up on your offer. Ye'll be well outnumbered, from what I can tell. I'm a dab hand with a gun or explosives. Saw barrels of petrol up there. Gave me an idea or three."

Squirrel studies him a moment. He says, "This is surprise."

"I might be more useful up top than down here, once you lads are gone. And I owe them fuckwits right and proper."

Squirrel grins. "I can trust a man who acts out of vengeance. It is one of most predictable of emotions."

He offers his hand, and they shake.

"One more wee complication. There's a female assassin who snuck her way into the mine. About yea high, ice-blond, Eurasian. Goes by Ash. Ring any bells?"

"Female assassin?" Squirrel consults his hulking associate. Who shrugs. "No."

"Okay. Thought I'd check. How many men've ye got?"

"Just the four of us."

"Guns in the bin, gentlemen. Let's fore to go. Oh, an' bring your winter gear. Skyhook's not the only complication topside."

Dez crawls through first with the heavy plastic bin, filled with the Russians' MP-443 Grach sidearms and their HK MP7 machine guns.

Squirrel is next, carrying a winter-camouflaged snow parka. Then the two Russians Dez spotted on guard duty. The massive guy, Moose, is last. It's a tight fit for him.

"Right, then. Skyhook won't see us coming. This could be good for a laugh."

Squirrel says, "I am liking your style."

Dez leads as they take the stairs up to three, then two, then the habitat level. Mayor Brandywine awaits them there, as does Trisha Jean and her bodyguard.

The mayor looks glum. When they reach that level, Squirrel stops. "You are leader in town?"

"I am."

"We did not kill your people. You have my word."

Burt Brandywine hesitates, then nods.

They get to the elevator debarkation room. Three townies are there with two shotguns and a rifle. Petra is there with Dez's winter gear. Trisha Jean and Rusty stand off to one side.

Dez gets the heavy metal grates in front of the door to retract into the ceiling and floor, then opens the elevator's twin doors. He puts the bin of guns in the open elevator on the far left. Then he reaches for his borrowed winter gear.

"Dez," Petra says. The look in her eyes is sorrowful.

"Pfff. It'll be a lark. I'll be seeing ye shortly."

Her look says she's not buying it. They hug, and it lasts.

Rusty Townsend holds his Secret Service firearm out toward Dez. "It won't be a lark. You'll be outnumbered."

"An' ye've an assassin runnin' about and playing merry hob. Keep it."

Dez winks at Squirrel. "'Sides. They won't see us coming, will they?"

In the infirmary, Dyson Patterson checks on his drugged patients and makes sure the door is closed. Then he draws the sat phone from where he hid it behind a cabinet. This phone has been hardwired to a secret comms line between the mine and the surface, which Patterson's allies rigged earlier, allowing it to work underground.

"Finn. The Russians and Limerick are on their way up. There are only four Russians. I spotted HK MP7s and sidearms. They know they're outnumbered but they figure they have the element of surprise."

Over the line, he hears Aiyden Finn's rage-heavy voice. "Roger that. We got a surprise for them, all right."

"Good. Out."

Patterson disconnects and turns.

Inspector Frank Watts of the Royal Canadian Mounted Police is on his feet, holding on to his gurney with his unbroken arm, groggy but awake. "What the hell did you just do?"

Patterson said, "Cleaned up loose ends."

He moves quickly, spinning Watts around, grabbing him by the shoulders and his chin, and jerking. Watts's spine snaps. The dead cop falls straight to the floor.

In the elevator debarkation chamber, Dez says his goodbyes to everyone. Moose and Squirrel stand passively, holding their camo'd winter gear, which they've yet to don.

Dez turns to them. "Shall we?"

And one more Russian, a fifth man Dez hadn't seen before, enters the room and puts an arm around Trisha Jean's throat, the barrel of a Grach against her temple.

Moose and Squirrel draw two hidden guns from their parkas. They focus up on the townies with their long guns.

"Weapons down now!" Squirrel shouts. "Now!"

The townies, caught off guard, lay their weapons on the ground.

Rusty surges toward the man holding a gun to Trisha Jean's head. The Russian behind her sneers, tightens his arm around her neck.

Rusty stops short, grim determination on his face.

The Russian adjusts his stance and kicks Rusty in the gut. The agent folds in two, landing hard.

"Little dog," Squirrel sneers. "Big bark."

Moose gathers the machine guns from the white bin and distributes them to his fellow soldiers. Another Russian takes the townies' guns and pats them down.

Dez says, "Fecking hell. Ye got what ye wanted!"

Squirrel turns to him and places the barrel of his own weapon against Dez's chest. "What I fucking want is what those fucking scientists have! That is why my superiors sent me to this godforsaken afterthought of a country! My orders are clear: I go home with it or I do not go home. The fucking scientists, they would not open door for me, but when they watch me execute one civilian every fifteen minutes outside of big, fancy door, I think maybe they change their mind!"

Dez takes a step forward. Since there's a barrel against his chest, and since Squirrel's arm is extended, that step forward means a step backward for Squirrel.

Whose trigger finger knuckle grows white.

Dez keeps his voice soft. "Ye've erred in your thinking, mate. A whacking great mistake. Ye don't even know it yet."

Squirrel narrows his eyes. "You are big, tough man, yes? You have very much bravery. I think maybe you help with . . . how do you say in English? An 'object lesson'?"

Dez flashes him the V symbol with the first and ring fingers of his right hand. "I'm a peaceable sort, me."

Squirrel growls something to Moose, then backs away from Dez.

Moose hands the leader his pistol and his machine gun, setting his parka on the floor. The man is six-six, made up entirely—from Dez's point of view—of barely contained violence and Carrara marble. He makes fists that are considerably larger than a normal human's.

"Mister Leader Man," Squirrel addresses the mayor. "I want to demonstrate why your people should be on best behavior, yes? My associate will now beat this man to death. I think it important your people watch and learn."

Moose approaches Dez, smiling down at him.

Dez shows him the peace symbol again. "Told ye. I opt for peace."

Moose's grin grows.

Dez says, "Nikolai? How do you say 'three fools' in Russian?"

The leader blinks. "Is *tri duraka*. Why?"

Dez's hand flashes, and he pokes Moose in both eyes with his extended fingers.

"Boink."

Moose screams and falls straight down to the floor. Those fists of his are now larger-than-life hands, covering the upper half of his face.

Dez uses his snow pants to wipe aqueous humor off his fingers, up to his first knuckles.

Moose writhes on the floor and bellows.

Nobody moves.

Rusty climbs to his feet, holding his gut. "'Three fools.' Because you didn't know if there was a Russian word for 'stooges.'"

Dez winks at him.

Moose howls in agony. One of his men kneels and tries to pry his hands away from his eyes but Moose is too strong. Lying on his back, he stomps the heels of his size-fifteen boots on the cement floor.

Squirrel steps up and pistol-whips Dez.

Dez sees it coming and rolls with it. The butt of the gun grazes his forehead, and he falls backward, but the blow isn't bad.

"I fucking kill you!"

Dez is on his hip and one elbow, hand to the forehead. "Believe I already told ye, mate. You made a whacking great error. Ye told me ye planned t'kill me. Since I know I'm dying soon, it gives me carte blanche to do as I please, yeah?"

Squirrel is shaking with rage. If his finger wasn't indexed, he'd have accidentally discharged his weapon by now. He fights to gain a little emotional control, as his giant friend continues to writhe and howl on the floor.

He points his gun at Trisha Jean but keeps his eyes on Dez. "What you have done is assured that this fucking cow is the first in line to be executed in front of the level five door! She dies first, then everyone in your party. *Then* the villagers, yes? Had it gone in other order, scientists would have opened door before long, and your people would be spared."

He turns to Trisha Jean. "This man signs your death warrant. Be sure to thank him."

# CHAPTER 48

The Russians escort Petra, the State Department team, and the eighteen townies down to level four. They seem not to know about Dyson Patterson in the infirmary, for which Dez is grateful. The physician seems a nice enough fellow, and someone ought to survive this.

Just before they leave the habitat level, Squirrel speaks to his men in Russian. They cover the hostages with their machine guns. Squirrel returns to the elevator site, where his friend lies, blinded. A few minutes pass, then they hear a single shot.

Squirrel returns. Hate seems to ripple out of his eyes like heat off a tarmac. It's clear he has put his friend out of his misery.

Dez is racking his brain, looking for an out. Nothing comes to mind. He's livid with himself he didn't do a more thorough search of levels three and four, in order to uncover the hidden Russian. But then again, he thinks, the mines are fairly vast. The man might have hidden out there indefinitely.

Squirrel waves his gun. "Move."

The two parties walk single file down to the second level, through it, then down to three and then four. The townie whom Ash had coldcocked, en passant, now lies dead, gutted with a knife. A few residents gasp or cry when they spot him.

Dez turns lazy eyes toward Squirrel, who gives him a vicious smile.

When they get to the barrier, two of the Russians go over the top first, while Squirrel and one other guard the hostages. Then the civilians are ordered over the top.

It's crowded down on the final level, before the great door to the Fuchs Underground Neutrino Collector. Four Russians, four from the State Department, and eighteen townies; twenty-six in total. The hostages are ordered to the far side of the narrow, forty-foot-wide staging area.

One of the Russians approaches menacingly toward Trisha Jean. Rusty steps in front of her, physically pushing her back.

Squirrel saunters his way. "I have question for you."

He knees Rusty in the balls. Rusty keels over, turtled in on himself.

"How did a little man like you get to be anyone's protector?"

Trisha Jean looks ready to drill the man a new alimentary canal.

"Is time for demonstration."

Dez says, "Your way's fine. Slow, but it'll work. Eventually."

Squirrel turns to him.

"Whereas I could open the door for ye."

Squirrel's eyes narrow. He hesitates.

"Is bullshit."

Dez shows him the tattoo of Janus on his arm. "Opening doors is what I do, mate. Beginnings and gates, transitions and times, dualities and doors, passages and endings. I'm clearly not State Department. I'd be a fecking lousy diplomat." He turns to Trisha Jean and the women from Fuchstown. "Sorry."

Then back to Squirrel. "The only reason these folks brung me along is to open the elevator. Which I done. And to open this door. Which I could. That's me one talent in this here universe. Well, that, an' I recently learned to chiffonade herbs."

Squirrel is clearly thinking. Dez believes the man would have no compunction against killing everyone down here. Hell, he just killed his lieutenant because moving with a blinded giant was going to add a degree of difficulty to his mission.

But the snowstorm is going to abate at some point. And Canadian law enforcement and military will show up. Squirrel has no way of knowing when.

If he has to choose between a slower, homicidal way and a quicker way, he might opt for the latter.

"Then do it."

"I've a tablet computer up in one of the rooms. Go get it for me. I can break the algorithm for the door inside of five minutes."

"No. Is trick."

"No. Is not. Look, you thick twat. Get me the tablet computer and I'll get you and yours away from here fast as a bunny. Yeah? Don't, and go through with page one-oh-three of the *Evil Henchmen Playbook*, killing hostages every fifteen minutes. That route will take you, if you're lucky, thirty minutes. Maybe as much as an hour and a half. My way takes five minutes."

Squirrel is thinking.

"Hell, change the deadline. Kill a hostage every ten minutes. That'll still take you well over an hour."

"Thank you for putting that suggestion in his head," Rusty says, rising, his face beet red, one hand still cradling his testicles.

Squirrel's brain is whirling. His eyes dance from Dez's, to his men, to his hostages.

"If you fail, I will rip off your balls and feed them to you before I kill you."

Dez grins. "That sounds fair. Deal."

He tells Squirrel he's bunking in one of the miners' rooms but doesn't remember which. "It'll be the one with a big oul' tablet on the bed, yeah?"

Squirrel sends one of his men to get it.

Now the odds are twenty-two to three. Although the three have machine guns and, in a confined space, they could shred the hostages with one squeeze of their triggers.

Behind the Russians, Dez spots the failed cerite mine. He remembers his briefing: They began mining down here but found no seams. So they leased this level to a combine representing the Massachusetts Institute of Technology, CERN, and Triton Expediters. That means this played-out mine shaft goes for some distance, but not too far, he suspects. It also isn't lined with overhead lights. If he could get the Russians disarmed, he might be able to get the hostages into the mine. Which would . . .

What?

Dez has no clear idea.

And he's running out of options.

# CHAPTER 49

One of the Russian soldiers trudges up to level one to find the Englishman's computer. He wants to get out of this hellhole as fast as possible, and he's had his doubts about the mission commander, Nikolai Zolotov. He speaks a little English; he heard one of the Canadians or Americans call him Squirrel and worked damn hard not to laugh out loud. Zolotov is not famous for his self-deprecating humor.

The soldier gets up to the top level. The Englishman told them he's bunking in one of the rooms. The soldier will just have to search them. He heads toward the habitat ring but stops as he hears voices.

They're speaking in English. Perhaps some of the villagers, or perhaps members of the U.S. State Department delegation, had avoided being rounded up?

The soldier unslings his MP7 and follows the sound of the voices. Surprisingly, it takes him back to the elevator debarkation room.

He spots the soles of the boots of his big colleague, who was blinded by the Englishman, then put out of his misery by Commander Zolotov.

He sees a Black man in khakis and a sweater. Speaking to several armed men in snow-camo suits. All of them are armed.

He ducks back. He counted as many as eight newcomers.

He races down to level two, hoping he's far enough from the newcomers to use his walkie-talkie.

Squirrel answers the hail and talks to his man for about thirty seconds. Dez doesn't know what's going on, because he doesn't understand the lingo. But clearly something went awry up top.

Squirrel considers the situation. He appears unsure of how to respond. Then he rattles off quick instructions via the walkie-talkie, while also nodding to his two men down here on five.

He turns to Dez and makes a *come here* gesture. "Limerick?"

"Aye?" Dez steps forward.

Behind him, one of the Russians rears back the butt of his machine gun and smacks it into his head.

Dez pitches forward, barely catching himself before he face-plants.

Squirrel had pistol-whipped him upstairs but Dez saw that one coming and was able to ride with the blow, minimizing the pain. This shot, though, rattles his brain thoroughly. Nausea rolls through him, his vision blurring.

Petra moves toward him, and Rusty grabs her shoulders, holding her back with a quick shake of his head.

Squirrel speaks to Trisha Jean and the mayor. "That takes care of the only wolf among the sheep. My two men will guard you. We have a situation upstairs. I will attend to it. Then we will worry about getting this fucking door unlocked. Behave, and you have a chance of surviving all this."

He throws the strap of his MP7 over one shoulder, dashes up

the tall flight of stairs, then onto the platform and over the barricade to four.

The two Russian soldiers train their guns on the townies and State Department team.

Dez is on his hands and knees, his vision warping, his forehead down to the cool cement floor. He'd like to avoid passing out or puking, neither of which will contribute materially to everyone's escape. He tries to rise, and his body disobeys. For now, at least, he's down for the count.

Squirrel gets to level two and his waiting man. "You're sure?" he whispers.

"The mercenaries from the surface. I think so. They wear snowsuits. There are maybe seven of them, maybe eight. With sidearms and machine guns. A few of them appear to be injured and bandaged."

"Come," Squirrel hisses. "We need to know what they're doing."

"I thought Dez and the Russians were coming up?" Aiyden Finn says, taking in the elevator debarkation room.

Dr. Dyson Patterson gives him that dopey, stoner's smile. "Russians suckered everyone. Took the townies and the Americans to level five."

"Jesus. I just wish you'd activated the damn elevator earlier. We wasted way too much time up there."

Patterson shrugs. "Couldn't while the townies were up here. Once the Russians took them, I got you in. Stop bitching."

Finn gives him a glare.

Patterson says, "I know where the find is stored. De Brienne showed me before Limerick cleaned his clock."

Aiyden Finn shakes his head. "De Brienne's a damn fine fighter. How the hell did that happen?"

"From what I understand about the shit in New York and St.

John's, and now here, I'd say Limerick's better." Patterson looks to the various visible wounds Finn's guys carry. One man, Bukowski, has his rifle strapped across his shoulders and is using two flat-edged shovels, improvised as crutches, to stay upright. Both of his legs are wrapped. Blood is seeping through the bandages. Others sport lesser bandages on their arms and legs.

Patterson leads the seven injured mercenaries—Dez's frag bomb did a number on almost all of them but Finn himself—to the same storage facility where his coconspirator, Joel de Brienne, had hidden their sat phone and weapons. One of Finn's men gets busy with a crowbar, removing the lid from a wooden crate with the words MACHINE PARTS stenciled on the side.

Two guys remove the lid. Finn and Dr. Patterson peer down at a cylindrical, uneven shape, more or less the size of a thermos, in both Bubble Wrap and a canvas blanket.

"It's heavier than it looks. Careful."

Two guys lift it out. The late Joel de Brienne had foreseen the weight problem and had stashed a standing dolly nearby. The guys set the find on the iron pad of the dolly.

"This is all Mr. and Mrs. Cray need. Get this topside and call for an evac," Patterson says.

Finn bristles, being ordered around by this guy he's never met face-to-face until this moment. He'd love to stay; to find Limerick and serve up a little payback. But he knows that's not the mission's priority. Besides, being a mercenary for an international corporation like Skyhook means plenty of downtime. Even if Limerick survives his encounter with the Russians, Finn and a couple of his most loyal guys can always hunt the runty Englishman down in the weeks or months to come.

"Let's roll," Finn says.

One guy pushes the iron dolly out and toward the elevator room.

That's when Patterson sees one of the Russians peek around the corner and quick-ducks back.

"Russians!"

He sprays the corridor with a short blast from his Sten gun.

Finn's men go for their own weapons.

Patterson doubts he hit anyone. And sure enough, the Russian's weapon appears around the corner for a quarter second, and the man fires blindly back at them.

Finn, Patterson, and their men dive for cover.

# CHAPTER 50

On level five, everyone hears the burp of machine guns, firing way up on a higher level. The sound is faint from down here but unmistakable.

Trisha Jean whispers to Rusty, "The Skyhook soldiers. They breached the mine."

One of the two Russians turns from watching the hostages and dashes for the stairs. He takes one knee, aiming upward to the top of the stairs.

Dez gets one boot planted. He's up on that foot and one knee, both hands on the floor. Dizziness whirls around him.

The other Russian steps past Rusty and aims his gun at Dez's broad back. Rusty grabs the man's MP7 and forces it down, aiming it at the floor. In the same instant, he slams his forehead into the Russian's face. The blow smashes the man's nose and cracks teeth.

The Russian releases his grip on the machine gun, and Rusty jabs the butt of it straight up into the man's gut, as hard as he can.

The Russian grunts and pitches forward. Rusty spins the gun and clubs the guy in the back of the head. Exactly as this same guy clubbed Dez, moments earlier. The man falls, barely conscious, and his arm becomes entangled in the gun's shoulder strap.

The Russian guarding the stairs hears the commotion and turns back toward the hostages.

Rusty tries to pry the gun strap free of the downed man.

Dez's legs are jelly. He rises, staggering, putting his bulk between the Russian's weapon and the hostages. He thinks, with a little bit of luck, he'll survive long enough to reach the guy and deck him. Or just pin him. Giving the others a chance to grab his weapons. If the twenty-one other hostages have two machine guns and two sidearms, well, then it'll be a more or less fair fight.

If giving them that is to be Dez's legacy, he'll be okay with that.

He takes his first step forward and spots Ash, emerging from the darkness of the failed mine.

The petite woman wears black workout togs, a black cap, and black, wrist-length gloves. She'd been invisible in the played-out mine.

She's on the Russian, literally climbing his torso, both hands on his shoulders, the sole of her sneaker on his chest. She moved at him laterally and her extra hundred pounds gets him off-kilter, spinning and falling.

The Russian lands on his back.

Ash lands on one foot and one knee. But that knee was positioned above the Russian's windpipe, which she crushes as she lands. Her weight also snaps the man's spine. Death is instantaneous.

She rises and side-kicks his machine gun. It spins across the room, coming to rest at Trisha Jean's feet.

Everyone stares at her. She watches them back, her face blank.

Dez drops to his knees. He sways, barely upright.

"Hallo, love," he mutters. "Jay-sus an' it's good to see you." Then falls over.

### ST. JOHN'S

Vincent Cray gets a sat-link call. His bunker-buster bomb, his backup mercenaries, and his wife are airborne and en route to Fuchstown. They'll be there in less than twenty minutes.

# CHAPTER 51

Rusty untangles the machine gun strap from the Russian he knocked out.

He looks around at the former hostages. "And for all of you who've asked: That's how a guy like me made the protection detail."

Trisha Jean and Petra both hug him. Trisha Jean also grabs the other Russian's machine gun up off the floor.

The townsfolk and State Department team are still huddled at one narrow end of the room. Dez is more or less in the middle; Ash and the soldier she killed at the other end, at the bottom of the stairs.

Everyone hears sporadic gunfire from the higher levels of the mine.

Dez uses his arms to leverage himself up to his knees. He manages to stand, but he's wobbly as hell.

Petra is at his side. "Easy. You could be concussed."

Dez rests an arm like a log around his lover's shoulders. "Been concussed. This is just a headache."

Petra holds up his hand. "How many fingers?"

"Thursday."

He actually makes her smile. Tears glitter in her eyes.

Dez looks around. "Everyone all right?"

Trisha Jean says, "Rusty kicked himself some Russian booty."

"Excellent. Ash?"

The petite woman stands motionless, emotionless.

"Appreciate what ye done. Not a hundred percent sure why ye done it, but I owe you me life."

Ash nods. Yes, he does.

"Firing your weapon would've alerted the other Russians, had 'em running back here," Dez tells her. "Taking him out the way ye did was smart."

Trisha Jean joins Dez and addresses Ash. "There's a whole lot more we *don't* know than we *do* know. But I think we know we can't let you into the neutrino sector. Not even after you saved us."

Ash does not react.

Dez groans, moves stiffly to the metal door and its console. "We get everyone through to the other side. Ash and me can play hit-and-run through the mines. Three-dimensional chess. Take the piss with the Russians and Skyhook alike. If Ash's willing."

She still stands apart. She's like a black hole. She emotes nothing.

Dez uses the door buzzer to send through an SOS again. As before, it works. A shadow flicks on a far wall behind the thick glass view port, and Dr. Sophia Araki appears.

She cranes her neck from side to side, seeing no Russians but spotting the townsfolk.

Mayor Brandywine says, "Dr. Araki?"

Obviously, they'd met in town.

"Mr. Mayor. Secretary . . . Jackson, I believe? The Russians are gone?"

"Not gone. Distracted," Trisha Jean says. "They're still in the mine. In a gun battle with those mercenaries I told you about. We want to get the residents of Fuchstown through to your side. Are you amenable to that?"

The physicist looks scared.

Rusty moves to the foot of the tall stairs, gun on the barricade above them. Trisha Jean hands the second MP7 to one of the women from Fuchstown, who nods and joins Rusty. She looks like she's handled guns most of her life.

Ash stands apart, hands laced behind her back.

Dr. Araki still looks frightened and unsure.

Trisha Jean keeps her voice soft. "We're not safe on this side."

"If the Russians haven't left, they'll never let us out."

"The Canadian military will get here once the storm passes. The U.S. State Department knows I'm down here, too, so I wouldn't be surprised to see a couple dozen Marines join 'em. Time is a luxury we can afford and the Russians can't. But only if you grant sanctuary to these civilians."

Petra adds, "Please."

A squawk of gunfire from above makes everyone flinch. It sounds closer than before.

Dez is studying the solid-state, titanium-steel surface of the high-tech door. If he had the tools to burn or blast through, he might be able to get to the wiring and possibly manipulate the controls. But he was bluffing about using his tablet to get them in. There are no ports on this side, USB or otherwise, and the frame around the keyboard appears to be a solid bit of steel with no fasteners to loosen.

If Trisha Jean can't appeal to the physicist's humanity, they could be screwed.

Then the crowd of townies parts, and Ash steps up between Dez and Trisha Jean.

And she does something Dez hasn't seen her do before.

She smiles softly.

Dr. Araki's eyes grow large. Tears form.

"You . . . you brought my daughter?"

Dez and Trisha Jean turn to each other.

"Hand t'god: *That*, I did not see comin'."

# CHAPTER 52

Dr. Sophia Araki taps several keys on her side. The pneumatic steel door hisses and begins recessing into the steel wall, then sliding sideways.

Gunfire erupts up on four and briefly limns the space over the barricade.

Rusty shouts, "Quick is good!"

Dr. Araki waves. "Come through! Come through!"

Trisha Jean and Petra act as doormen, getting everyone through in an orderly manner.

Dez joins Rusty and the armed townie at the base of the stairs. "Right, then. Smartly, if ye will."

The woman peels out first, heading for the door. Dez nods to Rusty, and they dash together to the sounds of the skirmish above.

The space on the nether side of the door is all metal: metal-grid flooring, metal walls, and aluminum ceiling tiles. As soon as Dez is through, Dr. Araki adjusts the controls, and the door hisses closed.

Dez studies the console on her side, making sure he'll know how to use it when the timing's right.

A young woman in a hoodie with FERMILAB stenciled across her chest steps around a corner. She's wearing a tool belt and a baseball cap backward, with a smear of grease across her forehead. She looks North African but sounds American and Midwestern. "We were monitoring from mechanical. C'mon. We don't have enough bunks for everyone, but we've got food."

She begins leading the townies farther into the Fuchs Underground Neutrino Collector. Dez gestures to Petra, who helps lead the townies toward food and rest.

Leaving Dez, Trisha Jean, and her bodyguard standing to the left of the now-secure door, and Dr. Sophia Araki and the woman she just called "my daughter" to the right.

And Dez can see the resemblance. It was faint, because Ash has some Asian genes in her and Sophia Araki does not, and because Ash's hair is dyed snow white. But it's there.

They don't hug.

"How . . . how are you?" Sophia finally asks. She sounds timid.

Ash dodges the question. "I'm here to get you out."

"But . . . how? Asha, my god. I haven't seen you since . . ." She lets the sentence wither and die.

Trisha Jean jumps into the void. "Doctor, our primary mission here is to see if you and your team are all right, and to find out what happened down here. I wasn't bluffing about the Canadians and the Marines. Help *is* on the way." She touches the woman's forearm gently. "I really need to know what's going on down here."

Dr. Araki is having difficulty dragging her eyes off her daughter. Finally, she does, inhales deep, turns to Trisha Jean.

"No."

"Sorry?"

"No. *I'm* the one who's sorry. But at this time, it is not my intention to explain to you or to anyone what happened down here. Get us out. Get me to Switzerland and the rest to the States and Italy and the UK. Get us home, and I'll tell you everything."

Trisha Jean is at the end of her rope. It's been an agonizingly long four days since she and her team boarded the C-130 in New Jersey. Dez can see how close she is to snapping. She forces a smile. "Well, bless your heart."

"I'm sorry. This is the way it has to be," the physicist says. "Come. You're probably dehydrated. We have plenty of water and coffee and juice. Plus, food. Plus, restrooms. I'm not sure where we'll put everyone but our staff is amazingly resilient. They'll figure something out."

She begins leading them away.

Dez pulls Trisha Jean aside and whispers, "A bit of advice?"

The diplomat nods.

"Whatever's scared her so much, maybe we let her play it her way? Getting everyone safe was mission one. Figuring out the mystery can wait."

A beat, then Trisha Jean hugs him. "God, we owe you so much. Thank you."

"Glad to help."

"How's your noggin?"

"If there are two of you, then I'm right as rain."

He doesn't tell her that he almost keeled over, stepping across the threshold to this side of the facility. The blow to his skull rang his bell but good.

They follow the physicist. Dez isn't one to make snap judgments about others' families, but the reunion of Sophia Araki and her daughter has been less than demonstrative.

Level five reminds Dez structurally of level one. Up there, the central facilities such as the break room and infirmary were in the middle, with the residences aligned in a doughnut around them.

The corridor that Sophia Araki has led them into also is curved. But this one is all metal.

Dez sidles up next to Ash. "Asha Araki?"

Ash says, "Ash," without looking his way.

"'Course."

Dez spots doors to rooms on his left but none on his right; rooms on the concave side from his perspective but not the convex side. That, he guesses, is because the area to his right is filled with water or some other liquid. It's the neutrino detector.

He turns to Rusty. "We're safe. But we might have to conjure a way to rescue Dr. Patterson. He's still up there."

Trisha Jean shakes her head. "Dez. Someone let the Skyhook soldiers into the mine. I've been asking around. Dyson was bad-mouthing you, keeping the townies riled up. Also, and not for nothing, but our one-and-only cop and two Canadian Coast Guard members were kept sidelined in the infirmary when they'd have been mighty helpful. I'm afraid the good doctor works for the Crays."

Now Dez is really worried about his cranium. He should have sussed that out himself.

# CHAPTER 53

The Russians are fighting the mercenary group, both sides pretty well armed. But Dr. Dyson Patterson no longer is all that concerned about who wins.

As the running firefight heads from level one to lower areas, Patterson grabs the standing dolly and the find, in its canvas and Bubble Wrap, and moves it to the embarkation room. He's also brought along one of those hinged, boxlike metal clipboards, with data about the find. He gets everything and himself into the industrial elevator and hits Up. He remembers Limerick telling everyone the elevator can only be controlled from down here, or via Limerick's tablet. The surface controls were sabotaged by De Brienne.

Once he heads up, there will be no way for Patterson to get back down.

Twin sets of elevator doors close side to side and up and down. The car begins ascending.

He gets to the surface igloo. He draws his sat phone and sends a text to the Crays.

He steps to the igloo's exterior door. A forklift blocks the entrance, thanks to that pain in the ass Limerick. The right side of the forklift is blackened by the frag explosive he'd rigged, which took out some of Finn's men and injured damn near all of them. Blood spatters the doorframe.

Patterson doesn't think any more opposition is lurking but he's not careless by nature. He steps outside, Sten gun raised, and checks to his left and right. Clear.

He hears the drone of an airplane engine. Not that far away.

He draws his sat phone and calls the only saved number. It connects to the Crays. He steps back in, out of the still-powerful snowstorm.

"Patterson?" It's Vincent Cray.

"Mr. Cray. I have the find. I'm on the surface and alone."

He expects to hear *well done* or *took your time* or *await further orders.*

What he hears is that Vincent has dropped his phone and is shouting from a distance. "Valerie! Valerie! Stop the plane! Stop the fucking plane!"

Patterson feels a chill run through his spine. What the hell?

"Mr. Cray? Vincent?"

Nothing.

He steps back outside.

The engine he heard earlier is definitely closer. It's flying above the cloud ceiling. Fixed wing, not a helicopter. And big, powerful engines. Maybe another Hercules? Could be.

It draws closer.

He shouts over the storm, "Vincent!"

Nothing.

He listens.

He thinks, maybe, the aircraft has just changed course. It's something in the bass rumbling, the acoustics of its mighty engines.

And if the storm isn't playing tricks on his ears, the plane has just passed overhead. He was hearing it from the west. Now it sounds like it's east of him and the Doppler curve tells him the plane is flying away from him.

He steps back inside.

"Mr. Cray?"

This time Vincent answers. "Here, Doctor. Everything okay there?"

"Ah. Yes, sir. I thought maybe that airplane was my lift home?"

"It is but you're not clear. Not yet. See if you can operate the town's snowplow. You have to get that runway cleared. That plane you hear? It's just refueled. They can circle over the storm until you give them the word. Then we'll get that bird on the ground and get you out of there. With the find."

Patterson inhales, expels it. He'll be glad to be out of this shit show. "Yes, sir. Hey, a question: Finn led a team to kill this guy Limerick in St. John's?"

"Yes. Limerick proved more . . . resilient than anticipated."

"Do you know why he's on this FBI/State Department team?"

He listens to the elongated pause. "No."

"Well, you lucked out. They sent this guy to open the doors to the mine. That's his thing, I guess. He opens doors. If Finn had killed him in St. John's, we'd all still be on the surface playing canasta."

A second passes, then Vincent Cray laughs. "Oh, you are kidding me."

"No, sir."

"Well, goddamn. I guess we are lucky. Okay, where's Finn?"

"In the mine. Confronting the Russians."

“Okay. When they’re done, let Finn know a new cadre of help is on its way. They’re traveling by helo. Should be there within an hour.”

“Will do, sir.”

# CHAPTER 54

Dr. Araki says, "Ms. Jackson, everyone? May I introduce Professor William Sato. Project director, theoretical physics. And Dr. Matteo Bernardi, University of Bologna, metallurgy and applied physics."

Dez isn't sure what he was expecting from a project director, but not this frumpy-looking Asian American guy with a bag of Cheetos in one hand and orange stains on his Homer Simpson T-shirt. Professor Sato wears cargo pants that are too big for him and bulbous yellow Crocs. His hair is long and unkempt, and he wears a messy mustache that currently has an orange hue to it.

Dr. Matteo Bernardi is tall and thin, hair swept back, wearing stylish glasses and an AC Milan jersey. "Good to meet you," he says, his English only slightly tinted with an Italian accent.

Dr. Sato, the Nobel laureate, smiles big. "Hi. Did you bring meat?"

Trisha Jean looks to Dez, who looks to Trisha Jean. She says, "Ah . . . meat?"

"Meat." He eats a handful of Cheetos and keeps talking as he chews. "Steak. Hamburger. Anything. At this point, I'd take a game hen. And I fucking hate game hen."

Sophia Araki smiles as if apologizing. "We voted to be a vegetarian facility, early on. Some of us adapted. And some didn't."

Dez says, "If you was expecting a rescue party or DoorDash, I regret t'tell you we're the former."

William Sato sighs. "Damn. Okay. Whatever. Can you get the radio working?"

From the briefing they all received before heading to Canada, the radio in the neutrino site is working. It's just been turned off.

The girl they spotted before, with the baseball cap and grease stain on her forehead, breezes into the community room where the State Department team has gathered. Before anyone else can speak, she says, "Sorry, Doc. If it was fixable, I woulda fixed it. No can do."

"Shit. Okay. Well . . . welcome. I guess."

The girl turns away and winks at Dr. Araki. Her bulky tool belt is well laden with hammers, screwdrivers, a massive tape measure, and thick, yellow leather gloves.

Dez glances around, realizes that Dr. Araki and her daughter, Ash, have positioned themselves with the State team between them.

Sophia Araki turns to her colleague. "Bill, the Russians are fighting that other force we were told about. We're not clear to leave yet."

"Then we should give them what they want and get the hell out of this shithole," says the renowned professor of physics from the Massachusetts Institute of Technology. He munches his snack and wipes orange dust off his fingers with his T-shirt.

Dez beams at the others. "I like him."

Trisha Jean advances on Professor Sato. "Sir? What do the Russians want?"

"Our data."

"On neutrinos?"

He nods.

Petra steps forward. "Petra Alexandris. Triton Expediters. Do you—"

Professor Matteo Bernardi's mouth drops open. "Good lord. You're our benefactor."

Petra gives her a brief smile. "One of them. Dr. Sato, do you know why the Russians want your neutrino research? Are they building a neutrino weapon?"

Sato laughs. He gestures around to the conference room table and its chairs, and to two mismatched couches. "Sit. Relax. Coffee's there."

Dez beelines to "there." He spots a foosball table, a couple of pinball machines, and—his heart skips a beat—an upright piano. Dez has been missing his guitar, which is in a wrecked helo topside. He always thinks best when he's playing music.

He also spots a bottle of aspirin and dry swallows a couple.

The girl with the mechanic's tool belt also has a walkie-talkie. It chirps, and they hear a voice say, *"Haddy? Can you come down here. Over."*

She whisks it up and heads for the door. "On my way."

Dez turns to the head scientist. "Why call this joint a neutrino collector? You're not. Collecting 'em, I mean."

Sato shrugs. "Well, we're collecting data *about* them. And besides, I thought the acronym FUNC was funny."

"Oh. Well, for the record: It is."

Sato addresses everyone. "What can any of you tell me about neutrinos? Our so-called ghost particles?"

Dez suspects the man likely was born in a lecture hall and emerged from his mother's womb holding chalk.

Rusty says, "Dez picks physics for two hundred."

Dez adds sugar and a creamer to his coffee cup. "Neutrinos are almost massless and nearly as plentiful as photons," he says over his shoulder, smiling so the others won't realize his head is killing him. From the look on her face, Petra's not fooled. "They've no charge, hence the name. Come from black holes, our sun, nuclear power plants, an' such."

"Very good," the professor says around a mouthful of his snack. "Why 'almost massless'?"

"'Cause they can change between, what, three different flavors?"

Trisha Jean says, "Flavors?" She's next to Dez, helping herself to a cup of tea.

Sato says, "Just an expression. And there's a theory about a fourth flavor, Mr. . . . ?"

"Dez to me mates."

"Dez, it is. Electron, muon, and tau, and maybe sterile." He addresses the others. "And as Mr. Muscles here says, only an object with mass can oscillate between flavors. A neutrino's really, really itty-bitty. Its mass is below zero-point-eight electron volts."

Rusty raises his hand. Sato points to him.

"You, yes."

"Who cares?"

Dez snorts a laugh. "Exactly. Or more to the point, why would the Russians care? Ye can't built a neutrino weapon. A trillion neutrinos are passin' through me right this very second. An' also through the steel in these walls, the rocks outside them walls, and the Earth. They touch nothing above the atomic level."

The Italian physicist, Dr. Bernardi, leans both forearms on the conference room table. "You have a good understanding of the basic physics. Neutrinos are wonderfully exotic and could help us understand the basic structure of the universe. Why is there mass in our universe and not just light? Why do we live in a matter universe, and not an antimatter universe? These are fundamental, building-block questions. But the Russians could learn that in a Physics 101 class at any university. What we're doing here is utterly fascinating, and utterly of no use to the Russian military. So why they want our research is a mystery."

He smiles blissfully. The Italian sounds enraptured by the particles.

Professor Sato wads up the Cheeto bag and throws it in a trash bin, the far side of the room, as if it were a free throw. "Swish. That's what we're working on, by the way. The CP violation."

Rusty turns to Dez. "Which means . . . ?"

"That bit's over me head."

Sophia Araki translates. "In this case, C means charge and P means parity. CP-symmetry tells us that the basic laws of physics should be the same if a particle is interchanged with its antiparticle—that's the C—while inverting its spatial coordinates—that's the P. And with neutrinos, it doesn't quite work out. It's one of the biggest question marks out there. Does the flavor change for neutrinos and antineutrinos happen at the same rate? If they oscillate differently, well, that could tell us why our universe consists of mass and light, and not just light."

Sato belches. "Anyway, if the Russians want it, I'd give it to them in a heartbeat. Who the hell cares? I just want to get out of here."

Trisha Jean says, "How will you solve these puzzles? If you don't mind my asking."

Sophia Araki points to the curved, concave wall behind her. "On the other side of this is fifty thousand tons of liquid argon and something like fifteen thousand light sensors. We can't see neutrinos, but our sensors can see the very faint, blue light they emit when a neutron collides with an atom of argon in what we call the Swimming Pool. The track of that blink of light tells us the direction the neutrino was traveling in. Where the subatomic particle came from is important. And also whether it's actually one of the flavors of neutrino, or an antineutrino. That's what we're looking for."

"It's great stuff," Sato says, popping open a diet Sprite. "So cool. But with all the comms down, this billion-dollar facility might as well be a Game Boy."

He scratches his considerable belly through his T-shirt.

Another walkie-talkie, sitting in the middle of the table, squawks. Sophia Araki reaches for it.

They hear the voice of the girl they met. *"Hey. Could someone ask the Englishman if he could come down to mechanical? I need some help. I think he's an engineer."*

Dez wonders how the girl, who appears to be all of twenty, could know that.

Sophia toggles the radio. "We'll be there in a second."

# CHAPTER 55

Sophia Araki leads Dez out of the conference room and into the curved hallway again. They approach a metal ladder that leads both upward and downward. "Think of this facility as Saturn," she says. "The Swimming Pool is the big, spherical planet, and all of the facilities for us humans are in the rings. We've got our own food supply, which is holding out just fine. We recycle our own water and air."

"Did ye notice the buildup of carbon dioxide yesterday?" Dez asks.

"No."

So this level has its own $CO_2$ filters.

She reaches for the ladder and Dez stops her. "Just so ye know? One of them Russians hit me in the melon with a gun. I've a bit of vertigo. Best let me go first, yeah? Don't wanna get dizzy an' land on you."

"One of my graduate students was an EMT in Afghanistan. Want him to look at your injury?"

"P'raps later."

Dez climbs down one floor. Sophia joins him.

"Your Professor Sato seems t'think the radios are broken, yeah? And I think you an' the lass we saw—"

"Haddy."

"Aye. The two of you are lettin' the man think that. But from what we were told, the radio's just off, is all."

Sophia again leads the way. "I'll explain when we're well clear of this facility and at home."

She leads him to a room with a wall plaque that reads MECHANICAL. Inside is a humid mess of pipes and wiring conduits, and three workstations. One wall, again, is convex. The girl with the backward cap and the Fermilab sweatshirt is there, as is a guy in his early twenties. They are messing with what looks to Dez like the mixing board of any recording studio he ever played guitar or piano in.

"Thanks, Doc," the girl says. "You're Dez? I'm Haddy."

Dez switches to Arabic. "At a guess, I'd say . . . Moroccan. And Haddy's short for Hadiya."

She grins. She stays in English. "Not bad."

"Which doesn't explain how ye know I'm an engineer."

Haddy says, "You told us."

She turns and begins adjusting knobs on the mixing board. "Wayno and I are the team's grease monkeys. I don't know anything about ghost particles, but I know how to keep all the tech running. We have fifteen thousand light sensors surrounding the Swimming Pool. I keep 'em running."

"Which ain't half-impressive, mate."

She grins over her shoulder at him. "With the doc's permission, I took several of the sensors offline and repurposed them. I've been scanning radio waves instead."

Dez says, "Radio w— Holy hell! Have you been monitoring comms this whole time?"

Haddy smiles at the physicist from CERN. "I told you he was quick." To Dez, she says, "Yes, sir. You guys, the Russians, the newcomer soldiers, the citizens of GoFuckYourselfVille."

Sophia says, "Haddy . . ." with a mild rebuke.

"I also tapped into the PA system in several of the level one rooms." She's still adjusting her monitor. "Let's pretend this is the opening credits for an episode of a TV series. Previously on this series: The Russians snuck into the mine. Then your mercenary types chased the townies down here. Someone sabotaged the elevator. You guys from the U.S. of A. arrived; you got the elevator running again. Your friend—who you call Trip Jacks and I'm guessing *that's* a good story—she negotiated with the Russians to leave. And the Russians backstabbed you."

Dez says, "Ten out of ten. I'm thinking you're about three different kinds o' brilliant."

Haddy grins again. "I got game. Hey, who's blondie-blonde. She's hot!"

Sophia says it again, "Haddy . . ."

"Sorry, sorry. Not PC. But *tssss*." She makes a sizzling sound. "Yow. Anyhoo, Wayno here picked up something we figured you should know."

Dez shakes the hand of the graduate student he assumes is Wayno.

"Okay, this is playback. From just a few minutes ago. Ready?"

She hits Play.

*"Patterson?"*

*"Mr. Cray. I have the find. I'm on the surface and alone."*

Just as Trip Jacks predicted: The betrayer amongst them is Dyson Patterson.

A beat, then (and more distanced):

*"Valerie! Valerie! Stop the plane! Stop the fucking plane!"*

A beat.

*"Mr. Cray? Vincent?"*

A longer beat.

*"Vincent!"* This time Patterson sounds like he's out in the storm.

Another delay. When Patterson speaks next, he's likely back in the igloo.

*"Mr. Cray?"*

*"Here, Doctor. Everything okay there?"*

*"Ah. Yes, sir. I thought maybe that airplane was my lift home?"*

*"It is but you're not clear. Not yet. See if you can operate the town's snowplow. You have to get that runway cleared. That plane you hear? It's just refueled. They can circle over the storm until you give them the word. Then we'll get that bird on the ground and get you out of there. With the find."*

*"Yes, sir. Hey, a question: Finn led a team to kill this guy Limerick in St. John's?"*

*"Yes. Limerick proved more . . . resilient than anticipated."*

*"Do you know why he's on this FBI/State Department team?"*

*"No."*

*"Well, you lucked out. They sent this guy to open the doors to the mine. That's his thing, I guess. He opens doors. If Finn had killed him in St. John's, we'd all still be on the surface playing canasta."*

*"Oh, you are kidding me."*

*"No, sir."*

*"Well, goddamn. I guess we are lucky. Okay, where's Finn?"*

*"In the mine. Confronting the Russians."*

*"Okay. When they're done, let Finn know a new cadre of help is on its way. They're traveling by helo. Should be there within an hour."*

*"Will do, sir."*

Haddy stops the playback.

Dez sighs.

Sophia says, "The find . . . ?"

"No idea. 'Twas hopin' you lot might know what it is."

All three of them shrug.

"Hell's teeth. S'pose someone needs t'figure out what the Crays are stealin', and why. Also, another set of mercenaries would not be good news for us."

"You and Secretary Jackson told me the Canadian military is on the way. Maybe the Marines, too."

"Aye, but when? We haven't been exactly overbrimming with luck of late, yeah? The gods an' goddesses help them what help themselves."

Haddy moves to an equipment locker and scrounges through plastic trays. She comes up with a headset wired to a belt clip. "I can rig my monitor to this. You'd be able to eavesdrop on everyone else's comms. And communicate with us, too."

Dez eyes Sophia Araki. "Once again reminding us that your comms aren't broke, love."

She raises a palm to him. "Which I will explain. When we're safe and away from here. I told you."

"That ye did." He turns to the girl. "What're you? Twenty?"

"Next February."

"Jay-sus. You're twice as smart as I'll ever be. Wouldn't mind being your intern for a couple of weeks. Ye'd teach me a trick or two."

Haddy almost levitates, soaking in the accolades.

Sophia says, "Are you seriously thinking of risking your life to stop the theft of whatever? You could wait it out here."

"The Crays are mad, bad, an' dangerous to know. Superrich and sociopathic. They've been willin' to spill plenty of blood for whatever 'the find' is. Don't think the world's a better place with them having this MacGuffin."

"So, even though you have a head injury, you want to wade back into danger to stop . . . something." Sophia smiles quite kindly. "You're a good man but possibly also just a bit crazy."

"Then you'll hate this next bit even more. I'm bringing your daughter."

The smile disappears. "No."

"Might not be your call, ma'am. An' of everyone in our party, she's by far the most qualified for this. I include meself in that list."

Dez takes the headset from Haddy. "Ta, love. You're feckin' brilliant, you."

He leaves.

Sophia Araki says, "Oh, god . . ."

Haddy grins. The grin slowly fades. She whips around to Sophia, throwing her palms over her mouth. "The hottie's your daughter?"

Wayno puts an arm over Haddy's shoulder. "Dude. You are so dead."

# CHAPTER 56

Dez climbs back up to the main level that encircles the massive globe of liquid argon. His head is still ringing a bit but that's subsided. He backtracks to the conference room.

Everyone stands or sits, some talking, some just resting. Petra is at the big table. Dr. Matteo Bernardi stands over her chair, showing her something on a laptop. Dez smiles, realizing the Italian is hitting on her. Well, that happens to Petra.

She spots Dez and says, "Come look at this."

Dez moves that way. The laptop is showing a display of light blue flashes. The flashes are moving like a bunch of iridescent hands on an analog clock.

Dr. Bernardi says, "We can isolate solar neutrinos from cosmic ones, or from those generated at nuclear power plants. One of the big problems in physics is the 'missing' solar neutrinos. We don't get as many from our sun as the physics predicts."

"Aye. What's this, then?"

Petra looks up at him. "It's amazing. See how the paths of these subatomic flashes are moving? Like . . . I don't know. Fans at a tennis match, their heads turning in unison."

Dr. Bernardi smiles at her. "That's good."

Petra gestures to the screen. "Matteo tells me their sensors are showing the motions of the sun in the sky. Even though we're way underground. I'd never seen anything like this."

And indeed, like heliotropes, the light blue paths are definitely tracking something moving off-screen; the path of the sun.

"That's bloody fantastic," Dez says. "This is the research Triton's paid for. Best enjoy it."

Petra says, "Oh, I am."

Dez stands straight and addresses Trisha Jean. "Might I have a word with ye? Ash, too."

Dez, Ash, Trisha Jean, and her bodyguard gather at one end of the conference room. Dez begins by addressing the woman in all black. "You're an assassin. A pro. Knowin' that, I made the assumption then that ye'd come here t'kill someone. You know what they say about them what assume. I'm as thick as molasses, me, an' I apologize."

Ash nods. She remains otherwise unreadable.

"Trip: There's more bad news. That brainy kid from Fermilab? She's been monitorin' everyone's comms this whole time. She knows the score; she an' Sophia both. An' she's discovered that Dyson Patterson's outside, in the igloo, with whatever 'the find' is. The thing the Crays have been seeking. A plane'll be landing once Patterson clears the runway, to take it an' him. Plus, another cluster of mercenaries are inbound. Here in sixty minutes or so."

She says, "Oh my God."

"Ash? If you're game, I think the two of us should head out there. Stop the plane from taking whatever the find is. An' see if we can't dissuade the incoming mercs from playing silly buggers with us. Are ye game?"

Ash says, "Yes." She hardly blinks.

Trisha Jean taps her own forehead. "You got clobbered, Dez. Are you up for this?"

"I'd say them aspirin an' that coffee cleared most of the cobwebs. Feeling better." And he is.

Trisha Jean lowers her voice. "This neutrino facility. The Russians can't want their research. Can they?"

"I don't see how. It's fascinating stuff, aye, but useful? For the military? I've no idea what their play is."

Rusty says, "And the, quote, 'find,' unquote?"

"Same. Could be anything. Could be alien bodies. Could be a near mint copy of *Action Comics* number one. All's I know is, the Crays are dangerous. And more gunhands are headin' our way."

Rusty says, "All right. I'll come with you. Trip Jacks is safe enough here."

Dez shakes his head. "Joel de Brienne infiltrated the townies, yeah? Dyson Patterson infiltrated our team. If I was a bettin' man, I'd say the chances that someone infiltrated the physics team are great enough, we should assume it's so."

"Agreed." Trisha Jean reaches out and squeezes Rusty's shoulder. "You're stuck playing babysitter."

"Yes, ma'am. Dez: I left the two MP7s up by the door."

"Ta. Ash?"

Ash looks up from under her black ball cap. Her eyes appear to be enormous. She nods.

"Let's fore to go."

# CHAPTER 57

At the great door, Dez dons his new headset and clips Haddy's comms unit to his belt. He picks up the MP7s and hands one to Ash.

She sets it back down. "They jam."

She draws her own G43X, pulls out the ten-round mag, slams it back home again. She wears a combat holster low on her right thigh.

Dez sighs and sets his machine gun down, too. "That they do."

He's got one of the Russians' sidearms, a Grach. "Don't much trust any gun I haven't cleaned meself, but beggars an' all."

She nods. She's a compact, tightly bundled package in all black, and Dez has the sudden illusion that when they open the titanium steel door, she'll shoot out of the gate like a greyhound.

"If Finn's mercs an' the Russians have chopped themselves t'bits, well, that's Christmas, innit? If not, we do 'em quick and get topside. I don't want that incoming aircraft to take off again. An' I want to dissuade the new batch of mercs from bothering us."

Ash nods.

"Araki. Your family's Iranian, then?"

Ash nods.

"Did your mother study physics there?"

Ash nods.

"When this is all over, ye'll have t'tell me how you went from bein' the daughter of a renowned physicist to a paid assassin."

The mechanic, Haddy, arrives and hands Ash her own headset and belt-clip comms unit. Haddy begins typing on the door's control panel. She peers out to the other side, leaning left and right, seeing maybe two hundred degrees of the room. "They could be hiding just out of sight."

Ash nods.

Dez says, "Can ye open it only a meter or so? Then close it up fast?"

"Sure can."

Ash steps up to the door. She turns to the mechanic and nods.

The door whooshes open exactly one meter.

Ash barrel-rolls through, drawing her weapon en passant, landing on her back, gun out, arm locked, checking to the left and to the right of the door.

"Clear."

Dez rolls his eyes at Haddy and jabs a thumb in Ash's direction. "'Clear.' Yack yack yack. Can't get this one to shut up. Right, then. Button it up tight, soon as I'm through. You open it for me, or for Ash. But for no one else."

"Roger Dodger."

Dez steps through and the door hisses shut.

Ash has risen, standing next to him. She is screwing a sound suppressor onto her weapon. Silently, they move to the tall stairs and the barricade beyond. They can hear no shooting now.

Halfway up, Ash speaks in French. "If we survive, I will tell you the story."

"Ta, love."

"You deserve to know. And it won't matter to me. I'll be dead as soon as I return to Paris." Dez climbs over the barricade first, quietly as he can, a Russian Grach pistol in hand.

The fourth floor is empty. At least, as far as he can see from here. He looks back over his shoulder and nods, then finishes climbing through.

Ash scampers deftly in his wake.

They don't have the time to check the mines on any level, but they do stop to listen. Dez brought a palm-sized flashlight that Haddy lent him. He peers into the level four mine shaft; him to the left of the shaft, Ash to the right, her gun held professionally, left hand supporting her right wrist.

They see the little electric tram but nothing else. Dez shrugs and deactivates the flash.

They begin creeping through the man-made portion of level four.

They find their first body. One of the Skyhook mob. The guy's been shot in the groin. It clipped his femoral artery, and he bled out. Likely within seconds.

Dez sets the Grach down, picks up the man's SIG Sauer. He checks the mag, checks that there's a round in the chamber. He frisks the man and comes up with two more clips. "Much better weapon," he whispers.

Ash nods.

They've heard no gunfire.

They creep through the level. Ash moves with the directed strength and grace of a ballerina: no wasted energy, never off-balance, her core strength on display. Dez tried unarmed combat with her earlier and hadn't laid a hand on her. He can see why.

She raises a fist to the left of her head, and Dez freezes.

She points to her own ear. She heard something.

Dez nods.

Ash advances, the heels of her sneakers never touching the cement. Dez advances in her wake. She crosses to the right of the corridor they're in so Dez crosses to the left. That way, when they come to the next intersection, they'll have the widest possible field of fire.

She stops a bit shy of the intersection. She shows no emotion. She almost seems to be closing her eyes.

Then she moves forward, one step. Her arms rise and *whut-whut.* She fires twice, the silencer doing its job.

Dez hears a grunt and a body fall. Hears a gun clatter to the floor.

She fired to her right down the intersection. Dez covers her to the left. Sees naught.

When he turns, she's crouched over a body, all her weight on the balls of her feet, feeling for a pulse. She finds none. She frisks the man, reaches for his radio.

Dez kneels next to her. This guy's one of the Russians. "No need," he whispers, and points to her own headset. "Russians aren't broadcastin', and neither's Skyhook. Everyone's comms-dark."

Ash nods and leaves the radio. She rises.

They advance to the stairs that lead to three. Dez points to his own chest. Ash takes a covering position, twenty degrees away from the bottom of the stairs; less likely to hit Dez with friendly fire, should opposition appear up top.

Dez gets to the platform on level three. He crouches and quick-glances out. Then turns to her and nods.

She makes not one sound scampering up the metal stairs.

"Talk about ghost particles," he whispers.

And is surprised to see a spritely little smile, which evaporates just as quickly.

They both tense as their headsets click.

*"Patterson to airlift! I should have a path clear in fifteen minutes! Over!"*

He's shouting. He sounds as if he's out in the storm, and they heard the reverberation of a diesel engine. He's in one of the Skyhook-brand snowplows, Dez assumes, clearing the airfield.

*"Ah, roger that, mate. Circling well above the storm. No sign of the Mounties. Over."*

The pilot sounds Australian.

*"ETA on the backup? Over!"*

*"They're twenty minutes out, more or less. Over."*

Their headsets click as Patterson disconnects his sat phone.

"That lass Haddy's a feckin' genius!" Dez whispers.

A giggle reaches them. *"I heard that!"*

Ash rolls her eyes and begins advancing down three.

They come upon another Skyhook mercenary. This man took a bullet to the back of his head.

Dez takes two magazines from him. Now he's got four beyond the one in his SIG.

The next body also is from Skyhook.

Dez taps his comms. "Haddy, love? How many mercs did Skyhook have?"

From the safety of the neutrino facility, she says, *"I heard someone say seven total."*

"Ta, love." To Ash, he whispers. "Three down, four t'go."

"Only one Russian left. What did your friend call him?"

"Squirrel."

They hear shots fired. A spray from a machine gun. It's faint enough, it's likely on level one.

Ash takes point, and they move forward.

They spot two more dead Skyhook soldiers on level two. Now the odds ahead of them are two to one in favor of the mercs.

"An' it couldn't've happened to a nicer bunch of fellas," Dez whispers.

He takes point up the stairs to level one with Ash on his six. Again. When it's clear, she joins him on this much-larger level.

They spot a Skyhook soldier. He's seated, leaning against a wall, bleeding from his mouth and nose. Blood drools out of an unseen wound under his Kevlar. Two shovels turned crutches lie on the ground near him. His legs are bandaged, and blood seeps through the material. Dez thinks this guy was front and center when his improvised IED blew up at the door to the igloo.

The man has a SIG in hand. He spots them. He groggily raises the weapon.

Dez kneels and takes it gingerly from him. He holds his finger to his own lips. "Shhh."

Ash kneels and produces a butterfly knife Dez didn't know she possessed. The handle whizzes through the air, too fast to observe, and she deploys the blade. She grabs the man's hair, tilts his head to the right, and slides the knife into his neck, just under his ear.

She severs his spinal cord, and the light disappears from the man's still-open eyes.

"Jay-sus," Dez whispers.

Ash looks calmly in Dez's eyes, cleans blood off her blade with the man's snow-camo pants. The little blade whirls and gets stowed away within its handle again.

She emotes nothing, just rises to her feet.

"One versus one," she whispers.

"Squirrel versus Finn."

They hear a single shot fired. A handgun this time, not a machine gun. It's close.

Ash leads. They creep toward the storage area. They hear nothing. When they get to the infirmary, Dez taps her on the shoulder. She nods. She takes one knee, right arm extended, left hand in support, left elbow on her upturned knee.

Dez creeps to the door. He slowly turns the handle and, when done, slams his shoulder into the door. It bangs open. Anyone hiding behind it would be pancaked.

He steps in.

Captain Cora Charbonneau and her copilot, Tulsa, lie dead. Both shot in the back of the head, a double-tap each. Inspector Frank Watts is dead as well; his neck broken.

If this is the work of Dr. Dyson Patterson—and Dez suspects it is—he's now hoping to lay eyes on the man one last time. Dez looks forward to signing him off.

He emerges and shakes his head. Ash rises.

They hear a sound coming from the break room, which the townies had turned into a sort of city hall. It's the *sheck* of someone slapping a magazine into a handgun.

Ash holds up her fist again. Dez freezes. She points to her own eyes, then points in the direction of the corridor that leads to the ring of living quarters. She spotted something.

She pulls Dez aside. She points toward the doughnut of living quarters that surrounds the central core. Using her finger, she points to herself, then makes an O in the air.

She wants to sneak the long way around the doughnut, to come up from behind whoever's hiding there.

Dez mouths the word *alive* to her. A beat, then she nods.

She holsters her gun, turns, and sprints silently away.

Dez holds his position.

He knows the woman is fast—damn fast. Too fast for him to fight. He doesn't think it'll take long.

He waits. He hears a grunt.

A man falls to the floor. Unconscious but, Dez thinks, alive. It's Finn. The tall, redheaded fella Dez first met in the parking lot of the hotel in St. John's.

Ash appears from behind him and nods once to Dez.

Dez steps back a few paces and finds the office that Mayor

Brandywine had picked out for himself. There are three chairs around a small table. Dez takes one and steps back out into the corridor.

He gets to the edge of the break-room door.

"Nikolai?"

The Russian leader, Squirrel, rises from behind a felled table that he's been using for cover.

Dez hurls the chair, hard as he can, into the room. He sidearms it, so it's spinning.

"Ugh!"

He enters quickly. Squirrel is on his back, dazed, arms akimbo, gun a few feet away, bleeding from a cut over his eyebrow. Dez pushes away the chair that clobbered the Russian in midair.

"Clear."

He hears Ash enter behind him. He gathers the man's gun and tosses it to her. He pats the Russian down. Squirrel is stunned but awake. *"Shto eta . . ."*

Des takes the man's headset and comms, tosses them to Ash. The man has a long, vicious-looking combat knife, which Dez takes.

He rises, passes Ash, heads for the corridor, and gathers Finn. The man is coming to, moaning. Dez pats him down, removes his extra cartridges. He removes the man's comms unit and tosses it down the corridor. Finn also sports a fixed-blade combat knife.

Dez gets him up and frog-marches him into the break room.

"Who the . . . fuck . . . ?"

"'Tis your oul' mates. Pleased as punch."

Dez tosses him into the room. He lands and rises to his knees. He's been shot and is bleeding from his leg.

Squirrel rises to his knees. He, too, is bleeding from a wound in his shoulder. Both men are huffing, gasping for air, in great pain.

Dez says, "Your men are dead. You're the last rats of the bunch.

Me and Ash are heading to the surface. Finn, we've a surprise or two for your incoming mates. Here."

He tosses both knives to the floor between the men.

Dez moves to one of the vending machines in the break room. It's six feet high, about three feet wide and deep. He places his massive hands to either side of it and lifts.

He grunts as it rises. He backs up, backs up. It's plugged into the wall, and the plug pops free. Dez backs all the way up to the doorway to the break room.

Ash already is out in the corridor.

Dez maneuvers the vending machine until it's blocking the door. The thing weighs hundreds of pounds.

Trapped in the room now, Finn gasps. "Limerick . . . wait . . ." He eyes the knives between himself and the Russian leader. Both are on their knees, both bleeding, both gasping in pain.

"Fuck . . . you," Squirrel says, reaching for a knife.

"Was lovely knowing ye both. Best of luck to ye."

Dez turns and leads Ash to the elevator debarkation chamber. And away from the diminishing sounds of a desperate knife fight and two trapped and wounded warriors.

# CHAPTER 58

Dez and Ash stop to gather their snow jackets, hats, and gloves. The left leg of Dez's polyester snow pants is blackened and half-melted, thanks to the townies' firebomb.

They get the heavy metal grates in front of the elevator door to recess into the floor and ceiling, then get the elevator door open.

They climb into the vast car, gloves in their pockets, guns extended to the opposite door, which will open topside. The car is soot-stained from the propane bomb.

The elevator rises to the ground level. It jerks to a stop. The doors hiss open. Ash emerges and zigs left and low. Dez emerges, zags to the right.

No one is in the igloo. Small drifts of snow line the curved edges of the floor, thanks to the bullet holes in the walls from the helicopter gunship. Dez spots something new. It's a standing dolly, with something on its pad the size and shape of a thermos, wrapped in cloth. He ignores it for now.

Ash gestures to the fenced-off tool area. "Goggles."

"Aye? Missed that," he says, moving that way. He gets two sets of goggles, under-hands one to Ash.

"Step one is t'stop them incoming mercenaries, yeah?"

Ash holds up her smaller-than-average Glock and gives Dez another fast-as-lightning smile. "How?"

"I always say, if someone brings ye a gift an' you fail to thank 'em, that's just plain rude, innit."

Dyson Patterson has been running the snowplow like a riding lawnmower: a long strip heading north, then a long strip next to it heading south, then north again. Methodical. Clearing a lane for the plane that's circling Fuchstown. The cabin on the plow is closed and has an electric heater near his feet, so it's not as bad as he feared.

He's done. He stops to glug stale water from a bottle he spotted inside the cab. He wants this job over with, and he wants to be airborne as fast as possible. He checks his watch. It's just past 1 A.M., Saturday. They've been here since Thursday.

He peers into the night. He can see the silhouette of the small but functional terminal building, where he patched up Frank Watts's broken arm. He spots their upturned Super Puma helicopter leaning against it, nose up, tail down, one rotor ripped off when it touched tarmac.

He looks to the other Puma; Finn's ride in. It was a rough landing; rough enough to kill three of Finn's guys. Surprisingly, that bird stayed upright on its skids and looks less damaged than the bird Patterson and the State Department team arrived in. He knows that's an illusion; neither bird will ever fly again. As he watches, the wind kicks up and Finn's helo—now essentially a coffin—rotates a little, the skis gliding over the ice. Seeing it move like that, with three cadavers in it, is disconcerting.

He activates his sat phone. "Airlift? You're clear. The runway's yours. Over."

*"Ah, roger that. On final. Over."*

Patterson starts up the engine again and turns the plow ninety degrees.

His sat phone chirps.

He shuts down the engine again—way too loud inside the cabin—and answers.

He hears the telltale *whoop-whoop-whoop* of a helicopter and a stranger's voice. *"Patterson? Cavalry's arrived. We're ETA in thirty seconds."*

Patterson says, "Roger that. Land near the igloo. I got the runway clear for the Hercules."

He peers toward the ink-dark silhouette of the igloo. A good fifty yards from him, Finn's downed helicopter skates in the wind, turning counterclockwise about five degrees.

*"I see it. Roger that. Think I can bring her down despite this wind. Hang on."*

Patterson peers into the night. Nothing. He waits.

The running lights of the helo break the cloud ceiling. It's just to the west of the igloo, holding steady.

Huffing, Dez puts all his weight into the tail section of Finn's downed Super Puma, pushing it counterclockwise, his boots slipping on the ice.

He gets it turned another five degrees. Then another.

He turns and sees a newcomer helicopter hover into view. It's perhaps thirty feet off the ground.

"That's enough!" Ash bellows over the storm. "I see them!"

And she lights them up with the mounted fifty-caliber gun that Finn and his mercenaries brought.

Patterson watches the incoming helicopter explode in midair. Flames and wreckage expand in every direction. The rotors disconnect and whirligig off into the night.

Then the burned-out hulk of the helo drops straight down like an anvil. Crashing into the ground and igniting another explosion.

"No!" Patterson bellows. How in the hell?

He sits there, aghast. Unbelieving. One second the helo was dropping slowly, under control. The next it's a fireball.

What could have . . . ?

He twists in his seat, looks to Finn's helo. Finn's gunship, and its fifty-caliber mounted gun.

Limerick. It has to be.

Patterson brought along his Sten gun and left it tucked behind his seat. He reaches back, draws it out now.

He checks his clip in the growing light of the cab. Then realizes: the growing light can't be coming from the exploded helo. It's way too far away. And the light is coming . . .

He twists in his seat again and sees the running lights of a massive C-130. The big ship has just cleared the cloud ceiling. It touches down, the wheels leaving the snowpack for a second, then touches down again. And screams, straight and smooth down the runway.

Patterson drops his gun, claws for the door, and leaps free a second before the leading wheel collides with the snowplow, the plane's landing gear snapping under the impact.

# CHAPTER 59

Dez and Ash watch as the C-130 keels over, one landing gear busted, then begins to spin down the newly plowed runway. For the second third of its run, it skids sideways relative to the runway. For the last third, it's gliding tailfirst. It comes to a halt.

Dez spotted a pegboard with keys inside the igloo. He swipes a key for one of the big Skyhook tractors parked near the igloo, this one with tank treads instead of wheels. He and Ash climb on, and Dez heads toward the now inert Hercules, a half mile away.

The forward, starboard passenger door has been opened. They find a guy in the snow, on his hands and knees, puking. Blood drooling from both of his ears. So out of it, he doesn't even see the newcomers.

Dez and Ash board the C-130 with its crippled landing gear, leading with their guns. They find three more crew members. Two with broken legs, one unconscious. They separate the men from their sidearms.

Ash checks the cargo as Dez speaks to the two conscious crew on the flight deck. "Here's your marchin' orders, then. You're to stay in this nice airplane of yours until the Canadian military or the RCMP arrives. Ye snapped your left front landing brace, ye clumsy oafs, so there's no getting airborne again. Step outside the Herky, and we'll do to you what we done to your mates in the helicopter. Are we clear then, me darlings?"

He is very clear.

Dez hears a noise behind him and turns.

The first thing he spots is Valerie Cray, raising a SIG Sauer and aiming it at his heart.

The second thing is Ash, moving like, well, a ghost particle. She's on the British woman, too quickly to see, dragging her down, the SIG skidding free.

Ash is behind Valerie, legs around the woman's waist, one arm around her throat, both of them reaching for the gun that skittered across the fuselage floor. Valerie elbows Ash in the gut.

Dez reaches down and grabs Valerie in a one-armed bear hug, lifting her boots off the floor, pinning her arms to her side. He wraps one massive arm around her waist and her arms, his other arm around her throat, gently cutting off the flow of blood to her brain. Putting no pressure on her airway.

She struggles mightily, kicking at his shins, trying to headbutt him.

"Not my idea of foreplay, darlin'. Just relax."

Ash rises, both guns in her hand.

Valerie keeps struggling.

"Nap time," he croons. "There's a good girl."

Her struggling ebbs. She goes rag doll in his arms. Dez nods to Ash. "Find us a bit of rope, will ye?"

Together, they get Valerie's wrists tied behind her back with bungee cords, get her into a seat, and secure the safety harness around her.

Only then does Ash catch Dez's eye and cock her head toward something at the rear of the plane. She rises and Dez follows her. She points to a device, something very large and cylindrical.

"Jay-sus," he whispers.

She nods.

"Now, that," he says, "is a big fucking bomb."

*"Oui."*

With the plane's crew sorted, and Valerie Cray tightly bound and seat-belted into one of the cabin seats, Dez and Ash trek back to the igloo via their borrowed tractor. Dez makes a stop first, finds an industrial snowmobile with a wagon on skids. He returns to the C-130, and Ash waits in the igloo.

When he returns, Ash is studying the thermos-sized thing, which she picked up and placed on a workbench. "Heavy," she says as he steps up.

He spots a metal clipboard that closes like a folder. It's near the dolly. He reaches for it and studies the documentation Patterson left behind. "This is interesting."

Ash peers at the papers in his hand. She looks up at Dez and shrugs.

"A Distant Early Warning bunker. A Cold War relic. It's about three klicks north of here. That's where Finn an' his mates were going to hide if that plane had delivered its payload. Gives me an idea."

Ash gestures to the lumpy thing all wrapped up. "And this?"

Dez studies the papers in the clipboard folder. He shakes his head. "The root of all evil."

# CHAPTER 60

Trisha Jean Jackson is having tea with Dr. Sophia Araki in her personal quarters, inside the neutrino facility. The physicist invited her in. "I . . . have so many questions for my daughter. And about my daughter."

Trisha Jean holds her mug in both hands, warming her palms. "I'd imagine so."

The little apartment is quite homey. Sophia opted for three oil paintings on three walls that feature windows and outdoor views; to fool her brain into thinking she isn't living underground. She has a love seat and a full bookshelf, and a good sound system, and a vase with fake flowers on a coffee table. She wears thick, wool socks and sits with her feet tucked under her, idly stirring her tea with a spoon. "Why did Dez insist on taking Asha out there to face those men?"

"Because she's highly skilled in combat." Not a lie, just not the complete truth.

"We haven't seen each other in so very long."

Trisha Jean sits on a comfy chair facing the couch. She's got her feet up on the other end of the love seat, her swollen left knee appreciating the break. She waits patiently.

"I'm . . . I'm a widow."

"I didn't know that."

Sophia nods. "My husband was half Persian, half Japanese. He was a brilliant chemistry professor. I'd been his graduate student, then his lab assistant. And then his lover. When he moved from Tehran to London, he took me with him and we married."

Trisha Jean sips her tea. She's a diplomat, a negotiator, and, most important, a poker player. She knows this story will take exactly as long as it needs to take. And that the telling of it is important to her hostess.

"He also was violent. So angry, always so angry." Sophia keeps her eyes on her mug and the spoon. "He took it out on me. As, I think, he had with his first wife."

She stirs and stirs but hasn't tasted her tea. She looks up. "I have no idea why I'm telling you this. I've told no one else. Not ever."

Trisha Jean reaches down and massages her swollen knee a little. "With all that's going on, maybe this felt like the time to . . . I don't know. Unburden yourself."

Sophia thinks a bit, then nods. "Perhaps. Or perhaps the appearance of my long-lost daughter has prompted a confession of my failures as a mother."

Trisha Jean waits.

"When Asha was eighteen, I found her packing her belongings in a backpack. She told me she was leaving. She held me and kissed me. Then she told me that I would be free of my husband the following day."

The little spoon clinks rhythmically against the sides of the cup.

"And the next day, the Métro Police came to tell me that my husband had been robbed and stabbed. He'd been visiting a prostitute, they told me. Well, he'd done so before, often. I believed them. They said he'd been robbed of his wallet and watch and phone, and that he died on the scene. And I was free of his abuse. Just as Asha had predicted."

Trisha Jean sits through about two minutes of silence. She's used to houses that groan and settle, ringing telephones, the shush of nearby traffic, wind. The underground bunker is absolutely without sound. She finds it unnerving but she doesn't break the silence.

"I never saw my daughter again until today. And I never found out what price she paid to set me free."

Sophia finally looks up, tears glittering in her eyes.

"I don't know her story," Trisha Jean says. "And if I did, it'd probably be her story to tell, and not mine. She's here now. This would be your chance to find out."

"Asha knew—she *knew*—in advance, that her father would be killed. I don't know how that's even possible." Tears roll down both cheeks. She daubs at them with the back of one hand.

Trisha Jean looks the physicist in the eyes. "No wonder you never talked about this to anyone." Secretly wondering if Ash arranged for her father to be killed or just took care of it herself.

The PA speaker on the wall near the door buzzes. It's Haddy. *"Doc? Dez and Ash are back."*

"Thank God," Trisha Jean says, lowering her legs and standing. "Thank you for the tea. I need to debrief with Dez and, well, I'm honestly not sure what you need to do. I read your curriculum vitae. You got postgrad degrees like Altoids got mints. You'll figure it out."

She heads for the door.

Sophia Araki says, "Do you have children?"

"I do, yep. Boy and a girl. Both all grown up and got jobs and everything."

"You're proud of them."

"They're wholesome and churchgoing and they irritate the holy hell outta me."

A little laugh bursts free and Sophia wipes tears off both cheeks with the back of her hand. "Thank you. I needed that."

Trisha Jean winks at her and leaves.

She's got a bum knee and she's stuck in a joint that uses ladders, not stairs, for getting around. That's the bad news. But Dez and their pet assassin survived and returned, and that's the good news. Trisha Jean's a diplomat. She takes the wins she can. She'll worry about the rest later.

Before getting to the conference room, Mayor Burt Brandywine finds Dez and offers his hand. Ash stays a couple of steps back, quiet and watchful.

"Looks like you two made up?" the mayor observes. "That was kinda silly, saying she was some sort of an assassin."

"'Twas." Dez smiles. "'Some sort'! She's the best damn assassin I ever met. Feel foolish, downplaying her skill sets."

Brandywine gives him an unsure, you're-pulling-my-leg smile. "Anyhow, are we safe?"

"From the Russians, and from two sets of mercenaries: yes."

"Then the residents want to get the hell out of this hole in the ground."

"Can. But best be warned, there are bodies on the mining levels, and more corpses topside. And they'll be there till the storms pass and the Canadian authorities get here."

Brandywine clenches his jaw. "I'll . . . I'll tell the others. We just want to see the sky. Even if it is a stormy sky."

Dez offers his hand, and they shake again. He gives the mayor one of the research facility's walkie-talkies. "Understood. And the radio's fixed. Shout if ye need help."

★ ★ ★

In the conference room, Professor William Sato is seated in one chair, his legs up on the conference room table, studying a scrolling set of data points on a tablet computer. He wears thick reading glasses, one hinge taped on. He glances over the tops of them as Dez and Ash enter. Dez is carrying the metal clipboard folder.

Petra is still seated right where she had been before, eyes on the laptop that shows visually the patterns of neutrino strikes within the massive sphere of liquid argon.

She rises and hugs Dez, hard.

"Done," he whispers.

She won't need the details now.

Silently, Ash removes her black cap and black wrist gloves. She shakes her white hair free. No emotion shows on her face.

Trisha Jean and Rusty Townsend enter, and she throws a hug around Dez's neck. "Hey, hunk. You done good?"

"We done good."

That gets Professor Sato to set down his tablet. "Can we get out of here now?"

"Well, the storm's still ragin'. And there are a few men topside in an airplane, though I think we put the fear o' god into them."

Ash gives him a little nod.

"The storm looks to be easing, maybe just a little," Dez tells everyone. "Hoping help comes soon."

He adjusts the comms controls on his belt. "Haddy? I know the radio's busted all t'hell, but maybe, with the threat over, you might, y'know, baby it a little? See if there isn't some life left in her?"

Dr. Araki enters the room and goes to the PA system, toggling a switch. "Haddy? I concur. Now is the time to try again."

*"That's a roger, Doc."*

Sato seems to fully buy the story the ladies concocted about their lack of communications. He says, "First thing? The very first thing? Barbecued brisket."

Trisha Jean says, "Texas or Kansas?"

"I got my master's in applied mathematics from UNC Chapel Hill. I'm Carolina barbecue all the way."

"Sides?"

The Nobel Prize laureate peers at the ceiling, pondering. "Well, baked beans."

She says, "That's a given."

"Collard greens."

"Sure."

"And . . . coleslaw."

Trisha Jean nods. "Me? Imma go with hush puppies, macaroni and cheese, and lessee . . . cornbread."

The physics professor stares at the diplomat for a full ten seconds. "Well, fuck. Now that's all I want."

"I know, right?"

Sato drops his feet down off the table, stands, adjusts his way-too-large pants and heads out the door. "I eat one more thing with tofu and someone's getting hurt."

Ash makes an all-around nod that seems to mean *excuse me* and exits also.

Trisha Jean looks to Sophia Araki, her eyebrows raised. Now would be a good time to talk to her daughter.

Sophia hesitates. Before she can act, Petra looks up from the laptop that she's been studying. "Professor? May I ask you about something?"

Petra gestures to the laptop she's been studying.

Sophia circles the table and peers at the screen, then at the notes Petra has been jotting on a legal pad. The color drains from her face.

She closes the conference room door and sits. Now it's just her and Dez and Petra, plus Trisha Jean and Rusty.

Petra says, "As I understand it, this represents the direction that the neutrinos were traveling when they hit an atom of . . ."

"Liquid argon," Dez says, sitting.

Sophia Araki sits. "Oh, dear."

Petra nods. "Matteo Bernardi explained all this to me. William Sato was willing to give the Russians your data. That's when you and Matteo and your mechanic shut off all comms and told him they were broken. With the Russians holding the lower two levels of the mine, you decided the only play was to wait them out."

Sophia stirs. "Their leader told me they controlled all four levels of the mine. Is he . . . ?"

Dez says, "He an' the top dog o' the mercenary group took each other out. We checked when we got back down. An' he was the last of the Russians."

"Good."

Trisha Jean addresses Petra. "What did you find?"

Petra adjusts the laptop so everyone can see the screen. "As I understand it now, most neutrinos come from cosmic sources like black holes or our sun. Also from nuclear power plants."

Petra adjusts the image on the laptop. They watch as tiny blue streaks flicker off the screen. They're all moving together, as if coming from a source that is rotating clockwise but off-screen. Like a field of sunflowers following the sun. She showed Dez this before.

"These are solar neutrinos. Matteo explained it to me. He said, as the sun crosses our sky, the direction these neutrinos are coming from changes, too. It's like watching a sundial."

"That's correct," Dr. Araki says.

"Now here . . ." Petra changes to a different image. More pale blue streaks now, and they're not shifting position. They also are coming from haphazard sources, crisscrossing one another. "Matteo told me these are cosmic neutrinos. They come from outside our solar system, right?"

"Likely black holes and supermassive black holes, yes." The physicist nods.

"And these . . ." She adjusts the screen again. This image has far fewer blue streaks than the other two images. And they seem to be tracking something that is traveling laterally. Left to right on the screen, or right to left.

"Them's not coming from the sun," Dez says. "Nor from outside this solar system. At a guess, I'd say they're terrestrial."

Petra smiles and nods.

Rusty has just filled a coffee cup. "Okay, but why are they moving? Nuclear power plants don't move."

Petra smiles and waits. Dr. Araki sighs, crossing her arms, looking crestfallen.

It's Dez who finally catches up to Petra. "Jay-sus! Of course they do! If they're aboard nuclear submarines!"

Sophia turns to Petra. "I take it you've studied some physics?"

"No. I run the bank that pays for these submarines. And I study where our money goes. I am not unfamiliar with the world's nuclear fleets."

She points to one of the horizontally moving streams of blue flashes. Then another. "If we're focused on the Atlantic right now, I'd hazard a guess that this first one is American. Los Angeles class. Their reactor output is around, I don't know, a hundred and sixty megawatts. This one? Vanguard class. Only 'bout twenty megawatts from their reactors."

Trisha Jean's jaw falls. She shakes her head. "Holy hell. You can tell that by looking at their neutrino flow?"

Petra says, "It's a guess."

Trisha Jean leans back. "Goddamn. I'm used to being the smartest lady in any given room. I don't even make the top ten in this hole in the ground."

Sophia gives Petra a soft smile. "The secretary is right about you. You are remarkable. None of my graduate students found the pattern, but you did."

Petra shrugs.

Rusty says, "So, you're telling us that your sensors down here can track nuclear submarines in the Atlantic."

Sophia smiles wanly. "No. Our sensors could track every nuclear submarine on Earth."

A stunned silence fills the room.

Trisha Jean shakes her head in shock. "Does Professor Sato know this?"

Sophia inhales and holds it, pausing to configure her answer. "Bill is brilliant. Completely, totally brilliant. Matteo and I are smart, but Bill? He is one of the greatest minds of his generation. And as naïve about the real world as an infant. His mind is always a billion miles away. MIT had to ban him from driving because he caused so many accidents. I found the submarine pattern first and told the others what we'd discovered. Bill communicated with a colleague of ours in St. Petersburg and joked about it. And shortly after that, the offers started coming in. First from Russia. Then the Chinese. They offered to make Bill the chief scientist at TRIDENT. The Tropical Deep-Sea Neutrino Telescope, the largest neutrino detector on Earth. Even bigger and dramatically more sensitive than IceCube in the Antarctic. Both of which make ours look like an Erector Set. Bill was over the moon. He was ready to accept. And to give them this technology. I told him the unbelievable harm that it could do; how it could unbalance the fragile peace between the West, the Chinese, and the Russians. And he just didn't care."

"So you stopped him."

"That's right. Matteo and I and the staff. We voted. We shut off all communications with the world. And while we've been waiting to be rescued, I've worked on nothing other than a plan to help the world's navies hide the emission of neutrinos and antineutrinos from their power plants."

"You'll give it to the Americans?" Trisha Jean asks.

"I'll publish it on the internet. All three superpowers will keep their submarine fleets hidden. Also the French, and English, and yes, even Iran, as much as I despise the regime. The status quo will be maintained."

Trisha Jean cradles her forehead in both hands. "Oh, mama. That's . . . whew. That's something we gotta talk about."

Dez laughs and reaches out with one boot to gently jostle her chair. "You're State. Not Defense. An' last I checked, the doc here don't work for Uncle Sam. She's got Swiss citizenship, yeah?"

Petra adds, "And Triton Expediters will finance the work. For every nation's fleet."

Trisha Jean rubs her temples with her fingertips. "I coulda been a schoolteacher. You know that? Majored in education for two semesters. That job woulda had a whole lot fewer headaches. And I wouldn't have had to deal with wiseasses."

Petra reaches out and squeezes Trisha Jean's forearm.

Dez catches Petra's eyes. "Jay-sus, but you're brilliant."

Petra is not one for false modesty. She cocks an eyebrow at him and nods.

Rusty says, "So that explains the radio silence from Planet Neutrino, and our pesky Russians. What we don't know is what the Skyhook idiots were after."

"I can answer that." Dez reaches for the metal folder/clipboard on the table. "Found this topside. Along with a mineral deposit that somebody unearthed in the mine."

Rusty says, "Not cerite, I'm guessing?"

"Nope. According to the documents we found, it's iridium."

Trisha Jean says, "Which is . . . ?"

"Extremely rare element. Almost totally absent from the Earth's crust. Found in places like, ah . . ." He scans a document. "Myanmar, Brazil, Russia, South Africa, an' the like. But in very small quantities. Like, a total of three tons per year is extracted from ores."

Trisha Jean says, "And the Crays found some here?"

"Someone found it. Kept it a secret. Reached out to the Crays t'see if they was interested. They said yes. Finn and Patterson was tryin' to smuggle out a wee bit that the geologist extracted, so's it could be tested."

Rusty shakes his head. "That's what all this fuss is about? Some precious but rare element? That seems like . . . kinda small potatoes."

Dez smiles. "Ye'd think. But iridium sells for a hundred and seventy-five American dollars per gram. And that chunk Patterson got to the surface? My guess is, it weighs twenty-five pounds. All by itself."

Sophia Araki's eyes flutter as she does the math in her head. "That would come to . . . ah . . ." Her eyes pop. "My God."

"Aye," Dez says. "That chunk up there's worth about two million dollars. An' who knows how much iridium is down here?"

Petra shakes her head. "The mine. The daily shift is about eighty men. It doesn't make sense to me that one person would find iridium and not tell their coworkers. How long would a secret like that last in an enclosed space like a mine? How long would *any* secret last?"

Trisha Jean says, "She's not wrong. One guy found this and hid it from all the other miners? And the townies?"

Dez shrugs. "Depends on who found it, yeah? An' where."

# CHAPTER 61

Twenty minutes later, Dez goes exploring and finds Ash in one of the more isolated corridors of the neutrino facility. She's sitting on a metal walkway, feet dangling over the side, her arms crossed on one of the horizontal, metal support bars, chin on her forearms.

Dez says, "Mind if I join ye?"

She nods.

He sits and also lets his feet dangle. They're both facing the enormous metal sphere that contains fifty thousand tons of liquid argon.

"Ye said you'd be dead the moment ye return t'France."

She speaks without lifting her chin off her crossed forearms. "Yes."

"Care to explain?"

She does not respond, and Dez is happy to just sit a spell. He reaches into his pocket. "Look what I found."

He produces a small bag of peanut M&M's. He rips it open, takes one. He holds the packet out in her direction.

A beat, then Ash takes one.

"I couldn't stay in the conference room. You all interact and talk so much. You and Petra love each other. Trisha Jean and Rusty love each other. It's . . . I find it difficult to take it all in."

Dez starts counting, holding up fingers as he does so. "That was . . . thirty-seven words. Which brings the total number of words I've ever heard out of you to about, say, forty."

She turns her enormous eyes to him. She gives him a small, sad smile.

"I am introverted."

"No, you kill people. There's a difference."

He takes a candy and holds the bag out. She takes another. She chews it thoughtfully and swallows.

"There exists this . . . group." She speaks barely above a whisper. Their voices echo off the giant sphere before them. "It is very old, or so I am told. It was started before World War I."

He leaves the last M&M for her. She takes it. Dez folds the little packet and slips it into his pocket. No need to litter. They're guests down here.

"They come to people in dire need. They offer to fix some problem. And in exchange, you indenture yourself to them for ten years."

Dez nods. "Spoke to Trip Jacks. She told me the story. You was living in London, eighteen years old. Your da was abusive to your mum—"

"And to me."

"Ah. And how one day ye predicted he'd be a threat no longer, come the morrow. Then you upped stakes an' left, and your da died the next day. Stabbed in a robbery gone wrong."

Ash sits quietly. After a while, she says, "I'm twenty-five. My service would have ended in three years. Provided I obeyed all of their rules."

"And I assume runnin' off to Newfoundland doesn't qualify as obeying all their rules."

"No."

"Question: How'd ye know your mum was in the barney down here?"

She blinks at him.

"In trouble. How'd ye know she was in trouble?"

"My contact with the organization to whom I am indentured. They have connections everywhere. In governments, in organized crime. They knew a Russian special forces team was impersonating the staff of a mineral company and coming here for the scientists. They didn't know why."

"An' they told ye not to come rescue her? And that the punishment for going AWOL is death?"

"Yes."

Dez reaches out and touches his palm to the massive metal sphere holding back fifty thousand tons of liquid argon.

"Makes no sense. Why even tell ye, then?"

Ash shrugs. They sit.

"This group have a name?"

"They call themselves the Tontine."

"They killed your da for you."

"Yes."

"And in exchange?"

"The person who stabbed my father likely made a similar deal with them, some years earlier. For saving my mother, the Tontine's price was to train me to kill, too."

"Why you?"

"I'd been a gymnast. In Iran. I made the Olympics team at age fifteen. I was the daughter of two brilliant scientists. I have a very high IQ. They felt I had . . . potential."

Dez huffs a mirthless laugh. He's still touching the metal sphere with his palm. "Smart and athletic, plus small and lovely, and ye look like a threat to no one. The perfect cover for an assassin."

"Yes," she says. "I was given two years' training. Fighting, weapons, surveillance, evasion skills. I had my first kill the week after I turned twenty. He was a police officer in Kraków. He was quite corrupt. He had . . . How do you say? Dirt?"

"Aye. He had dirt on others." Dez is fairly certain Ash has never told anyone this story. Once he got her to open up, the tale is just pouring out.

"I shot him from less than ten feet away. He was looking at me. He looked so . . . surprised. I used a handgun. A G43X."

"'Cause ye've got small hands."

"Yes. Killing him, watching him die. It was horrible and also . . . mundane? Does that make sense?"

"Does, aye. I'm a soldier, or used t'be. I'm good at killing. Done it a lot. Still try to avoid it when I can. I understand being good at it and hatin' it."

She turns her head, studies him. "You didn't kill me that day in Paris."

"Didn't need to."

Ash says, "I understand."

"The Tontine will kill you for disappearing?"

She nods.

"If they simply let people go after their ten years of indentured service, don't ye think someone would have heard of them years ago?"

Ash pauses. "Yes."

"So it's likely that ye don't get a going-away cake and a party. Like as not, at the end of ten years, they kill you."

"Yes."

They ponder that for a while.

"Can ye explain it to them? Ye came to rescue your mum. Again. Which is how you got on their radar to begin with."

"Their rules are few but simple and always enforced equally."

"You could hide."

"Forever?"

"Good point. We could maybe intimidate them? Threaten to upend the apple cart?"

She turns to him again. She says, "We?"

"You saved me life last night."

"You could have killed me in Paris. We're even."

"Well. Let's not dwell overmuch on gettin' our sums right. I'm in this thing now, and that's all there is to it."

Ash watches him for a while.

They hear the beat of sneaker soles on metal stairs. They turn as the science team's mechanic, Haddy, draws near.

"Dez? We picked up a faint radio signal. Just for a couple of seconds. I'm not sure, but I think it's the Canadian Army."

"Good news," he says, gently caressing the sphere. "Haddy? This place has seismic security, I'm guessin'."

The staff mechanic nods. "Sure."

"I'm asking, 'cause in the event of a quake, ye'd not want fifty thousand tons of liquid argon spillin' into the habitat ring. Aye?"

"That'd be a big no. That would kill us all."

Dez smiles up at the girl. "So, in the event of a leak . . . ?"

Haddy shrugs. "The argon dumps downward, not outward. That's what we've got the sixth level for."

# CHAPTER 62

Dez, Petra, and Trisha Jean meet up with two of the physicists, Dr. Sophia Araki and Dr. Matteo Bernardi. Trisha Jean shows them her tablet computer, with its depiction of the five underground levels.

"There is no sixth level."

"That schematic is out of date," Sophia tells her. "We had to have a way to flush all of the argon, in the event of a disaster. One that didn't involve killing the staff."

Dez says, "So, as you was setting up the neutrino collector site, ye also excavated an extra level. And nobody bothered to update the schematics."

The two physicists shrug in unison. Matteo Bernardi says, "Is this a problem? Did we violate some sort of Canadian land-use code?"

Petra gets there. "Oh. Oh, I see. Dez thinks the sixth level is where the iridium was found. If it had been found in the main mining levels, every worker would have heard about it."

Dez grins at her. "Took me ages t'get there, love. You got it in a blink."

She says, "We have to get a sense of how much iridium is down there. It'll tell us what the Crays are willing to do to get it."

Trisha Jean huffs a laugh. "You mean, beyond homicide and domestic terrorism?"

"I'm afraid I do. I believe Vincent and Valerie Cray aren't just killers. Especially her. I think she's a psychopath whose violent tendencies have been hidden by the family's millions, and a team of lawyers and PR people."

Dez runs a hand through his hair. "Jay-sus. If the find's big enough, what wouldn't that nutjob do? 'Fraid Petra's right. We need t'get into the sixth level."

Matteo Bernardi shakes his head. "It's not safe. We've never been down there ourselves. It was excavated just to take the fifty thousand tons of argon. There are no stairs or ladders, no lights, no electricity. It's just a very, very great hole in the Earth."

Petra says, "How was it excavated?"

Sophia Araki says, "We don't know. When the mining operation found no cesium at this level, they leased the facility to our universities. The sixth level was excavated in case of an emergency, the neutrino facility was built atop of it, and then our team moved it. I'm not at all sure there's even an entrance to the sixth level. We've never seen it, at any rate."

Petra turns to Trisha Jean and Dez. "This was before my company added the money needed to complete the site. We didn't know about the sixth level, either."

Dez turns to the physicists. "Could I borrow Haddy? If there's an entrance to level six, she's more likely than anyone else to have sussed it out."

Matteo crosses his arms. "We have three of the greatest minds in physics working here. But Haddy is the only one who's kept the facility running. She is quite literally the most important person on the team. To put her at risk . . . ?"

"Girl's dead brilliant, aye. But I'm guessin' she knows every square inch of this place better than anyone. Yeah?"

The two physicists nod.

"Then she and me will do a bit of exploring. Nothing dangerous. You've me word."

Dez finds Ash, first, and tells her the plan. "If it's a crawl-space issue, I think we've already established you can get into places I can't."

Ash nods.

The two of them head to mechanical and find both of the resident grease monkeys, Haddy and Wayno.

"Ye've not been introduced proper-like. Ash, these two keep the place runnin'."

Haddy, nineteen and Moroccan American, stammers and makes an awkward little wave. "Um. Hey. Yes. Hi. Hello."

Wayno snorts a laugh, and Haddy smacks his shoulder.

Ash just nods.

"Right, then. We're lookin' for a way to get to the sixth level of the mine. Wondering if either of you know if there's an entrance."

Haddy doffs her massive tool belt. She's wearing a hoodie with SKATERGRRRRL stenciled across the front and a baseball cap worn backward. She's trying not to make eye contact with Ash. Dez has seen it before: lust at first sight.

"Mmmmaybe?" Haddy says. "We haven't found one, but I know a couple of places we can look."

Haddy comes up with three flashlights and takes Dez and Ash through an intricate maze of metal-gridded walkways and ladders. The neutrino collector site is larger than Dez imagined, just looking at the schematics. The habitat level is, as one of the physicists described, a horizontal ring around the massive so-called Swimming Pool. But down here, a few levels below the living quarters, it's dark, cramped, and humid. Dez has never served aboard an old-school diesel submarine but he imagines this is what it feels like.

Haddy weaves easily through standpipes and bundles of wiring, leading them unerringly. Ash, petite and balletic, has no problem keeping up. Dez, with his bulk, barely gets through a couple of intersections.

"If anything goes kerflooey down here, Wayno and I get pinged," Haddy calls back, her voice echoic in the all-metal space. "They built this facility pretty good. There's very little to fix."

"How'd you get so good at mechanical systems?"

Haddy is on all fours, crawling under a pipe. She grins back. "My mom rebuilds classic Harleys. I grew up in her garage."

"Now, that's what I call homeschooling."

Haddy laughs.

Bent low, she climbs over a set of iron braces laid out in an X pattern. She shines her flashlight ahead. "That might be it."

Ash hops deftly over the braces and crouches next to her. Dez has to lie on his back and squeeze his fifty-inch chest under the braces, but he gets through.

He sees where the women are aiming their flashlights.

It's a door. Two feet by two feet, iron, with a locking wheel in the middle. Again making Dez think of submarines.

Dez draws closer. He reverses his flashlight and smacks the butt end against the door, three times.

"Sounds like there's air on the other side. Ye think this leads to level six?"

Haddy shines her light straight up.

The ceiling is convex. They are directly beneath the Swimming Pool. "It's that or Narnia."

Ash flashes her a quick smile. Haddy turns four or five shades of red.

Dez pretends not to notice. "Have ye gas masks and oxygen tanks?"

"Yes. Several, in case of an argon spill. Should I go—"

Ash places a hand on the girl's knee. "I can go faster. Tell me where."

"She's not braggin'. I'd not seen speed till I met this one."

"Um, yeah, sure, okay, it's, ah, can you get back to mechanical?"

Ash nods.

"Wayno will show you."

And with a blink, Ash is simply no longer there.

Haddy waits for nearly thirty seconds, then lets loose with a whooshing exhale. "Oh, man, that's fire."

Dez laughs. "You're not wrong. But just so's you know, you're attracted to someone's who's more than a wee bit of a lunatic."

Haddy laughs. "Something else Mom and I have in common."

# CHAPTER 63

Ash returns with Wayno, the other mechanic. They bring three small oxygen tanks and three masks that fit over the nose and mouth. Also, three sets of goggles. Wayno stays a few junctions away from them because it's crowded near the mysterious door.

They mask up and suggest that Wayno gives them some more space. "Will do," he calls out, and retraces his steps.

Dez hunkers low and takes a knee. "Interesting."

The women draw nearer.

"The handle's not dusty. The floor is, and mine's not the first boot print here."

He grips the locking wheel and turns. They hear the dull metallic *thunk* as he disengages the door cleats from the doorframe.

"That's been well oiled," Haddy says.

"Noticed. Ready?"

Dez opens the door. Air whooshes past them.

The women crawl closer, shining their lights in.

On the other side of the door is a massive rock cave. Three shafts of light penetrate the dark, exposing a steel ladder, work lights on a stand and attached to a car battery, and two largish tool kits.

"There." Dez levels his light beam on a portion of the rock wall. They spot a seam of silvery-white metal that glints dully when the flashlights hit it. In the center of one of the seams is a round hole.

"That's where the sample of iridium came from, all right."

Ash touches Dez's arm. She's right beside him, in the square door. She shines her light elsewhere in the cave.

And highlights several of the silver-white seams.

"Jay-sus," Dez exhales. "There's our answer. This'd be worth billions. Maybe tens of billions."

He closes the door and dogs the hatch. The hinges don't squeak.

They unmask.

"There's no lengths them psychos, the Crays, wouldn't go to for this find. We've no more Russians to worry about, and we've offed two sets of mercenaries. But we'd be dumb as dirt t'think the danger's past."

They near mechanical, with Haddy and Wayno ahead, carrying back supplies. Dez keeps his voice low.

"The Crays had a mole on our airplane. An' they had a mole amongst the Fuchstown civilians."

"And on the neutrino team," Ash whispers. She's figured that much out for herself.

"Aye. Someone's been down there on level six recently. That sample of iridium Patterson got to the surface? The Russians couldn't've gotten down here, nor the townies. Only someone from the science team."

Ash nods.

"Maybe you, me, an' Rusty take shifts, keeping watch, until the Canadian military gets here."

She nods.

"I'll take first watch. Where are you bunking, then?"

Ash gives him a small smile. "I imagine in Haddy's quarters."

Dez side-hugs her. "That might well be the first non-crazy thought I've heard from ye since we met."

# CHAPTER 64

Dez, Rusty, and Ash take turns on sentry duty that night in the neutrino facility.

And in the morning, Haddy gleefully informs everyone that the Canadian military has arrived. And as Trisha Jean predicted, they have U.S. Marines with them.

Deputy Assistant Secretary Jackson and Petra Alexandris of Triton Expediters serve as spokespeople for the State Department, and for the scientists. The three physicists say they prefer to let the two professional negotiators take point.

The storm has eased off considerably, and it still takes the better part of a day and a half for the military and for the Royal Canadian Mounted Police to figure out who's who in Fuchstown, in the mine, and in the neutrino research facility. The entire site and the town above it are one gigantic crime scene.

The RCMP find the bodies of seven Fuchstown residents hidden in a storage locker connected to one of the prefab homes in the town. Mayor Burt Brandywine holds a prayer vigil and a town meeting with the surviving eighteen citizens, and they agree to abandon their town for the time being. They'll be flown to the capital of Newfoundland and Labrador, St. John's, where the Canadian government will put them up until the multipronged criminal investigation is complete.

The crew of the wounded C-130 are arrested and held on charges of conspiracy to commit murder. A little investigation shows that the plane traveled through Canadian and U.S. airspace under the auspices of a mission for Skyhook Technologies.

Surprisingly for Dez, Valerie Cray is not found on board.

The bodies of fifteen mercenaries cannot be recovered quickly from the burned-out wreckage of a helicopter that crashed, so that grim detail will have to wait for now.

Three more bodies are found in yet another helo.

From within the mine itself, authorities remove the bodies of two Canadian Coast Guard pilots and Inspector Frank Watts of the RCMP. They uncover the bodies of five Russian special forces soldiers and seven international mercenaries.

Before the survivors are airlifted to St. John's, a team of journalists from CBC Television fly to the site with the permission of the RCMP. They show no bodies, but they do a stand-up interview with Trisha Jean and Petra.

Between the two of them, they explain that Petra was on site at Fuchstown to find out if Skyhook Technologies—specifically, Vincent and Valerie Cray—was doing anything illegal.

Trisha Jean takes up the narrative, pointing to a now-unwrapped core sample. "We have evidence that the Crays were attempting to smuggle out this sample of iridium. It comes from a much, much larger iridium deposit in the mine. We estimate that it could be the largest iridium deposit on Earth, or one of the largest. It could be worth tens of billions of dollars."

As the reporters Gatling gun questions at them, Petra raises a palm to quiet them down. "The find could be worth tens of billions of dollars . . . for the Canadian government. Because the seams that were discovered are not on the fifth level of the mine. Not in the Fuchs Underground Neutrino Collector site. I'm the former senior legal counsel for Triton, and it is my legal opinion that the iridium doesn't belong to the universities that funded the neutrino research. Nor to Triton. The site is under Canadian soil and is subject to all appropriate Canadian laws."

As the flurry of questions comes anew, Dez stands behind the thicket of journalists and smiles approvingly. This had been Petra's little bit of legerdemain. Make it impossible for the Crays to claim they own the iridium. Because to do so, they'd have to admit to staging the attack on the town and the mine.

"Speaking for the U.S. State Department, I concur," Trisha Jean says. "We are of the opinion that the Canadian government should hold on to the iridium until such time as mining rights can be sorted out. And that cannot happen until the criminal investigations into all these murders are completed."

Trisha Jean Jackson tells the media that she's been in contact with the U.S. State Department, which is taking the accusations against the Crays and their company seriously and will begin working with the Justice Department for a combined investigation.

And since the neutrino facility is partially funded by CERN, an investigation by Switzerland and Interpol begins as well. Switzerland is not in the European Union, but Skyhook has its corporate headquarters in Paris and New York, so the EU announces an investigation, too.

Dez enjoys the show the women put on for the media. It won't bring back any of the lives taken. But it will rob the Crays of billions of dollars. And for Dez, that's enough.

For now.

* * *

It takes everyone a while to realize that Dyson Patterson apparently escaped. The authorities look into him and realize that he was never a Canadian; never in the Canadian military. He's an American and a former Delta soldier wanted on two continents for war crimes.

Dez is pretty sure that Patterson rescued Valerie Cray and got her out of town. He has no idea how. But the two of them are in the wind.

# CHAPTER 65

As the last of a train of winter storms plays itself out on the Newfoundland coast, Dez, Petra, the State Department team, and the entire neutrino research team are airlifted to St. John's. But not before Dez rescues his duffel bag, as well as his beloved bass guitar, from the ruined helicopter on the edge of the town's airfield.

With the townies airlifted out, that leaves only the military and the RCMP in charge of the ghost town, the mine, and the research facility.

Within three weeks, Dr. Sophia Araki will publish a paper on the internet explaining how neutrino research facilities could be used to track nuclear submarines. She also will publish the directions for how to scatter the signal from neutrinos and antineutrinos, so that such submarines cannot be tracked.

And within six months, every nuclear submarine on Earth will be equipped with what will become known as an Araki Shield.

The offer to let Dr. William Sato run the largest neutrino research facility in the world, the one owned by China, is rescinded. Sato will return to MIT. And to eating meat.

In a big, sturdy CH-47 Chinook—a tandem-rotor heavy-lift chopper—Dez and Petra sit, Dez with his guitar, tuning it, as Trisha Jean and Rusty move their way. Trisha Jean takes a seat and keeps her voice low. "Ash ain't with us."

"This is her play," Dez said. "And based on her saving our lives, I'm inclined to let her play it. Trip Jacks?"

The diplomat ponders it for a bit. "She did save our lives. And she didn't kill anyone under State Department protection. I'm with you. The less said about her, the better."

Once they get to St. John's, everyone gets debriefed by the RCMP, by military police, by American intelligence agencies, and by U.S. State Department personnel. Trisha Jean vouches for Dez.

Dez admits to killing no one at or below Fuchstown. Trisha Jean and Rusty feign ignorance.

Baffled but unsure what else to do, the authorities release Dez from custody.

Dez gets back to the very hotel he stayed at near the St. John's Airport, Tuesday last. He's waiting in line to check in when it dawns on him that he's been without an internet connection for most of a week. He checks his voice mail messages and spots a vaguely familiar name. He gets to his room—a different one this time—and returns the call.

"FBI Special Agent Neal Conway."

"Wotcher. Desmond Limerick, returning your—"

"Oh! Yeah, right. Tom Fairweather's been awaiting your call. Can you hold?"

Dez does, drawing out his beloved, candy-apple-red bass guitar and fiddling with a few chords.

"Mr. Limerick."

"It's Dez to me mates. How's the noggin?"

The leader of the FBI's Hostage Rescue Team says, "I'm on the mend, thank you for asking. Mr. Limerick, I'm told I, once again, owe you a very large debt of gratitude."

"Dunno 'bout that, mate. A handful of brilliant women did most of the heavy lifting. I just did what they told me to do."

"I've spoken to Secretary Jackson. Her version is different. So thank you."

Dez says, "I imagine you've questions?"

"Answers," Fairweather counters. "You'll want to know about Dyson Patterson. We're about eighty percent certain he works for Vincent and Valerie Cray. The secretary tells me Ms. Cray was actually up there. In the company of mercenaries."

"Aye. Was."

"Then Patterson got her out. He was special forces. He's trained in running exfiltrations."

"Figured as much. I'm the only one who saw Valerie Cray. Guess my word wouldn't be enough for an arrest."

"I'm afraid not, no," Fairweather says. "The secretary also filled me in on the Russians, and the iridium deposit. And how you thought there might be a sleeper working for the Crays amid the scientists."

"Do. Ye might want to take a look at Dr. Matteo Bernardi, University of Bologna."

"Why him?"

"One of his degrees is in metallurgy. Doubt any of the other scientists, or the support staff, would recognize iridium if it bit 'em on the arse."

Fairweather doesn't laugh, but Dez can hear the man typing on a keyboard. "That's a sound bit of deduction, Mr. Limerick. May I ask you a question now?"

"'Course."

"I debriefed with Secretary Jackson. The only person she didn't mention was Elisabet LeCroix of the Canadian National Research Council. I'm now informed that there is no Elisabet LeCroix of the Canadian National Research Council. The secretary said she couldn't fill me in any better."

"She was the quiet, petite one, yeah? Didn't interact with her much." Dez subconsciously rubs the ear that Ash kicked.

A beat, then the FBI special agent says, "I'm relatively convinced that you and the secretary are protecting her. And I get the sense I'd be smart to let this drop. So I will."

"You're a good man, Tom."

"I'm also going to tell you something in confidence, Mr. Limerick. This is on a need-to-know basis, and I think you need to know."

"All ears."

"The FBI has been conducting an investigation into Vincent and Valerie Cray, and into Skyhook Technologies. For some time now."

"Aye?"

"You have a knack for making friends *and* enemies. And we believe the Crays are formidable enemies. Vincent's father created Skyhook and ran it until his . . . suspicious death. His son, Vincent, was the only witness when his father fell to his death at a ski resort in the Alps. A board of directors now runs the day-to-day operations of Skyhook. Providing materiél for mining around the world."

"Rumor has it Skyhook cornered the market on mining in failed states."

Fairweather says, "It's more than a rumor, sir. We think their niche market—if you can call it that—is helping warlords and narco dictators extract anything valuable from the ground to prop themselves up."

"Lovely." Dez sets aside the guitar, kneels, and takes a lidded water from the room's minifridge. He cracks it open. Flying dehydrates him.

"Here's the confidential part," Fairweather says. "And I would consider it a personal favor if nobody ever finds out how you know this information."

"Done."

"The Skyhook board, and the Skyhook lawyers and marketing people, have kept Vincent Cray out of several courts and several jails. He's been accused of grand theft, of perjury, of bribing public officials, of hiring armed men to injure or possibly to kill business rivals."

"Sounds about right."

"And, Mr. Limerick, that makes him a paragon of virtue when compared to Valerie Cray. Also born rich, British upper crust, her father in banking, her mother in the fashion industry. Growing up, British MI5 suspects her parents paid considerable amounts to hide their little girl's spates of violence. They have investigated so-far-unconfirmed stories of tortured pets from when she was a tween, and expensive cover-ups of boyfriends who were driven off roads, or driven *over* by their own cars. Even stabbed."

"A ray of sunshine, her. We met. Lovely woman, with all the charm of diphtheria. Question, then: How in the world have these fuckwits not driven themselves out of business?"

"That's the Skyhook board of directors. They have two jobs: to make a profit any way they can, and to keep the Crays out of the headlines. Which may be a full-time job."

"Nice work if ye can get it."

"As for Valerie Cray, I asked friends in the U.S. Intelligence

Community to run a psych profile on her. I've seen the report. She presents with significant psychopathy. Worse yet, she's got a genius-level IQ. She's smart and sadistic. And from what I've been told you were up to in Newfoundland, you just made her angry, sir."

Dez sips his water, sits on the bed. He shrugs. "Can't run an' hide from a person who's rich, smart, and demented, yeah? Best to confront 'em."

Special Agent Fairweather says, "If I were talking to anyone else, I'd warn them not to take that route. But then, I'm not talking to anyone else."

"Ta." Dez accepts the somewhat byzantine compliment.

"I'm sending you a packet of information. We know where they are right now. They're in St. John's, too. We also know about their holdings, and their corporate offices in New York and Paris."

"Ta, mate. I owe ye one."

And with that, Dez gets a small, brief, dry chuckle from the special agent. Which is all that he could hope for.

"Mr. Limerick, as far as I'm concerned, the Federal Bureau of Investigation is not even close to catching up to what we owe you."

# CHAPTER 66

Valerie Cray swings wide and clips Dyson Patterson in the face.

He spins away, feeling blood flowing.

Vincent Cray grabs his wife around her waist and lifts her physically off the floor, dragging her away from the man who used a snowmobile to rescue her and to escape arrest or death in Fuchstown, getting her to the house they bought in St. John's.

*"You had our iridium! You had it! You had it!"* she screams.

"But I got your crazy ass out!" he shouts back.

If Patterson expects to be rebuked by Vincent, he's surprised just to get a smile.

Patterson puts his palm to his face and pulls it back. He's got three bleeding gashes on his cheek.

Blood drips from Valerie's nails. She struggles in her husband's grip, her sneakers off the floor.

"Hey! *Hey!*" Vincent shakes her like a maraca.

She tries to free herself but he's pinioned her arms. She tries to bite him. She kicks at his shins.

Vincent laughs. Still holding her as she thrashes, he nods to Patterson. "Go get lost, will you? And put some Neosporin on that. You'll find some in my toiletry kit."

Patterson says, "You sure I don't need antivenom?"

*"Fucking useless cocksucking son of a whore . . . !"*

Vincent laughs. "Honey? Chill."

Thirty minutes later, Dyson Patterson is sitting on the side of a bed, his bare feet on the floor, holding a hand mirror and studying the three long scratches on his left cheek. They aren't deep, and they stopped bleeding pretty quickly.

He's naked. He's cold and fatigued. He grew tired of playing the humble, stoner doctor for those State Department idiots. He grew tired from Aiyden Finn firing indiscriminately into the igloo, knowing his ally was in there. He grew tired of the Fuchstown yokels. And now, he's growing increasingly tired of Valerie Cray.

Vincent Cray kneels on the bed, leans forward, and kisses Patterson's tight-as-a-tick trapezius muscle.

"Your wife's insane."

Vincent kisses his deltoid muscle; he can feel the muscle twitch. He laughs. "Her insanity is a feature, not a bug."

Patterson half turns, studying the naked man behind him. "She's dangerous."

"She's fun. She's unpredictable. Yes, she's batshit crazy. She's also very good in bed. Hey, nobody said marriage is easy."

Patterson gives him a half smile. "You know, she might not be the craziest person of your relationship."

"She'll be all right," Vincent says, and pulls Patterson down onto his back. "I've got news for you: She's already moved on from you to this Desmond Limerick guy. She met him, you know. Tried to seduce him."

"Limerick told me, yeah."

Vincent smiles in the dark and straddles him. "Poor Limerick. My honeybunch just made him her new pet project."

# CHAPTER 67

Dez is starving. He opens his hotel room door and looks down. Ash stands there, now in a black leather biker jacket, leggings, and clunky boots. She looks like an anime character.

He has no idea how she got from Fuchstown to St. John's. Maybe she stowed away aboard the Chinook. She's small enough, it's possible.

"You've made an enemy of these people, the Crays."

Dez laughs. "An' you're the second friend in as many minutes to tell me that! Come on in."

Ash stiffens a little, shocked by the word "friend."

"Thought you'd done a bunk. Did you get t'say farewell an' adieu to your mum?"

Ash looks his way. "I came to save her. We don't know each other anymore. Maybe we never did."

Dez is no family psychologist; he lets that one glide by without swinging. "Tell me 'bout them fuckers, the Tontine."

"The Tontine is . . . difficult to describe. They're gentlemanly. Quaint. They have a moral code of sorts."

"They're feckin' tossers."

She gives him that pop-on-pop-off smile. She's not a woman who smiles often, so it's gratifying. "Yes. But more: They follow an orderly system. They are the guardians of the status quo. You're an X factor. If I were to give you to the Crays, I might be able to buy my way back into the Tontine's good graces."

Dez nods. "Thought much the same. Could work."

Her already-large eyes go wide. "You don't object to my suggesting it?"

"Sound strategy, if I'm bein' honest."

She studies him. He waits.

"If there was profit to be had in double-crossing the Crays, that, too, could buy me their goodwill."

"Then you'd be an assassin again."

"My debt would be paid off in three years. And I'd be alive."

"The Crays will come gunnin' for me, or so says a trusted ally. An' me oul mate Rafik, whom ye met briefly in Paris, he used to remind me that the best defense is a good offense."

Ash says, "You are going after the Crays."

"Dunno how. Also don't see a good alternative."

"I will help."

"It's help I'll accept. Question: Can you contact the Tontine? Tell them I want to parlay?"

She thinks about it. She maintains eye contact. He can practically hear the gears whirling in her head.

"Why would you do that?"

"'Cause I can't do naught about 'em until I know who they are."

Ash studies him. "Earlier, you called me your friend."

"Did I? Suppose so."

She is quiet and still. A few beats, then she says, "Would you sleep with me?"

Dez barks a laugh. "I'm plannin' to sleep with Petra Alexandris, if the gods are willing. Also, you're a decade me junior, love. That's an insurmountable obstacle."

Ash says, deadpan, "I could mount it."

Dez laughs hard, wipes tears from the corners of his eyes. "That might well be the greatest double entendre in the history o' the English-speaking peoples! Come along, love. I'm starvin.' An' I'm buying."

Down in the hotel lobby, Ash disappears in the blink of an eye, and now Dez sees why. She spotted Trisha Jean Jackson and Rusty Townsend checking out.

Dez ambles their way.

Trisha Jean throws a bear hug around his shoulders. Rusty shakes his hand.

"The RCMP cleared us for departure," she says. "We're heading to New York. There's a seat on the plane if you want to come along."

"Ta, but I think maybe I'll stay a bit. Never got to see any of St. John's, what with the storm an' all."

Rusty peers at him. "You might've made an enemy or two. Or, you know, thirty. You sure you wanna stay?"

"I'll be fine, mate. Get back to your wife. Tell her she married a very, very good bodyguard."

They shake again. The diplomat and the Secret Service agent gather their bags and head to the door.

"Trip Jacks?" Dez calls out. "Try not to fleece anyone on the ride home."

She reaches into her coat pocket and produces a pack of Bicycle Playing Cards. She winks at him, and they leave.

★ ★ ★

Dez rolls into the dining room and is surprised to find Ash sitting at a table in the corner with Petra Alexandris. He joins them.

He and Petra kiss. He sits. She says, "I have a theory that you're contemplating doing something very dumb."

"That's only because ye know me so well."

"I ordered you a stout."

"See?"

His beer comes. Also, a vodka martini for Petra and water for Ash.

When the waiter takes their food order and leaves, Dez says, "The loony couple behind all this? There's a chance they want me head on a pike."

Petra says, "I've never met anyone who makes friends as easily as you do, and I've never met anyone who makes enemies as easily as you do. Usually, you make the right sort of both."

"Might have to take matters into me own hands. Which means I want you well gone before the balloon goes up."

Petra lays a hand atop his. "My presence here would reduce the number of chess moves available to you. You can't protect me and go on offense. I understand."

"Knew you would, love. Problem is, I don't even have a play in me head yet. Just know I can't do naught."

Petra sips and thinks. Ash seems to be watching her. Studying her.

"We hurt the Crays financially by stopping them from stealing the iridium, or laying claim to it. They're facing criminal investigations in the Americas and in Europe. Are you sure they're not going to disappear until this is over? They have the money to do it. Anywhere in the world."

Dez shrugs. "I know next t'nothing, which is how I am with most things. A mate of mine in the FBI says they won't take losing well. Says they'll want to come after me. Don't plan to wait around and find out."

Petra turns to the quiet girl by his side. “And you?”

Ash studies the room.

She speaks just above a whisper. “Limerick is not comfortable killing people. He might need someone who is.”

# CHAPTER 68

Dez sees Petra off at the St. John's Airport. One of the Triton Expediters' private jets awaits her. They kiss and embrace on the public side of security.

"I owe you. Again."

"You mean for the fabulous sex?"

Petra laughs and punches his shoulder. "I already miss you."

"An' are ye going to be all right? Running Triton again?"

Petra kisses him again. "I might be through running Triton the way my father did. I think it's time to run it my way."

He watches as she moves through security.

Then he heads back to the airport parking lot. The information that Special Agent Tom Fairweather sent Dez includes a mobile number for Vincent Cray. Sitting in a rental Jeep, Dez calls the number.

It goes to voice mail.

"'Allo. Desmond Limerick here. Ye don't know me, but I thought we might want to parlay before—"

He hears a click.

"Well, well, well."

"An' you'd be Vincent Cray, then. How's with you, my son?"

The man on the line pauses. "You interfered with our work, Mr. Limerick. You dealt us a significant setback. How do you think I'm doing?"

Oddly, Cray does not sound angry. Dez would go with . . . bemused?

"It's Dez to me friends. Let's be honest, mate. You sent that lot to New York to bribe me. You sent them idjits to the St. John's hotel with guns aplenty. And yes, I'm stayin' at that same hotel again, just in case ye was wondering."

"That's helpful, Dez. Thank you for telling me where you are. And you're right: I'm Vincent."

"The pleasure's mine."

"Why did you call?"

"Thought maybe we could get a drink. Talk things over."

Now Dez is sure there's bemusement in the man's voice. "A drink."

"Like gentlemen, aye."

The man chuckles. "Do you really think you can talk your way out of this?"

"Well, dunno what *this* is, exactly. Somewhere between an imbroglio and a contretemps? A *mishigas*, p'raps?"

"Son of a bitch. Now I really do want to have a drink with you. Care to come to the place we're staying? It's—"

"Know where it is. I think gatherin' in public might be more conducive to me long-term health. Also, your wife tried t'shoot me. Quite recently, it was. Shockin' as hell."

Vincent says, "Yeah, she does that. I spotted a bar just off the harbor and about a block from that big Anglican cathedral." He names the place.

"I can find it, aye. When?"

"How about in thirty minutes?"

"Done. See you soon, squire."

Dez disconnects and looks at Ash, sitting in the shotgun position. They go online and find the bar.

Dez is expecting a double cross, and he's expecting that the Crays won't anticipate Ash's presence. She's in the Jeep, keeping watch. So he's more than mildly surprised when Vincent Cray walks into the tavern alone.

Special Agent Fairweather sent photos of the man, along with the FBI investigation notes.

Vincent Cray is tall and appears athletic. Handsome, early fifties, with graying hair clipped short and a strong jaw. He's wearing a well-lived-in bomber jacket and jeans and scruffy boots. You'd never know he is copresident of a company worth billions with operations on five continents.

Dez picked a booth well away from everyone else. The tavern is dark and fairly quiet, the floors warped old wood, the bar itself burnished redwood. Dez liked it straightaway. He asked for a bottle of Irish whiskey and two shot glasses, and he sits facing the door.

Vincent Cray spots him, shakes his head, smiling. He walks over and sits.

Dez offers a massive hand across the table. Vincent takes it.

"Dez. You've got nuts the size of bowling balls."

Dez cracks open the bottle. "If I'm being honest, 'twas fairly cold up north. Everything shrinks, if ye get me meaning."

Vincent laughs. He produces a pack of cigarettes and a small box of wooden matches. He lights up.

Dez pours into both shot glasses. Vincent picks his up. "Your health."

"An' yours, squire."

They drink. Vincent's one of those guys who can hold a drinks glass and a cigarette deftly in one hand.

Vincent sighs. "Hey. That is nice. Irish?"

"Is."

"You cost us many, many billions of dollars, Dez. Billion with a B. That's . . . substantial."

Dez sits sideways on his side of the booth, one boot up on the well-worn wooden seat. "You sent mercenaries to practically kill an entire village. You sent your lad Finn with a feckin' gunship. Your charming wife went all Queen of Hearts on me. 'Off with his head!' You infiltrated the townies, and the State Department team, an' even the boffins in the neutrino facility."

Vincent reacts, but just a little. His poker face isn't perfect. He didn't know that Dez knew about the third mole. "What's your point?"

"That you had every opportunity to win, an' you didn't. An' you believe that's my fault?"

"My wife does." Vincent reaches for the bottle and pours for them both.

"Mad at me, is she?"

"You could say that. Twice she's met you. Twice she's walked away empty-handed."

"She's an interesting sort, your wife. President of the garden club, I'd imagine. Friends of the Library."

Vincent sips his whiskey, smiles. "On the other hand, an investigator for one of our law firms says you might—*might*—be fucking Petra Alexandris. *That* would be a get. To you, sir."

He holds up his glass. Dez feels anger boil up but he keeps his face neutral. He does not toast.

"No comment? No bragging?"

Dez sips.

Vincent shrugs and drains his shot glass. "You know, turning down Valerie is going to be one of those regrets you pine over on your death bed. She's . . . unbelievable. Not that many guys say no to fucking Valerie."

"Took all me manly willpower to resist."

Vincent smiles. "How about me, Dez? Would an offer to fuck me get a yes?"

"Not highly likely, no. And meanin' no offense, 'course. You're a fine specimen of a man, you are."

"Thank you. So you're saying our failure in Fuchstown was of our own doing. That . . . what? We didn't try hard enough?"

"Skyhook's worth loads. Early on, before all the skullduggery, if ye'd used a pittance of your wealth to flood the area with lawyers, likely could've made the case that the iridium belonged to yez. Might've been a peaceable way to reach your goals."

"That probably would have meant sharing the iridium," he says. "We're not big on sharing."

"So you chose to kill all them people, to sabotage the facility, to lie, cheat, an' steal."

Vincent Cray says, with strange gusto, "You bet!"

Dez sips. "Ah, but that's fine whiskey, that."

"Good stuff."

They sit for a bit. Vincent rattles his box of matches in his hand.

"Don't understand the math of it," Dez says. "You find the largest iridium site in generations, an' you rejoice. Problem is: If ye try to sell that much of the stuff, the price would plummet, yeah? Makes no sense."

Vincent smiles. "In business, you don't always make a profit by selling. Sometimes, you make it by not selling. Like, for instance, iridium. It's used in high-temperature applications, electrical contacts, in catalysts and cancer treatment. It's used in spark plugs, especially for electrical vehicles. So what if I offered to give the U.S. auto industry as much iridium as it wants, for free? Their cars suddenly get cheaper, and they flood the market. Or vice versa. Give the iridium to China, let them win."

"Or give it to neither for a hefty . . . ah, how would ye say it? A status quo dividend?"

Vincent smiles big and points to Dez. "Exactly. We could display a massive chunk of iridium in the lobby of our New York or Paris headquarters, and everybody who looks at it would wonder if we're about to drop a guillotine on their production of vehicles. We could be the arbiter of the entire market of EV cars. Or of a dozen other high-tech sectors of the economy. That's not money, Limerick. That's influence. That's power."

"If you say so." Dez sips his drink.

"Now let me ask you one: So what'd those Russians want with the mine? Or was it the scientists?"

"Don't think we'll ever know," Dez lies. "My turn: Why put your HQ in New York and Paris?"

Vincent looks like he has a foul taste in his mouth. "The board acquired both buildings in a hostile takeover. Can't stand either of them. Haven't stepped foot in them for, I don't know, years. Valerie and I have our own headquarters. You'll see it soon."

Dez doesn't know what that means. "I assume, where your lady wife is involved, the modifier 'hostile' proceeds everything."

Vincent laughs.

"And will the two of you be coming after me for revenge, then?"

Vincent says, "Yes. We pretty much have to, from our perspective."

"Rich people never *have* to do nothing, mate."

Vincent laughs. "More money, more problems."

"Likely true, that. An' I can't talk ye into a truce?"

Vincent shakes his head.

Dez drains his glass, then refills Vincent's, then caps the bottle and stands.

"I find it a pleasure to talk to a man who's honest an' straightforward. Know where I stand now, don't I? Rare thing, that."

"Wish you'd taken the bribe, Dez. Wish you'd fucked Valerie."

Dez grins. "Bein' your enemy probably is less risky than being her lover."

Vincent laughs. "True, true."

"Ta, squire. The bottle's paid for, so sit and enjoy it."

Vincent smiles up at him. "We'll see you soon."

Dez ambles out of the tavern.

So now it's war.

Dyson Patterson sends two men to the airport hotel to do a reconnaissance. They spot no U.S. or Canadian law enforcement waiting to pounce. Nothing appears to be amiss.

They bribe a clerk in registration and find out what room Limerick is staying in.

Patterson himself comes this time, and with just two men. Aiyden Finn brought four guys to this very hotel to take Limerick out before the trip to Fuchstown. They failed. Well, Finn's now lying in a Newfoundland morgue somewhere and Dyson Patterson isn't, so that suggests who was the better soldier. Or at least the smarter one.

In the corridor outside Limerick's room, Patterson stations one man at the elevators and one man at the fire stairs. Patterson raps three times on the door, then draws his gun. He can see light through the peephole in the door. The moment that goes dark, he'll fire through the wood.

The peephole doesn't go dark.

Patterson gestures to one of his guys, who hurries over, takes a knee, ands runs a bypass on the door lock.

That man throws open the door.

Patterson enters first, gun leading. He checks the main room. Nothing. One of his guys checks the bathroom. One checks the little clothes closet that features five empty hangers, an upright ironing board, and an iron.

Patterson checks under the bed.

The room's phone rings. Patterson and his guys turn to it. It keeps ringing.

Patterson suddenly knows who it is. He picks it up. "Fuck you."

Dez says, "When it comes—an' the bullet's coming, Dyson, my lad—when it comes, 'twill be for Inspector Frank Watts of the RCMP. For a brilliant pilot name of Cora Charbonneau. And for Tulsa, her copilot."

"Yeah, then—"

Dez hangs up.

# CHAPTER 69

With the storms over, Vincent and Valerie Cray and their staff begin the process of moving all of their belongings out of the old house in St. John's and back into their headquarters.

Dez rented a Jeep and followed one of the cars at a safe distance. Now he stands at Battery Lookout with binoculars, overseeing St. John's Harbour. He whistles, high-low, then hands the glasses to Ash.

"Will ye look at that, then."

She lifts the glasses and peers at the superyacht in the harbor, and the tender boats moving back and forth between it and the Crays' party on the docks.

"That is a very large boat."

"That ain't an aircraft carrier, love, but it's fecking close."

They head to a coffee shop called the Percolator. Dez looks up the Crays' superyacht. "That wee beastie out there is *Le Grand Requin*

*Blanc.* The Great White Shark. Damn near a hundred meters stem to stern, and eighteen thousand gross tonnage. Can take fifty-plus passengers and a crew of thirty-six. Top speed of twenty-one knots. Has its own helicopter and helipad, its own minisub and a moon pool. Jay-sus, but that's one hell of a battle cruiser."

He hands his tablet computer to Ash, who scrolls through the web page. She looks up at Dez with her enormous eyes.

"If you owned such a thing," Ash whispers, "you would feel safe aboard her. *Oui?*"

Dez begins to grin. "Now that you mention it, suppose you would."

A waitress heads their way with a coffeepot, one of those globe-shaped things from the 1960s. She refills Dez's coffee and asks if Ash wants more water. "Either of you named Limerick?"

Dez glances around to see if he can spot trouble. "I am."

"There's a phone call for you. We don't usually let customers take calls here. The guy said it was a matter of life and death."

She leads them to a landline phone mounted on a wall in the coffee shop's tiny and airless kitchen. The phone dangles from its cord, spinning a little. Dez retrieves it. Ash stands close enough to listen. She has her hand on her gun, holstered to her belt under her biker jacket.

The man on the call sounds British and upper crust. "Good afternoon. Do I have the honor of addressing Desmond Aloysius Limerick?"

"That would be me, aye."

"Sir, we know about the incidents that recently unfolded in Newfoundland and Labrador. And we have been told that you wish to . . . parlay."

Ash mouths the word *Tontine.*

"That's right."

"We have confirmed both your attendance and that of several representatives of Mr. and Mrs. Cray. And, we suspect, one other."

"I know her as Ash. Others as Asha Araki. Aye, she was there."

"Intriguing. The woman to whom you refer has, of late, been absent from her post. A most disturbing set of circumstances."

"I should think so."

"When one conducts business, one expects their employees to be where they are needed, when they are needed. We are loath to suggest disciplinary procedures. Yet sometimes one must."

Dez finds himself enjoying the oddly prim banter. "One might quibble with the designation 'employee.'"

"A distinction worthy of reconsideration, yes. What do you know of our, ah, endeavor?"

"Next to nothing. Nor, bein' honest, do I wish to. My own past has been described on occasion as opaque. It would be rude of me to pry into the inner workings of your organization."

"Yes," the man drawls. "Your past is well shrouded, sir. We assume someone in the upper echelons of the British clandestine services owed you a rather large favor."

"Something o' the kind, aye."

"Very good, Mr. Limerick. Very good. Yes. We would be amenable to a meeting."

"Splendid! Do you mind waiting a few days? I've a few people in need of being killed."

The voice says, "A limousine is pulling into the parking lot of the Percolator, even as we speak. I'm afraid it's now or never, sir.

"Oh, and Ms. Araki, who is standing to your left, can wait for you at your booth. The second one from the end."

Dez steps out of the quaint coffee shop and spots the shiny black limousine. A driver in a black suit and peaked cap stands next to it, his gloved hands crossed in front of him.

The Tontine has been running surveillance on Ash. And on himself. And he hasn't even realized it.

Dez crosses to the perfectly waxed car. The driver sounds British. "May I have your mobile, sir?"

Dez hands it over.

The driver opens the left rear door. Dez climbs in.

The limo is large enough that three people could sit facing forward, and three people could sit facing backward. He spots a small, compact, but complete wet bar.

A gentleman waits for him in a somber suit. The man might well stand six-four, Dez guesses. He's possibly in his late seventies or early eighties, exceedingly thin, with swept-back white hair and quite a thick mat of it. He's deathly pale, with cornflower-blue eyes. The scarecrow sits facing forward so Dez takes a seat opposite him.

His host gestures to a cut crystal bottle at the bar to his right; to Dez's left. "This is a 1925 Grande Champagne Cognac. One of the best I have ever tried. May I?"

He sounds very Eton and very, very Cambridge. "I'll have a splash. Ta."

The man pours for them both. He holds his glass, palm up, and swirls it. His hand is enormous; as large as Dez's, the skin almost translucent.

"It was very good of you to come on such short notice, Mr. Limerick."

"Dez to me friends."

Dez sniffs the cognac. Tastes it. It's superb. "I've never had better."

The old man swirls his drink. "Most of my taste buds died in the nineteen-seventies. This could be petrol for all I know."

Dez grins.

"This vehicle is swept for listening devices," the old man says. "We may speak freely in here."

"Fine, then. What's the goin' price for Ash's head?"

The scarecrow sips his cognac. He smiles, which makes him

look more cadaverous, not more cheerful. "All life is precious. One does recoil from putting an actual monetary value on the life of anyone made in His image."

"You trained an assassin."

"And quite a good one, thank you." The man dips his head, accepting Dez's comment as a compliment. "We were disappointed in her decision to vacate her position in Paris without so much as a 'by your leave.' Young people can be impetuous."

"But ye do plan to kill her for it."

The old man winces, as if finding the violent verb offensive. "Ye-es. Yes, I suppose that is the prudent option."

"An' I'm asking: What would it fecking take to stop that from happening? Hmm?" Dez asks, then sips his cognac.

The old man smiles again. "I've always envied those who can swear in daily conversation. My mother passed many decades ago, and I can still feel the rap on my knuckles when I even contemplate it."

Dez has hoped his swearing would unnerve the old bugger. The guy's sangfroid seems impenetrable.

"My goal herein is t'save Ash's life. I want her out of her contract. Immediately."

The gaunt man nods, pondering this. He crosses his legs at the knee, adjusts the crease in his trousers. There is more than enough leg room between them for this. His suit has a fine chalk pinstripe on the deepest of blue.

The moment lingers.

"Would you be willing to replace her?"

Dez barks a quick laugh. "No feckin' way. See, I think bein' an assassin's a bad thing. I think *ownin'* an assassin's a bad thing. Having me, or someone else, take her place, well, that's the moral equivalent of doing naught. Innit?"

"I quite see your dilemma. And while I am loath to put a

numerical value on a human life, I also cannot say that the young woman in question is without monetary value. She is an asset that is worth something to us. Partly because of the two years of training in which we invested in her. And partly because she is terribly, terribly good at what she does. Even if she wishes it otherwise."

Dez sips his drink. "So we're back to talking filthy lucre, which is a language I understand, mate."

The man is silent for a while. He swirls his drink in his upturned palm. His pendant shoe does not bob. He stares at the limo's fine carpet.

Then he looks up. "You say you don't know anything about the Tontine."

"Not a bleeding thing."

"We have been around for quite a long while. Winston Churchill was a member of this organization, as was Joachim von Ribbentrop."

Dez barks a laugh. It echoes in the limo. "Churchill and a Nazi officer! Not bloody likely, mate!"

"Quite correct," the old man says with supernal calm. "One man fought with all his might for king and country. One man fought with all his might for the Third Reich. They were implacable enemies. But they found, from time to time, that their needs aligned. And on those quite rare occasions, 'discretion' was the watchword of the day. Both men were capable of putting aside their obvious differences to achieve . . . quiet goals."

"That sounds like twenty pounds of zebra shit in a ten-pound bin, mate. But for now, let's say you lot really are that old. And that connected. What's it to do with Ash and our situation today?"

The man doesn't directly respond. "The young woman in question has told you how she came to our attention? The problem we solved for her? Her subsequent contract and training?"

Dez nods.

"What you do not know is that we've done the same for many,

many generations. When we quietly need an assassin, we train one. When we need a thief, or a spy, or a saboteur, or a seducer, then we train them and deploy them. All for the goal of . . . world stability."

"Stability for rich, white blokes."

The old man sips his cognac and provides that death's-head smile again. "Well, yes. Quite."

"An' when these indentured servants are done serving, they're killed."

"Oh, no. They're paid handsomely and told that if they ever speak a word of the Tontine, they *will* be killed. Along with their loved ones. When the young woman is in the final days of her contract, she will meet others who have moved through our ranks and who now are free to do as they wish. She also will be shown documentation of those who disobeyed our covenants, and who paid the ultimate price for their lack of discretion. Had she not . . . *strayed*, let us say. If she had not strayed, she would have been free to do that which she wished in only a few years' time, and with a sizable stipend for the rest of her life."

"We're travelin' in circles, mate. This conversation's right back where it started, innit. What's it take to spare Ash's life?"

The old man shows a hint of embarrassment. "Good lord. In my old age, I have become something of a chatterbox, haven't I? The point I was attempting to make—and doing so poorly—was that the Tontine seeks world stability."

Dez waits.

"The actions of Mr. and Mrs. Cray—quite specifically in what Western leaders refer to as 'failed states'—do not lend themselves to stability. Those two people controlling a majority of the world's iridium does not lend itself to stability."

And Dez's smile grows. "You saying: I take out Skyhook, an' their third-world, narco-state, man-who-would-be-king shenanigans, I could buy out the last three years of Ash's contract."

"I am saying we would be inclined to lift the sanctions upon the young lady."

"Not good enough. I want her contract ripped up. I want her free."

The old man nods. "And have you, perchance, asked the young lady if that is her wish as well?"

Dez pauses.

And the answer is, in fact, no. He has assumed Ash wanted to stop being an assassin. But he hasn't exactly asked her.

"The offer stands, sir. If the Crays were to meet some sort of untimely end, we would be amenable to lifting all sanctions against the young woman about whom we speak. Take the offer to her. See how she responds. What say you, sir?"

Dez waits a moment. He gulps down the rest of his booze, sets the glass aside, and offers his hand.

The old man sets down his drink as well, and they shake. His grip is powerless, his skin like parchment. Dez doesn't dare squeeze hard or the old man's entire arm likely will fall off like a flower petal.

"Done."

"And might one inquire, Mr. Limerick: Do you have a plan to stop the Crays? Knowing they want you dead, and that they have a veritable army at their disposal."

Dez beams. "Haven't the foggiest feckin' clue how to start. Something'll come to me. Usually does."

The old man chuckles. "Quite."

He doesn't press a button or raise his voice, but the driver opens Dez's door for him. Dez steps out. The driver closes the door and touches the brim of his hat with his gloved hand. He hands Dez his mobile.

"Sir."

Then climbs in behind the wheel and starts the purring engine.

## ABOARD *THE GREAT WHITE SHARK*

Vincent Cray spots Dyson Patterson in the forward lounge of the third of five decks, watching the onboarding of the Crays' household equipment and personnel. Patterson turns to him and says, "Okay with you if I increase the security on board this thing?"

"They'd better be good."

Patterson says, "There's an outfit I've used before. Occidental Ventures. They're expensive but good."

"And they can be counted on for discretion?"

"Occidental Ventures is known in the field as Occasional Vultures. One of the guys I know has a tattoo across his back that reads 'shoot, shovel, shut up.'"

Vincent smiles. "I like it. Make the call. As many guys as you can get. Money's no object."

# CHAPTER 70

Dez has squirreled away quite a bit of money. Some from his military days; some he stole from a corrupt and powerful woman he met in Portland, Oregon. He has enough to buy a Zodiac and two sets of scuba gear; one from the children's section of a sporting goods store, because none of the grown-up ones would fit Ash.

A little after midnight, they paddle out to the *Le Grand Requin Blanc*, with its flying bridge, its five living decks above water, and its helipad and helicopter. "I've lived in smaller towns," Dez whispers as they paddle nearer.

The superyacht grows larger. A couple of times, Dez notes guards walking the main deck. Nobody has spotted their black inflatable boat or their black scuba gear.

"A question I've been meaning t'ask. The old bloke from the Tontine offered to drop the death contract on you. I said I wanted that, but also to end your contract early. And the geezer asked me if I'd discussed this with you."

They paddle softly. The storms are gone but not the cloud covering.

"I need to think about this."

Dez shrugs. "You could stop being a killer, love."

"Yes," she whispers. "And then become . . . what?"

"Whatever ye'd like."

They paddle.

"I need to think about this."

Well, that's as good as Dez is likely to get tonight. They draw closer to the sea behemoth.

"We have only my gun," Ash whispers.

"If we need 'em, we'll find plenty aboard this tub. Can I ask ye another question before we do this?"

*"Oui."*

"Your mum is back at CERN. In Switzerland. I checked. Could take ye. Give ye a chance to talk without all them guns waving about."

She is silent a bit. They paddle. She whispers, "I felt it necessary to save my mother's life. But the daughter she had no longer exists. I am not that girl. I'd prefer she never finds that out."

That's the last time Dez asks.

"How does a moon pool work?" she asks.

"It's a hole in the bottom of the boat. Divers and submersibles can come and go safely. Also, with subterfuge."

"Why does a hole in the bottom of the boat not sink the boat?"

"They maintain a stable, air-filled space that prevents water from flooding the chamber. In a submarine, ye'd do that by pumping air into the chamber. On a boat like this, it means the chamber's ceiling is high enough to stay above the waterline."

"And we'll be able to dive under the boat and simply swim up through the moon pool?"

Dez says, "Wanna find out?"

# CHAPTER 71

The helipad aboard *Le Grand Requin Blanc* is large enough that two commercial helicopters can occupy the space. But not if one of them is a Chinook heavy lift. For that flying monster to settle in, the Crays' personal helicopter has to fly out to the St. John's Airport and wait.

Vincent and Valerie Cray are on the helipad with Dyson Patterson as the Chinook's big starboard side door glides open. The man who steps out is Black and very dark-skinned. He is built like a soldier and moves like a soldier. He approaches Patterson, and they shake.

Patterson does the introductions. "Chike Ibrahim of Occidental Ventures, this is Vincent Cray and Valerie Cray."

The Nigerian shakes their hands and gives each a quick head nod.

"I have twenty-five men with me, as requested," he tells Vincent.

"Enough to defend this ship?"

"Enough to defend Cairo, if it came to that, sir. My men are as good as you will find." His voice is low and musical, his pate shaved and with a goatee. "I am told the threat primarily is from one man?"

Valerie's eyes flare. "He's beaten the men who came before Dyson. He's smart. He has military training. He's good with technology."

Chike Ibrahim looks around the base deck of the impossibly big yacht, with its five residential decks stretching upward, then its flying bridge, then its four radomes. "Well, possibly not this good, eh? You are in safe hands."

Vincent says, "We're sailing for France. The only place we're vulnerable is here in the harbor. Once we put to sea, we might not need all twenty-five of your guys."

"I agree. When do you sail?"

Vincent checks his watch. Ibrahim's men are debarking the helicopter, bringing with them their automatic rifles and ballistic vests. Four of the men carry a long and apparently heavy wooden crate. "We haul anchor in a couple of hours."

"Very well. What more can you tell me about this man?"

Patterson says, "Put together like, well, like you, only shorter. British, or maybe Irish. I'm not sure. The U.S. State Department brought him along because he's good with doors. He's the reason they, and I, even got into that mine I told you about."

"He is here in St. John's?"

Vincent says, "Yeah."

"And . . ." He pauses, turns back to Patterson. "What do you mean, 'good with doors'?"

"He's like a picklock. Some kind of breaking-and-entering expert. I watched him rewire controls to an elevator I know for sure my predecessor eighty-sixed. He—"

Chike Ibrahim raises his right sleeve and points to his own forearm. "Does he have a tattoo? Of a two-faced god?"

Patterson feels his hackles rise. "Yeah. He does."

The Nigerian soldier draws a small radio and activates it. He speaks in a foreign language. Igbo, although neither of the Crays nor Patterson recognize it as such.

But all three can tell he is issuing orders.

He returns his radio to a belt holster. Valerie says, "What? What did you recognize?"

"Your Mr. Limerick is a gatekeeper. We have dealt with his kind on few occasions. There is virtually no door that man cannot go through."

The Crays exchange surprised looks.

Ibrahim says, "I have studied your great ship. You have a moon pool, yes?"

Valerie says, "Yes. But—"

He draws his radio again. "We will secure it at once."

Vincent smiles. "What, you think that sawed-off asshole just swam out here and climbed on board my ship via the fucking moon pool?"

Chike Ibrahim says, quite simply, "Of course."

Unaware that Dez and Ash did just that, but nearly four hours earlier. And have been on board ever since.

As the superyacht begins moving out of the harbor, Dyson Patterson heads to his quarters to catch some sack time. He's glad his old friend Chike Ibrahim is here to take command of vessel security. It's good to have allies.

He steps into his quarters, drops his holstered gun and his phone and wallet on a side table, whisks off his sweater and undershirt, and washes his face and neck in very cold water. He wants to stay awake until *Le Grand Requin Blanc* is at sea.

He returns to the main room of his living quarters to see if he needs to order more coffee packets from room service.

Dez Limerick stands by the porthole, looking out at the night.

"Hallo, Doc. Wotcher?"

Patterson glances at the side table, absent his gun, phone, and wallet. He looks the other way and spots the small young woman with ice-white hair, whom he hasn't seen since the mines. The faux Elisabet LeCroix, or Ash. She holds an automatic with a sound suppressor.

"Fuck," he exhales.

"Dyson, me oul' darling. I'm no expert, but I believe you broke the Hippocratic oath in Canada."

Patterson holds his hands out to his sides, palms forward. "How'd you get on board?"

"Quite easily, come to find out. Look, let's not play silly buggers, yeah? You done Inspector Watts and them two air-rescue pilots. Should kill ye for that alone."

"And you killed Joel de Brienne, Aiyden Finn, and . . ." Patterson laughs softly. "Dude, I honestly lost track of how many Russians and mercs you killed. Don't you think it's a little late for either of us to take the moral high ground?"

"You betrayed people, my son, not I. But, if you give us a few straight answers about this glorious tugboat, and if you get me onboard the flying bridge, I'd be willin' to let bygones be bygones."

Patterson says, "Bullshit. You want revenge."

"You was military, I'm told. Me, too. Revenge is a mug's game. I fight for tactical or strategic advantages. I fight in cold blood."

Patterson gestures over his shoulder to the petite woman with the gun. "She doesn't."

"That's where you're wrong. She kills in blood far, far colder'n anything you or me could produce."

Ash emotes nothing.

Patterson gives Dez a shrug and his lopsided stoner smile. "Then I believe you. Soldier to soldier. The Crays have about six new guards. Just arrived. Rent-a-cop types. But screw you if you think you can get onto the bridge. I don't have access, ace."

Dez says, "See? A man who understands that taking care of number one is the best any of us can do."

"I was Delta. We were good, but we were never suicidal. And I walk away?"

Dez grimaces. "Well, ye would, aye. Except, we was watching when a great deal more'n six rent-a-cops arrived via the Chinook. And the lad in charge? That's Chike Ibrahim! A top man in a mercenary firm me old unit used to run into from time t'time. Occasional Vultures. Which means ye lied to us about—"

Patterson hops backward, lands on one foot, and kicks Ash in the gut.

She fires, but only after the blow lands. Her bullet thuds into the ceiling of Patterson's quarters.

Patterson moves quickly into Dez's space. He throws several blows and kicks, a fast-fast combo. Dez blocks them, backing up. He doesn't have much backing-up room.

When Dez's heels hit the wall, he's expecting Patterson to advance. So Patterson changes up and spins back to Ash. She's doubled over from that kick to her gut. Patterson's on her in an instant, grabbing a fistful of her white-blond hair, yanking her head back, her throat bared. He superimposes his much larger hand on her tiny one and wrenches the silenced gun out of her grip.

"Ah ah ah," he says as Dez approaches.

"That was a mistake, lad."

"Think so?"

And Ash jams her butterfly knife into the underside of his neck. Straight up, through his throat and the root of his tongue, into his brain stem.

She yanks the knife free.

Patterson looks at her in surprise. Then dies. He's still looking at her in surprise. Then the corpse's legs give out, and it crumbles to the concrete floor.

Holding her gut, Ash crouches and uses Patterson's jacket to clean blood off her knife and knuckles.

Dez watches.

She rises, eyes on Dez. The knife dances. The blade tucks back into its handle, and she slides it into her jacket pocket.

Dez sighs. "For the record, love. If he'd have told me the truth, I'd've let him live."

"He was dead the moment he threatened my mother."

# CHAPTER 72

The Skyhook Technologies board of directors has been in an emergency meeting for most of the day. Well after the sun sets, and as the Crays' superyacht gets set to clear the harbor, the board places a call to the couple.

Vincent and Valerie maintain an office and living quarters on the fifth of five decks of *Le Grand Requin Blanc.* Half of the deck is their luxury apartment. Another quarter is a dojo Valerie has set up for their daily workout. Another quarter of the space is the office they try to avoid whenever possible, because that always requires interacting with the board.

One full wall of their office is a state-of-the-art, floor-to-ceiling flat screen. When they log in, the board members appear to be life-sized. Wendell, the vice president of personnel management, is there. The title is a euphemism. Wendell's only real duty is keeping Vincent and Valerie Cray out of headlines, out of courts, and out of prison, worldwide.

From the stern faces, the couple are pretty sure this isn't a friendly call.

"We're hemorrhaging," their chief financial officer tells them. "Since the allegations of, ah, your misconduct in Canada, we've had four future contracts on two continents evaporate. Concurrent mining operations in the Horn of Africa, in Mexico, and in Central Europe are all on pause."

Vincent sits at their perfectly empty conference room table in his khakis, sweater, and Timberlands, his feet up on the table, crossed at the ankles. He has his ubiquitous box of wooden matches in his left hand. He looks as cool as a sip from a mountain creek.

Skyhook's head of PR says, "There's, ah, more. And it's, um, not—"

Valerie stands at the starboard window, watching the forests of St. John's pass. "Spit it out, please."

The PR guy inhales deeply. "Ah, Aiyden Finn. He apparently wrote a, well, confessional of sorts. In the event of his death, it was sent to us. The media don't have it yet. But they will. He claims—it's crazy, I know, nuts—but he claims Ms. Cray . . . well, shot his predecessor."

Vincent looks at his lovely wife. Backlit, those skintight leather trousers and those sky-high heels are serving her well, he muses. "I'm guessing Finn wanted some insurance."

"Well, yes, sir, but since the accusation's obviously a falsehood, we're already on it. We have interviews prepped for *The Wall Street Journal* and Bloomberg. We'll be turning down all interview requests for you, of course, on the advice of Legal."

Legal, sitting to his left, jumps in. "Yes. Absolutely. No interviews, no public appearances."

Vincent is shaking his box of wooden matches, listening to them rattle. "We're hosting a charity golf tournament outside of Tokyo next weekend."

Wendell, their babysitter, shakes his head. "Sorry, Vincent. The media will be on it like piranhas. Also, Legal is getting deluged by demands for information and documents. From the Canadians, the U.S. State Department, the EU . . . everyone."

Vincent smiles calmly. "So? That's what you get paid to handle. Right? Paid pretty fucking well. Handle it."

The chairman of the board sits forward. "Look. Vincent, this isn't like some of the . . . escapades you and your wife get into. This is a serious international incident!"

He says, "Then, if I were you guys, I'd handle it like a serious international board of businessmen."

And he shuts off the transmission.

Valerie stands at the window, arms crossed.

Vincent shakes his matchbox, near his ear, listening to the rattle. "I thought losing out on cornering the world's iridium market was the essence of the bad news. But the hits just keep on coming."

Valerie speaks to her reflection in the glass, and to the back of Vincent's head. "If Finn had gotten out of there, he'd have blackmailed us. Me."

"Looks like. Glad he died in the mine."

"I'm not. I want to have killed him myself. I want to taste his fucking blood."

"Here's what we do: nothing. Let the lawyers and the PR guys and the accountants and Wendell worry about the fallout for Skyhook. They get paid to do that. You and me, we focus on Limerick first. We came after him, and when we get to Paris, he'll be coming after us. No doubt whatsoever."

When she doesn't respond, Vincent says, "The guy reminds me of me."

His wife turns, eyebrows arched. "And not me?"

He laughs, legs still up on the conference table. "Oh, hell no. You're all rage and fire. Limerick's military. A strategist. He won't back down before another predator, but he'll calculate the odds. He'll move with precision."

Valerie studies him. He smiles over at her.

"Good," she says. "Let him come to us."

He smiles. "That's my girl."

The ship's PA system whistles a military, maritime tone. Vincent lowers his legs off the table and reaches for the controls. "Yes?"

It's the ship's new head of security, Chike Ibrahim, the Nigerian. *"Sir. There is something you ought to see. On the helipad."*

It gets cold fast out here on the water. The Crays throw on parkas and gloves and meet Chike Ibrahim about a hundred feet from the ship's helipad. Occidental Ventures' big Chinook took off long ago, and the company helicopter is back.

Ibrahim points to a large barrel, standing on end, at the nearest edge of the round helipad.

"That was not there twenty minutes ago," the soldier says.

Vincent says, "Is that . . . Do you think it's a bomb?"

"That is possible, sir. It's a large barrel. An ammonium nitrate/fuel bomb that size could sink this ship."

The Crays exchange looks.

Ibrahim says, "I have a man on board who is an expert with explosives. I've called for him. We shall let him—"

In her tall heels, leather trousers, and fur-lined winter coat, Valerie Cray stalks past him. "Our opponent is Desmond fucking Limerick. He is not going to kill everyone on board the ship."

She walks toward the barrel. Chike Ibrahim looks to Vincent, who raises both palms in an *I'm not going to stop her* gesture.

Valerie marches up to the barrel. She has no problem prying the lid off. She peers down into it for a bit.

Vincent and Ibrahim glance at each other. Vincent shrugs. They walk toward the pad, joining her, one to her left, one to her right.

The body of Dyson Patterson has been stuffed in the barrel. About a third of his body is submerged in his own blood. He bled out inside the container.

Valerie reaches for Patterson's head, adjusting his position. She sees that his throat has been slit. It's a clean, short cut. Almost surgical. Professional.

A cheap phone has been taped onto his shoulder. Once all three are peering in, the phone lights up. Vincent pauses, then reaches in, pries the tape free, and lifts the cheap phone.

Vincent studies the lit phone and says, "Huh."

Chike Ibrahim, gun drawn, peers around the great ship. "Sir?"

Vincent holds the phone out to him. "It's for you."

A beat, and Ibrahim accepts it, still holding his gun in his left hand.

He sees his name on an incoming email. He opens it. A video is queued up. He shows it to the Crays.

Valerie says, "Play it."

"It could trigger a—"

"Play it."

He does.

The face of Aiyden Finn appears. A very much alive Aiyden Finn. He looks directly into the camera. *"I'm hoping no one ever sees this. The moment we extract the iridium from Newfoundland, I'm going to send a copy of this to the Skyhook board of directors with my resignation. I watched as Valerie Cray shot my predecessor, Craig Loesser, in the chest. You could see in her eyes that it meant nothing to her. I've seen soldiers show more emotion while peeling potatoes. My guys and me buried Loesser's body in a quarry seven miles due west of St. John's. When this job is done, I'm tendering my resignation. This tape will be my insurance policy, to make sure I don't end up like Loesser. I'm sorry, but Mrs. Cray is a lunatic. If something goes wrong between now and then, well, let this be my deathbed confessional."*

The tape stops.

"Limerick," Vincent says. "He's hacked into the board of directors' system. He's inside Skyhook."

The phone vibrates. An incoming call.

The Crays lean in to listen. Ibrahim accepts the call and puts it on speaker.

"Chike Ibrahim! *Alsalam ealaykum!*"

Vincent says, "The hell is that?"

Ibrahim says, "Peace be upon you."

"Name's Dez Limerick. The two of us never met, formal like, but we connected more or less when me oul' unit stopped the hijacking of that tungsten delivery outside of Marrakech. What, three years ago, was it? 'Bout that. Time flies. How's with you, mate?"

Ibrahim peers around the ship. He spots eight of his men, all with automatic rifles. There's no sign of Limerick.

"Fella name of Loesser ran merc ops for the Crays, and her ladyship shot him. Then it was Aiyden Finn who died—quite badly, if I'm being honest—in a knife fight with a Russian. Then it was America's sweetheart, Dyson Patterson. See below, stewin' in his own juices. Which leads us to yourself, me good lad. Dunno what kinda retirement nest egg ye've been saving up, but, well . . . ye might not be needin' it after all."

Valerie speaks up. "You won't be able to hide from us forever, Limerick. You should have accepted our offer—offers—when you had the chance."

"Aye. Coulda used the gelt, truth told. And I wouldn'ta minded sleeping with you but fact of the matter is I'm not up to date with my tetanus shots."

The color drains from her face.

Vince knows that look. Mount Valerie is about to experience a pyroclastic event.

"'Sides: Who says I'm hiding? I'm—"

Chike Ibrahim disconnects the call. His eyes rake the scene.

"I know who this man is. I know what happened in Marrakech."

Vincent looks his way. "Yeah?"

"You are not safe."

"Seriously?" Vincent chuckles. "Are you suggesting we evacuate the ship, which will be on the high seas in a manner of minutes, despite the highly trained soldiers standing between us and him?"

Chike Ibrahim looks directly at Vincent. He seems surprised by the question.

"Of course I am."

# CHAPTER 73

Chike Ibrahim speaks into his radio, issuing orders. Then turns to the Crays. They watch as six of the Nigerian's men come running in their direction, automatic rifles at the ready.

"I am calling back our Chinook. It is bulletproof. We will secure this deck and all of the higher, forward-facing decks, until you are aboard. I have told my pilot to pick a destination but not to tell me over the radio. When I'm aboard, he will tell me where we are going. After you are both off this ship, my men will take as much time as necessary to find this man Limerick."

Valerie says, "I'm staying. I want his blood. He'll—"

Ibrahim says, "Either you are following my direct orders, regarding your security, or when the Chinook arrives, my men and I will climb on board and will leave. And our PMC will refund your money."

"Fuck you! I won't—"

Vincent grabs his wife by both shoulders, standing behind her. "Honey? Let's do as the nice man says."

"Fuck it! I—"

Vincent squeezes. Hard enough to leave bruises on her shoulders, even through the coat sleeves. "Honey? We will do as the nice, heavily armed man says."

He turns to Ibrahim. "Do you think the asshole's still on board?"

"Probably not. Easy enough to call from the shore. Less dangerous for him, as well. But I take no chances. Yes?"

"Fine by me."

Occidental Ventures' helo stays at the St. John's Airport. It has to get refueled because the pilots hadn't anticipated a long-distance flight tonight. The refueling and resupplies take the better part of ninety minutes, then the big bird lifts off the ground.

It's barely fifteen minutes later when the Crays, the mercenaries, and the yacht crew hear the deep bass whoosh of the twin-rotor helo, drawing near. One of Ibrahim's men spots the running lights first and radios it in.

One of Ibrahim's lieutenants, up on the flying bridge, is running a radio check. Calling each of their twenty-five men and asking for a quick call-off.

*"Gunther . . . ? Here . . . Rodriquez . . . ? All's quiet on the aft of deck three, over. Garrick . . . ? All quiet here. . . ."*

Ibrahim speaks into his radio, then turns to the Crays, who stand surrounded by six of the mercenaries.

"Your helicopter lifts off first. Then ours lands. We get you aboard."

Vincent says, "We haven't packed."

"Two of my men are packing for you."

Valerie says, "They're pawing through our clothes? In our quarters?"

"Yes, ma'am. You are staying here. In the midst of these good men."

*"Wiśniowski . . . ? Present. . . . Khamphir . . . ? All's good. . . . Mattson . . . ? I've got the engine room, all clear. . . ."*

Vincent says, "Gotta say. I didn't quite see Limerick as a slit-the-man's-throat type. Taking out Patterson like that? That's cold. Didn't think he had it in him."

Valerie looks quickly his way. "I don't believe he does. Could he have an accomplice?"

Ibrahim, his head on a swivel, says, simply, "He could."

The Skyhook Sikorsky lifts off from the pad. The big Chinook hangs about twenty meters off the bow, waiting for the clearance. As soon as the much smaller Sikorsky is away, the Chinook pilot positions for a landing.

*"Aubert . . . ? Oui, here. . . . Carvalho . . . ? All quiet. . . . Becker . . . ?"*

The Crays turn to see two men hauling their suitcases, heading their way.

"Once you are safe, we will—"

*"Becker . . . ? Check in, Becker."*

Ibrahim raises a hand, palm out, to the two men with the suitcases. "Wait! Stop there!"

He raises his radio. "Becker? Becker, check in now. Becker!"

The lieutenant on the flying bridge says, *"Nothing here, Chief. Does anyone know where Becker was supposed to be?"*

Ibrahim said, "He was to guard the GAU-21 and the extra munitions. He—"

And at that moment, the forward floor-to-ceiling window of deck two explodes.

And bullets from a tripod-mounted machine gun begin strafing the Chinook.

The big plane is bulletproof, yes. But not against the heavy, fast shells of the GAU-21, designed by the U.S. Navy for use on fixed-wing aircraft. The belt holds six hundred rounds and it can fire a thousand rounds per minute. The massive slugs slam into the ship at almost three thousand feet per second. They penetrate the armored hull like it were cheesecloth.

Chike Ibrahim tackles both of the Crays, slamming them to the deck, his body over theirs. The six men around them turn toward the bright flashes of heavy-duty machine-gun fire. They begin firing at deck two, but from this distance, see no chance to actually hit anything.

Ibrahim and the Crays watch as the huge Chinook takes round after round. It drifts to the starboard, the tail coming about. Ibrahim is convinced that the pilot's been hit.

They all watch, aghast, as the bird sets down on the very edge of *Le Grand Requin Blanc*. Balances there a second, then begins toppling over into St. John's Harbour.

The fifty-caliber grows quiet. Chike Ibrahim lies atop the Crays, barking orders into his radio. At some point, he gets the couple to their feet. Ibrahim and the Crays and the six bodyguards walk quickly but carefully toward deck one. Moving together, the couple in the middle of their seven heavily armed protectors.

Vincent says, "He wasn't aiming for us. If Limerick had wanted us, we'd be splatter on the deck."

Ibrahim agrees but is playing this by the book.

Reports come back over his radio. Four of his men have made it to deck two. They find two of their own soldiers dead. One shot twice in the head, one with a slit throat. The GAU-21 was deployed, all right, its iron tripods bolted to the deck.

They find another soldier, bleeding out, on a walkway that circles deck two.

A big Polish soldier kneels over him and applies pressure to his chest wound. "Was it the Englishman? This Limerick?"

The dying man shakes his head. "Was . . . girl . . ." Blood seeps from his mouth. "Pretty girl. Pretty . . ."

He dies.

The Pole swears a blue streak. He reaches for his radio.

Just as he's about to call Ibrahim, the deck shudders under his boots. The entire superyacht quakes.

Someone on the radio shouts, *"Smoke! Coming from the engine room! We got smoke!"*

It's late. The Crays and their six guardians are in the yacht's kitchen. Both entrances are being watched. The yacht dropped anchor to avoid drifting with the engines fried.

Chike Ibrahim and the ship's captain conduct a survey. To see who's alive, who's missing. If any equipment is unaccounted for.

Other than the three dead on deck two and the pilots of the Chinook, no other mercenaries, and none of the ship's crew, seem injured.

But the inventory comes up short.

Valerie slams her palm into the door of a walk-in refrigerator. "He's still here! Limerick is on board! *Why can't you fucking find him!*"

Chike Ibrahim walks into the kitchen. Shaking his head. "I would say not."

Vincent says, "He, what? Swam?"

"Your personal two-man submarine is missing."

# CHAPTER 74

It takes most of the day for the harbormaster to tow *Le Grand Requin Blanc* back to St. John's. In the meantime, Chike Ibrahim has used an encrypted line to contact his superiors at Occidental Ventures.

The private military contractor rents a warehouse space near the harbor. It's not pretty, but it stands apart from other commercial buildings with good line of sight in 360 degrees. No one knows what Desmond Limerick will try next, but Ibrahim has enough men to guard this site.

At dawn, he parks the Crays and their luggage in the warehouse.

"We have an armored cargo plane. It will be here in seven hours," he tells the couple. "We will fly you to an undisclosed location. Yes?"

Valerie is too tired to be psycho. She climbs on a desk in the warehouse, on her back, hands folded over her chest, and closes her eyes.

Vincent grips Ibrahim's shoulder. "That works. And thank you. We—"

His cell phone vibrates. He draws it out.

The readout says the call is coming from the late Dyson Patterson.

Vincent shows the mercenary leader. Ibrahim nods. Vincent makes the connection. He says, "Hey, Limerick."

Dez is in his rented Jeep, not four kilometers away. He's routing this call through a server in Estonia that will make it impossible to track. Ash sits next to him, looking quiet and diminutive in her winter coat.

"That wasn't you on the GAU-21," Vincent says. "Who's your little friend?"

"Was telling her: Ye shoot down one helicopter with a great fecking machine gun, well, them things happen. Shoot down two? That's a bit excessive. But if she shoots down a third one, it'll be time to admit she's got a problem."

"Helicopters are just things, Limerick. I can replace them with money. And I have more than enough money to come after you till the end of days."

"Regarding that, Mr. Cray, sir. I'm hopin' there's a way out of this situation in which we've found ourselves. Are ye amenable to a trade?"

He waits.

Vincent says, "Trade?"

"Aye, sir. See, I know something you don't. Nor does the lovely Mrs. Cray. Is she there? Say hello for me, will ye, then?"

"What is it you think you know that we don't?"

"Well, as to that. I know that the Canadian authorities now are in possession of the Fuchs Underground Neutrino Collector. Which includes the massive iridium find on level six. With which, ye'd have cornered the market in iridium."

"Get to the fucking point."

"Your metallurgist, Matteo Bernardi."

There's a pause. Dez is betting that the Crays have no idea he knows about the Italian physicist who first contacted them. His goal here is to keep them off-balance. Keep them guessing.

"He left all his mining equipment down on level six," Dez says. "Ye know. From where he drilled that core sample. So before we left, I drilled a few of me own. Twenty-six of 'em, to be exact. An' I hid 'em. Off-site."

Vincent starts to say something but Valerie overrides him. She sounds like she's on the edge of snapping. "You lying fucker! You want us to believe you took twenty-six more core samples? Fuck you! No way!"

Vincent says, "Why would you do that?"

Dez laughs. "That'd be a trick question, yeah? The first core sample must've been worth two million dollars! Now I'm sitting on more'n forty million dollars' worth of the rarest Earth element! Not working for charity here, ye know."

It's Valerie again. "You're lying! But don't worry, I know how to get the truth out of a guttersnipe like you!"

"Jay-sus but you're a flirt! Leave off, darlin'. The men are talking."

The more he pushes her buttons, the more Vincent Cray will have to expend energy to keep her in check. In fact, Vincent sounds like he's physically struggling with something when he says, "And . . . damn it! . . . and why should we believe you?"

"I'll tell ye where my iridium core samples are, and you send someone to find 'em. If I'm lyin', there's still a bounty on me head, yeah? And if I'm not, well, you can cook up the paperwork to show you've had the samples for weeks now. Hell, months. That'd bolster the argument that, whoever sent them mercenaries up to Canada, wasn't you. Why would ye? You already own the find. And you can run a chemical analysis of the iridium an' the ore it's in t'prove that both samples came from the same mine."

He waits. He hears Valerie Cray's voice, but maybe one of the mercenaries is restraining her some distance from the phone. Or two of the guys. Or all of them. Dez does not envy whoever pulls that duty.

Vincent's voice loses a little of its anger. "Limerick? That actually might work. But here's a new angle on the deal. If we get there and you've lied to us, we're going to kill Trisha Jean Jackson. She's got an ex-husband and two adult kids. They also die. And her bodyguard, Townsend. I've done my research; he's got a wife named Lauren. She dies, too. You were staying in New York before this, working at a restaurant. Our private investigators say her name is Sly Colehouse. My investigators said you got pretty close. She's dead. You had a landlady in New York? A Mrs. Welliver? Dead. Oh, and I saved the best for last. Petra Alexandris of Triton Expediters? I'm going to play with her. Then I'm going to let Valerie play with her. Then she'll beg us to kill her. But, of course, that's if you're lying."

"Square deal," Dez says. "I'd've loved to be a rich man, but I'd much rather be a living one. You've me word."

Vincent says, "All right, Limerick. We have a deal. Just remember those friends of yours, and their families. They'll pay the price if you're fucking with us."

"I'll remember, my lad. I'll be leaving St. John's now. When I'm twenty-four hours gone, I'll call again an' tell you where to find your iridium. You start setting up the story that Skyhook's had it for ages. And after that, Bob's your uncle. Cheers."

Dez hangs up.

He smiles over at Ash. Who watches him intently.

"Thoughts?"

"The way you move through doors," she says. "The way you moved without being seen. By men who were looking for us. Your ability to control your process through hostile space. I have never seen anything like that."

"That's me training, love. Took years to learn that."

Ash keeps watching him. As if she's seeing him, or facets of him, for the first time.

# CHAPTER 75

When Occidental Ventures' armed and armored aircraft arrives, Vincent Cray convinces Chike Ibrahim that they have to wait for Limerick's next call. "His plan could actually work. We could make a legal case that we own the rights to the iridium. All of it. Not just the core samples he stole."

"This man is a trained soldier, sir. If he seeks your death, don't use his playbook."

But Vincent won't be swayed.

Four hours later, the call comes in. The Crays and the mercenaries are still bunking in the harborside warehouse.

"Limerick?"

"Vincent. Ye've a pen?"

"Just fucking tell me where my iridium is."

"'Twas too heavy to drag far, even usin' the town's motorized snow sleds. Me mate and me took it to a Distant Early Warning bunker. A Cold War relic. It's about two miles north of Fuchstown."

Vincent knows of it. Valerie spotted it on a map while they awaited the arrival of their backup mercenaries at the mine. "Our iridium is there?"

"Is."

"It will take our crews the better part of a day to get there and to get back. If you've lied to me . . ."

"We've been over that, mate. Know the threats, thank you very much."

"Limerick. If the find is there, then you and I are squared. I tell you this because Valerie told me she'd be square with you, too. But just so you know: Valerie sometimes changes her mind."

"The prerogative of all women, the world over."

"This is my way of telling you: Even if you're being truthful, it would be a good idea to stay the hell away from Skyhook for the rest of your natural life. Am I clear here?"

"Reading you five by five, squire."

"You won't hear from me again, Limerick," Vincent says. "Unless you're lying. Then you will."

He hangs up.

He turns to Valerie. "Call Ibrahim please. I'll arrange for his men to—"

She says, "No."

Vincent's eyebrows rise.

"We sent a virtual army and all the weaponry they could possibly need. And they failed. We sent a second set of mercenaries. And they failed. This time, *we* go."

Vincent smiles at her. They step closer, and he embraces her, kissing her.

"You're right. We'll need men to help us get it back to France, but you're absolutely right. We do this one ourselves."

The Crays fly out on Chike Ibrahim's armored bombardier with Ibrahim and four of his men. "When we get there," Vincent tells them, "you'll stay with the plane until we say otherwise."

"Limerick could be here."

"Limerick could have killed us on the deck of our yacht and didn't," Vincent says. "Just do as you're told."

Valerie is on the sat phone in one corner of the plane. She disconnects and moves toward the men. "We should have the place to ourselves when we land."

Vincent turns her way. "The Canadian authorities?"

"Gone. We're flying in the wake of yet another storm, and my source tells me the military and RCMP abandoned the site for the duration, for safe measure. They'll be back in twenty-four hours. We've the airfield, and the town, to ourselves."

Their pilot makes for Quebec, then brings the bombardier down low and turns toward Fuchstown. Hopefully, low enough to be off Canadian radar. It takes little time to get there, and the storm they've been chasing has moved off.

They're worried that the new storm might have made the runway unusable, but their pilot assures them he can land. The crippled C-130 has been towed out of the way, sitting beside two of the three wounded or destroyed helicopters on-site.

The landing is uneventful.

Ibrahim's men deploy two powerful Polaris sleds. The Crays change into snow gear and goggles. Vincent says, "Monitor the airwaves. If the cops or military come, let us know. If we find what Limerick promised, we'll let you know. Understood?"

The mercenary leader nods.

Vincent and Valerie Cray take off, using a GPS guide lashed to Valerie's handlebar. The sun won't set for hours yet, and they've a windless, blue day in the wake of the latest storm.

The trip is enjoyable, both of them grinning.

They spot the ancient Distant Early Warning bunker, from which Canadian military in the 1950s and '60s watched the sky for Soviet-era bombers and missiles. Their research tells them this site hasn't been in use since 1982. It's low, made up of concrete blocks.

They pull up and cut their engines. "Look," Vincent says.

There's a corrugated iron awning covering the door. That awning protected the ground from the latest storm, and they see snowmobile tracks leading to and away.

"Limerick told the truth."

Valerie says, "He still has to die." She dismounts the snowmobile.

"I made him a promise."

"I didn't."

They lodge their goggles down around their necks and remove their thick mittens. Vincent draws a two-way radio and contacts the bombardier.

*"No sign of the military,"* Chike Ibrahim tells them. *"No one knows we're here. Over."*

"Good. Get ready to deploy the other snowmobiles and the trailer. We'll get back to you soon. Out."

They move to the metal door. Only about twenty feet of the bunker is aboveground, and the part they can see slopes away. The bunker itself is largely subterranean. "Limerick picked his site well," Vincent says. "You could hide, well, anything up here forever."

His wife smiles at him. "You respect Limerick."

"I do. He's smart and resourceful."

Her smile ratchets up several degrees. "He'll be fun to play with."

"I couldn't stop you if I wanted to."

"No. You couldn't."

Vincent reaches for the C-shaped iron handle on the door. He yanks. The door doesn't want to budge. He yanks again. The hinges, rusty and old, squeak. The door cracks open.

They activate both flashlights and peer inside.

Vincent Cray says, "Jesus. Oh, Jesus."

His wife spins to him. Kisses him. Passionately.

And the bunker-buster bomb, which Dez and Ash found aboard their C-130, explodes.

Chike Ibrahim watches the mushroom cloud, five kilometers or so to the north, for a full minute.

He tries several times to reach out to the Crays by radio. He's not sure why he even bothers.

He turns to the pilots. "Take us home please."

# CHAPTER 76

## NEW YORK CITY

A day has passed.

Upon returning, Dez checks with his landlady, Mrs. Welliver, and is pleased to find out his old room hasn't been rented out. He and Ash move in. The landlady, in her oil paint–stained overalls and with her infectious smile, notices his new "lady friend" and seems pleased.

Until this thing is wrapped up, Dez sleeps on the floor and Ash has the bed.

They are in New York because the Tontine contacted Ash and asked them to be here. They don't know for how long.

Petra Alexandris calls Dez from the Triton Expediters campus in Los Angeles.

"Was just thinkin' of you," he says wistfully.

"I think of you all the time. I heard the news. The Crays returned to the scene of the crime. They had some sort of massive bomb with them. Maybe to get back into the mine? Maybe to bury evidence? The news says it blew up prematurely and killed them."

"Aye."

"I am reliably told by my many, many military contacts that several of the world's hot spots likely will cool off now, without Skyhook's profiteering."

"I'm glad t'hear that."

"You saved my life. Again. I owe you. Again."

"Was less dramatic than that, love."

"Which is why I will never tell a living soul that the story of the Crays having a big bomb, and it going off prematurely, is, to use a Limerickism, 'twenty pounds of zebra shit in a ten-pound bin.'"

Dez grins. "I've no idea what you could be thinking about."

"No," she says. "But I concur. It was the right move. As always."

Chike Ibrahim is having one last drink at an outside table of a bistro in New York before being reassigned to a mission in Bangkok. He's leaving tomorrow from JFK.

Someone brings his drink, plus an identical one. He looks up. It's Desmond Limerick.

Dez sits.

"You."

"Aye. Was wonderin' how we are. You'n me."

Ibrahim studies him, quietly. Then shrugs. "I came with twenty-four trusted soldiers. I walk away with fewer. But it was the Crays who initiated the violence. Not you. I respect that you outthought me. Not many men ever have."

"My beef was with Psycho Barbie an' her hubby. Not you. Wanted to make that clear."

"You did. But how did you know I or my men wouldn't be at the bunker in Canada?"

Dez digs out his phone. He goes to a video, hits Play, sets his phone down.

The black-and-white video shows the Crays arriving at the bunker on snowmobiles.

Dez stops it. "Took a surveillance camera from the igloo when I stole their whacking great bomb. Repurposed it. Had you been there, I'd've called them freaks an' told them this was me final warning. To leave me an' mine alone or else."

Ibrahim nods. "So even before you left Canada, you knew it might come down to ending them as a threat."

"Did."

Ibrahim ponders that. Finally, he says, "Tactically sound."

"Ta."

They finish their drinks. Dez rises first.

"Limerick, my friend. If you ever feel like getting paid what you deserve for your remarkable talents, look me up."

Dez shakes his hand. "Safe travels, mate."

# CHAPTER 77

The next day, Ash's phone vibrates. She looks at the readout and hands it to Dez.

A voice, male, possibly German or Austrian. "The newspapers tell of a tragic accident in Newfoundland and Labrador that took the life of the co-CEOs of Skyhook Technologies."

"So's I hear. Well, mining's dangerous work."

"Truly. There is a club on the Upper West Side. Near the park. If I give you the address, would you be good enough to pay us a visit? Feel free to bring young Ash."

Dez and Ash take a taxi to the club. He's guessing the place was built in the early to mid-1800s. The inside is dark, mostly browns and greens and grays, and decidedly masculine. He spots paintings of terribly important-looking gents, some in powdered wigs. Dez never quite got the purpose of the powdered wig, but then again, he's unlikely to offer fashion tips to anyone. A doorman asks for their cell phones, then they're deposited in a library.

"Your host will be along in a moment, sir. May I get either of you a drink?"

"Would love a stout, if ye've one."

"On more or less the chocolate side, sir?"

"Whatever ye have is fine. Ash?"

Ash turns enormous eyes to the servant and whispers, "A Clover Club, please."

The man blinks. Then does so several more times. "I'm, ah, not sure I—"

"One egg white, a quarter ounce of raspberry syrup, one and a half ounces of gin, three-quarters of an ounce of lemon juice. Shake the ingredients to emulsify, add ice, shake again. Grenadine will work if you've no raspberry syrup."

He gives her a little bow. "Excellent, miss. Please wait."

Dez's eyes are as wide as saucers.

"What?"

"Was a time you was laconic, is all."

Ash takes one of the matching green leather chairs. "Clarity over brevity."

Their drinks arrive. One full wall of the joint is a floor-to-ceiling bookshelf and Dez has never in his life been able to resist a bookshelf. These tomes are dust-free and very old. Most look like they've actually been read. He pulls out a few, scans them. He spots bits of paper used as bookmarks, and also notes jotted in the margins of one. People who love books collected these; not people who think books make them look impressive.

"Mr. Limerick."

He turns as a gentleman enters. Not the same gent from the limo he met before. This guy's mid-sixties, hair swept back, wearing an expensive suit and shined shoes. He shakes Ash's hand first, then

Dez's. He pours himself a whiskey from a decanter and sits opposite Ash. Dez takes a third chair.

"You have had a productive few days, Mr. Limerick." Definitely Austrian, Dez thinks.

"The deal was, I sign off the Crays, you lift the contract on Ash's life. And you free her from the last three years of her contact. Let her be Asha Araki again. Aye?"

Ash shuffles in her chair. She normally is as still as a statue. Dez senses something's up.

The Austrian gentleman smiles benignly and sips his drink. "I am told that the reason you were asked to come with Ms. Araki was so that she can confirm that which we are about to tell you. Miss?"

She nods.

The man says, "The contract is lifted. Her debt is not."

Dez says, "Had a deal. An' you don't want me as an enemy. Tell your puppet masters that."

But it's Ash who replies. "Dez." She reaches over and places her tiny hand on his enormous fist. "They offered to lift my debt. I . . . declined."

He turns to her, studying her.

"Come again?"

She inhales, holds it, lets it out. She makes eye contact and maintains it. "When you saw me in Paris, eighteen months ago, I told a handler that I didn't want the posting. Didn't want to do this anymore. But for the past few days—and much to my surprise—I've come to realize I actually do. I like that I have this talent. And if I agree to stay on, the Tontine will give me right of refusal on all future assignments."

Dez takes a moment to let that absorb. "You're jokin'."

"I never said I wanted out of my contract." It's said with a little heat; nearly the first words he's ever heard from this woman that contain any true emotion. "You presumed so. Just as you presumed I traveled to Canada to kill someone."

Dez has no reply to that.

Ash softens her voice. "Since I was eighteen, this is all I have ever known. And I am good at it."

She gives his hand a squeeze.

Dez sips his extremely good beer, just to buy himself some time. The Austrian gentleman waits, smiling, picking invisible lint off his trousers.

Dez forces a smile. "Your life. Not mine. Your call. Not mine."

"Thank you."

"Just know: There could come a time our paths cross again. But . . . dunno if it will be as allies."

Ash stands by his chair and kisses his cheek.

She says, "I know."

She nods once to the gentleman, then leaves.

Dez dredges up a smile for the other man. "Women. Eh?"

The Austrian smiles kindly. "Thus was it ever."

Dez stands. The man sets his drink down and rises. They shake hands.

"I will add only this, Mr. Limerick. We wish you all the luck in the world."

Dez makes the journey back to his apartment.

He decides to stay a couple of days. He wants to eat in Sly Colehouse's restaurant, and to see his kitchen mates. He loves this city.

He returns to his rented room and finds Mrs. Welliver out front, a canvas on an easel, painting. The plump Englishwoman has a stain of cobalt across her left cheek. She is painting the street scene.

"That's quite good," he tells her.

"Thank you, dearie."

"Me, I couldn't draw a straight line."

Her eyes dart from her painting to the street and back. "The entire façade changes as the light changes, doesn't it, dear? For me, here, this city and this century, just as it was for Monet or Pissarro, all those years gone by."

Dez grins. "That's a thing, innit? Splendid."

Mrs. Welliver adds a couple of brushstrokes to her canvas and sighs. "Desmond? Did it ever occur to you to ask: Why did the Tontine want that nice Egyptian gentleman killed, eighteen months ago, in Paris?"

Dez is stunned. "Bloody hell!"

She bats her eyes at him. "Keep your friends close an' your enemies closer. Isn't that the line, Desmond?"

"I'm . . . I'm without words. And no. I never asked."

"Your Egyptian had no serious enemies. His work drew some opposition but hardly enough to kill him."

"Then why?"

She smiles. "We didn't want him dead. We wanted to see how you reacted. Could you take on two trained assassins? Would you kill indiscriminately? Were you as smart as you are strong?"

She looks and sounds like the stereotypical English granny.

"An' why's that, then?"

"We had heard you planned to retire. We were recruiting a gatekeeper, dearie! Would've thought that was obvious by now."

"Feckin' hell! Excuse me language."

She chuckles.

"Ye do know there's not a chance in the world that I'd work for you lot. Aye?"

She finds an already paint-dirtied rag and tries to wipe paint off her brushes. "Is that so?"

"Is."

"Desmond, we wanted the Crays to stop meddling in failed nations. We wanted them not to corner the market on an important element. We sent you to make sure those things didn't happen. And you succeeded splendidly."

He thinks about this a while.

"Ash," he asks. "Is she really Sophia Araki's daughter? Or was this all an elaborate ruse to get me on the Crays' radar?"

"Oh, that part was real enough. Every bit of it."

Dez's mind shudders like an old-school film reel, frozen, the frame over the light bulb melting. "Jay-sus! It was you lot told her her mum was in trouble! That Russian forces were comin' for them scientists. You knew she'd up stakes an' head to Canada!"

"We did."

"Then why sentence her t'death for it?"

"Oh, that part was a ruse, Desmond. We had no intention of killing Ash. You've absolutely no idea how talented that young lady is. She's an assassin unlike any we've seen for generations. No, we let her think that we would kill her as part of our recruitment test for you."

"You have to know I'd never have anything t'do with that madness."

"We take little at chance." Mrs. Welliver smiles sweetly. "We thought this might be another opportunity to see just how good you are. And my, but you're good, dearie."

She shakes her head, stowing her supplies in a fold-open fishing kit.

"Ash might have killed you. She had no idea we'd arranged for you to be there. She still doesn't. The Russians might've killed you. Those Skyhook lads might've killed you. And yet, here you are. Big as life." She shakes her head, beaming.

"I'll not work for the likes of you."

She starts laughing, her eyes twinkling. "Oh, Desmond!"

"What?"

She shakes her head and uses a knuckle to wipe a tear of laughter from her apple cheek. "Not all that long ago, a very rich man wanted to take a wee bit of California, to make it his fiefdom, and to rule from his little throne. We were concerned enough to have people on hand. When what happened? You came along and swatted him on the nose with a rolled-up newspaper! Not long after that, a titan of technology was involved in a hostile takeover with organized crime. That wouldn't lead to stability, it would not! But we needn't have worried. Desmond Limerick was there!"

Dez just studies her.

"Desmond, you delightful man! Who's to say you haven't been working for us all along?"

She folds up the easel, her painting tucked away. She smiles at him, the sun in her eyes.

"Do have a lovely day now."

And she toddles off.

# ABOUT THE AUTHOR

**James Byrne** has worked for more than twenty years as a journalist and in politics. He's the author of more than a dozen novels, including the Dez Limerick thrillers, most recently *Chain Reaction*. He lives in Portland, Oregon.